From Death to Birth

LIZ DELSIGNORE

ISBN: 979-8-9924362-0-4

DEDICATION

In loving memory of my father, James, who I miss dearly every day.
To my best friend, Bobby, who has always been there for me throughout the
years.

DEDICATE

ACKNOWLEDGMENTS

Thank you to Nicole Hendricks, who provided insight into how chaotic the
Labor and Delivery wing can get (as well as giving birth).
I appreciate the support from my friends and coworkers, who have put up
with me and provided emotional support during the writing of this novel.
Thank you to my editor, Loki Cornelow, for your friendship and putting up
with my shit.

FOREWORD

I met Liz in a Facebook cul- er, international community dedicated to a weasel-necked cat from New Zealand. We bonded over our own cats- her boy Vinny, my tiny tabby Smudge, and two orange morons Apollo and Kismet (who appear in this book!). Yes, it's true… Kismet eats paint and thinks that headbutting you in the face is love.

One of the first non-cat related things I learned about Liz is that she loves her dad. This book is a wonderful showing of a daughter's love and dedication to her father. Along with pouring her heart into it, she also did a LOT of research into things like the Vietnam War, her dad's information, and even at one point what year electronic money transfers were created! Jimmy lived a full life, and it's a privilege to have gotten to edit this. While this book is a fictional biography, the love that Liz has for her dad is entirely non-fiction.

I want to mention, specifically, the relationship between James and Frankie-theirs was a gentle, imperfect love that didn't need to be shouted from the rooftops, because it was a constant, quiet, whisper throughout their lives together. You'll get to see their strengths and their weaknesses, and how their devotion to each other was unmatched.

There are parts of this story that are 100% drawn from real life. Apollo and Kismet exist, and they're as dumb as they are sweet. Like I mentioned, Kismet has an obsession with pulling paint off the doorframes, and Sam the vet tech really did tell me that he's just really, really stupid.

All in all, editing this book has been a journey that I've loved every minute of. I've got a friend for life in Liz, and it's been absolutely spectacular to see her vision come to life. Thank you for bringing me along on the adventure.

- Loki (the editor)

1: THE AFTERLIFE

Am I having an out-of-body experience? What's happening to me? I rub my eyes to wake myself up and scan my surroundings in an attempt to get my bearings.

Bright beams of white and gold light surround me, and I realize I'm sitting on a cloud. Don't ask how the physics of that happens... I can't figure it out either. The sun's beams flash in my eyes, almost blinding me. As I stare into the distance in front of me, I see the Pearly Gates. Saint Peter is standing at the front, holding a golden staff in all his glory. He's referencing what looks like the biggest book I've ever seen, albeit written in a dip pen onto parchment paper, the cover being a fine brown leather. There seems to be a line of people in front of me, too.

This is it. This is Judgment Day for me. I'm now coming to terms with the thought that my earthly body has died, and now I'm about to find out if I'm going to Heaven, Purgatory, or Hell. I don't know how I got here. I mean, yes, I'm dead and now awaiting the afterlife, but how did I end up in this exact situation? Did I accomplish anything while on Earth? Was I happy? How was my love life? What did I do professionally? Was I good-looking? Does anyone miss me? It's questions like these that are racing through my head faster than professional drivers on a Formula 1 racetrack. There are so many more questions I have, too, and not enough answers to go with them. At least not satisfying answers.

There are easily hundreds—no, thousands—of other souls standing alongside me, each of us waiting our turn to be judged and our fate decided. Visible from anywhere in the highest altitude of the skies is God. He is both massive and glorious, and He alone will decide my destiny. While His expression is calm and loving, Saint Peter has far more of an analytical way of carrying himself. Being the sole recipient of the keys of heaven certainly comes with a strong sense of discernment. Those being banished down to Hell for eternal suffering are sent without a moment to waste. For those souls who have proven themselves

1

righteous and good, Saint Peter steps aside and opens the Pearly Gates to allow their entry into the kingdom of Heaven.

Seeing others go before me and come face to face with God is wrecking my nerves. Some are begging for mercy, even if they spent a life full of gluttony, lust, greed, wrath, and envy. Some allowed pride and sloth to get in the way of a more fulfilling life while on Earth. What we all have in common, though, is that we understand Heaven is the ideal place for our souls to end up in this afterlife. Heaven is vast, glorious, plentiful, and peaceful. Earthly pains experienced by people are made at peace here. Food and resource insecurities simply do not exist, as anything you could need is abundant. The idea of being with loved ones who passed before them brings them comfort and a renewed sense of love.

To the left of this line sits the Rainbow Bridge. This is where all the pets and animal companions who have ever passed away are sent. If they had human companions during their time on Earth, they would be reunited with them here—assuming the humans are allowed into Heaven. Once their human companions are allowed into Heaven, they are reunited for eternity. Those who were hurt or maimed are made whole and strong again. Any wrongs that were committed on Earth are corrected and made right. Peace and harmony are bestowed on both the spirit of the humans and their animal companions as they cross the Rainbow Bridge together, never having to be apart again.

My mind and heart begin to burn with questions once again. I want to say I'm nervous, but there's just one problem – I don't remember anything I did while on Earth. How can I be nervous about being judged by God when I can't remember what even happened in my life? I could have been an awful person, but I could have also been a good person. I could have been somewhere in between, too. If I was wealthy, did I share my wealth or use it for good? If I was poor, was I a beggar? Did I ever marry, and if so, what was her name? Was I loved by animals or repelled by them? I wish some of my memories on earth followed me to the afterlife, but that is tragically not the case.

After what feels like an eternity, I finally get to the front of the line. There He is. God. I can't believe I'm here for any number of reasons.

"James...," He says.

That's my name? James? That would have been nice to know a while ago.

"Y... yes, Heavenly Father?" I feel myself shaking, my knees trembling, my heart pounding out of my chest. I'm sweating profusely and anxiously await what is about to determine my destiny for the rest of eternity.

"You have come to me today because your earthly body has died. Throughout your life, you have sinned no more than any other human being. It is no surprise that my son, Jesus, died for the original sins of mankind. The Holy Spirit has remained strong in your heart throughout your many years on Earth, and you have been a fervent follower of mine while in the flesh," He says.

"Yes, that sounds correct."

"You have also practiced, to a notable degree, a virtuous way of life—even if it didn't always seem that way to you at the moment. In you, I see humility, charity, chastity, gratitude, temperance, patience, and diligence..."

I feel more beads of sweat making their way from head to toe. Here it comes. Here's the decision.

"James Antonio Rossi, welcome to the kingdom of Heaven."

Oh, my. What a relief. I feel as if I can breathe again, although I wasn't physically holding my breath the entire time I've waited here to receive the good news. Wait...my last name is Rossi? My middle name is Antonio? Interesting. Very interesting. I would say that that's not what I expected if I had any expectations.

Saint Peter steps aside as he opens the gates of Heaven. I cautiously take a few steps forward, entering the most beautiful, majestic, and breathtaking scenery you could ever hope to experience. Angels live throughout. I soon get to see all my long-gone loved ones—my father, mother, other relatives, and my friends. The experience is overwhelming. Suddenly, I am flooded with every positive feeling—love, acceptance, happiness, gratefulness, relief, and freedom, to name a few. Tears begin to stream down my face as I come to terms with being reunited with those I love.

Now that I'm here and know my name, I know I have one duty—to find out who I was on Earth. It's time for my spirit to turn back the clock.

2: SIXTY-TWO

I'm in my sixties, and I'd be lying if I told you that I'm in the best shape of my life.

My body is frail, and my health is declining. Based on what Jeremy, my supposed brother six years my junior, tells me, I was diagnosed with testicular cancer approximately five years ago. The cancer has mostly been slow-moving, but he says that about two years ago, it started to spread more aggressively. Unsurprisingly, this caused those around me great concern. I'm 62 years old, so I'm not young, but I'm also not a fossil. How neat...I think? Was it worth it?

I don't have children, but I have a beautiful, doting wife who I've been dutifully married to for 37 years. Even in middle age, she is breathtakingly gorgeous. Her name is Francesca Regina Mancini Rossi. Her parents, Eugene and Anna Mancini, brought Francesca and her three brothers to the United States from Cosenza, Calabria, Italy. She is of a small frame, standing at 5'2" (about 157 cm for those who use metric). Her eyes are glacier blue, closely resembling the purest form of water. Long, coarse strands of dark brown hair once graced her oval face but are now various shades of grey and white. She possessed a bosom that was proportionate to the rest of her, which helped to fill out her slender figure. By modern beauty standards, and especially to me, she's a stunner.

Jeremy is living at our Las Vegas, NV home with Frankie and I. He's been staying with us since his late wife, Giulia, passed away. She passed from a fatal heart attack while she was asleep. It's about 8:17 AM, and he's sitting at our kitchen table reading through the sports section of today's edition of the *Las Vegas Review-Journal*. About a foot away from his right hand is his coffee cup— he takes his coffee black.

By Frankie's account, we moved here from Ohio in 1977—I was 25, and she was 24. Before that, my parents—Giovanni and Maria Rossi—immigrated from L'Aquila, Abruzzo, Italy. Like many other foreign-born families that immigrated during the Second Wave, both of our families were searching for a

4

better, more prosperous future. None of us particularly miss shoveling snow in the Ohio winter, making sure the roads are salted and plowed, or having to put snow chains on our tires.

Our cat, a 12-pound, 10-year-old calico girl named Chloe, is sleeping on the left armrest of the black leather sofa in a ball peacefully. The Cat Distribution System gifted Chloe to us when she was only six weeks old, seeing as we found her in a dumpster in the parking lot of a Smith's grocery store after we got done shopping on a Sunday afternoon. We checked everywhere for her mom, but after about two weeks of searching, we concluded that mom was either dead or abandoned Chloe. On the way home the day we found Chloe, we stopped at a PetSmart to get some essentials for her: a litter box, litter, dry cat food, treats, a tree that's taller than me (this thing is 6', and I'm only 5'10"), and a few different types of toys. The whole trip cost us a pretty penny, but Chloe has been a spoiled cat ever since. It took Chloe a long time to learn to trust us, but the investment was worth it. She loves to cuddle when one of us goes to take a nap and goes between my and Frankie's room and Jeremy's room at night. Chloe also doesn't know a stranger and is very sociable for the rare times we have guests over.

At about 9:35 AM, Jeremy's phone lights up and vibrates from a phone call. I'm not sure where he went off to, but probably the restroom or the backyard, if I had to guess. I glance over to check who it is, and it's my nephew David. Jeremy has three sons—David is the oldest, Thomas is the middle, and Cody is the youngest. David moved to Tampa, Florida, about twenty years ago and has children of his own, so he doesn't call all that often. He usually doesn't mind if I pick it up when he's not around, so I do.

"Hey David, how's it going?"

"Oh, hey, Uncle Jimmy. Can I speak to my dad?"

"You know, David, I'm not sure where he is right now. He left his phone on the kitchen table, which is why I picked it up. Would you mind giving me a minute so I can look for him?"

"Yeah, sure. I'll stay on the phone."

My house is thankfully not unbearably large and is about 1,600 square feet and two stories. I can move around reasonably well, and stairs aren't a huge burden. I go upstairs and walk to Jeremy's room. The door is closed, so I knock a couple of times.

"Jeremy? You in there?"

"Yeah, what's up?"

"I have David on the phone for you. You left it downstairs on the kitchen table."

"Oh, shit? Here, I'll take it."

Jeremy opens the door just a crack, enough to stick his hand through and grab the iPhone from me, and closes the door. I'm not one to eavesdrop, so I go back downstairs, where I find Frankie making breakfast. I haven't seen her all morning, so I assume she either just woke up or just now decided to cook.

It's a little late in the morning to just be waking up for her, though. Frankie is usually awake by 7:00 am on most days. She looks around the kitchen and catches my eye.

"Oh, there you are. Are you hungry, honey?" she asks.

"Yes, of course. What are you making?"

"Breakfast burritos with Beyond Sausage, egg, red bell pepper, mushrooms, green onion, and potatoes. I've been craving this for some time now." Frankie told me many years ago that she's been a vegetarian since she was nine years old. I'm an omnivore by nature, but I've never minded eating plant-based. I don't eat meat all that often anyway—mostly if we go out somewhere nice. Honestly, that's probably part of the reason why we've lived so long.

"That sounds great, sweety! I'll just be over on the couch--"

"Oh, no, it's ready now. Would you mind getting your brother and telling him breakfast is ready?" She finishes wrapping the last of the breakfast burritos and plates the three of them.

I go about halfway up the stairs, then yell, "Jeremy! Breakfast is ready!"

"OK, be right there," he yells back. Within about three minutes, Jeremy begins his descent to the kitchen to join us for breakfast.

"What did you make today?" he asks Frankie.

"Breakfast burritos," she responds and lists out the ingredients again to Jeremy.

"Oh, man, that sounds *delicious*!"

She smiles and brings over the three plates, each containing a rather fat breakfast burrito. Jeremy gets up to make a fresh pot of coffee and gets a glass of water to bring to the table. He sits down and makes himself comfortable.

Frankie looks expectantly at me. "Honey, do you want to say grace?"

"Sure." The three of us hold each other's hands as we sit around the table together.

"Lord, bless the food we are about to eat, the hands that prepared it, and hope that it provides nourishment to our bodies."

"Amen," the three of us say in unison.

I grabbed my burrito and took a big bite out of it.

"My God, Frankie. You've outdone yourself with these!"

"I'm glad you like it, honey." She smiled and kissed me on the cheek.

"I don't *like* it, I *love* it! You should make these more often. For sure."

"I can certainly make that happen. What about you, Jeremy?"

Jeremy looks up, his mouth busy from chewing. He waits a second to chew and swallow before responding.

"I agree with my brother. This is one of the best breakfast foods I've ever had, and you know full well that I can be a picky eater."

"Well, I'm certainly glad you're both enjoying it. I've been wanting to make these burritos, or at least something like it, for quite some time. Just never got around to doing it until today."

The three of us didn't talk much while we were eating. I suppose we're all feeling more hungry than sociable. At least I know I'm like that and have been this way since my youth. When I'm hungry, I don't talk. I just focus on eating.

3: SIXTY-ONE

Ring, ring. Ring, ring. My cell phone's ringing. Who's calling me at 1 pm on a Wednesday? When I looked at the caller ID, it has a 330 area code, so it's from someone back in Ohio.

"Hello?"

"Hello, is this James Rossi?"

"Speaking, who's this?"

It was a man on the other end of the line. "Hi, this is the Mahoning County Coroner—"

I heard crying in the background. I can't make out who's crying, but it's hysterical and uncontrollable sobbing.

"Who died?"

"Mr. Rossi, I'm sorry to inform you, but your parents have passed."

"Wh—what? How? When?" My voice began to shake. Mom and Dad are *gone*?!

"We were called along with medical staff by a…Ralph Mancini? What's your relation to him?"

"He—he's my brother-in-law. How did he end up calling you guys?"

"He told the dispatcher at 9:30 am that he came to drop something off for your parents and intended to visit, and when they weren't out and about in the house, he went searching. He said that their bodies were stiff and cold by the time he arrived. When I came on the scene at 9:41 am, I determined that the cause of death for both was a heart attack about two to three hours prior."

"Well, w—why are *you* telling me instead of Ralph or another family member?"

"They asked me to. I'm truly sorry for your loss, Mr. Rossi."

"Thanks, I guess…"

The line dropped, and the call ended. Without a moment of hesitation, I dropped my phone to the ground, and began sobbing hysterically as well. My parents are gone. This can't be… This just can't be…

I look through my phone contacts, and locate Jeremy. I wonder if he knows. I press the phone icon to call him.

It rings twice, then I heard him pick up.

"Hello?"

"Jer? Have you heard the news?"

"What news, Jim? You're making me nervous."

"I just got the phone call that Mom and Dad are dead." I started crying again.

"WHAT?!" Yeah…That's about how I expected him to react…

"Ralph apparently found them dead when he was going to visit them. It was the coroner that called. I heard crying in the background."

"Jim, I—I don't know what to say." It was at this point that I heard his voice start to shake, and within seconds, he's crying.

"I can't believe they're gone…"

"How did they go?"

"The cause of death was ruled a heart attack. Ralph called 911 and they were already cold and dead by the time he got there."

Jeremy cried harder, and didn't have the energy to speak. I could tell—I know my brother.

"I--I'm gonna hang up now," he said.

"Alright. Call me back if you need anything. Love you little bro."

The line goes quiet. I further burst into tears, unable to control myself either. A few minutes later, my phone rings again—this time, it's Frankie.

"Hi honey," she says.

"Hi…" I said hesitantly, my voice still shaking from all the crying.

"Oh my God, what's wrong?"

"I was told not that long ago that—that—my parents are dead, Frankie…"

"Oh, honey… I'm so sorry… That's tragic. Where are you? Home?"

"Yeah… I'm at home."

"I'll be home in ten minutes. Are you going to be okay?"

"I'll be okay for ten minutes."

"Okay, I'll hurry home. I love you."

"I love you too, Frankie."

I ended the call at that moment.

Eight minutes later, almost to the second from the time I ended the phone call with Frankie, I hear her key jostle in the deadbolt of the front door. She's home.

I was sitting on the couch, my puffy, red face buried in my hands and a box of Kleenex in front of me on the living room table. Frankie comes up to me and sits down to my right.

"Hi, dear."

"Hi." She wraps her arms around me, and I turn my body slightly so that I could lay my head in her chest. She rubs my back with one hand while she's embracing me, and we sit there in silence for a couple of minutes. I'm trying my best to calm my breathing back down and stop crying, but it's difficult.

"Honey?"

I look her in the eyes, tears still rolling down my cheeks.

"Huh?"

"I know you love your parents *so* much. I love them, too. It'll be alright..."

"I... I have to go back to Ohio. For the funeral. Jeremy, too."

"Who's going to pick you up from the airport and all that?"

"I guess I'll figure it out. One of your brothers?"

"I'm sure one of them can help. Do you want me to call one of them?"

"Please... Joe if he's available. I guess I get along with him best."

"Alright, give me a minute."

Frankie gets up to dial Joe's number, and gives him a ring. I didn't hear much, since she went into the bedroom to make the phone call. What I did catch was her briefly explaining the situation, and it sounded like it was going well from what I could make out.

She came back to the living room ten minutes later with a slight smile on her face.

"Joe said he's available whenever you need him to pick you up and drop you off from Cleveland airport. Do you want me to come with you to Ohio?"

"Yes, please. Thank you for calling him, sweety."

"You're welcome. I love you so much, Jimmy. Forever and always."

~ * ~

A few days later, Frankie and I were on a plane back to Ohio to bury my parents. I've been through a lot, but having them both go at the same time is on another level.

The ceremony was being held at my childhood church—Saint Nicholas. Everyone was there, even people I don't remember. Uncle Greg, Mom's two sisters, all of Frankie's brothers, and her parents. There were cousins that flew in from all over the country, most of which I forgot their names.

It gets to the point where I'm asked to address everyone at the lectern in the church, to say a few words. I'm the older son, so of course everyone expects me to have it together. At the moment, that is the *opposite* of how I'm feeling. I do not have it together. I do not have the emotional resolve for this right now. But I need to try.

The room is dead quiet--you could hear a pin drop. I positioned myself behind the lectern, and took a deep breath, with everyone's eyes fixated on me. I'm not used to the spotlight, so this is pretty uncomfortable.

"Friends, family, and loved ones... My parents, Giovanni Rossi and Maria Polce Rossi were among the strongest, most resilient people I've ever known.

Dad, with his unending patience and ability to keep everything stable at home. Fixing my and Jeremy's toys growing up when they would break. Encouraging us to chase our dreams, whether that was playing football, going to school, or—for me—wrestling with the fact your oldest son was being shipped off to Vietnam.

Mom, with her kind and patient heart, always making sure we didn't go without. She would tell me we'll be okay when the going got rough. She cooked all of our meals, and made sure that we did well in school. She made sure that Jeremy and I grew up to be gentlemen who respected women, became productive members of society, and empathetic, caring humans.

There are not enough hours in the day, nor enough words in the English language, to communicate how much I love and appreciate them. They gave everything they could to make sure that our lives were the best they could be. They never went to bed angry, and always told us that we're loved and appreciated.

Mom, Dad,... I love you. Until we meet again."

The once silent group of people began clapping, some wiping their own tears in the process. I lost my composure as I started to cry when leaving the front of the room, returning to my seat in the front row pew.

The rest of the ceremony moves on, but I don't. My parents were gone, and if there's one thing that terrifies me about death, it's the finality of the act.

4: SIXTY

Today, we are celebrating Frankie's 59th birthday, making the date January 25. She's a few months my junior. It's currently 12:05 PM.

Something you need to understand about Frankie is that while she *says* she doesn't want me to make a big deal out of something like her birthday, she *loves* it when she's surrounded by her closest friends and relatives. I've reached out to all of her brothers. Ralph is the oldest, and Vincent is the second oldest. After that, you have her brother Joseph, and Frankie is the baby of her siblings. You can imagine that having three older brothers meant that they were all fiercely protective of her growing up, and they still are, honestly. They certainly gave me a run for my money and low-key threatened me to treat her right when she first brought me home to her family. Of course, this was while we were still living in Struthers, Ohio—a suburb that's part of the Youngstown metro area. Vincent and Ralph still live in Struthers, so they've flown into Vegas to be able to see Frankie.

In addition, I've contacted Frankie's best friend, Rosa. They have been best friends since childhood, so they've experienced every stage of life by each other's sides at this point. I'm thankful that Rosa lives in Vegas with us as well.

The best thing about this is that Frankie has no idea I've organized any of this. She's going about her day running errands, not once considering that she's going to come home to her brothers and her best friend for her birthday.

I decided not to invite the whole family out from Ohio and other states in the Midwest and East. With both Frankie and I being full-blooded Italian, the family sizes can get ridiculous—especially as you throw a wider net to include more generations. Not to mention, our kitchen isn't the biggest, and I don't have the energy to get more chairs for a bunch of people.

On today's birthday menu for Frankie, I've made her favorite dish—vegetarian lasagna. For the appetizer, I just made a Caesar salad. For dessert, I've made almond biscotti and some chocolate tiramisu. No matter how much Frankie may try to deny it, the woman's certainly got a sweet tooth. Plus, who's going to say no to biscotti and tiramisu? I've been awake since about 6:00 AM, prepping, cooking, baking, and cleaning everything so that it'll be ready by the time Frankie gets home in about an hour. Vincent, Ralph, and Rosa are bringing a gift with them, and they should all be arriving within the next thirty minutes.

About fifteen minutes go by, and Rosa is the first to arrive. She knocks on the door twice, I look through the peephole, and let her in.

"Hi, Jimmy! Long time no see," she says as she hugs me.

"It has been some time, eh?" I said as I hugged her back.

I go to the water fountain in the kitchen and pour some cold water from a pitcher into a glass to hand to Rosa.

"Oh, thank you, Jimmy. I'm parched. How's Frankie been?"

"She's just been doing her own thing. You know how she is. You've known her longer than I ever have."

I hear the doorbell ring, and my head jerks subconsciously to look towards the door. I got out of my chair to go answer it. On the other side of the door are Vincent and Ralph; it seems they've come together in a rental car.

As I open the door, Vincent outstretches his arms and says to me excitedly, "Hey Jim! Long time, no see!"

"Hey Vincent," I say as I go in to hug him. I greet Ralph the same way and hug him as well.

"Please, make yourselves at home. Would you like water or anything?"

"Sure, I'll take a glass. That'll be great," says Ralph.

"Make that two," said Vincent.

I grab two 8-oz glasses out of the cupboard and fill them both with cold water. I then place them on the table in front of Vincent and Ralph.

Both brothers take a sip out of their respective glasses. Ralph looks at me and asks, "Where's our sister?"

"You know, that's a good question. Let me give her a call."

I search for Frankie's contact in my iPhone, select it, and tap the call button. The line starts ringing out.

"Hey honey," I hear her answer.

"Hi, sweetheart. When do you think you're going to be home?"

"Oh, I'm on my way home. I'll be there in about ten minutes. I'm just over on Fort Apache and Patrick Lane."

"Great, sounds good. See you soon, love."

"OK, love you. Bye."

The line goes dead, and I hear a click.

I turn to my brothers-in-law and say, "She'll be here in ten minutes."

"Oh, awesome! Should we hide, or how are we doing this?"

"Nah, we can just hang out here. Seeing all three of you will be plenty." I smiled.

"Rosa, you doing alright? Can I get you anything else before Frankie gets here?"

"No, I'm okay for now. Thank you for the hospitality, Jim."

"Alright." As I turn my back to my guests, I take the lasagna out of the oven. Oh, *damn*, this smells awesome! Maybe even better than the breakfast burritos that Frankie made that one time.

Fifteen minutes go by, and I hear the door handle jostle. Someone's turning the key. Frankie's home!

She pushes the door open an inch, then another inch, and finally fully lets herself in.

"Surprise!' we all yell in unison.

"Oh… Oh my God! Jim, you didn't have to do this for me!" Frankie, usually calm and collected, suddenly bursts into tears, realizing who is here.

My face lights up as I see her smile and cry at the same time. It's such a great feeling to see her beautiful face smile so candidly.

"I know you haven't seen your brothers or Rosa in a long time, so I have been planning this for months to get everyone here."

"Oh, Jim… I'm so glad I married you all those moons ago. You have always known how to make me happy, and today is no different. Thank you. I've missed all of them, and you brought them here."

Frankie goes over to hug her brothers and Rosa individually and gives them a peck on the cheek, in the way we Italians do when we greet each other. Especially considering how long it's been since we last had everyone together at the same time.

"You cooked too?! What did you make?!" I've never seen her this surprised before, I don't think.

"I did. I made your favorite—veggie lasagna. For dessert, I also made almond biscotti and chocolate tiramisu."

Her voice shakes as she chokes back even more tears, which I know are out of joy and happiness. She then comes over to me, her eyes welled up, and her arms outstretched.

"Thank you, Jim… Thank you. You know how much it means to me to have the people I love. Including you. I love you so much."

I give her a long hug, embracing her small frame and gently rubbing her back in the process.

"Well…shall we eat? The lasagna should be rested and cooled off enough by now."

"Yes, let's eat!" Vincent said.

I grabbed the chef's knife out of the block and uncovered the top of the lasagna pan, which I covered with foil earlier to retain some of the warmth after I took it out of the oven.

"Frankie, how big of a piece do you want?"

"Oh, um… I don't know, just a medium-sized piece. I trust you to cut the right amount."

"Alright." I carve out a 4-inch by 3-inch piece of lasagna for her, and I give her one of the corners, then put it on her plate. Frankie has always loved the corner pieces due to the little bit of extra crunch along the edge. I handed her the plate with the corner piece of lasagna, as well as a fork. She thanks me and puts it on her placemat at the table.

Next, I cut a piece for myself, which measures about the same size as the one I just did for Frankie, except I cut along the height next to the corner piece I just gave her. I, too, bring it back to my chair at the table. Vincent, Ralph, and Rosa follow suit, and finally, we're all about to dig in. But first, we need to say grace.

"Ralph, do you want to do grace?" I asked.

"Sure. It seems only fitting."

Ralph clears his throat and begins to say grace.

"Lord, please bless our beloved sister a very happy 59th birthday, and may she have many more birthdays to come. Also, bless the lasagna we are about to devour, and I'm sure it will be delicious. In Jesus's name, amen."

"Amen," we say in unison.

The clicking, cutting, and stabbing of forks and knives monopolize the sound in the room for the next few minutes, as everyone is readily digging into the vegetarian lasagna I made.

"Damn, Jimmy, who taught you how to make lasagna like this? It tastes damn close to our mother's recipe," Ralph exclaimed.

"Ha, well, Mama Rossi taught me a thing or two as well about cooking. I'd like to think I did learn quite well."

"She most certainly did. Shit, this is delicious," added Vincent.

Rosa looks at me for a moment and finishes chewing before she begins what she's about to say.

"This is almost better than *my* lasagna!" she adds.

Truly, I'm glad that everyone is enjoying themselves and thinks the lasagna is tasty. I agree with them—I'm proud of myself for how it turned out.

"Is anyone interested in a glass of wine? I've got a Sangiovese from Tuscany called Brunello di Montalcino I haven't opened yet. It's been a few years, so it has aged a bit."

With everyone chewing, they all look at me and nod affirmingly. I grab four wine glasses and divide the wine evenly among them. I then serve the wine to everyone and myself and sit back down.

"To Frankie's 59th birthday and our beloved family and friends."

"Cheers," we said while clicking our glasses together and taking a sip.

"So, Frankie, got any good shows you're watching lately?" Rosa asks.

"Well…I do seem to like *The Crown*. A lot of people seem to hate the British royals, even think they're annoying, but I rather enjoy the dramatics."

"What channel is that on?"

"Oh, it's on Netflix. Don't you have Netflix, Rosa?"

"Well, kind of. My grandson added me to his account, but I don't use it too much. I tend to watch my soaps during the day."

"Ah, yes, that's right. You've never been much into Netflix. You should give it a try; there are lots of shows and movies to watch beyond the crap that's on

TV."

"Maybe I'll try it when I get home. I just need to figure out how to use my damn TV first. It's one of those smart TVs. Do you think you could help me with that?"

"Uh… Jim set ours up when we got our TV. Honey, would you be willing to help Rosa with it later? Or whenever she has time?"

I finish chewing the lasagna that's in my mouth and wipe my face. "Sure, that's fine. She can just call me, and I'll do what I can."

"Okay, great! Hey, Vince, how are those Ohio winters treating you? Still shoveling snow?" Frankie asks.

"I got this kid next door helping me out back home. He's a young man of about thirteen years old. His name is Robert; he doesn't seem to mind. He comes over to shovel once he's done his driveway."

"Oh, how very kind of him. What about you, Ralph? Sick of the snow and ice yet?"

"You know, I complain about it every winter, but yes, I still do shovel my snow. I have one of the grandkids come help when I'm not feeling in the best condition, too," Ralph responds.

"I'm so glad that we haven't dealt with snow since we moved out here in Vegas," I interject.

"Yeah, yeah. Way to rub it in, Jimmy."

"Look, you could have moved many moons ago. You didn't have to stay."

"You're right, but we wanted to stay close to the grandkids."

I looked at Frankie, then back at Ralph. Frankie and I exchanged a look at what appeared to be a mutual agreement.

"Can't say I can relate. Never had any."

Ralph looks at me quizzically for a moment, and then the words finally escape from his lips. "Do you ever regret not having kids?"

I thought for a moment, then looked at Frankie. "No, not really. We've had a pretty good life, especially since we moved here. We've traveled a lot when we were younger—like going to Europe for two weeks, doing a tour of South America, doing an Alaskan cruise, and much more. There's been a lot more opportunities here than we found in the Youngstown area, too."

Ralph raises his eyebrows and nods his head. "You've got a fair point there, Jimbo."

By the time Ralph finishes annunciating that last syllable, I realize everyone's plates are empty.

"Anyone save room for dessert? There's tiramisu and biscotti."

"Yeah, I'll have a small piece," Vincent says.

"Same for me," says Ralph, then Rosa.

"What about you, birthday girl?"

"Yes, a small piece is fine by me, too, honey. Thank you."

I proceed to cut four 2-inch by 2-inch pieces of tiramisu and plate them for everyone. I brought the empty plates that once contained lasagna back to the kitchen sink and rinsed them off individually, along with the silverware that was used. I add a candle to Frankie's helping and light the wick with a lighter that I had in my pocket. I bring the tiramisu over, as well as fresh silverware. Once I sat back down, I looked at Vincent, and he knew what was about to happen next just from that.

"On a count of 3, follow my lead. One... two... three..."

Then we started singing in unison. "Happy birthday to you! Happy birthday to you! Happy birthday, dear Frankie! Happy birthday to you!"

Frankie's beautiful face turns beet red, blushing hard, yet it's obvious that she feels grateful to be able to celebrate another birthday.

Slowly but surely, everyone took a bite of the tiramisu. Everyone seemed to let out a collective sigh, and I saw Vincent and Ralph allude to needing to loosen their belts by a notch or few.

While everyone finishes their tiramisu and/or wine, Vincent strikes up more conversation.

"So now that we're all about to go into a food coma, what's next?"

"You want to play a game of bullshit? You know, the card game?"

"Oh man, it's been *forever* since I've played bullshit. Sure, get the cards out."

I headed upstairs to get my deck of cards and return with them. I'm surprised I was able to find them so quickly—it's been a minute since I've played any sort of card game, especially this one. I take out the jokers and distribute the remaining cards evenly among us face down.

"Alright, Frankie, you go first. Then we'll go around the table to the right."

She fiddles through her stack of cards for a minute, being cautious not to expose any of her cards to anyone else at the table.

"Two of Diamonds," she says as she puts a card down in the middle, face down.

Vincent is next since he's directly to her right.

"Three of clubs." Next is Ralph.

"Four of hearts." I'm to Ralph's right.

"Five of spades."

Rosa looks more carefully through her cards. "Six of clubs," she says.

Finally, it's my turn to stir the pot. "Bullshit," I exclaim.

"Damn, Jim, already?" Vincent questions.

Rosa quizzically looks at me and turns the card over that she just put down so that it's face up. It's a six, alright...but it's a six of *hearts*, not clubs. I admire her bravery, but I know this game well.

"Take them all, Rosa!"

Unsurprisingly, she rolls her eyes and scoffs at me. I love annoying people with this game. It's fun. I look through my stack of cards.

"Seven of spades."

Of course, as the game naturally goes around and around the table, "bullshit" was called several times on each other. I ended up winning, considering I've always been good at this game. I would usually let Frankie win, but the competitor in me loves the dopamine rush of victory. By 4:00 pm, everyone has left, and Frankie and I have the house to ourselves again.

5: FIFTY-NINE

At 59 years old, you could safely say I've seen a lot of shit by now. By the time you reach my age, there's not a lot that can get under your skin.

Since I don't have any children, I don't have grandchildren as a result. My brother Jeremy carried the burden of perpetuating the Rossi family name. It just didn't appeal to me for some reason. It's not that we necessarily had a bad childhood, but I guess I never had the paternal urges like he did. Oh well. I don't regret it.

I very much recognize that these thoughts and beliefs make me very different from most people in my generation—the Baby Boomer Generation. The generation that would leave behind a gargantuan wealth and economic stature to those after them. The generation that would change history. Although they've been gone for some time now, my parents were *furious* with me when I said they were not getting any grandchildren out of Frankie and I. They were beside themselves with anger.

I walked over to the end table by the couch and grabbed my iPhone—where I seemed to have left it. When did that get over there? Am I just getting old and don't remember?

Anyway, once it's in my hands, I unlock the screen with my PIN so I can check my messages and any missed calls. At first glance, I have three unread iMessages and a missed phone call. The phone call seems to be from Rosa. Dutifully, I returned her call—only to reach her voicemail. It appears we are now engaging in a game of phone tag.

"Hi, you've reached Rosa. Sorry, I missed your call. Please leave me your name and number, and I'll get back to you as soon as I can. Thanks!" *Beeeeeeep.*

"Hi Rosa, it's Jim. Just returning your call. Hope all is well. Talk to you soon. Bye." I promptly hung up the call after that.

I sit down on the sofa and turn the channel to ESPN. Surely, there's got to be something to watch on a Sunday in early September, right? This *is* football season, after all. The game is at commercial break, but I see on the description

20

when it comes up who's playing—the Packers are playing the Vikings at U.S. Bank Stadium in Minneapolis. I'm sure this isn't going well for the Packers, considering they're the worst in the NFC North right now.

The game comes back from a commercial break, and unfortunately, the worst sports broadcaster of all time is one of the two at this game today—Cris Collinsworth. Ugh, I hate him for so many reasons. It's just that Collinsworth puts his biases on display and doesn't shut up about them the whole game. The Packers are losing, to no one's surprise, 31-17 right now. Not only did we just come back from a commercial break, but *halftime* just ended, too. At 14:05 into the third quarter, I see a flag come out—then another, and another. There end up being about five flags thrown on the field in a short period. NFL referee Brad Rogers runs out, sporting the typical referee uniform you expect, surrounded by the other officials while they consult him.

The call in question is that the Packers' offensive line didn't have enough players at the line of scrimmage, so it would be considered illegal formation unless Brad Rogers saw something different. Here comes the verdict.

"Illegal formation, offense, five-yard penalty from the spot of the foul, repeat second down," he says, as he additionally signals the call with his hands. Once again, both teams lined up at the line of scrimmage—this time with the required number of players to avoid the same call.

I feel my stomach rumble and look at my iPhone to get the time. It's 9:43 AM, and I've somehow not eaten breakfast yet—even though I've been awake at least two and a half hours. I look in the fridge and see that we still have eight eggs left out of the dozen. Towards the back of the fridge, I see a couple of plastic containers—one contains strawberries, and the other contains raspberries. Looking around the kitchen some more, I noticed we had some wheat bread left, as well as a new bottle of maple syrup. Frankie is just coming down the hall, seemingly from our downstairs bathroom.

"Sweetheart, have you had breakfast yet?" I ask her.

"No. Were you making something?" she responds.

"I was about to make some French toast with the strawberries and raspberries, as well as some scrambled eggs."

"That sounds wonderful. Thank you, honey. I appreciate it very much." She smiled as she finished uttering the last word and kissed me gently on my lips. My God, I love this woman with all that I have, and I always will. After all these years, I don't love her any less than I did the very first time we told each other, "I love you." As a matter of fact, with each passing year and decade, my love for Frankie has only grown *stronger*. I realize that many would probably be jealous of our marriage. It's a marriage that has stood the test of time—through sickness and health, through thick and thin, for richer or poorer, and for better or worse. Love like this *does* exist, but I'll be damned if I said it was easy. It was most certainly not easy, and my heart goes out to young people these days trying to find Mr. or Mrs. Right.

I crack four eggs into a large bowl and throw the shells into the trash, turning on the gas burner beneath the pan I'm going to use. Then I untie the twisty off the loaf of wheat bread and get out four pieces. Two for Frankie, two for me. I cut each slice of bread diagonally and set the pieces aside while I whisk the eggs thoroughly. I start to dunk four of the diagonally sliced pieces into the beaten eggs, then place each of them into the pan on the stove with heat under it, which is covered in spray butter to prevent the eggs from sticking everywhere on the pan. Specks of grease start flying, and the popping starts to fly onto my bare hands. "Ow," I mumble under my breath, running my left hand under cold water in the sink to ease the immediate pain. I let the four pieces currently in the pan sit there for about a minute before grabbing the tongs to flip them over. While those are cooking, I grab two large plates from the cabinet just above the stove to put our food on. I turn over the four currently in the pan and let it sit for about another minute before plating two on one plate and then two on the other. I pour myself a glass of orange juice before repeating the process with the remaining four pieces of bread.

After finishing the French toast, I whisk and scramble the remaining eggs in the carton while sprinkling shredded cheddar cheese into the pan as well. Frankie has always liked her eggs this way, and what self-respecting Italian doesn't have a cheese obsession? Once the eggs are done, I scatter the strawberries and raspberries on the freshly cooked French toast and call for Frankie, who seems to have changed the channel from the football game to KTNV 13 Action News. I walk over to being just behind her and gently put my right hand on her left shoulder.

"Breakfast is ready, beautiful," I say as I kiss the top of her head.

"Oh, fantastic!" She immediately springs to her feet and walks towards the kitchen. I place one of the plates of food directly in front of her at the table, then go back to get mine and retrieve the bottle of maple syrup.

"Anything to drink? Coffee? Tea? Water?" I inquire.

"Have you made any tea yet?"

"No, not yet, but I can put some in the kettle. I'll get you a glass of water while I make it?"

"Sure, that's fine."

"What kind of tea are you wanting, hon?"

"Do we have any of that peppermint tea left?"

"We sure do."

"Yes, let's make that."

I fill the kettle with water up to the marked fill line and place the bag of tea within the metal container inside the kettle. After closing the lid and turning it on, I return to the dining table with two forks and knives in my hands. I make a second trip to get our glasses of water, then finally sit down and get comfortable.

I liberally pour some of the maple syrup on my French toast, making sure that most of the surface is covered. As I take my first few bites, I notice that Frankie has caught my gaze.

"How did I get so lucky?" she asks me.

"What do you mean?"

"Jim, we've been married for decades. Even now, there's no one I would rather be with. I love you so much, and you have always meant the world to me."

"I love you too, beautiful. It didn't take me long to figure out that you were the woman of my dreams many moons ago, and I knew I would want to spend the rest of my life with you. You were always very different from anyone I've ever met. You continuously inspire me to be a better man, even now. Not just for me but because of who you are. You're incredible inside and out, and marrying you was the best decision I've ever made in my life."

6: FIFTY-EIGHT

I opened the garage door with my remote, just getting home from Electric Chair Salon (my barber). I see Daron every two weeks because I've got hair that grows fast. I should count my lucky stars, though, since I'm not bald, nor do I have the desire to shave off what's currently there. After pulling into the garage and opening my car door, I was immediately met with the sound of Frankie crying. I could hear it through the door that goes to the rest of the house, so she must have been in the kitchen or somewhere right on the other side of the wall. Frankie's not one to cry often, so I wonder what happened.

I walked in the door, and made my presence known. Kismet was…somewhere in the house, but I'm not entirely sure where.

"Honey, I'm home—"

Frankie was sitting at the dining room table, at least ten used tissues immediately near her, and her face red and puffy. Oh no… Something had to have happened. Something bad if she's this hysterical. I approached her from the right side.

"Holy fuck. Frankie. What *happened*? I'm not going to ask if you're okay because you're obviously not…"

"I… My dad's dead… He lost his battle with heart disease…"

"Oh, sweetheart…"

The only way I know how to respond is to hug and hold her. After being with Frankie for most of our lives, I know that she doesn't want solutions in the moment. I know that nothing I say in that vein right now is going to help her.

I brought her head to my chest, and she wrapped her arms around me while she sobbed uncontrollably. Frankie and her dad were close, although not as close as her and her mom. Either way, she spoke to both of her parents frequently enough that it mattered.

I felt my shirt dampen quickly from her tears. I can't stand the thought and sight of her being like this, but such is the cycle of life. I wish I could do something to help her, and I can't pretend that I don't know how it feels. Losing the people (and animals, since they're family, too) you are closest to, that you love so dearly, is one of the most heartbreaking, gut-wrenching experiences you can ever go through.

"Can I help with anything, dear? Have you drank enough water today?" I asked her. For all the crying she's doing, I'm almost certain that she hasn't drank enough water to replenish what's been lost. She's also generally bad at drinking water to keep her hydrated on a baseline level.

"W—water, p—please," she said between each trembling breath.

"Alright, I'll get you some," I said, patting her head gently before walking to get a clean glass from the cabinet.

"Ice?" I asked her.

"Y—yes," she responded.

I grabbed some ice from the freezer, and dropped the cubes into the cup before I poured in the water. I brought the glass over to her, placing it on the table a few inches from her hand.

"Do you want me to give you some space? Or do you want me to stay here with you?"

"S—stay, p—please…"

"Okay. I'll stay with you, beautiful."

I pulled up another chair to sit directly next to her, and ran my left hand through her hair. I kissed her forehead tenderly, and slightly pulled away so she could get her emotions out.

While we're sitting in silence together, I hear the pitter patter of paws closing in on us. I look around us in every direction, and realize that those are, in fact, the orange paws of Kismet.

"Oh, hi Kismet."

Kismet quickly jumped into Frankie's lap and put his paws onto her chest. Frankie unconsciously put her hands around Kismet to support his fat ass. Kismet then begins to headbutt Frankie from her chin, believing that doing so will resolve all of her problems and heal her broken heart.

"Hi, baby boy…" she said, taking deep but even breaths to soothe herself some. She began petting him, then went to give him head scratches. Kismet smiles at Frankie, happy and content with the attention she was giving him. His smile reinforces how empty that little orange head is, void of a single brain cell and any thoughts. She takes notice, and squeezes him tighter in her embrace. Kismet complains about this change, but tolerates it for the sake of Frankie's emotional state.

"I love you, Frankie." I grabbed a clean tissue and wiped the few tears she still had running down her face.

"I love you, too, Jimmy. Thank you for staying with me."

"Of course. Anything to make my baby girl happy and at peace."

Her face flushed red the moment I said "baby girl". I have called her that throughout our entire relationship, and it seems that the effects haven't worn off with the decades that we've spent together. I love this woman more than any words can express, and I know for a fact that she still feels the same way. We made vows to each other 'til death do we part, through sickness and health, through happiness and despair. I am thankful for her every day I wake up next to her, and fall asleep with her, and all of life's experiences in-between.

7: FIFTY-SEVEN

I heard my phone vibrate on the dining room table for a moment, then it began to ring…and ring…and ring. Whoever it was, they weren't going to let up without me answering this phone call.

I jogged over from the living room, which was maybe twenty feet away. I looked at the caller ID, and noticed that it was my brother. I answered the call.

"Hey, Jer," I said.

He's sobbing uncontrollably, to the point where he's inconsolable. What happened?

"Jim, she… she…"

"What is it? What happened?"

"Giulia… She's… She's gone…"

"What do you mean *gone*, Jeremy?"

"She… didn't… wake up…"

"Did you try CPR? Feel for a pulse on her neck or wrists?"

I listened as my brother struggled to compose himself at the tragedy that just wrecked the family that he helped create.

"Hold on. Stay here," he said.

"Alright, I'm right here for you," I said, trying to reassure him that I was here for whatever happens.

What I heard next from his end of the phone was one of the worst experiences of my life up to this point. I heard him wail and scream with abandon. I listened quietly while he failed to calm himself. Everything in him had exactly zero restraint.

"Jer, do you want me to come to your house? Do you think that would help?" I offered. It turns my stomach to hear my brother act this way without someone to offer him a sliver of comfort.

"Yes…" he said.

"Okay, I'll be right there as quick as I can."

"Thanks. S—see you soon, J—Jim."

He hung up the phone after that. I quickly grabbed my keys, wallet, and phone, then headed out to Jeremy's as quickly as I could.

When I say quickly, I mean I risked catching a speeding ticket or few on the way there. From my home, I took Pecos Road south to the 215, then took that to the Valle Verde Drive exit. Once I got off on Valle Verde, I went just past Paseo Verde Parkway into his community. Upon arrival at his home, I noticed that the garage door was already open. He must have left it open since he was expecting me. I tried the handle of the door that goes into the house, and it was also unlocked already. I let myself in, and announce my presence. It's actually pretty early...

"Jer, I'm here," I called out.

"Bedroom," I heard him respond.

I walked towards the master bedroom, which is where him and Giulia stayed together. All of the kids have moved out several years ago, making my brother an empty nester at this point. Now he is a widower.

What I walked into was Jeremy lying on the bed in the fetal position with a box of tissues coming up on the last small handful next to him. By this point, he must have just stopped crying within the last couple of minutes. His face was still puffy and red, but his voice and heart rate have started to stabilize a bit.

"Jer... I'm so sorry..."

He rolled onto his right side to face me while I sat on the left edge of the bed. He reached up to grab me for a hug, and I leaned into it. He started to cry again, and I just let it happen. His tears began to soak my shirt, but I don't care.

"Thank...you..." he said between sobs.

"For what?" I asked.

"F—for coming... to be... with me..."

"Jer, you're my brother. You know I'd do anything for you, man."

I felt him embrace me tighter as his tears and emotions flowed.

"A—are you staying?" he asked.

"I'm here for as long as you need me," I said.

He tried to calm himself again. It seems like he wants to talk about everything, but I can't be certain. As I'm ruminating on what could possibly happen next, Jeremy sat up in bed, his back against the wall while still on the bed.

"Okay..."

"Tell me what happened, Jeremy. As much as you're able to tell me right now."

Jeremy takes a few slow breaths, inhaling and exhaling with discernible thought and effort before he begins to respond. He wipes the tears that are currently trailing down his face.

"Well... I went to go do some yard work earlier. Pull weeds, clean the pool, that sort of thing. I would like to think that I was being pretty quiet, and since I started early, I let her sleep in."

"Okay, good. What happened next, Jer?"

"Well, when I came back in a couple of hours later, I was curious to know why she hadn't woken up yet. By this point, it was about 9 am. She is usually awake long before then. When I came back into the bedroom, I noticed her still in bed, but…she wasn't moving."

"Oh, fuck, I'm so sorry."

"So, the next thing I do is that I was looking for any sign of life. Her chest wasn't rising and falling like she was breathing. I checked her pulse on both her neck and wrists. I tried to put my ear to her mouth, but that was kind of difficult since she was laying on her stomach with her head turned to the right side. I…I think she was already gone by that point."

I turned the rest of my body towards Jeremy, and gave him another hug. This one was more "proper", in the sense that we were both at least sitting upright by now. He put his chin on my right shoulder.

"My heart breaks for you, little bro. I'm devastated, too. I would be lost without Frankie," I said.

I didn't know how to comfort or reassure him otherwise. As much effort as I put into being a safe person to open up to for the people closest to me, that doesn't mean I'm always able to find the words to do so. I've discovered that sometimes, it's easier to be quiet and let the moment happen organically. Although we've had our fights and disagreements growing up, the only person I love more than Frankie is my brother. We've truly been through hell and back together.

"Thanks, man. I appreciate you coming over here on a whim, too."

"Don't worry about it, Jer."

"I love you, bro."

"I love you, too, fucker."

Jeremy chuckled slightly at that, which I'm going to take as a positive. He's always been one to look at the glass half-full. In his authentic Sagittarian nature, he's historically been one to believe that everything will work out on its own.

"I'll help you with whatever you need, bro. Funeral arrangements, telling the boys, anything you need," I offered. Jeremy was about to have so much on his plate that it's going to make his head spin, on top of his corporate job that can sometimes suck the soul out of his life force.

"I couldn't ask for a better brother, Jim."

I smiled. "Thank you, Jer. I appreciate the kind words."

"Are you hungry? I'm starving."

"Yeah, I could eat," I said.

"Let's go get brunch," he said.

"That sounds like a great idea. I'll drive."

He grabbed his keys, and I fished mine out of my pocket as we headed to my car. He closed the garage door behind us. The two of us went to get brunch, and despite the circumstances, it was nice to spend time with him. Just the two of   us,   like   old   times.

8: FIFTY-SIX

I walked into the men's room at work on the casino level, minding my own business. All I had to do was take a leak. Suddenly, I hear a familiar voice that I haven't heard in a very long time...

Typically, I find the urinal that's not near anyone else to do my business. The familiar voice begins to get louder as he comes closer to me. Do my ears and eyes deceive me? Is that who I fucking think it is?

I hurry up and finish taking a piss before I dare initiate any kind of conversation. There are few occurrences more awkward than someone trying to talk to you when you have your dick in your hand as you empty your bladder.

"Uncle Greg?" I call across the restroom.

He makes eye contact with me, wasting no time scanning me. That is, without a doubt, Uncle Greg.

"Jimmy?!" He seems just as surprised as I am that we're having this conversation. In the men's room. While I'm at work.

"Crazy to see you here..." I told him.

"Yeah, no kidding. What are you doing here? What's with the suit?"

"Uncle Greg, I work here. I have for a few years. I'm actually the Vice President of Gaming..."

"No *shit*! When did you even move out here?"

"About thirty years ago at this point."

I witnessed his jaw drop to the floor in disbelief.

"So... In your twenties? Are you married? Have any kids?"

"Yes, I'm married. My wife's name is Francesca, but she mostly goes by Frankie. Kids, no. I never felt any desire to have them, and she didn't either. I just don't feel that children are necessary when I love my life the way it is."

"Ah, makes sense... You remember my wife, Angela? We had our first child about a year after we first met you."

"Oh, that's cool. Did they have kids? I assume you're a grandparent by now?"

"Yes, we have eight grandkids."

I felt my heart jump out of my chest and catch in my throat. Eight. Fucking. Grandkids?! Does no one know what a condom is in this family?

"Wait, how many *kids* did you have to have eight *grandkids*?"

"Four. One girl, and she's the oldest. The rest are boys."

I did some simple arithmetic in my head after receiving that information. Eight grandkids, four kids, so that's…an average of two each? Unless it happened differently.

"Oh. Wow. Y'all are busy."

"My daughter had three. The second-oldest son had two. The second youngest son had two. The youngest has one."

"Thank you for clarifying the math, I guess?"

God, this is so awkward. I am terrible at small talk. I always have been. I just want to get to something more interesting than talking about how much Greg raw-dogged Angela for her to pop out four kids.

"Yeah… So anyway, this is my first time coming to the Silverton. Angela's out in the casino right now waiting on me to come back. I told her that I would play blackjack with her," he said.

Thank God. I can get back to work and out of this terribly awkward, boring conversation.

"Oh, yeah. Of course. I'll let you get back to it. I have to go back to my office to get some work done anyway."

"Of course. No worries. We'll be here for another few days, so don't be a stranger if you see Angela or I running around again."

"Good to see you, Uncle Greg."

"You, too, Jimmy. Take care."

I picked up my pace to leave the men's room, considerably quicker than when I first made my entrance. I made a beeline for the elevators that would take me back to my office.

My God, what a strange and unexpected interaction. I haven't seen Greg since I lived in Ohio. We have never kept in touch by phone or anything over the years. It's not that he was a bad guy or anything. Life just happens that way, and we lost contact. Dad never gave me Greg's number, nor have I bothered to ask for it in all these years. Out of all my family members, both my side and Frankie's family included, I have talked to Greg the *least*. It's exceedingly random to run into him out of millions of potential people in my casino at this exact visit to the men's room.

When I finally got back to my office, I closed and locked the door behind me immediately. I didn't need any more surprise visits from people I haven't seen in literal *decades*, or surprises like that in general. I threw my keys onto my desk before I went around the other side to sit in my chair. The sun was out still, but not for long. It was already 3:30 pm in the middle of November, which means that the sun goes down just slightly earlier every day in the fall here. By the time I leave at 5:30 pm, or whenever I do since I sometimes get kept later, the sun is already down and I turn on my headlights immediately upon getting into the car.

I spent the next two hours in meetings that I didn't schedule. Brian scheduled one of the meetings, as he needed to meet with all of the vice presidents to determine how we were going to close out the fourth quarter and do some projections for quarter one of next year. The other… well… truthfully, it was a waste of time. That seems to be the case with anything related to HR, though. If you ask me, HR is one of the necessary evils of being in a big business. You know they're there. You know you have to behave. But sometimes, you don't *want* to behave. I guess it's a little easier to get away with shit when you're higher up the food chain.

9: FIFTY-FIVE

I was taking a shower, as normal, and I washed my balls and dick because I'm not disgusting. On one of my testicles, the left one specifically, I feel…what is that? I look at it a little closer. Is that a lump? Some sort of growth? I don't remember that being there. I know my own body well enough to know that that is a new development. I was just about done in the shower anyway, and all I had to do was rinse the body wash off my physique.

I grabbed the towel that was hanging on the shower door, and I dried myself off normally everywhere else. I take extra cautionary measures to touch it while it's wet, and also while it's dry, to see if the sensation is different under each condition. It doesn't seem to matter. Upon touch, it's rather sensitive. If I get it in *just* the right way, I experience pain.

"Frankie? Are you around?"

I hear a faint "what" come from the direction of the closet. She must be looking for something in there.

"Yeah, what's up?"

"Can you come here for a moment, dear?"

"Sure, be right there."

I listen as her footsteps inch closer to the bathroom, and finally comes up directly next to me.

"What did you want me for?" she asks.

"Do you see that?" I pointed out on my left testicle the problematic area.

"Oh, wow… Yeah, I don't remember that being there."

"Should I get it checked out, you think?"

"I would. You seem worried about it."

"What kind of doctor do I even call for this?"

"You have a urologist, don't you?"

"Well… Yeah. I haven't been to him in a while, but I do have one."

"Call them first. Have him look at it. He should be able to help you from there. At least that's what I would think. If something like this happened to me,

I'd call my gynecologist first."

It's Sunday, so most medical offices aren't open on the weekend apart from emergency services, which are 24/7.

"I see. That makes sense, I suppose. At least it logically checks out."

"Do you still need me in here with you, dear? You're buck-ass naked and still seem to be dripping wet from the shower."

"Oh... Yeah... Let me dry off and get dressed." I was mildly embarrassed, but Frankie has seen everything hundreds of times by now since we've been married for so long. Not much can surprise her anymore. I've seen the same with her.

I finished drying off, then walked into the bedroom to grab a clean pair of briefs, and a clean shirt and shorts from the closet. Frankie seems to have gone elsewhere now since she wasn't in the same room anymore. I let my hair air-dry in the meantime, which usually occurs quickly.

~ * ~

As soon as I remembered to, I called around looking for an appointment with a urologist the next day. To my surprise, I was able to get one for the same day. That scarcely ever happens when it comes to scheduling doctor appointments, especially when it's a specialist.

I showed up to the appointment on time, and was promptly asked to provide my prior health information as well as that of my insurance. I waited around 45 minutes to be called back.

Once I was called back, a nurse took my vitals before showing me to a patient room. She said that the doctor will be in shortly, so I waited patiently. I took a seat on the patient bed, my feet hanging off the ledge.

Twenty-five minutes later, I heard a knock on the door.

"Come in," I said.

The door handle jostles, and a male doctor comes in wearing light blue scrubs, a stethoscope around his neck, and black sneakers. He's accompanied by a nurse who has a paper-thin gown in her hands. She hands it to me, and tells me to keep it on my lap for the time being.

"Hi, my name is Dr. Flores. I see you're a new patient?"

"Yes, I am."

"Can you verify your first and last name, and date of birth?"

"James Rossi. September 28, 1952."

"What brings you in?" Dr. Flores asked.

"So... I've been having swelling in my nuts for a while, and I noticed recently that I had some kind of weird growth on the left one."

"What do you mean by a while? How long has this been happening?"

"Probably about a month. I never said anything to my wife until just recently, though."

"I see. Anything else? You said that you saw a growth that isn't typical either, right?"

"Yes, that's correct. There has been some pain in that general area, although I haven't really thought anything of it." Why did I wait this long to come see a doctor? I feel like an idiot.

Dr. Flores looked at me for a moment, scanning my facial expressions before he broke eye contact to contemplate how to communicate what was about to happen.

"Do you go by James, Jim, or Jimmy?"

"Jim or Jimmy, preferably."

"Alright. That robe that she just handed to you when we walked in... I'm going to need you to strip down completely, and put on the robe, the opening facing the front. Tie the strings at neck level. There's also a drape in there of the same material that you just rest over your penis. We'll give you a few minutes to change and knock before we come back in."

"Alright."

I obliged the request, and it didn't take more than a few minutes before they knocked and came back in. I permitted them to come in.

Upon re-entry, Dr. Flores puts on gloves before he rearranges the high-fashion garments (the medical gown and drape) in a way that allows him to examine my undercarriage with painstaking detail. It was mildly uncomfortable, but I let him do his thing. It's for my own health, I guess.

"Well, Jim, I don't know how to tell you this..."

"Go on..."

"Jim, you may have cancer. I can't say for sure without a biopsy, so we'll schedule one for you as soon as possible. It's a minimally invasive procedure, and we'll send the tissues off to pathology."

I looked at Dr. Flores with my mouth agape, both of my hands going through my hair simultaneously.

"C... Cancer? What? If it *is* cancer, I mean."

"There are options. Some are more invasive, like removing the testicle that is affected. Chemotherapy is another, but first, we need to be 100% certain of what we're dealing with."

Tears began to well in my eyes at the idea that I may be a cancer patient. Never in my wildest dreams did I imagine that... this would happen to *me*.

"Go on..." I told Dr. Flores.

"If pathology does come back that it's cancerous, Jim, then we'll go over your options—and any further testing you may need—at that point. Please understand something, though. If it *is* cancerous, expect treatment to be aggressive and move quickly."

"Do I... need to do anything else?"

"Is there any family you can call to take you home? Most people want to be with someone after news like this, as you can imagine..."

"Yes, I can call my wife, Frankie."

"Do you have any further questions for me before I let you go, Jim?"

"I—I'm going to need a while to process this. At the moment, I don't think I have questions, but I'm sure I will soon enough."

"Alright. Well, sorry to have been the bearer of bad news…"

"It is what it is," I said.

"Check out with the front desk on your way."

"Will do."

After he left the room, I sat there. Alone. Confused.

Cancer? Me? Fuck…

Frankie will not take this well. As a matter of fact, I know she's going to burst into tears, and in short order. I love her with everything in me, and I know she feels the same way towards me. This is going to crush her.

Not only will it crush Frankie to hear this news, but it's going to crush everyone who knows and loves me. I sat in the patient room for what I thought was a few minutes, and it became apparent that I was there a bit too long. A nurse walked in, and didn't see the doctor with me. Just me, with my face buried in my hands.

"Sir, did you already see Dr. Flores?" she asked.

"Yes, he left a few minutes ago. I'll get going to check out. I just got news that I may have cancer…"

"Oh, I'm so sorry, sir…" she said. "Yes, when you're ready, please head back around to check out. I'll leave you to it."

"Thanks."

She shut the door quietly behind her as she went on her way as well.

I finally made my way back around to the front desk to check out, headed down the elevator to the first floor, and made the dreaded phone call to Frankie to come pick me up. She was about to get some of the worst news of her life.

10: FIFTY-FOUR

It was a relatively normal Saturday evening. When I came in to work, I clocked in immediately, but someone stopped me before I could make it out to the casino floor.

Standing before me is the President of the company. W—what did he want? I haven't had anything worrying or concerning happen lately... Not for a while, as a matter of fact.

"Jim! Great to see you," he said.

"Hey, Brian... I don't usually see you out and about?"

"Yeah, I know. Would you mind coming to my office with me?" he asked.

"Sure, I don't see why not."

He escorts me to the elevator, then we go up to the eighth floor. I don't usually come up to this floor unless I need something.

After navigating what feels like a maze fueled by elevators and tourism, we arrive at his office a few minutes later. Brian opens the door effortlessly, suggesting that he didn't previously lock it before he left the office to come find me. He entered first, and I followed closely behind. I gingerly closed the door behind me.

"So... why am I here, Brian? I hardly ever see you, but I'm sure you have a reason," I said.

"Yes, I do have a reason," he said.

"Well...?"

"Have a seat, Jim."

"Brian, you're scaring me."

"Alright, Jim. Here's what's going on... You came to the Silverton a few years ago, and were made Director of Gaming within two years. That is uncommon, as that progression typically takes longer. Well... Pending your acceptance, we are extending to you another promotion."

My jaw dropped to the floor and my eyes grew a few sizes.

"Brian, w—what are you talking about?"

"Jim, how does Vice President of Gaming sound to you?"

Me? Vice President of *anything*?! What the hell? Please tell me this isn't a joke or a prank…

"You're being serious?"

"Yes, very much so." His facial expression matched the intensity and veracity of the words he was speaking.

"Wow. Yes. I accept."

I find myself at a loss for words. Never in my life did I imagine I would get any executive-level job title, although I am not disappointed that it's being offered to me in this very moment.

"Do you have any questions, Jim?" Brian asked me. His piercing blue eyes looked me up and down as I contemplated a response. It's mildly uncomfortable, but I've dealt with far worse.

"Well, hm… What additional responsibilities am I going to have with this new role?"

He laughed before he answered.

"Meetings. More meetings than you will ever know what to do with. If I'm being honest, you won't even be on the casino floor much now. You're going to have your own office, and have even more people reporting to you."

"My…own office? What office?"

I've never had my own office. This is such a trip.

"Well, since that VP position has been vacant for a while until now, there's a pretty big office a few doors to the left of this one that can be yours. Then there's another one directly to the right. I guess you could have your pick."

"Can we go to these offices now?"

Brian takes a cursory look at his watch, and the judgment he just made seems like a positive one.

"Yeah, I've got some time. Let's go."

I opened the door and waited for him to exit the office behind me before closing it again.

"Go down five doors to the left. That will be the first office. Then the one directly to the right of it is the second."

I followed his directions, and try the handle of the first office that he mentioned. It's locked, of course.

"It's locked," I said.

Brian promptly looks through his giant key ring, filled with at least a couple of dozen different keys. I wonder what all of them go to. He tried to insert three different silver keys, and finally, the fourth one was capable of unlocking that office door. He turned the handle and pushed open the door, allowing me to go ahead of him.

"Go ahead," he said, gesturing with his left hand.

I walked into the office, and was immediately stunned. Caught off guard. Amazed. The floors are completely covered in light oak hardwood, each piece expertly aligned. Towards the back of the office is an executive desk made of dark mahogany, with a computer monitor sitting on top of it. I went over to look at the rest of the setup. A slide-out drawer contained the keyboard and mouse, each on its own pad. Behind the desk was, what looked like, a brand-new Herman Miller black Aeron chair. Towards the front right corner was a small cup that contained a few pens, a yellow highlighter, and a single yellow #2 pencil. Around the perimeter of the office were bookshelves, lined with titles that had to do with gambling, business operations, and finance. There were also several binders and storage boxes packed with paper files of documents containing years past. Just past the door on the right side sat a small two-seater black leather sofa, and a couple of wooden chairs with red cushions to the right of it. The blinds on the windows were open about halfway, and the blinds themselves were free of dust. For a position that Brian says has been vacant for some time, this office has surely been kept in pristine condition.

"Well, what do you think of this one?" Brian asked. "Do you want to take a look at the other office?"

"Be honest with me. Is this one nicer, Brian?"

"I would say so, yeah."

"Then I'll take this one. This place is fucking immaculate."

Brian chuckled. "Yeah, Housekeeping does keep this one in great condition. Someone must have hinted to them that we were filling this position soon."

"Yeah. I'll take it," I said confidently. This is beyond anything I have ever dreamed of, and I'm so grateful to be given this opportunity.

"Sounds good, Jim. We'll get your nameplate created and affixed just outside the door soon."

That's crazy... I can just imagine it now: *James Rossi – Vice President of Gaming*. I could definitely get used to that.

11: FIFTY-THREE

Once again, Frankie and I find ourselves in a hospital. Not because anything bad is happening, but the opposite. Jeremy, the little shit of a brother that I thought for decades wouldn't even get married, is about to become a *grandparent*. What the hell? Is this real life?

This time, because my nephew Cody and his wife Emma live further away from us, the newest addition to the Rossi family is being born at Valley Hospital.

You know, I've always been awkward around babies. It's not that I hate them necessarily. It's that I don't really know what to do with them. I'm not around them enough these days because all of Jeremy's children—my three nephews—are grown at this point. Since we moved away from Ohio in our early twenties, Frankie and I also weren't around for the maturation of *her* nieces and nephews. On occasion, she does express regret that she hasn't been there for more of their lives, but her brothers have also not held it against her. They know they have every opportunity to visit us as well, and understand that effort has to go both ways.

Cody and Jeremy are sitting next to each other in separate chairs, while Emma is laid out on the patient bed. For as much effort as she's trying to put forth into keeping calm, the discomfort of contractions is visible on her countenance.

"You doing okay, love?" Cody asks her.

"As much as I can be… Oh, fuck, there's another contraction…" she said.

Although Frankie doesn't consider herself maternal for anything other than cats, she still has some empathy for Emma enduring indescribable pain.

"Are you having a boy or a girl?" I asked. Both the Rossi and Mancini families are chock-full of boys, with very few girls in between.

"A little girl," Emma says, smiling. Thank fucking God. Sometimes, even *I* need a break from the constant testosterone and competition, and I say that in my fifties. Between Jeremy and I, plus my three brothers-in-law, there are just too many guys around.

40

"Oh, how sweet," Frankie added. "What are you naming her?"

"Olivia Gianna," Emma said.

"Did Cody pick Gianna?" I asked, since that would make the most sense. For once, Emma was one of the only non-Italian people running in our family.

"Yeah, how did you know?"

"Because it's a pretty Italian name, and we're all full-blooded Italian in this family," I said, chuckling.

She laughed in agreement. There was no possible rebuttal that would make sense in this context.

"Oh... Oh no..." Emma said.

"What?" I asked.

"She—she's coming. Olivia is coming."

Emma frantically presses the call light, and not even thirty seconds later, a nurse appears in the patient room.

"You buzzed?" the nurse asks.

"My baby is coming..." Emma says impatiently.

The nurse pokes her head out of the patient room, and yells to the rest of the labor and delivery wing. "Baby is on the way!"

Three other nurses, plus an obstetrician, rush through the door. The obstetrician puts on his gloves, mask, and glasses, then begins guiding Emma through the birthing process.

"Emma, I'm going to be right here with you. Try to relax as much as you can. When you're ready, start pushing," he said.

Emma nodded, giving a valiant effort to keep her composure under the pressure of the situation.

"Ready?" he asks.

"Y—yes," she responds.

"Push, Emma. Push."

Wasting no time, Emma starts to push with all of her might. This reminds me of when my brother was born for how much energy is put into every single push Emma is having to endure. She screams with every push, and the other nurses are keeping a close eye on her while the doctor crouches at the foot of the bed, waiting for Olivia. His hands are in front of him in a way that would support and catch her.

Finally, Emma's efforts pay off, and Olivia Gianna Rossi was born. The first girl of her generation in the Rossi family was finally born.

"Time of birth, October 10, 2005, 4:55 pm," the doctor said. A nurse took down the information readily. The doctor immediately took Olivia's height and weight after cutting the umbilical cord and cleaning her off, then handed her to Emma.

To nobody's surprise, Emma began crying uncontrollably the moment that Olivia was placed in her arms. Despite the weird food cravings, hormonal fluctuations from hell, and everything else that came with growing and gestating a tiny human, she swears that it's worth it. Judging by the look on Frankie's face, she seems to disagree with that sentiment strongly. It's a good thing I don't have any paternal drive, either, or this marriage would have become awkward many years ago.

"Wow, she looks just like you, babe," Cody said.

Emma looked at him in disbelief, and I don't blame her on this one. She definitely looks more Rossi than...whatever Emma's genetic makeup is.

"I'm not too sure about that, dear."

"She may look more like a Rossi now, but that could easily change as she gets older, you know," I said.

"That's true," Emma agreed. I was trying to give her some sliver of hope that little Olivia wasn't just a female carbon copy of the Rossi men. One thing is for sure: Italian genes sure do permeate through everything and become dominant, even when you mix with other cultures.

Throughout the commotion and series of events going on at the present moment, I looked over at my brother. He's not one to cry that much, if at all, but he was *sobbing*. I've never thought of him to be particularly sentimental— that was always more characteristic of me than him, even in childhood.

"Wow, Jer, I never see you this emotional..."

Jeremy tried to catch his breath between sobs.

"I—I know..."

"How does it feel to be a grandpa already?"

"S—still trying to come to terms with that..."

"Do y'all want to have some privacy?" I asked. I was hungry, so it was a good excuse to leave the hospital anyway.

"Y—yes, please," he said. He was still stumbling on his words, struggling to catch his breath and steady his heart rate.

"Alright, we'll head out then. You know how to reach me if you need me, Jer."

I looked over at Cody and Emma.

"Congratulations, you two."

Both Cody and Emma nodded in agreement at me, almost in perfect unison no less.

I grabbed Frankie's hand, and we left Valley Hospital to go to my car, and went to dinner from there. Frankie seemed relieved the moment we stepped foot outside of the hospital, and her sense of well-being and comfort has always been my top priority.

12: FIFTY-TWO

After spending over an hour at Smith's (our main grocery store that we frequent in Vegas) because Frankie insisted that we go up and down every aisle in existence, the two of us were finally headed back to my car with a shopping cart full of...whatever the hell we bought.

I parked towards the back of the lot, and was merely a few feet away from the dumpster. As Frankie and I were loading groceries into the trunk, with some in the back seat, we heard a high-pitched, kind of squeaking sound emanating from the dumpster.

"Hold on a second, honey," she said, putting down the bag she had in her hand a moment earlier. She goes over to the dumpster to investigate, and I heard her audibly gasp as she takes a look at the interior contents.

"Oh my God, Jim! It's a kitten!" Frankie exclaims.

"That's what I heard? A kitten meowing?"

"Yes! She's so cute. Come here."

"How do you know it's a girl?"

"Calicos are 99.9% female. To find a male calico is extremely rare. Come here!"

I know she's going to want to bring this kitten home. I hope it's at least in decent health, so we don't start out with hefty vet bills. I approach Frankie from the right side to look at the kitten.

Oh... Oh my God. She's tiny. She's screaming. She's cold. Most importantly...she's *adorable*. I wasn't really looking to get a new addition to the family along with our grocery haul today. Her bright green eyes expressed distraught, but it was obvious that this kitten wanted to fight to have a better life.

"Can we take her home, sweety?" Frankie asked.

There it is. The exact question I was waiting for. I knew it.

"Let's stop by our vet on the way home first to see if she belongs to anyone or not," I insisted.

"I wouldn't think so if we're just finding her in the dumpster of a Smith's."

"Okay. Just to be safe, though."

I turned over the engine for Frankie while I finished loading all of the groceries from today's Smith's haul. She took the kitten into the front seat with her, trying her best to calm it down enough to relax and not run amok in the car or parking lot.

After I finished loading everything, I get back into the car and we make our way to our vet, which mercifully isn't too far.

We walked into the vet's office on the cat side, since there's a dog entrance and a cat entrance. Sometimes I wonder where people take their exotic pets, like snakes and other uncommon animals. The two of us approach the reception desk.

"Hi, we have brought our cats here for years. We just found this little girl in a dumpster in the Smith's parking lot, and would like for her to get scanned to see if she belongs to anyone. How old she is would be helpful to know, too."

Frankie shows the tiny screaming calico to the receptionist, and we watch as her eyes widen. She lets out a kind of squeal, likely because this kitten is pretty adorable.

"Oh my God, she is precious!" the receptionist exclaims.

The kitten squirmed in Frankie's hands and squeaked loudly again.

"Can we get her scanned and see if she belongs to anyone? Because if not, we would like to keep her," Frankie insisted.

"Absolutely. I'll bring her right back and get her scanned," the receptionist responds. Frankie promptly hands over the kitten, who is now squirming even more than before.

The receptionist, accompanied by a vet tech, came out a few minutes later with a grin across their faces.

"Well, it doesn't seem that this kitten is microchipped. I assume that you've kept an eye out for anyone looking for this kitten?"

"Yes, I haven't seen any signage or anything saying that this kitten is wanted by someone. Also, the fact we found her in a dumpster..." Frankie said.

"Ah. Right. Well, if you want to keep her, then she's yours to keep," the vet tech said. When I looked for her name badge, I saw something clipped to the bottom of her shirt. It looked like it said Hayley, but I couldn't be sure. My vision's not the greatest these days in general, but I'm also farsighted.

"Thank you... Hayley? Is that what your name badge says? Sorry, I can't see that well."

"Yes, my name is Hayley," she said, smiling. "Did you want us to do a health check on the kitten since she's still back here?"

"Please, that would be great," Frankie said.

"Alright, I'll be back in a bit. Meanwhile, you can come back with me and I'll put you in a patient room while you wait."

We followed Hayley back to a small patient room, and got some glares from other people along the way. I mean, we kind of just waltzed in here without an

44

appointment, and got brought back pretty quick. I can't imagine how long everyone else was waiting to get the same thing. Hayley closed the door behind her upon departure.

"You didn't notice anything immediately wrong with her, did you, dear?" I asked Frankie.

"No, she looked fine other than being cold in that dumpster."

"Alright. Well, hopefully she's just normal and we don't have to do anything except introduce her to our home," I said, trying to reassure both of us.

Frankie laid her head on my left shoulder, at which point I lifted my arm so that she could be somewhat more comfortable on my chest and wrapped it around her. I ran my right hand through her hair, and I heard her utter a relaxed sigh in response to my touch.

Thirty minutes later, Hayley returned and opened the door with one hand, the screaming kitten in the other.

"Well, good news. She's healthy, and doesn't have any problems. She's just tired and will take some time to adjust to your home. You must have found her just in time."

Both of us sighed in relief, practically in unison.

"Oh, thank goodness," Frankie said.

"What are you going to name her?" Hayley asked.

"Chloe seems like it would fit her. What do you think, sweety?" Frankie suggested.

"Yeah... Chloe sounds nice," I agreed.

"Alright, Mr. and Mrs. Rossi. I will get Chloe added to your records. Is there anything else you needed from us today?"

"No, I think we're good. We're going to take Chloe home now," I said.

"Yeah, we're good," Frankie agreed.

"Have a great rest of your day, you two...and congratulations on your newest little addition. Chloe is adorable."

"Thank you so much, Hayley. You've been a real help," I said.

Frankie grabbed Chloe from Hayley, and I opened the doors to exit the vet's office, and we headed back to my car to head home.

13: FIFTY-ONE

I was supervising the high-limit poker tables, minding my own business, when I heard my name being called from a short distance away.

"Jimmy!"

I looked around in every direction to determine where the person calling my name was. I see my boss heading directly for me at a brisk pace.

"Oh, hi," I said. He doesn't usually come to the casino floor like this at random. I'm not sure what he wants.

"Jim, can you come with me to my office?"

"Right now? Who's going to watch the pit?"

"We'll find someone. Yeah, right now."

"Sure, I'll come with you."

Typically, if your boss specifically asks you to come to their office, it means that something significant is about to happen. I hope that whatever is about to happen is positive because my heart is in my throat, beating a million miles per minute.

The two of us traverse the casino floor, making our way through the various pits—blackjack, poker, craps, roulette, baccarat. We take an elevator up to the sixth floor, go down a hallway, and finally arrive at my boss's office. He inserts his key into the deadbolt, unlocking it and having me follow behind him before closing the door.

"Have a seat. Make yourself comfortable," he said.

I obliged the request, and sat in one of the two chairs that were situated in front of his desk. I take a look around and realize that he keeps this office in pristine condition. Books line the shelves along the wall, and are perfectly categorized by author's last name. I'm not in here very often, which would be a good thing, so it's not like I have much to go on for background knowledge.

"Do you want water or anything, Jim?"

"Sure, that would be great. Thank you."

He opens the mini fridge, takes out a small water bottle, and brings it over to hand it to me before taking his place in his own chair behind the desk. I promptly twist the cap off the water bottle, taking a drink of it to calm my nerves. I don't remember doing anything wrong? Why am I here? I guess I'm about to get those questions answered, and more…

"Jim, do you have any idea why you're in my office right now?"

"I've been thinking about that since you called my name. No, I don't have any clue."

"I've been keeping an eye on you since you joined our team here at the Silverton two years ago. I must say, I am impressed. You have a great temperament and an even better work ethic."

"Okay…" Well, this was going better than I expected.

"Effective immediately, assuming you accept the position, I'm pleased to offer you the position of Director of Gaming."

"Wait… Are you serious?"

He laughed. "Of course I'm serious. I've put a lot of thought into this, and already have been given the green light by *my* bosses to do this."

"Yes, I accept! Wow, thank you so much. I can't even begin to tell you how happy and appreciative I am right now."

He smiled, flashing his pearly whites in a grin that reached his eyes.

"As you can imagine, you are also receiving a raise with the promotion. It'll be an additional $20,000 per year. I'll get with HR to make the appropriate changes, but you'll see it on your next pay stubs after this current pay period finishes out."

My eyes grew a few sizes in that moment. An extra $20k annually?! I was already pretty comfortable with where I was financially, but Frankie's going to be *really* happy about that news.

"I'm speechless. Thank you so much."

"You deserve it, Jim."

"Do I need to do anything else?" I asked.

"Nope, you're all set."

I got up from my chair, making sure to remember to take the water bottle with me as I walked to the door.

"Do you want me to close the door?"

"Yes, please. I appreciate it," he said.

"Alright. Again, thank you so much. I'll catch you later."

"Sounds good. Have a good evening, Jimmy."

I opened the door and stepped outside of his office, carefully shutting the door behind me. As I walked back down the hallway we came through towards the elevator, I grabbed my cell phone out of my pocket to call Frankie. She's always been very supportive of my career, and she was definitely going to be thrilled with the news of my promotion.

I scrolled to Frankie's contact, and pushed the Call button, bringing the phone to my ear immediately. It rings three times, at which point I hear her pick up the phone.

"Hi, honey," she said.

"Frankie, guess what?"

"What's that?"

"I got a promotion!"

I heard her gasp on the phone before she spoke.

"Oh my God, congratulations sweetheart! What's your new title?"

"Director of Gaming."

"I'm so proud of you! Don't you have to get back to work right now?"

"Yeah, I do. I'm heading back down the elevator to the tables right now. I just wanted to tell you right away."

"Oh! I see. We can talk more tomorrow after we both wake up since I'm already asleep by the time you get home most days."

"Okay, we'll do that. I love you so much, Frankie. Have a good night. I'll see you when I get home."

"I love you, too, Jimmy. See you later."

I ended the call, and the elevator beeped as we reached the casino level. The doors opened for me, and I started to make my way towards the poker tables I was supervising before I got called into my boss's office.

The rest of my shift went alright, but once I got home at 2:00 AM, I felt the weight of exhaustion hit. I managed to eat a snack, brush my teeth, strip down to my briefs, and get into bed with Frankie. Within a few minutes, I was cuddling her and quickly fell asleep.

~ * ~

I woke up a few hours later. I opened one eye and rolled onto my side to check the time. 9:17 am. I guess I'll get out of bed…

I stumbled out of bed, heading downstairs with my mind half there and half not, groggy as fuck and honestly still half asleep. Once I reached the bottom of the stairs, I looked around for Frankie. She's not in the kitchen, nor the living room… Is she in the garage perhaps? Or, more surprisingly, is she in the backyard? She's not one to have a green thumb, so we've never kept a garden of any sort. Here and there, since we've moved to Vegas, we've tried to keep different plants alive that we've found at the store, but the heat kills off everything.

I put on a pair of sandals before opening the glass door that goes into the backyard. I feel a sense of relief as I see Frankie setting up some pool items for herself – a bikini, flip-flop sandals, a book that's on top of the table in the backyard, and a deck chair.

"Good morning, darling," I said to her. She looked around for a moment, determining which direction I was coming from.

"Good morning," she said as she yawned. "Did you just wake up?"

"Yeah. I rolled out of bed and came to look for you."

She walked closer to me so that we could have a conversation without yelling halfway across the backyard.

"So, tell me about this promotion you just got at work."

"Ah, yes. Well, it's effective immediately. My boss said that I will see the pay raise effective next pay cycle, as he's going to get with HR pretty quickly."

"You said your new title is... a director? How much of a pay raise is it?"

"Yes, Director of Gaming. It's an additional $20,000 per year."

"Wow, that's a steep pay raise. Congratulations, sweetheart. I've always been proud of your ambition and work ethic."

"Thank you, Frankie. I'm so thankful for you. You've always been there for me and with me, and I can't fully express how much I love and appreciate you."

"I love you, Jimmy."

"So... what do you want to do now?"

"Go change into trunks and let's go in the pool for a bit."

I nodded and quickly obliged her request. I ran upstairs, looked through my dresser to find my swim trunks, and changed into them. I came back downstairs with a towel to dry myself off afterwards. When I went back outside to meet Frankie, she was already in the pool. I put my towel on the table next to her stuff, got in the pool next to her, and once again lost myself in her beautiful eyes.

14: FIFTY

Thanksgiving just came and went. People who traveled to Vegas for the holiday have now returned to their homes out of state. The madness is finally settling down from *that* holiday as we now prepare for Christmas full swing.

Andrew, whom I've known since kindergarten, moved to Vegas a few years after I did. He, too, got sick of Ohio—the winters of shoveling snow, the humidity, the mosquitoes trying to get every ounce of your blood, and honestly, getting away from his toxic family. I don't blame him one bit. I left Ohio in search of more and better opportunities for myself.

Andrew and I are exactly two months apart in age, and tomorrow (November 28), he's about to turn fifty. Hard to believe that it's been half a century since he's been running his mouth without any serious repercussions (such as ones that threaten his life). I'm often surprised because this man talks shit like it's going out of style.

For the record, I kept my 50th birthday celebration low-key in September. Frankie and I went to a movie together, and came home to have dinner afterwards. I've never been one to like flashy and elaborate displays and parties.

I grabbed my cell phone out of my pants pocket, and texted Andrew. This is how the conversation goes:

Me: Hey man, happy birthday!
Andrew: It's not until tomorrow though.
Me: I'm not allowed to say it a day early…? lol
Andrew: I guess that's true. Thanks.
Me: Do you have any plans tomorrow?
Andrew: No… The wife didn't say anything. Or anyone for that matter.
Me: How would you feel about coming over for dinner?
Andrew: Is Frankie cooking?
Me: No, I am.

Andrew: Since when do you know how to cook, man?
Me: Since forever, Andrew. She's happy to most of the time, but I'm not completely useless in the kitchen. My mom taught both Jeremy and I how to cook. You just have never had my cooking. Well, most people haven't.
Andrew: Then fuck me, sure, I'll come over. Can I bring my wife?
Me: Of course you can. What kind of question is that?
Andrew: Alright, what time do you want us to come over?
Me: 5:00 pm.
Andrew: Sounds great. Appreciate it, man. I'll let her know in just a minute. Wait… What are you making?
Me: That's for me to know, and for your Mexican ass to find out tomorrow.
Andrew: Lol, whatever you say, Jim. I look forward to finding out.

I returned my phone to my pants pocket. I'm so thankful to have the Blackberry 5810, or else this conversation would have been far more laborious to type out on my end. I guess I've liked texting since it became more common, since it's quicker and easier to talk to people.

Frankie's currently out to brunch with her best friend Rosa and a few of her girl friends. Before heading out, I located a notepad and pen, and scribbled down all of the necessary ingredients I'd need to buy. I can't be sent into a grocery store without a list, or else I will start buying tons of random shit.

I grabbed my car keys, started the car, and headed to the closest Smith's for groceries. Kroger acquired Smith's Food and Drug in 1998, so it was just a few years ago.

On the menu, I have Mexican-style empanadas as the appetizer, fajitas for the entrée (both vegetarian and carne asada options are available, plus all the other fillings, as Frankie is a vegetarian), and churros for dessert. Everyone has an inner fat kid who loves churros. It doesn't matter what your ethnicity is.

Once I got to Smith's, I tried to be as quick and efficient as possible in locating all the necessary ingredients. I think I did alright, though Frankie does admittedly know the store *way* better than I do. I always feel somewhat lost without her in here, and when I come alone, again… I buy stupid shit like Gold Fish or bags of candy that don't have anything to do with what we're having for dinner. Frankie does occasionally ask what my problem is, and quite honestly, I'm not sure.

I go up and down the aisles, looking for the exact ingredients that I need. I did have to ask a couple of the store employees for help finding a few things, but I have it under control. After what felt like forever and checking every item off my shopping list, I head to the front of the store and get into a checkout lane. When I say my cart is full, I cannot understate it. This thing is fighting for its life under the weight of all the food within it.

Once I paid and barely made it to my car with my life, I loaded everything up into my car. Some items went into the backseat. Others went into the trunk. I felt like my car was almost full to the fucking rim with how much I just bought. I am a gentleman with manners and common sense, so I return the cart to where it's supposed to go instead of leaving it in the middle of a parking spot like some of these uncultured swine.

I got home, and Frankie has returned from her brunch with her girl friends. From the looks of it, she just got home as well.

"Oh, hi honey. Where did you just come from?" she asked.

"Smith's. Can you help me unload everything?"

Frankie raised an eyebrow. "Sounds like you have a lot of stuff. What all did you get?"

"I got groceries for empanadas, fajitas, and churros. Andrew and his wife are coming over for his birthday tomorrow. I want to cook for everyone."

Frankie gawked as she realized what was happening.

"You mean… I get the day off from cooking?"

"That's exactly what I'm saying. I'll even handle breakfast in the morning. Everything is vegetarian friendly, too. Meat will be on the side for anyone else."

She jumped me, which immediately turned into a hug. I wasn't prepared for *that* reaction, so I grunted slightly upon impact.

"You're the best," she said.

"Thanks dear… I try."

~ * ~

I woke up the next morning and started cooking immediately. I didn't even take a shower first. I kept my promise to Frankie that I would also cook breakfast I was going to get sweaty and repulsive anyway due to all the time I've had to spend cooking.

After slaving away in the kitchen for the entire day's meals, I finished all three courses of the dinner for tonight at the last second—4:55 PM. I told Andrew to arrive with his wife at 5:00pm, and no earlier.

Knock, knock, knock.

Andrew… I swear.

"Coming!" I yelled from the kitchen as I rushed towards the front door. As I opened the door, half expecting to see Andrew, I met a different kind of visitor. It was a girl in her twenties or thirties, holding up a picture of a dog.

"Excuse me, sir. Sorry to bother you. Have you seen my dog?" She darted her eyes to the picture.

"Oh, um… I don't think so. I don't really go out much apart from work and running errands. Same situation for my wife. I'm sorry."

She let out a deep sigh, despair evident in her expression. I felt bad for her, but I told the truth. Frankie and I just aren't around enough *outside* to be able to notice a particular dog.

"It's okay… Thank you anyway."

"No problem. I hope you find the dog soon."

She walked off, back down the driveway, and went to the house that was directly to our left. In addition to not going outside very much, Frankie and I have also not made any serious efforts to get to know our neighbors. Despite the fact that we have been in Vegas for quite some time now, it's just not the same as Ohio where everyone knows each other on a given street. The West Coast is far more independently minded and oriented, and people keep to themselves more than they try to create and foster a sense of community.

I closed the front door, but didn't lock it right away since Andrew should be here any moment. I walked over to the fridge and grabbed a clean glass out of the cabinet, then poured some iced tea into it. Frankie made a pitcher of it the other day. Of course, as soon as I finished taking my first big sip of it, I heard the doorbell ring.

I jogged towards the door, and when I got there, I looked through the peephole to check who it was. Thankfully, it's not some random lady or someone I'm not expecting. It's Andrew and his wife, Rachel—the two people I *am* expecting.

"Hey, Andrew!" I said, opening my arms to hug him. He did likewise. We haven't seen each other in a bit. I think it's been several months since we last spent any time together. I hugged Rachel as well and invited both of them in.

"Hey, Jimmy. Thanks for having us over," Andrew said.

"No problem at all! Happy birthday, man."

"Thank you. What the—*Puta madre, que incredible!*"

In all the years I've known Andrew, I don't think I've ever heard this man speak Spanish around me…

"Can I get you two something to drink? I have beer, wine, water, I think some Dr. Pepper?"

"I'll take a water," Andrew said.

"Same," Rachel added.

"Where's Frankie?" Andrew asked.

"She's upstairs. Probably just finishing getting ready."

"Who made all this food?" Rachel asked.

"Me," I said triumphantly.

Rachel's eyes grew three sizes, her mouth fell open, and she dropped her purse immediately. The disbelief in her expression and mannerisms was viscerally apparent.

"Jim. Did I hear that correctly? YOU made all of this?!" she asked.

"Yes. All me. I also made breakfast and lunch for Frankie and I. She hasn't stepped foot in the kitchen to cook all day."

"I had no idea you could even cook like this. What the fuck?" she said.

I heard Frankie's footsteps descending the stairs and getting closer to the three of us. When she came up to me, she gave me a kiss on my right cheek. I turned my head to give her an actual kiss on the lips.

"Well, *hello* there, beautiful," I said.

"It smells and looks awesome. You outdid yourself, babe," Frankie said.

"Everyone, have a seat, and I'll get the drinks situated. Frankie, what do you want to drink?"

"Whatever red wine we have that needs to be finished," Frankie said, although it sounded like she was going to laugh, but didn't. I obliged and poured Frankie a glass of the red wine that was about 80% gone. I ended up pouring the remainder of the bottle's contents into her glass, then promptly threw the bottle into the trash. After I brought the wine to Frankie, I sat down next to her.

"Andrew, do you say grace at all at home?" I asked.

"No, not really," he said.

"Alright. I will respect that. Everyone, dig in."

Unsurprisingly, Andrew was the first to grab the serving utensils and put what he wanted on his plate for the first serving. Rachel then dished hers, then Frankie, then I served myself last.

"God damn Jim, this is so good!" Rachel said. "It's pretty close to Andrew's mother's cooking."

I stared at her, mid-chew, to assess what she just told me. I haven't tried to cook anything Mexican in a while. I finished chewing before I started to formulate my response.

"Wow, seriously?"

"Yeah, and that woman can cook up a *storm*," Rachel replied.

"These empanadas are amazing, and so are the fajitas," Frankie added in approval.

The rest of the night went smoothly. Andrew and I had a chance to catch up on what's been going on with our lives since we last saw each other. At one point, Frankie and Rachel ended up on the patio together, talking about whatever independently of Andrew and I.

We did sing "Happy Birthday" to Andrew, which made this now-50-year-old man blush. God, I love seeing him blush…and that scarcely ever happens. It's just too entertaining to pass up any opportunity to pull that reaction out of him.

After Andrew and Rachel left, Frankie and I expeditiously went upstairs, changed, and went to bed. Within minutes, she slept peacefully, and I was snoring.

15: FORTY-NINE

I felt my phone vibrate once in my jacket pocket, then heard it start to ring. After looking around to make sure I would have privacy for this conversation, I reached in to answer it. It's…Frankie? She almost never calls me at work.

"Hi, love," I said.

"Hey, sweety. Can I come by the Silverton? You forgot your wallet earlier," she said.

I frantically checked my pants and jacket pockets. Shit. She's right. I *did* forget that at home. I wouldn't have noticed if she didn't call to say something until I needed it, too.

"You're right, I did. Good catch, dear. I'm by the high-limit poker tables right now. Do you know how to find your way to this pit?"

"I can figure it out," she said confidently.

"Alright, see you soon."

How the fuck did I forget my wallet? My main essentials for going anywhere are keys, glasses, and wallet. I would venture to say that it's the same for most adult men. I guess it's a good thing that I married a woman who looks out for me this much. Sometimes I wonder how she remembers half the things she does with so much detail and intention.

I ruminate quietly to myself, and let one of the poker dealers know that I need to use the restroom quickly, so I'll be right back. He nods at me, and I head towards the men's room, which is a decent walk from this pit. Once I do my business and am walking back to the high-limit poker section, I see Frankie, and she's…running. Why is she running? She knows full well I just barely started work an hour ago, and the night is still young.

"Hi, honey," she said when she finally approaches me.

Before I could say a word, one of the players at the table to my left—who is discernibly drunk as fuck, I should add—whistles in Frankie's direction.

"God damn girl, you are fine," he says. I noticed that he also bit his bottom lip directly after saying this.

Frankie turns herself around so fast I thought she might get whiplash from the action.

"Excuse me?" she asks.

I lean in to whisper in her ear, "Let me handle this." She nods and backs off the situation.

"Sir, that's my *wife* you're hitting on," I told him, looking directly into his eyes. He takes another big gulp of the beer he's drinking, as if to re-up on the audacity.

"Yeah, I bet she's a great lay, too," he said. Okay, what the fuck? I know he's drunk as a skunk, but the balls on this man…

"You either start showing her *and* my marriage more respect, or I'm going to remove you from the property myself."

He gets up from his chair at the table, setting his cards down face down, and stumbles his way over to stand right in front of Frankie. I'm going to have to throw this asshole out, aren't I?

"Why don't you leave this fucking clown and come home with me, beautiful?"

I turned to look at the facial expression she gave him, and it's one of pure disgust.

"That's it. I'm done playing nice. Come with me. Frankie, can I have my wallet before I bring security to 86 him?"

"Oh, sure," she says. She grabbed it out of her purse, and handed it to me. I put it in my vest pocket immediately.

"Thank you, sweetheart. I'll see you at home," I said as I kissed her quickly. I watched as she walks away to make sure nothing else weird happened to her.

"What? What do you mean…come with you?" the drunk said.

"I mean that you're coming with me, and you won't be allowed to come back here. Now collect your things and come with me."

"Man, I was just making a joke."

"The time for jokes is when *my wife* isn't around for you to hit on like she's just a piece of ass."

"She's a smoke show," he said.

"If you say one more dick-headed thing about her, I will make sure you're picking up your own teeth from Las Vegas Boulevard. I'm not playing these games with you."

He got quiet after that.

I'm trying to keep my calm, but I'm also not going to be taking any of this man's shit insulting my own wife! I still have to be professional in the process, too, which can be tricky when you're not in the mood for their antics. I've thrown out many people over the years, but it's been due to reasons like card counting, being sloppy drunk to where they're falling down in the middle of the casino, and other tomfoolery of that sort. Not because they're coming after my wife of 20+ years.

I grabbed the radio that I kept clipped on my belt during work hours, cued up, and called for security.

"Gaming to Security," I said.

"Go ahead," I heard a male security officer respond back to me within seconds.

"Can I get a dispatch to the high-limit poker section? I've got a man here who's had entirely too much to drink that needs to be 86'd."

"Of course. Is this Jim?"

"Yes, it's me."

"We'll be right over."

A couple of minutes later, a security officer shows up and approaches me.

"What happened, Jim?"

"You've met Frankie, right? My wife?"

"Yes, of course. She's come around a few times, hasn't she?"

"Right. Well, this clown thought he'd be cute and try to hit on Frankie, not to mention tell her to come home with him. You know as well as anyone in this company that I don't tolerate disrespect for Frankie at any time, or to any extent."

The security officer looked at me, then looked at the drunk.

"Yikes. You said 86 him from the property?" he asked.

"Yes, please."

"Will do, Jim. Come with me," he said to the drunk. Still wasted, the drunk reluctantly followed him, stumbling every third step and his breath reeking of shitty beer.

"Thank you," I mouthed to the security guard as the two of them walked away.

God damn it...why can't people ever mind their own business and relationships? Drunks are so exhausting. Now that that's dealt with, I can move on with the rest of my night.

16: FORTY-EIGHT

After several years at the Tropicana Hotel and Casino, I feel that it's time to move on and up. For the past several years, I have been a shift manager here, also known in the industry as a pit boss. As of a couple of weeks ago, I accepted an offer to become Casino Manager of the Treasure Island—a promotion and raise by way of a new job.

You know that feeling where you start something new—whether it's a job, a relationship, a project, or anything else—and you have that initial streak of excitement and energy? Then it wears off over time because the novelty dilutes and dissipates, and after a while, you feel like you've done everything and outgrown it? That's how I think about the Tropicana. I spent many wonderful years there, and it was one of the first jobs I got since moving to Vegas, but I am ready for a change. The Tropicana allowed me to cut my teeth in the hospitality and gaming industry, and I've met so many great people.

Today, I start my first day as Casino Manager, which is a step up in my career. You know, when I first moved to Vegas, I didn't think I'd end up in this specific position. I knew that Chauncy would have helped me with my first job out here, and he delivered on that promise. But to think that I'd spend 20-something years in hospitality and gaming is something I never accounted for. I've had the opportunity to go back to school, and I've considered it throughout all this time, but I've never pulled the trigger. I guess, to me, I've already "made it" in a sense, and don't feel a strong ambition to acquire further formal education. Plus, despite the fact that I am good at math and work well with numbers, do you think I'd remember how to do basic algebra again? I'd likely have to take remedial math courses just for that, never mind anything more advanced.

Whenever I start a new job, I always make sure to look my best on my first day. That's not to imply I don't *always* dress well for work, as I've been known to be bougie when I have to be, especially in professional and/or formal settings. Today, I chose a solid black suit, a light blue button-up long-sleeved dress shirt, a royal purple tie (because I think it's an awesome color), and black slip-on dress shoes. I noticed my bottle of Joop! cologne was running a bit low earlier, as I spritzed some on while getting ready.

Thankfully, the drive from my house to Treasure Island is also identical to the one to the Tropicana. They're not that far apart (by car, anyway) along Las Vegas Boulevard.

Once I parked in the parking garage, I searched for the elevators. I just realized that I was told to go to Human Resources first (before I go out to the casino floor), and I've never been there. How was I supposed to find where this office was without directions or a map?

As luck would have it, I saw another employee coming towards the elevators. He had a name badge on, which is the only way I would have known that he was an employee and not a tourist. I hope he knows where I have to go. He walks up to the elevator, and as he waits for the car to come to the third floor, I approached him.

"Excuse me, sir?"

He turns to face me.

"Yes? How can I help you?"

"Do you know how to get to Human Resources? Today is my first day, and I realized I wasn't given a map or anything when I was hired."

"Oh, yes, I can bring you to HR. What department are you coming into?"

"Gaming? Unless you call it something else? I'm going to be the new Casino Manager."

"Oh wow, wait… Are you Jimmy? I'm one of the blackjack dealers, and I think I heard about you coming on board."

"Y—yes, I'm Jimmy Rossi. Wow, word spreads fast here."

He extended his hand to me, and I gave it a firm shake. "I'm Evan. Nice to meet you, Jimmy."

The two of us walk into the elevator, and he pushes the button for the car to go to the fifth level. I would have never guessed that they would put Human Resources on the fifth floor on my own.

Once the doors close, the elevator car begins its ascent to the fifth floor. To my surprise, nobody else called it along the way, or else it would have stopped at one of the levels in between. Upon arrival on the fifth floor, the car did a *ping* sound, and the doors open once again.

We depart from the elevator, and Evan motions for me to follow him down a long hallway. There are doors on either side, but they aren't all guest rooms for travelers. Some are labeled as offices: Housekeeping, Lost and Found, typical ones of a hotel. Four doors from the end of the hall on the right, we reach our destination: Human Resources.

"After you," I said to Evan. He nodded, and knocked on the door first. We heard a voice beckon, "Come in." He turned the handle and walked in first while I followed immediately behind.

A woman sits behind the desk that is directly to the left of the walkway. She looks at Evan, then me.

"Hi Evan, and...who do we have here?"

"Oh, hi. My name is James Rossi. I go by Jimmy or Jim. Today's supposed to be my first day as Casino Manager."

"Yes! I do remember hearing about you coming to join us recently. You came from the Tropicana, right?"

"That's correct."

"Alright, have a seat in front of me. I need to have you sign a few things before I can send you out to the casino floor. Oh, before I forget... Do you have your ID handy, as well as your direct deposit information?"

"Yes. Let me get that for you."

I grabbed my wallet out of my ass pocket, and first took out the ID from the plastic slot, then removed a half-piece of paper that had my routing and account numbers on it from Wells Fargo. I handed both to her at the same time. I had to call my bank to get that information since I'm not one to carry paper checks on my person—those stay at home. If it doesn't fit in a trifold wallet, it doesn't come with me in my pocket.

"Thank you. Give me a few minutes to process everything."

"No problem. Take your time."

I folded my hands onto my lap, and looked around the office from the vantage point of where I was sitting. College degrees, certifications, pictures of the ladies' families... Nothing exciting, just typical décor for an HR office, I suppose.

After fifteen minutes, although it felt like a fucking eternity, she spoke to me again. She handed me back my ID and direct deposit information paper.

"Jimmy, I've got everything taken care of for you now. Here's your name tag, so just put that on your suit vest flap when you have a second. Do you need anything else from me, or have further questions?"

I sat and thought for a minute, then came up empty.

"No, I think I'm good."

"Alright, I have been instructed to put you in the blackjack pit today with Evan. He can start introducing you to the dealers on swing shift."

"Oh, okay. Sounds good to me." I looked over at Evan. "I guess we're going to become fast friends," I added jokingly.

Evan made a nervous smile and chuckled at the request.

"Evan, behave. He's your new boss," the woman said. Damn, has he spent that much time in HR?

"Will do," he said. He didn't look too enthralled that he was having to show me around and introduce me to everyone.

The two of us walked out of the office, and took the elevator down to the casino floor on the ground level. Once we got down there, Evan introduced me to the other dealers as they had time between games of blackjack. What I was more surprised at, however, was that no one gave me any bullshit today. Part of me was expecting tons of it on my first day, but I'm glad it didn't play out.

17: FORTY-SEVEN

I heard Frankie's cell phone ring on the nightstand while she was in the shower. The caller ID was…Joe? Now *that's* someone I almost never hear from. I pushed the button to accept the call.

"Hello?" I said.

"Oh, hey Jimmy… Where's my sister?"

"She's in the shower. How's it going?"

"Well… Not good. I guess I could tell you, but I would prefer to tell both of you at the same time."

The sound of water running in the shower suddenly stops, and I heard the shower curtain move. Frankie just finished and was starting to dry off.

"Joe, give me one second, please."

"Alright," I heard him say.

I went over to the closed bathroom door and knocked. Frankie may be my wife, but that doesn't mean we forego rules and boundaries in this house. Or ever, for that matter.

"Yes?" I heard her say.

"Honey, when you're able, come here for a minute. Joe called and said he wants to talk to both of us."

"Oh, that can't be good. Is he still on the phone?" she asked.

"Yes, he is."

"One second, please."

Just under a minute later, Frankie opened the bathroom door. One towel was wrapped around her body, and a smaller towel wrapped around her hair. I hand her the phone.

"Hello?" she says.

"Hey, sis. Can both of you hear me?"

"Yeah, we can both hear you," I said.

"I…have some bad news…"

"What is it, Joe?" Frankie questioned.

61

"I'm getting a divorce, guys." I heard his voice start to shake, and finally, he started crying. Joe wasn't known to be much of the crying type, although I could say the same about any of my three brothers-in-law. I looked over at Frankie, and she too was feeling some kind of way in reaction to Joe's emotions right now. I think even *she's* unsure of what she's feeling, but there is something there.

"Oh, I'm so sorry, Joe…" she said. Joe was the closest brother in age to her, and she would tell you herself that she was the tightest with him as a result.

"What happened, exactly? This can't have just popped up overnight."

"S—she—"

Joe sobbed harder.

"Well?" Frankie asked.

"She had an a—affair…"

Both Frankie and I went completely silent, mouths agape. Ending a relationship in general is already difficult, especially if it's been one that has spanned several years. Finding out that your long-term partner has stepped out on you after taking an oath to be faithful, both legally and ceremoniously, is a level of hurt that I hope that I never have to personally experience.

"I'm going to kill her," Frankie said.

"The fuck you are," Joe said.

"Joe… That sucks, man. For how long? Do you know who the other guy is?"

Joe let out an exasperated sigh as he tried to collect himself enough to continue the conversation.

"With her… best friend… that she told me… not to worry about…"

Frankie's eyes grew what seemed like three sizes.

"Fucking yikes, Joe," she said.

"Damn… It's always the ones that they tell you not to worry about, isn't it?" Frankie has never given me a reason to question her loyalty. To be fair, she barely likes people in general. However, I've had several of my friends and colleagues recount their experiences over the years where their wife/partner/fiancée cheated on them for any reason whatsoever.

Joe cleared his throat, and I heard him take a deep breath before continuing what he was going to say. Sounds like we might be hit with a lot of information at once.

"It's her supposed best friend, Ken. They've been friends since elementary school. I've met Ken before, and we even had him over to the house a bunch of times. I feel ridiculous. I'm so upset I didn't see this coming much earlier."

To be fair… I wonder whether I would have noticed the same thing earlier or not. Sometimes, people can be very secretive about hiding things, or I guess in this situation, *people*. I would like to think I'm observant, but at the same time, I'm a guy. I don't always pick up on everything, even if Frankie is telling me to my face what's going on. If I were a woman, I think I would read between the lines better and more efficiently. But as someone who doesn't have a user's manual for women, I'm not sure what to tell you. I'm lucky that Frankie and I have stayed together all this time. She is a godsend for putting up with my shit all these years.

"Have you filed yet?" Frankie asked, her tone very matter-of-fact. I could hear anger permeate her expression as she spoke those words.

"I'm going to talk to an attorney tomorrow. I've been collecting dirt on Lacey and Ken for months. How I found out was that I came home from work early one day, and I heard Lacey making a fuss about something from a distance… When I went to the bedroom to check it out, I saw shit that made my fucking heart drop into my stomach. Both of them are buck-ass naked, she's bent over, and he's just *giving* it to her. Never in my life did I think I'd have to see another man's bare ass while he's balls deep in *my* wife, and mother to our two children."

"I knew I didn't like that bitch," Frankie said.

"Fuck me, Joe, that's awful," I said. Where were the kids in all this, I wonder?

"The worst part is that the kids were home while their mom was in the next room over being a whore."

With every time he spoke, Joe was quickly going from heartbroken to angry, which then turned into rage. Frankie was starting to get uncomfortable, rather than going along with her brother's emotions.

"Alright, Joe… We have to get going. We have some errands to take care of still."

"Oh, right… I guess, thanks for letting me vent. I haven't had anyone to talk to about any of this."

18: FORTY-SIX

At Sunrise Hospital, our patient room was dead silent... but not for long. My niece-in-law Kaylee, who was due any minute, screamed the words that caused what feels like the entire floor's medical staff to swarm in: "THE BABY IS COMING!"

Within seconds, several Labor and Delivery staff rushed to room 1408 as Kaylee was about to give birth to Vince's first grandson, Liam. Henry Mancini, the oldest of Vincent's kids (and the first of my nieces and nephews by him), is about to become a father for the first time.

One of the nurses quickly double-checks information with Kaylee and Henry against the chart that they have on file. Kaylee is visibly grimacing and whining, alerting the medical staff to pick up the pace on getting this watermelon-sized baby delivered. (Judging by the size of Kaylee, Liam's going to be a big boy.) After the nurses have completed what they need to do prior to delivery, one begins the birthing process.

"Kaylee, I'm going to need you to take a deep breath... and then start pushing."

Kaylee obliged the request, and began to push with all her might, screaming and yelling in the process. For a moment, it looked as if the veins in her neck and arms were trying to break free. She threw her head back and pushed again, the second and subsequent efforts equally as ferocious as the first. Jesus, I haven't seen this much of a garden-variety train wreck since my brother Jeremy was born. I fully understand why women would not want to have kids if this is what they have to go through *every* time.

Baby Liam finally made his entrance into the world after enough commotion, pushing, screaming, and tears. A nurse quickly cleans him off, weighs him, and measures him before handing him to Kaylee.

"What are we naming him?" the nurse asks her.

"Liam Vincent Mancini," Kaylee says.

Vince begins to tear up. "You—you're naming him after me?"

"We are," Kaylee said, smiling.

"Liam Vincent Mancini, born July 7, 1999 at 10:36 AM. Ten pounds, three ounces, 20 inches in height," the nurse says as she writes down the information on the form in front of her on a clipboard.

"Holy shit, that is a *massive* baby," Frankie commented. I'm not sure if she meant to say that out loud, but...here we are.

Kaylee stared at her blankly, Vince raised an eyebrow, and Henry scratched his chin. All of them were confused by what just came out of Frankie's mouth. I'm the one who's always having to play peacemaker when shit goes awry—in true Libra fashion. I love Frankie, but sometimes she says the wrong thing at the absolute worst of times.

"Um... Thanks?" Kaylee said.

"Little sis, you were *tiny* by comparison," Vince said, laughing.

"Gee, thanks," Frankie fired back.

"Guys... Fuck. Can we please get along?" I interjected. I swear, Italians are some of *the* most temperamental people to be related to.

"Kaylee, this is the type of kid that 'Baby Elephant Walk' was written for."

"Francesca Regina Rossi!" I yelled.

"Okay, I'll be quiet." Frankie put her hands in front of her, palms facing outward.

"Frankie, can I talk to you for a minute? Alone?"

"Sure," she said. I watched as she squinted at me with a look of suspicion. I motioned for her to follow me out of the room and into the hallway. As soon as she came out to the hall, I closed the door.

"Sweetheart, talk to me. What's with the attitude today? This isn't like you."

"I... I didn't sleep very well or much last night. I'm also just kind of in a weird mood, honestly. No idea where it came from." She lowered her head in shame.

"Why couldn't you sleep?"

"If I knew, I'd tell you, Jimmy. You know that."

I sighed. This isn't Frankie's usual disposition. She's typically a bit more agreeable. Not always happy-go-lucky, as it depends on the day, but she's a lot more friendly on average. She's polite, if nothing else.

"Alright... Do you need a minute to collect yourself? Your brother just became a fucking grandpa himself, and this isn't what anyone expects from you, dear."

"Yeah... I'll come back in a few minutes."

"Thank you, beautiful. Take your time. I love you so much." I brought her into me, and kissed her on top of her head. She looked up at me after living in the moment for a few seconds.

"I love you, too, Jimmy."

I opened the door again, going back into the room with everyone else. Frankie will return when she's ready.

"Is she okay?" Kaylee asked, holding baby Liam in her arms.

"Yeah, she's fine. She's just having an off day." All things considered, that's the truth.

"Can I hold him?" Henry asked.

"Well… yeah. That's your son," Kaylee said, holding back an eye roll but drawing her brows together at the question. She hands Liam over to him gently and carefully, making sure that Liam's head is supported correctly to prevent mishandling.

"Kaylee, do you need anything?" I asked. The woman has just given birth. There has to be *something*…right?

"Yes. Can you grab me that glass of water on that little stand over there? I can't quite reach it."

"Of course." I located the half-full glass and brought it to her.

"Thank you." She slammed the remaining water within seconds.

"You're welcome. I'll be right back."

I slowly opened the door, looking for Frankie on either side of the doorway. I didn't see her there.

"Frankie?" I called out. I saw her emerge from room 1406, which was just across the hall. It must have been empty.

"Sorry, I had to go to the bathroom. That patient room was empty, so I just…went real quick."

"Oh, okay. Are you good to come back now?"

"Yes." She grabbed my hand and kissed my cheek.

The two of us go back into 1408, where Kaylee is laying back on the pillow and looks ready to fall asleep.

"Should we let you rest, Kaylee?"

Kaylee poked her head up just enough to look at me in the eyes, but did not fully get up.

"Yeah… I'm going to take a nap while I can."

"Alright. Vince, again, congratulations on being a nonno yourself."

"Thanks, Jim."

"Kaylee, congratulations. Henry… Good luck. You're going to need it."

Henry nodded at me, still holding Liam. Kaylee already fell asleep at this point.

"Let's head home, dear," I said to Frankie. I held her left hand with my right, and opened the door with my left. I let her go ahead of me, keeping close behind. I closed the door carefully and quietly.

We headed to my car, and I drove us back to our quiet, kid-free home. Just the way we like it.

19: FORTY-FIVE

"Jimmy, did you hear?" Frankie said as she nudged me awake. I had a rough evening, so I was groggier and more exhausted than usual as I opened my eyes. Frankie, I love you, but shouldn't you know better by now than to wake me up with conversation when I haven't even had my coffee yet?

"Hear about what?"

"Adam is graduating from Youngstown State."

"Wait, who the fuck is Adam?" I rolled onto my back from my side and proceeded to wipe the rheum out of my eyes. I let out a groan because why am I having this conversation when I still feel physically dead and haven't even sat up?

"Ralph's oldest son, dear. My oldest nephew."

"Oh, yeah, that's right... Wow, I didn't even know he was that old already."

"Ralph is nine years older than me. Actually, Adam is getting his Master's. The bachelor's came a few years ago."

"Well, shit. What's the Master's in?"

"Mathematics."

In the moment, I feel bad for my nephew Adam. Not because *he* did anything wrong, but because I feel I don't know the slightest thing about him. I almost forgot he existed until Frankie brought him up just now during the conversation. I don't see or hear from any of Frankie's brothers nearly enough to be able to remember the names of all my nieces and nephews, never mind be able to quickly recall details of their lives. It makes me feel like an asshole, but this is just the truth. I feel I should know Adam more than I do (which may as well be not at all right now). To me, it feels like I'm being a shitty uncle who only comes around when he needs something, even though that behavior goes against everything I know and feel about my own character.

"Frankie, can I be honest?"

"Yeah, of course."

"I honestly forgot Adam existed until you just brought him up."

Frankie stared at me in silence, her face showing an expression that was somewhere between confusion and offense. Maybe it was something else, too, but I can't interpret feelings and emotions very well in the first place.

"I—What—Are you serious right now?"

"Sweetheart, it's not like I talk to Ralph very often. You don't bring up Adam very often either, and Ralph's *your* brother."

Frankie sighed and rolled her eyes at me.

"I guess…"

"How soon is the ceremony?"

"Next week, I think."

"Well, I can't get time off approved for that short notice. Would it be okay if I got Adam a gift and shipped it to Ralph's? Unless you happen to have Adam's address?"

"I'm sure I can get Adam's address for you," Frankie said reassuringly.

"What would even be a good graduation gift for someone graduating with a master's in math? How well do *you* know him?"

"Adam likes sports, tech, and anything with a motor."

"What about a laptop? Can't go wrong with a new PC."

"Can you afford it, Jimmy?" She cocked an eyebrow at me.

"Of course. It's not like I'm buying gifts for everyone and their mom super often."

"Then yes, that would be a great idea." Frankie hugged me, laying her head into my chest. I ran my left hand through her hair, which was down and free-flowing.

"I'll go find something tomorrow before I head into work. Make sure to get Adam's address and a card that we can both sign. I'll mail everything out once it's all together."

"Will do. Thank you, sweetheart."

~ * ~

I kept my promise. I didn't have to be at work until 5pm, so once I woke up around 9:30 am (I got home around two in the morning, mind you), I had some coffee, showered, and got dressed to head to Circuit City. It's not a store I visit frequently, but I'm often entertained by the sheer variety of gadgets available here. I could spend hours in this store.

A male employee was bright and cheery as he greeted me. "Hello, sir, welcome to Circuit City." He's in his early twenties at most, is wearing rectangular glasses, a red Circuit City polo shirt, khakis, and black sneakers. His name tag states his first name—Dan.

"Hello," I said, to be polite.

"Can I help you find anything?"

"Actually…yes."

His expression lit up like a kid in a candy store, eager to learn about what I was looking for specifically. He smiled widely, and I could tell it was genuine because the smile reached his eyes.

"What is it that you're looking for, sir?"

"Please, just call me Jimmy. Anyway… I need to get a graduation gift for my nephew. He's getting his Master's in math next week or so. I just found out today, so I can't take time off work and fly out for the ceremony on short notice. But I figured that maybe a new computer would be a nice gift."

"Jimmy, you are a really cool uncle for this."

"Thanks."

"I've got just the thing for him. Follow me."

I followed Dan through the aisles of the store, being careful to not run into anyone or knock anything over. I said "excuse me" to at least three different people on the way. Finally, we reached the section containing the laptops and computers.

"What, specifically, were you thinking?" I asked him.

"An IBM ThinkPad!"

He showed me the laptop that was on display, and I manipulated it to try it out for a few minutes. Shit, I feel like I should get one of these for *myself*. This thing is kind of slick.

"Oh, yeah, I like this. How much?"

"$2,199."

Initially, yes, I had sticker shock. I feel that, as the childfree uncle, it is my responsibility to spoil my nieces and nephews when the opportunity arises…and this is a prime opportunity to do so.

"Alright, I'll take it."

"Oh… Uh… Well, okay then, Jimmy. Let's take it up front. Wait, do you need anything else?"

"No, I think that's it."

Dan went to grab an unopened box of the ThinkPad model that matched the one on display that I played with from the back of the store, then came back to where I was standing.

"Alright, follow me."

The two of us went back the way we initially came, for the most part, except this time, he brought the laptop with him behind the register. I followed his exact footsteps but came in front of the register instead. He scanned the barcode on the side of the box, then set it back down to free up his hands to complete the transaction. He looked at the screen to provide me with the total amount.

"Your total is $2,352.93."

I pulled out my wallet from my right pants pocket, then removed my American Express credit card.

"Go ahead and swipe, please."

I slide my card through the right side of the terminal, and heard the familiar beep that indicated that the card read was successful.

"Would you like a receipt?"

"Yes, please."

Dan pressed a button on the register, and a paper receipt came printing in front of me. He tears the receipt off the printer, and hands it to me.

"Here's the receipt. Thanks for coming into Circuit City, and I hope you have a great rest of your day!"

"Thanks, you as well." I shoved the receipt into the same pocket where I have my wallet, grabbed the box, and headed to my car. I unlocked the car with the fob, loaded the box in before I got into the driver's seat, and went home. The drive takes about fifteen minutes.

I wonder if Frankie has already bought a card. I guess I'll find out. I opened the garage door and parked to the right of Frankie's car. She's here, but the question is, did she *leave* while I was gone?

"Honey, I'm home," I call out.

"Oh, hey, I just got home a minute ago. I got a card for Adam."

"Ah, yes. Did you do that while I was out?"

"I left maybe two minutes after you did."

"Good, good. The computer is in the car still. Front passenger seat. Do we have another box to put it in with the card?"

"Yes, we should have some. I'll go find one."

As Frankie walks past me to go into the garage, I pull her into me and kiss her. She smiles as our lips meet. She then continues her search for a suitably sized box. While Frankie was in the garage searching, I heard a few things slam and drop. That can't be good, but I trust that she knows what she's doing. As long as nothing breaks that I have to fix or clean, we're good.

A few minutes later, she emerges with a triumphant smile in the doorway. I wouldn't say she's out of breath, but she does look somewhat frazzled.

"Got one!"

"Nice. Let's see if it fits."

I unlocked my car with the fob, and she goes into the front passenger seat to retrieve the computer. She puts that box into the one she found in the garage, and it's a snug fit, but still big enough to comfortably fit it and a card.

"The card is on the kitchen counter," she says. "You can go sign it or write something before we pack everything up."

"Oh, okay. I'll go do that real quick."

I went back to the kitchen, and found the card in the envelope. I read it and laughed. Frankie prefers getting funny cards because she enjoys making people laugh and smile. I'm not much of a writer, and I also don't consider myself overly sentimental. However, I picked up a pen that's next to the coffee pot (no idea when that got there, but I'm not going to argue it either), and began writing:

Adam,

Congratulations on getting your Master's degree! It's no small feat, and getting it in mathematics is especially difficult. I wish we could be there to see you walk across the stage at

Youngstown State, but it was such short notice. I hope you understand, and we wish you the best of luck in all your future endeavors. You're always welcome to visit us in Vegas if the mood ever strikes.

Love,

Uncle Jimmy and Aunt Frankie

I stood there thinking for a minute, wondering if there was anything I was missing… Then I realized that Adam doesn't have our phone numbers, so I put both of our cell phone numbers in case he wanted to contact us individually. It feels like we're never home at the same time, so there wasn't a point in putting the house phone number.

Once I felt satisfied that that's all I wanted to include in the card, I brought it over to Frankie for review. She opens the card and reads what I wrote.

"Aw, you can be sweet when you want to be. Looks good," she said.

Well… She's not wrong. I just have to *want* to be sentimental, I suppose. I put the card in the envelope, and licked the top flap to seal it. I handed it to Frankie immediately after, and she threw it into the shipping box that she quickly taped up.

"Do you want to go to the post office with me to ship it out?" I asked her.

"Sure," she said.

I placed the box into the backseat, and Frankie got into the front passenger seat. We headed out to the post office together, which I hope doesn't have a crazy long line.

Upon arrival, only one person was in front of us in line, so we got here in time. They didn't take very long either, as they already had their label affixed onto their parcel and were just dropping it off.

We get to the front of the line, and a postal employee calls us up. Frankie had Adam's address written on a small piece of paper, which she handed to the employee. I handed over my driver's license for both identity verification purposes, and to show the return address with less hassle. The employee was swift in getting the parcel weighed, labeled, and paid for. Without any hesitation, we went back home, and took a nap.

~ * ~

Five days later, I get a call from a 330 area code phone number that I didn't recognize. It wasn't saved in my contacts. I hesitated, but answered it anyway.

"Hello?"

"Uncle Jimmy? This is Adam."

"Oh, hey there!"

"Thank you so much for the ThinkPad!"

"No problem at all. Sorry we couldn't make it to the ceremony. Did it happen yet?"

"It's tomorrow. Seriously, thank you. Not even my dad gets me this kind of thing."

I laughed. "It's my job as the best uncle to get the nieces and nephews all the cool shit."

I heard Adam laugh in response to that statement. "True that. I know we don't talk a lot, but you have always been my favorite uncle."

"That means a lot, Adam. Thank you. Have you talked to Frankie lately at all? Or did you call me first?"

"I called you first. How is she doing?"

"She's doing great. We've been in Vegas for a while now. Come visit us one day, yeah?"

"I will have to find a few days off, but I can make that work."

"Just don't come in the summer if you don't want to sizzle out in this heat," I warned him.

"Good to know! Hey, I need to get going. I have so much shit to do before tomorrow."

"Okay, that's fine. Well, it was great hearing from you, Adam. Congratulations again on your Master's. Hopefully we'll talk again soon."

"Absolutely. Bye, Uncle Jimmy."

"Bye, Adam."

The call ended, and I resumed the rest of my day.

20: FORTY-FOUR

What in the love of all things holy is this cat doing? Is he... Is that... Paint in his mouth?! When I say this cat is orange, and has never seen the brain cell a single second of his life, I truly mean it and say that with my entire chest. I let out a deep sigh before walking towards Kismet, who is currently as ecstatic as a kid in a candy store. Except the "candy" he's eating is paint, and the store is my house.

"Kismet Fizzarolli Rossi, what the actual fuck are you doing?"

Kismet turns his head to look at me with his mouth full and his head completely void of logical or rational thought. Or any thought whatsoever. My walls are being scratched and torn apart by this fifteen-pound orange dumbass, and he looks very proud of his handiwork. His green eyes are dilated with pride and delight.

"Spit it out, Kis. Please."

He continues to stare at me. Cats have all these wonderful muscles in their ears to more effectively and efficiently ignore human requests and demands.

"Kis... Spit. It. Out."

He purrs louder, and something must have got through his thick but empty skull because he obeyed that time. I picked up the chunks of my wall containing paint from the floor that lay just in front of his body.

Kismet goes off to another corner of the house slowly, and the way he's walking could possibly indicate that something is wrong. He could also be sulking.

I guess it's a good thing I'm on PTO for a few days because I might have to take the furry idiot to the vet. That's exactly what I need right now—another reason to spend money.

I rolled my eyes as I went downstairs to the garage to look for the cat carrier. We don't keep it in a cabinet or anything within the house since we don't use it too often. Only when Kis needs to go to the vet, get groomed, or anything else that requires transporting him out of the house. Where did Frankie put this thing? It surely can't be that difficult to find a huge plastic cat carrier in a garage, right? To be fair, the garage *is* a hot mess right now, though. After searching high and low through every shelf, weird hiding spot, and crevice in the garage, I finally found the cat carrier.

I bring the carrier into the living room, and Kismet is nowhere to be found immediately. In under a minute, I hear the *thump, thump, thump* of Kismet coming down the stairs.

"There you are. Come here, Kis."

I go to pick him up, and I have to lift him with my legs. This fat orange lard-ass is a whopping 16.7 pounds. I put him into the carrier, quickly closing and locking the door. Glasses, wallet, keys, Kismet… Do I need anything else before I head to the vet? I think that's everything.

I load the carrier into the front passenger seat of the car. I prefer to do this since Kismet is not that bright and needs constant reassurance when we must transport him to the vet or anywhere else requiring the carrier. He hates the carrier being picked up by the handle, so I have to carry this thing like a human child. He's lucky he's cute.

I get in the car, close the door, and start the engine. As I open the garage door and start to back out, Kismet begins screaming. He wants to make sure that everyone hears him sing the song of his people. I wonder if his people are equally as dumb. Once the rear end of the car makes it out to the road, I shift into drive and head to the vet. These drivers are almost as dumb as Kismet. Almost.

Upon arrival at the vet's office, I get out of the car, then walk around the front to get Kismet in the carrier out of the front passenger seat. To his chagrin, I had to pick up the carrier by the handle in order to bring him inside the office. Once inside, I set the carrier on an empty spot on the reception desk.

"Hi, who do we have here today?" she says, looking at Kismet in the carrier.

"Kismet."

"Your name, sir?"

"James Rossi."

"What's going on with Kismet?"

"I found him eating paint. Again. Then he started acting weird, so I figured I'd just be safe and take him in."

"Oh. Okay then. Give me one second."

She did a few things on the computer, and I waited in silence patiently. Kismet was also surprisingly quiet.

"Alright, Mr. Rossi. I got you checked in. Just wait with Kismet for a few minutes, and we'll call you back."

I scoot the carrier on the floor next to a chair that I sit in. There are a few magazines here, so I picked up a copy of *Sports Illustrated* and started to flip through the pages. I probably end up reading about half the magazine before I heard our names being called.

"Kismet," a male vet tech called. He is approximately 5'5", average build, and of Taiwanese descent. He's wearing all black scrubs and black sneakers.

"Coming," I said, picking up the carrier and taking it with me to follow the tech. He takes me back to a small patient room, where I set Kismet's carrier on a table.

"My name is Sam Tanng. You can just call me Sam. What are we bringing in Kismet today for?"

"Well... See... He eats paint. He scratches my walls, then eats the paint. After I caught him earlier, he started acting weird. I didn't want to chance it, so I brought him in."

"So, we're just doing a check-up to see what's wrong?"

"That would help, yes."

"Alright, I'll take him and be back in a bit. Wait here."

"Okay, thanks."

Sam takes Kismet in the carrier out of the room, and I wait patiently. Five minutes pass, then ten, then... I looked at my watch, and maybe thirty-five minutes go by before Sam comes back into the room with Kismet.

"Mr. Rossi, I did a thorough examination of Kismet, and I don't see anything wrong. He behaved normally for me."

"Wait. What?"

"Sir, I don't know how to say this nicely..."

"Go on, I can take it."

"Kismet is being orange. He's exceedingly stupid, and that's all there is to it."

"So... What you're saying is... He's just a fucking idiot."

"Yes. That's exactly what I'm saying."

"Well, I guess that's a relief then."

"I'm not going to even charge you for the wellness check. Just please try to make sure he doesn't eat *more* paint."

"Oh, you're a gem. Thank you so much."

"You're welcome. Have a good rest of your day."

"You as well, Sam."

I walked out the way I came in, and the receptionist nodded and smiled at me as I made my way out to my car.

21: FORTY-THREE

"NO! This can't be happening!" I sobbed uncontrollably, wailing as I went rigid with disbelief. I held my hands over my face to catch my tears, but those tears were in a state of free flow.

Between my sobs, I heard footsteps pounding as they came up the stairs of our house.

"Apollo…" I said.

"What about Apollo?"

I held Apollo's lifeless body in front of Frankie. I found him under our bed when I was looking for something else in the bedroom, and his body was stiff and cold.

"Frankie, he's…gone…"

She goes to pet him, and comes to the same conclusion. Her eyes quickly fill with tears, and her voice begins to shake.

"NO! Our baby boy…"

"I know…"

"Jim, how did this happen?"

"I don't know. I came up here to look for something else earlier. For some reason, my gut told me to look under the bed. That's when I just found him…not breathing, and not moving."

"But…he hasn't had serious health problems, has he?"

"No, not really. This was a very unwelcome surprise."

"What do we do, Jim?"

"Well, I guess that depends… Do you want to know why he died?"

"Yeah, I guess…"

"Then maybe we can take him to the vet to see if they can determine a cause of death."

"Oh. True, I guess. We can do that."

"It'll have to be today, though."

"Let's just get it over with. I want to know, and it'll help us grieve, I think."

"I can agree with that. Put some shoes on and we'll head out now, I guess."
I grabbed a tissue to wipe my tears, and then I grabbed another one to wipe
Frankie's as well.

We both put on shoes, Frankie grabbed Apollo, and headed to my car. I
normally open Frankie's door for her, but my own emotions got the better of
me at the moment as you can imagine. I opened the garage door with the clicker,
and we headed to our vet. Mercifully, it wasn't a far drive.

I open the front door of the vet's office once we arrive, and Frankie follows
behind with Apollo in her arms. The receptionist greets us warmly.

"Hi, how can I help you today?" she asks.

"Well... We just found our cat dead not too long ago. We would like to
know how, when, and why he passed."

"Oh my GOODNESS, I am so sorry! What's the cat's name?"

"Apollo."

"Your names?"

"James and Francesca Rossi. Jim and Frankie, preferably."

"Alright, give me a moment. Let me have someone come get Apollo to take
him back."

"Thank you," Frankie said, her voice beginning to shake as she started to
cry again. I put my right arm around her shoulders and kissed the top of her
head. We were sharing pain and grief in real time right now, and that's not
something you easily replace or just "get over". We sat in two adjacent chairs
that lined the perimeter of the waiting room, and saw a lady in light pink scrubs
come out from behind the door that separated the practice area from the lobby.
Her dirty blonde hair was in a ponytail, visibly tousled, and her face told me
that it's been a long day.

"I'm looking for the cat named Apollo?"

Frankie and I turn to face her quickly.

"That's us," Frankie says, showing Apollo in her arms.

"Come on back," the vet tech said. We followed her back into a patient
room, and she shuts the door behind us.

"So... Reception told me that Apollo's gone?" she asked.

"Yes, that's correct," I said.

"I'm so sorry. May I see Apollo, please?"

Frankie slowly hands over Apollo's stiff, dead body.

"Here," she said.

The vet tech gently takes Apollo into her arms, fighting back a slew of
emotions herself.

"Thank you. I will have one of the doctors come in when we are ready. Hang
tight here for a bit. Open the door here and call out for us if you need anything."

"Will do," I said. She closed the door behind her, and for the first ten
minutes immediately following, Frankie and I just cried. Loud, hysterical, all-
consuming tears were falling twofold.

I looked around between crying fits at one point, and saw a box of tissues on the counter in the room we were waiting in. I got up and grabbed it, bringing it over and placing it between Frankie and I. She took a tissue out of the box to blow her nose and wipe her tears, and I did the same within seconds.

"D—do you have any idea… w—what it could b—be?" Frankie hesitated, crying between words.

"No… I don't…"

"M—maybe he ate s—something w—weird?"

"T—that's possible…"

Beyond that, we sat together without talking and let our emotions out before we heard the doorknob jostle again. It felt like an eternity for how much we both cried, but it may have only been thirty minutes. This time, instead of the vet tech we saw earlier, it was a male doctor. He is tall—I would guess about 6'1". His rectangular glasses reveal hazel eyes behind them, and his dirty blonde hair is neatly parted, with most of it falling to the right, held in place by gel.

"Hello, my name is Dr. Davis. Are you… James and Francesca Rossi? With the orange cat named Apollo?"

"Yes," Frankie answered.

"Well… First of all, let me start with saying sorry for your loss."

"Thanks," I said. "What took him?"

"It…appears that he was poisoned. Something he ate was malicious, and based on what I saw, it didn't take long. Additionally, cats often hide when they are dying. The tech said that you found him underneath your bed?"

"That's correct."

"It's possible that after he ingested whatever poisoned him, he went under there to go in peace. To some degree, he may have known you wouldn't look under there right away."

"I see… Wow…" Frankie said. She seems at a loss for words. We both are, really.

"Do you want to cremate Apollo?" Dr. Davis asked.

"We can do that?" I had no idea that was a thing.

"Yes. We will have him cremated if that's your desire, and you can pick up the ashes in a few days."

Frankie and I looked at each other. I could tell by the look in her eyes, which are still filled with tears, that she wanted this too.

"Yes. Let's do that."

"Alright, I will get that process started for you. Is there anything else I can help you with while you're here?"

"N—no. That was it," I said.

"The girls at the front desk will help you on the way out. Again, I'm very sorry for your loss. I deal with putting animals down daily, and the only thing that comforts me is knowing that they're no longer suffering. I have three cats of my own, and know it's one of the hardest things you'll ever experience."

"Thank you, Dr. Davis. You have been very helpful."

"Yes, thank you."

"Take care, you two. My heart goes out to you."

Dr. Davis walked out of the room, and closed the door to the patient room. After we stabilized ourselves again, we also exited the patient room and went back around to the reception desk the same way we arrived.

"I'm so sorry that it had to be like this today for you guys," the brunette behind the desk said.

"It is what it is," Frankie stated.

"That'll be seventy-five dollars for the cremation."

I reached into my back left pocket to grab my wallet, then promptly took out my MasterCard credit card. I handed it to the brunette.

"Thank you," she said as she grabbed it and ran it through to process the payment. She handed it back to me as soon as the transaction was approved.

"Would you like a receipt?"

"Yes, please."

I waited a moment for the merchant copy of the receipt to print, which I then took from her to sign the bottom. She handed me another copy to keep for my records.

"Thanks," I said, as I shoved the receipt into my wallet before putting it back into the same pocket. I held Frankie's hand as we walked out of the vet together to go home.

22: FORTY-TWO

It only took 42 years to do this, but I'm finally going to cross it off my bucket list: I will be attending The Game. If you're not familiar with the term in regards to college football, I'm referring to the annual matchup of The Ohio State Buckeyes vs the University of Michigan Wolverines (or, as Ohio State fans call it, That Team Up North). TTUN for short.

Of course, I'm going to make a whole day of it. I'm flying out to Columbus, Ohio the day before—November 18, 1994. In relation to today, that's two days from now, and yes, I have not even brought out my suitcase yet. I'm going to meet up with Frankie's brothers and Andrew. I asked Frankie if she wanted to go, and she declined the invitation. She's not as into football (or sports in general) the way I am, but she has no problem encouraging me to go if that's what makes me happy. The Mancini brothers and I have been planning this for months, so I'm sure you can imagine my excitement. I'm sure at least one of them is going to ask about her, but we're also just looking to have a good time at the game.

We're all flying out on the 18th and getting hotel rooms in Columbus because there's no way I'm missing the "dotting the I" ceremony. It's a tradition that's been occurring since 1936. A tuba player held the honor of doing this after the rest of the Ohio script was formed by the marching band on the field the first time, but in 1937, Glen Johnson became the first sousaphone player to take up that role, and it has remained with the sousaphone player since.

~ * ~

The four of us arrived at John Glenn Columbus International Airport (CMH) at various times on the 18th, and decided to stay at the German Village Inn within downtown Columbus. We split two rooms, each with two separate beds. I shared a room with Ralph. Vincent and Joseph Mancini took the other room, and both were adjacent. The hotel seems nice and meets our needs, but we're four men who are traveling without our wives. Travel tends to be easier under those conditions.

Thankfully, the hotel is a mere 2.2 miles from Ohio Stadium. Being that TTUN fans had to travel south to get here, there were a number of them in various rooms staying at the same hotel. Since there are four of us, we decided to hitch our own ride between the hotel and the stadium.

We arrive about fifteen minutes prior to kickoff, and thousands of people have already found and taken their seats, as well as hit up the concession stands. Upon approach at the main entrance, security patted us down and made us empty our pockets to make sure we didn't bring any crazy shit into the venue.

Our seats were pretty good—we were closest to the 25-yard line in section 23A, a few rows off from the very bottom of the section. Ralph purchased all the seats together as early as possible, and I sent him money via check to pay him back for mine.

Once we sit down, Joe immediately wants to drink. "Do any of you guys want to go get a beer with me before it starts?"

"Hm… I think I'm alright at the moment. Don't the guys usually come around and have beer for sale, too?"

"They do," Vince said. "That's often what I do at live sports events. I don't want to get up, and they come to me with the cold beer."

"I guess I'll take one. Whatever you get, I'll have the same," Ralph said. Ralph got out his wallet and handed Joe a few dollars to pay for his own beer.

"Alright, I'll be back," Joe said as he got up. He had to go up quite a few stairs, but somehow made it up, got beers, and came back before the Dotting the I ceremony and national anthem began.

"That was…quite the impressive feat, making it back so quickly. Were there just no fucking lines?" I asked.

A few minutes later, the game is ready to begin. Michigan wins the coin toss and receives the ball first. Although it's common to defer, that was not the case today.

Following the outcome of the coin toss, both teams take their places on the field. Wearing jersey number 38, kicker Mike Malfatt punts the ball out to the Michigan offense, the defensive line surrounding him on either side. The first few plays of the game past kickoff were…honestly kind of a bore. Maybe I feel that way because of unstated expectations. I'm not sure. During a play on 1st and 10, Michigan quarterback Todd Collins was sacked by #92 defensive end Matt Finkes for a loss of nine yards. It didn't take long before Michigan had to turn the ball over on downs, as their opening drive was mostly uneventful. So much for that. The Ohio State defense was something that they failed to overcome early on, which makes me happy. They gave *us* two points when QB Todd Collins fell into their own end zone at about the 2-yard line and caused a safety at 3:30 in the first quarter.

The second quarter saw some more interesting plays, which meant that Michigan's hopes and dreams were crushed further. Just after the start of the second quarter, 14:11, came the first scoring touchdown of the game. Ohio State quarterback Bob Hoying ran four yards for that touchdown, and the extra point by Josh Jackson went directly between the uprights. This brought the score to Ohio State 9 – Michigan 0. While Michigan struggled offensively, the Buckeyes didn't slow down. Despite their best attempts, they couldn't convert for another touchdown this quarter. At 6:22 in the second quarter, Josh Jackson lines up for a 26-yard field goal, and makes it successfully, bringing the score to 12-0.

At halftime, I decided to use the men's room, since I had a few beers in me by this point. I didn't drink at the start of the game, but decided a few minutes into the first quarter to go grab a couple because of the slow pace of the game. Naturally, there was an insanely long line outside the men's room. Everyone and their brother needed to empty their bladders at the exact same time, or at least it felt that way.

Starting the second half, the team looked confident, although head coach John Cooper knew deep down that his job was on the line if he didn't put this game into the win column. His record against Michigan during his tenure up to this point was 0-5-1, and the athletic director was having none of it. Third quarter felt like a repeat of the first quarter because nothing super exciting happened during it. I don't quite remember the time marker, but at some point, Todd Collins overthrew a potential touchdown pass to wide receiver Amani Tumer. However, the ball went out of bounds, and so did Tumer. The pass went through Tumer's hands, but not in them. For them, that's tragic. For the Buckeyes, that added fuel to the fire. This team was determined to change the narrative. At 7:57 during this quarter, Michigan kicker Remy Hamilton scored for their second and final time of the game, from 22 yards out.

The fourth quarter of the game sealed the fate of both teams, leaving myself and the Mancini brothers happy with the results. At 11:22, Josh Jackson successfully put the ball through the uprights from 36 yards out, bringing the score to 15-6. When Michigan tried to respond in kind, the result was disastrous. Michigan kicker Remy Hamilton went for a 35-yard field goal kick, which was promptly blocked by the Ohio State defensive line. The ball was spiked too high by the center before the holder could get his hands on it and place it. Within a split second of the ball making its way airborne, it was blocked, came loose, and quickly picked up by cornerback Marlon Kerner. Kerner wasted no time in taking the ball out to the 48-yard line. The Buckeyes didn't let the offensive drive go to waste once the play completed. At 8:35 in the quarter, Ohio State running back Eddie George completed a 2-yard running touchdown, and Josh Johnson's extra point was good.

Within the last five minutes of the game, it was obvious that the Michigan roster and head coach Gary Moeller had abandoned all hope of coming out of this game with a W. The final score was Ohio State 22 – Michigan 6, and the officials allowed the clock to run out with about thirty seconds left.

Once the game ended, the four of us made our way out of Ohio Stadium, hailed a taxi, and went back to our hotel room. The next day, the Mancini brothers returned to Cleveland Hopkins International Airport, and I made my way back out to Vegas, arriving at McCarran International Airport.

23: FORTY-ONE

I don't spend nearly enough time talking to or seeing my brothers-in-law, and they all know it, especially the oldest—Ralph.

To temporarily escape the bitter cold of the Midwest (read: Ohio) winters, Ralph has decided to fly out to Vegas for the New Year's celebrations. He's staying in the guest room downstairs for the few days he's here. He arrived yesterday, and he's leaving on January 3. Leaving on the second would probably be too much of a disaster, so he figured that an extra day won't hurt anyone. We rarely get to see him anyway.

At 6:57 am, I hear Ralph messing about in the kitchen from upstairs. I went to bed rather late, so getting woken up at this hour isn't a pleasant experience. Of course, he has no problem feeling right at home in our house. I don't mind him. I just don't like being woken up super early when I got home from work at 1 am.

Frankie was already up and about. I heard her footsteps slowly become less audible, and I assumed that she was heading downstairs to see what commotion Ralph was causing in the kitchen. After about a minute, I heard faint conversation, but decided that I would try to go back to sleep so I'm not feeling like a zombie this evening when the three of us are trying to enjoy the New Year's festivities and shenanigans.

I tossed and turned, pulling the comforter over my head to attempt to drown out everything—Frankie, Ralph, and anything happening outside. Our bed was only a couple of feet away from a window, and we have neighbors who seem to be active at all hours of the day. There are times that I question if they're even employed, or if one of them stays at home while the other is the sole breadwinner. I shifted around in bed until I was lying on my stomach, my head facing to the right (away from the sun's light coming through the window), my arms at my sides. I forcibly closed my eyes for a minute, then tried to relax again. After what felt like eternity, but was realistically only a few minutes I'd guess, I did fall back asleep, although not for very long. I would guess that I was able to sleep another twenty to thirty minutes before I gave up and decided to reluctantly get out of bed anyway.

I looked through the closet and threw on some black sweatpants and a light grey T-shirt, then went on my way to join Frankie and Ralph in the kitchen.

"Well, good morning, sleepy head," Ralph said sarcastically.

"Man, don't even try me… I got home from work at 1 am," I said. I was annoyed and needed coffee desperately.

"Oh, man… Did you just wake up?" he asked.

"Well, um… Sort of, but not really. You woke me up just before 7, then I unsuccessfully tried to go back to sleep for twenty to thirty minutes before I just gave up."

"Sorry, man. That's rough. Coffee? I just made the pot."

"Please. I desperately need the caffeine."

Ralph opened the cupboard that contains all of the drinkware, and grabbed a coffee mug. It seems Frankie has given him a lay of the land because he didn't ask where that was. He pours some coffee in it, and stops with about ¼ inch left from the top rim. He promptly hands it to me, and I grab some creamer and sugar to fix it the way I like. Once I felt satisfied with my adjustments, I took a sip from it. It's warm, but I'm not burning my tongue or the roof of my mouth.

"Did you sleep okay, dear?" Frankie asked.

"I mean… not really. Honestly, I slept like shit."

"I'm sorry. You can always take a nap later," she said. I appreciate her reassurance, but I'm *exhausted* beyond belief and recognition.

"Yeah. I guess."

I grabbed the handle of my coffee mug, which was sitting on the kitchen table in front of me, and started to drink it at a steady pace. The next thing I know, I've emptied the first cup, and I need to pour myself more. I go to fix myself the second cup of coffee, and doctor it the same way as the previous one. This one isn't as warm, so I chug it down as quick as possible, yet I still feel completely exhausted. I hate this feeling with every fiber of my being.

"Frankie, Ralph, do you guys need anything from me for the next little while?"

"I don't think so," Ralph said.

"No, why?" Frankie asked.

"Because I want to go back to bed, honestly."

"Oh, well… Go ahead. We'll try to not be too disruptive," Ralph added.

"Thanks, man."

I approached Frankie, and gave her a quick kiss on the lips. "I love you, sweety."

"I love you, too. Get some rest."

I rinsed my coffee mug out with water, and placed it into the sink before making my way back upstairs to our bedroom. Once I got there, I plopped onto the bed face down and promptly passed out.

~ * ~

I must have needed sleep because it was several hours later before I woke up from my slumber. When I say several hours, I mean the clock went from AM to PM. I think I passed out around 8 am… Not that I was checking the clock specifically. That might have been the best sleep I've had in quite some time. Frankie and Ralph didn't make much noise at all, as I was able to tune it out easily. I didn't notice Kismet next to me in bed licking himself and making atrocious noises of slurping until waking up just now either.

I rolled over to check the clock on the nightstand for the real time. 1:35 pm. Holy shit, I was out for a *while*. I can't complain, though—I feel great. I moved to sit on the side of the bed, rubbing my eyes to try and wake myself up further. I should probably shower. I feel disgusting and repulsive.

I strip down, grab some clean clothes and underwear, then head to the bathroom to turn on the shower. After a couple minutes of waiting for the water to get to my desired temperature—which isn't scorching hot nor freezing cold, but somewhere in-between—I get in and clean myself. Once I finish drying myself off, I get dressed and go back downstairs to see what they're up to. Kismet has gone off to do whatever chaos he's going to enact as well.

"Well, hello there Jimmy," Ralph said.

"Hi…"

"You passed out for quite a bit. Feeling any better?"

"Significantly. I showered, too. I'm sure you can tell by the wet hair."

"Of course," Frankie said.

"What are we doing tonight? Did you want to go to the Strip to watch the fireworks show they put on, Ralph?"

"That's a thing?"

I laughed. "Yes, Ralph, this is Vegas. Of course that's a thing. The Strip has the biggest fireworks show in the valley on New Year's Eve and the 4th of July."

"Then hell yeah, let's go! Sounds like a lot of fun."

"Alright, I'll brave the Strip for you. The fireworks start at midnight, so I figure we should leave no later than 10:30 pm so I can find a place to park. Of course, we can watch the ball drop in New York City at 9pm on TV as well if that's something you're interested in."

"It takes that long to get there?" he asked.

"Well, no, but the parking situation will be hot garbage due to the sheer amount of people who live here *and* visit for New Year's."

"Oh. That makes sense then."

"Yeah. Trust me, this city gets crazy. Vegas knows how to party, if nothing else. We *are* the entertainment capital of the world, after all."

Ralph sat there for a moment on the couch to contemplate something, though I wasn't sure the nature.

"Well, um, what do I wear?" he asked.

"Something warm? It's December. It may not snow here in the winter like it does in Ohio, but believe me when I say that I've experienced biting cold since moving here. It's a different kind of cold than you're probably used to. Whatever's comfortable that will keep you warm will do."

"Okay, I see. Makes sense."

~ * ~

At 9:30 pm, I went over to the guest room and knocked on the door to see if Ralph was dressed and ready to go soon or not. Frankie had already been getting ready for a while, and based on my knowledge of her, she won't be too much longer finishing up—ten minutes maximum. I'm the only one that's completely ready to go.

"Come in," I heard Ralph say faintly.

I opened the door, and he's got pants and socks on, but no shirt yet.

"I was checking to see if you were ready to go yet. Doesn't seem like that so far."

"Give me like ten minutes and I should be. I already showered and put on cologne. Just need to finish getting dressed and put shoes on," he said.

"Alright, sounds good. I'll leave you to it. Come out to the kitchen when you're ready. Frankie should be ready about the same time."

To my surprise, Ralph was done getting ready first. He put on way too much cologne, though, and I started coughing like crazy.

"Jesus, bro, did you spray the whole fucking bottle of cologne?!"

He laughed. "No, only a few spritz. It's just really strong at first."

Frankie waltzed downstairs a few minutes later, makeup done and dressed seasonally appropriate but still beautiful nonetheless.

"Alright, I'm ready to go," she said.

"Ralph? You good to go?"

"Sure am."

The three of us headed to the garage, where the car was parked. I opened the front passenger door for Frankie, and Ralph chose to get in the backseat behind Frankie. I went around to the driver's side, backed it out of the garage, and the three of us made our way to the Strip at 10:25 pm. I headed straight for the parking garage of the MGM Grand, which just opened its doors thirteen days before—December 18, 1993. To my surprise, there were still openings on the top floor, which was prime viewing for the fireworks show that would start at midnight sharp. I pulled into a spot on the perimeter of the garage that was facing the main Strip, turning off the engine once I shifted into park.

The three of us got out, and leaned our arms against the perimeter rail, eagerly awaiting the sparks and colors that would reign in the new year.

At 12:00 am sharp, the fireworks show that characterizes the main Las Vegas Strip every New Year's Eve began. Hues of green, blue, pink, and red start to burst and fill the night sky as the aerials pop everywhere.

"Happy New Year, guys," I said, then I quickly planted a kiss onto Frankie's lips. She's always wanted a New Year's kiss at midnight, and I just gave her one that she will remember.

"Happy New Year, Jimmy," Ralph said.

"Happy New Year, love," Frankie said, smiling.

We continued to watch the fireworks until cessation, and promptly got in the car to go home after that.

24: FORTY

Fuck me. What do you *mean* I'm forty years old? There's no way. How did this happen?

When we're little, we see adults as "old" past a certain age. That point in time can vary based on individual perception and even their upbringing. Age is just a number, as they say, but it's a number that people can (and do) often make snap judgments about you based on it. Haven't accomplished certain things in your life by a specific age? Judgment. Haven't made a certain amount of money by some arbitrary age? Questioning and judgment. Don't have kids and never want them, regardless of your age? Oh, the horrors. (That's definitely sarcasm.)

Because I must be a functioning member of society on my birthday, I find myself at work instead of doing…literally anything else that I want to do more. This is some weapons-grade bullshit.

Not only am I working today, but I'm also covering for someone in this pit. I'm not one to take the high-stakes tables on a regular basis, but I can manage it when I have to.

A man comes up to me as I'm supervising the high-stakes Texas Hold 'Em pit. He doesn't even look like a local, so he's got to be from somewhere else. Since it's fall, he's wearing a solid navy polo short-sleeve shirt and khaki shorts with tennis shoes. Nothing special. He doesn't look older than 35 either, but I could be mistaken. I've never been great at guessing age or anything like that, primarily because I don't like making assumptions about people that can possibly land me in trouble with them. He's slightly taller than me—6' in height if I had to guess. His hazel eyes look disconcerted, and his medium brown hair is somewhat unkempt.

"Excuse me, sir. Do you work here?"

"Yes, I do. How can I help?"

"Well, um… My wife was playing in this area about an hour ago, and she thinks she may have lost her purse in here. She hasn't been able to find it in our belongings in our room, or anywhere else we've been since we arrived in town yesterday. She swears that this is the last place she had it."

"Oh, wow… What does the purse look like? I'm sure I can ask the dealers in this area, and also check with Lost and Found."

"It's a Louis Vuitton St. Jacques in emerald green."

"Girl's got expensive taste."

"Yeah, I know… It was an anniversary gift one year."

"Well, shit. Do you want to take a walk with me to Lost and Found? See if they have it?"

"That would be great," he said.

He walked alongside me through the casino, up the elevator five floors, and down a hallway lined with guest rooms on both sides. Finally, we approach an unmarked door, which I knew from experience is the Lost and Found. I put my ear to the door to listen if anyone is in there right now. Usually, there's only a single employee at any given time, and of course, we all have human needs to use the restroom and all that. Since I didn't hear anything immediately, I knocked three times.

"Come in, it's open," I heard a woman say from the inside of the office. I grabbed the handle and turned it to let myself in.

"Oh, hello Lucy," I said.

"Hi, Jimmy! What can I do for you?"

"This gentleman said that his wife may have lost her purse in the casino. He approached me when I was supervising the high-stakes Texas Hold 'Em pit."

Lucy looks to my left to see the gentleman that I brought with me. His face reeks of panic and worry.

"Sir, can I get your name?"

"Richard Calimeris."

"Are you staying here with us?"

"Yes."

"What's your wife's name? Maybe someone could've found the wallet within the bag, and I can look for it."

"Carol Calimeris."

"What kind of bag is it? Do you know the make, style, and color?"

"It's a Louis Vuitton St. Jacques in emerald green. Fairly hard to miss that color and brand."

"Alright, Richard, give me a moment, and I'll go look for it. Stay here with Jimmy."

"Okay, I can do that."

Richard and I exchanged a look, and he seemed slightly less worried, at least visibly. I don't know what's going on inside his head unless he tells me, which applies not just to him, but anyone, for that matter.

"Relax, I'm sure it's fine." I was trying to be reassuring, but I know that can go either way when someone is worried sick.

"I sure hope so. She said your name is Jimmy?"

"Yeah, that's right. I'm the manager on duty right now."

"Oh, well, no wonder you're helpful. You must know what you're doing."

"I've been here for a number of years already, so I do know it pretty well by now, I'd say."

Ten minutes later, Lucy emerges with a green bag, her mood triumphant with her findings. She truly went through every single item in this Lost and Found, which is…not a small amount. People lose their shit all the time, and you would be surprised for the amount that *don't* come back to look for their belongings. Items as innocent as a pair of sunglasses, to a few wedding rings, and everything in between have found their way into this room.

"Richard, is this the bag you're looking for?"

"I—I think so. Can I see it for a minute?"

"Sure," she said as she hands the bag over to him by the handles. He quickly unzips the top, and checks for the wallet and opens it. I watch as a smile comes across his face, verifying that it was his wife's wallet, driver's license, and belongings.

"Oh my God! This is it! Thank you both so much! She will be elated to have this back."

"I'm glad we could be of assistance," Lucy said with a smile.

"Do you know how to find your way back to your room, or do you want me to help you along?" I asked him.

"I think I got it," he said.

"Sounds good. The elevator is just down the hall, the same way we came, and you can get to your floor from there."

"Thank you so much, Jimmy! I appreciate you."

To my surprise, he hugged me. Clearly, finding that handbag meant more to him than just the bag itself. He did mention that it was an anniversary gift, but it felt like his wife would kill him if it wasn't retrieved and found, too. After he pulled away from the hug, he thanked Lucy again as well.

"You, too, Lucy."

He made his way down the hall to the elevators, and the two of us watched as he disappeared into the distance after the doors of the elevator car closed behind him.

"Right, well, I'm going to head back down to the casino," I told Lucy.

"Yes, of course. Good to see you, Jimmy. It's always a pleasure."

"Same to you. Catch you later."

Just as Richard did, I walked down the hallway, the heels of my dress shoes click-clacking against the tile floor once I arrived in the area by the elevators. The doors slid open for me to enter, and I made my way back down to ground level to return to the high-stakes pit.

As the elevator made its way down, I adjusted my tie, fixed my suit jacket, and popped an Altoid mint into my mouth. By the time the elevator doors opened back up into the casino floor, I felt ready to tackle whatever else would be thrown my way the rest of the night.

25: THIRTY-NINE

On the evening of May 9, 1992, Frankie and I head to the airport to pick up a very important person—Mom. She has never been to Vegas before, never mind the West Coast, and she's here for Mother's Day. I never would have guessed that it would take this long for her to see the West Coast, but it's better late than never, I suppose.

It takes us about twenty minutes to get there. Vegas is rapidly expanding, and as more roads are paved and more homes are built, it's starting to take longer to get where you need to be. For every month and year that passes, this city grows more than the previous it feels like, and the economy is booming here as a result.

When we arrive, we park in the short-term parking garage, walk across the bridge, and are immediately greeted by several baggage claim carousels and sparse chairs scattered throughout. Once inside the building, we begin looking around, although Mom is hard to find. She's 5'1", which means just about everyone is taller than her. I'm able to see a little more than Frankie, but not by a lot. Anyone taller than 5'10" is going to be obstructive to my field of view.

Finally, I locate Mom at carousel 9 in the baggage claim, and realize that Frankie and I are at carousel 16. We have a little bit of a walk, but it's nothing terrible. When we're about five feet away from Mom, I take up a slight jog to hug her. I've missed her so much.

"Hey, Mom," I said, wrapping my arms around her and giving her a warm hug. I crouched down slightly so that she could put her head against my chest.

"Jimmy!" I felt my T-shirt dampen as I realized she was crying into it. Readily. "I've missed you so much."

She finally pulls back just slightly, still crying, then goes to hug Frankie. "How's my favorite daughter-in-law?"

Frankie seemed surprised to learn this new information.

"I'm the favorite? What about Giulia?"

Mom chuckled, wiping her tears with a tissue that she pulled out of her

92

purse.

"Oh, of course you're the favorite, Frankie. I've always loved you. That's between us, though."

The three of us laughed. Mom has always been funny, and loves to pull jokes on people.

"Where's your bag?" I asked.

"It should be coming around on the carousel soon," she said.

We sat in three adjacent chairs a few feet away from the carousel that was going to bring out Mom's bag.

"What color and style is the bag? That way we know what to look for?" Frankie asked curiously.

"Bright pink one with wheels and a handle. Solid color."

Dozens of bags begin to make their way around the baggage carousel, amassing a variety of colors, patterns, and even shapes. Staff seem to be pushing them out consistently, although there are gaps of a few minutes where no new bags make their way around. Judging by the look on Mom's face, it doesn't seem like hers has come around yet, and she's starting to grow impatient. Mom growing impatient is a rarity, so this was quite a spectacle to behold.

"Well, it doesn't seem to be coming along very quickly," Mom said.

"Just be patient, I guess. There are only so many passengers on any given flight," Frankie said in an attempt to reassure Mom.

"Yeah, well, I'm tired. I've been up since 6 am Eastern. What time is it now, Jim?"

I took a glance at my watch to read the time.

"It says... 9:05 pm."

"So, you're telling me I've been up for... about 18 hours. Since it's past midnight back in Ohio right now."

"Oh, yeah, true..." Frankie sounded like she didn't realize how *long* Mom had been awake, and how cranky Mom gets when she doesn't get her beauty sleep.

I feel like someone heard us because within about a minute of this interaction taking place, dozens more bags quickly started coming out. After a few rounds on the carousel, I saw Mom's pupils dilate as she recognized her bag come towards us.

"It's about time!" she said. She pointed it out, and I caught sight of it as well. Once it got to where I could reach it, I pulled it off of the carousel and stood it upright, extending the handle as well.

"Is that it? Just the one suitcase?"

"Yes, that's it. I packed light this time."

"I've never known you to pack light, Mom."

"Well... I've learned to over the years, I guess." She shrugged.

I leaned the suitcase towards me so that I could wheel it towards the elevator, and the three of us went back to my car in the short-term parking garage once we got off it. I opened the trunk and put Mom's suitcase in there before opening the passenger rear door to let Mom in, and the passenger front seat for Frankie, before I got into the driver's seat.

I started the engine, and just as we were leaving the parking garage, I heard what sounded like snoring. I quickly look behind me, and Mom is passed out. She *really* was exhausted.

"What about you, Frankie? How are you feeling?"

"I'm alright. I'm tired, too, though. Maybe not as much as her."

"I love you," I told her, as I grabbed her left hand with my right. I brought it up to my face and kissed the top of her hand.

"I love you, too," she said as she smiled, her eyes glistening despite the exhaustion.

We stayed quiet the rest of the time to allow Mom to sleep a little bit. Once we got to our house, Frankie gently woke her up.

"Hey, Maria, we're here." Frankie nudged her on the shoulder just a bit.

Mom groaned and mumbled something, but I couldn't quite make out what she said. She opened her eyes and took a second for her vision to adjust to the dark.

"Alright," she said, yawning. She unbuckles her seat belt and slowly but carefully gets out of the car.

I wait for her to situate herself upright, and I pop the trunk to retrieve her suitcase before I take her hand and walk her to the front door of our house.

"Frankie, can you get the door, please?"

"Oh, sure," she said, finding her keys in her purse. Frankie gets a few paces ahead of us, and unlocks the door, holding it open for Mom and I before she enters as well.

"Thank you, dear." I kissed her quickly once everyone was inside.

"My God, Jim, this is a beautiful home!" Mom said.

"Well, I can't take much of the credit. Frankie did most of the decorating and keeps it organized. I help, too, but it's mostly her."

"It looks great, Frankie. You turned a house into a home."

"Thank you, Maria, I appreciate that."

"Where's my room?"

"Oh, right. Do you want anything? Food? Water? Just want to go to bed?"

"I'm exhausted and just want to sleep right now," Mom insisted.

"Alright, I'll show you to your room."

I guided Mom down the hallway that connects to the kitchen and living room area, then opened a door on the left. The guest room has a queen bed, its own bathroom, and it looks like Frankie even left her a clean set of towels already. I placed her suitcase upright to the left of the door.

"We'll probably be up a little longer if you need something, but otherwise, have a good night, Mom."

"Thank you, Jimmy."

I backed out of the room and closed the door quietly, giving Mom her space to do as she pleases.

"Are you tired yet? Do you want to watch something on TV?" I asked Frankie.

"Nah… I think I'm ready to lay down, at least. Read my book a little bit. I don't want to do anything crazy right now."

We made our way upstairs to our room, and made ourselves more comfortable once we closed the door. Frankie picked up her book, and read a few pages before putting it down because she got too tired to stay awake and continue.

"Honey, I want to go to sleep. Can you turn off the lights?"

"Of course, my love."

I wasn't yet settled in bed, so I obliged to turn off the lights. Apparently, my bladder decided I needed to take a leak, too. Once I was done relieving myself, I turned off the bedroom light and crawled into bed under the covers next to Frankie. To my surprise, she already passed out peacefully. I kissed her on the forehead, closed my eyes, and went to sleep.

~ * ~

I was woken up early the next morning to the scents and sounds of Frankie making breakfast. Today is officially Mother's Day, which means that Mom isn't required to do anything but kick back and enjoy herself while Frankie and I make every bit of this trip (and holiday) an easy one for her.

As I lay in bed contemplating when to get up, I realized that I never actually got Mom a gift for Mother's Day. I've been so busy with work that I completely forgot to get her something. Surely this trip is enough? I've never known Mom to be materialistic. She was always more concerned with spending quality time with Jeremy, Dad, and I than she ever was worried about gifts. Honestly, gifts made her uncomfortable most of the time. I paid for the airfare to get her here, and Dad drove her to Cleveland Airport. She flies home on Tuesday. I took the days off because I don't get to see her very often, and I wanted to make her first trip out to Vegas a special one.

I looked for my boxer-briefs, some shorts, and a T-shirt to change into, then took a shower. Mom is somewhat of a clean and hygiene freak, so I'm not trying to smell or look bad (worse, homeless). After brushing my teeth and getting dressed, I walked downstairs to see Frankie finishing up whatever she was cooking, and Mom sat at the dining table with a plate and silverware setting already in front of her.

"Well, good morning, lazy ass," Frankie said as she laughed.

"Hey, shut it. You fell asleep first, dear. I also typically work swing or graveyard, so this is about normal for me."

"I know, I know. I'm just giving you a hard time."

"What are you making?" I asked, eyeing the stove and kitchen countertops that were filled with various pans, cooking apparatus, and food at the moment.

"French toast, eggs, and bacon."

"Since when do we keep bacon in this house, Frankie? You've been a vegetarian for as long as I've known you."

"I got some when you were at work on Friday. I figured you and Mom would want some."

"Oh, well... I appreciate that. I do like bacon."

"The bacon is almost done, and once it rests for a minute, everything will be ready. Oh, Maria, did you want coffee or anything to drink? We've got orange juice, tea, coffee, water..."

"Coffee and water. Thank you, Frankie! You're very sweet." Mom had the most genuine smile on her face. She truly meant those words, and looked happy to be here with us.

"Did you hear from Jeremy or Giulia, dear?"

Frankie looked up and to the side, racking her brain for recent memories and experiences regarding my brother, sister-in-law, and *three* nephews. David is the oldest one, Thomas the middle, and Cody the youngest. Jeremy and Giulia decided to finally stop procreating after Cody was born, feeling satisfied with having three sons to carry the Rossi family name.

"I... don't think so. Call them."

I obliged immediately. I grabbed the cordless phone, which sits atop the junk drawer in the kitchen. I dialed Jeremy and Giulia's number, and waited to hear it ring a couple of times.

"Hello?" I heard Jeremy answer.

"Jer, it's your brother."

"Oh, hey Jim. What's up?"

"Do you know what today is?"

"No, what...?"

"Mother's Day, bro."

"Oh... shit! It is! I need to call Mom—"

"Well, actually, you don't. You can come see her. We picked her up from the airport last night. I paid to have her fly out and spend Mother's Day in Vegas with Frankie and I."

"Shut the fuck up. Seriously?!"

"Yeah, seriously. Here, I'll hand her the phone."

I went over to Mom and handed her the phone, mouthing the name "Jeremy" to her silently.

"Well, hello Jeremy," she said.

"Hi, Mom!"

"Do I get to see all of you today? You, Giulia, and my grandsons?"

"Yes! We'll be right over as soon as we can. Maybe an hour so that we can get ready?"

"Sounds good. See you soon."

Mom promptly pushed the End Call button on the handset.

"It seems like we're going to see Jeremy and the gang soon?" Frankie asked.

"Yes, they are bringing the grandkids with them in about an hour."

After that, Mom finished eating her breakfast. Frankie and I were eating ours, and moments later, Frankie was ready to put the dishes and silverware into the sink with the pans and cooking utensils. Although she could have had every reason to ask Frankie to reheat it, Mom didn't opt to do that.

"Wow, Frankie, this breakfast is great. Thank you so much." Mom took a few sips of her water in between bites of food, and mostly kept quiet while she ate. That must be where I get it from—when we're hungry, we eat. Not a lot of talking occurs if it's that dire.

After Mom finished eating, and Frankie did the dishes, we sat on the couch, and Apollo came to join us. Apollo these days is not super energetic, but he's still a great cat. He still wants pets and attention as much as possible, even if he's becoming an old man.

Last year, we also decided to adopt another orange cat because apparently, we're gluttons for punishment. At this point, Apollo is twelve years old. We decided to get a younger cat to give him a friend, finally, after all these years of him being solo. His name is Kismet, and to say he is violently orange is still a huge understatement. This cat has never had the brain cell for a single day in his five years of life. Not only is he orange, but he's a Maine Coon as well, so he's bigger, fluffier, and far dumber than anything imaginable. He's lucky he's cute and that we love him because he would never survive on the streets. Kismet may think (whatever that means to an animal that almost never has the brain cell) that he can take down a tomcat in the streets, but he would be sorely mistaken. He would scream for rescue the moment that type and status of cat hisses at him. I should also mention that Kismet likes to scratch at walls and eat the paint. There is truly no hope for this animal.

An hour and a half later, I hear the doorbell ring, and sprang up to respond to it. Mom and Frankie didn't even seem to be fazed or care. I walked to the door and looked through the peephole, seeing my brother and Giulia at eye level on the other side. I unlocked the dead bolt and open the door.

"Well, it's about time you showed up," I said jokingly.

"Hey, bro," Jeremy said, hugging me, and Giulia followed suit right after him. I looked down and saw David, Thomas, and Cody, eager and happy to see me.

"Uncle Jimmy!" they said in almost perfect unison.

"How are my favorite nephews?!" I tried to hug them individually, but they ended up running past me inside, still full of energy as young kids. I don't know how Jeremy and Giulia handle it. I love them to death, don't get me wrong, but I'm tired after my *own* day, never mind having three boys. Jeremy and I were enough of a handful growing up.

"GRANDMA!" David yelled, running up to Mom. That kid does love Mom, and I don't think he's seen her in quite some time either. David jumped on the couch next to Mom, and she gave him a hug as well.

"Well, hello there, David!" she said, smiling. It was so nice to see Mom happy again. Thomas and Cody followed closely behind, although David is the most energetic of the boys. He always has been.

Mom looks in front of her over the top of David's head, seeing Thomas and Cody, who also want a hug from her. She wasted no time in obliging the request for both of them.

Jeremy and Giulia make their way in, taking their shoes off before they walk any further into the house. That's always been something that we've done at home in our family.

"Do you boys want to play in the back yard?" Giulia asked.

"Yeah!" Cody yelled excitedly.

I got up to open the sliding door that goes between the kitchen and the backyard, making sure to not let either of the cats out, but enough for the three of them to play.

"I guess that'll keep them busy a while, yeah?" I asked.

"Yeah, for sure. They'll tire themselves out eventually," Jeremy responded.

"What are we doing in here then?"

"We can flip through channels and look for a movie or show, I guess?"

I handed Jeremy the remote to the TV, and he flipped through channels halfheartedly before we decided to watch *Star Trek: The Next Generation*. That wouldn't be my first choice, but it was on, and it was sufficient background noise.

The boys barely came inside to take a drink of water, never mind eat. They must have ate already before they came by, since that's something Giulia would do. They played outside basically the entire time unless nature called.

"Maria, do you want anything to drink? Maybe a mimosa?"

"Francesca Regina, since when do *you* day drink?" I asked.

Frankie looked at me, surprised, like she felt she had done something wrong. I guess getting your legal first and middle name randomly can do that to a person. I always knew I was in deep shit when Mom would yell across the house "James Antonio Rossi!".

"Since when do *you* call me my government name?" she asked, cocking an eyebrow at me.

"Hmm… I guess that just slipped. But seriously, I've never seen you day drink, and I've known you since high school."

"Jim, we're pushing 40… I'm allowed to have a mimosa. It's Vegas, for Christ's sake."

"Yeah, I suppose. You have a valid point."

"So, Maria, do you want a mimosa?"

"Sure, I'll take one. Do you add any flavorings to it, or just straight champagne and orange juice?"

"I add a little bit of mango flavoring."

"Oh, my, that sounds amazing."

Frankie proceeded to prep two mimosas with champagne we had (but never opened), orange juice, and some mango simple syrup. I have to admit, it does look amazing.

"I guess I'll take one, too, Frankie," I said sheepishly. I watched as Frankie rolled her eyes, then got out another champagne flute for my third mimosa. She smiled as she mixed it, too.

"Jeremy, do you want one, too?" Frankie asked.

"No, I'm good. Thank you for the offer," he said.

Once Frankie mixed everything and poured out the three mimosas, she handed me a flute and Mom the other before bringing hers over to join us.

"Happy Mother's Day, Maria."

"Happy Mother's Day, Mom," I said.

Jeremy was only half paying attention but also repeated the "happy Mother's Day" greeting.

"Cheers," I said, as we clicked our flutes together. It was nice, for once, to have more than just Frankie and I in the same place at the same time. Lord knows it rarely happens anymore.

26: THIRTY-EIGHT

April 8, 1991. Frankie and I are in Ohio visiting my parents right now because it's Dad's 65th birthday. Tomorrow is never promised, and I haven't been back to Ohio in quite some time—especially since we moved to Vegas. It's not that I don't love my parents. It's that Ohio is sometimes a bit depressing to stay in for more than a few days.

These days, I'm less enthusiastic about making the trip east to visit the Buckeye State. I'm happy in Vegas as far as I'm concerned, and Frankie doesn't have serious complaints either. However, none of us is getting any younger, so I figured that it would be a good opportunity to enjoy beautiful spring weather in the Midwest again.

Frankie and I flew in last night, and we are staying in what used to be Jeremy's old room. There's a Queen bed in there, which works better for us than the two twin beds on opposite sides of the room that I used to sleep in.

We went downstairs to greet my parents at about 7 am. We haven't been here long enough yet to adjust to the fact that it would be 4 am in Vegas normally for us right now.

"Good morning," Frankie said while visibly yawning. "Do you have any coffee?"

I cocked an eyebrow at Frankie's request. "Dear, you hardly *ever* drink coffee."

She scoffed and rolled her eyes right back at me. "I'm tired, okay? A girl is allowed to be tired."

Yeah, she's not having my shit this morning. That much is abundantly clear right now.

"Of course, I just made a pot," Mom said. "Good morning, you two."

"Where's Dad?" I asked.

"He might be in the shed or garden. You know how he is. Never sits still. Ever."

"True. I'll go find him and tell him happy birthday. I'll take a cup of coffee as well."

I made my way outside before retrieving any coffee for myself, and started to look around for Dad. He was tending to the garden and pulling weeds.

"Hey, Dad."

He whipped his head in my direction, looking like I caught him by surprise. I must have.

"Oh, goodness, Jim. I didn't hear or see you coming. Don't scare me like that! Getting too old for this shit."

"I was just going to talk to you about that."

"Huh? How do you mean?"

"Happy birthday, Dad."

I watched as a smile came across his face and upturned the corners of his mouth. A reaction like that from Dad is rare, especially as he gets older. He also came up to me from a few feet away to hug me. I embraced him, but not too tight. His once strong and lean physique was declining, even if he was keeping himself active by doing gardening and yard work.

"Thank you, Jim. Did Jeremy and Giulia not come with you guys?"

"No, he had to work. He's always working. Doesn't seem to stop."

"Ah, well... That's too bad. Maybe he'll call later or something, I guess."

"That's possible. It's still pretty early back in Vegas. He might be asleep right now."

"True. I didn't think about that. What are Frankie and your mom up to?"

"They're just in the kitchen having coffee. Haven't heard anything about breakfast unless Mom started cooking something since I've come outside to talk to you."

"Makes sense."

"Did you want to do anything in particular today for your birthday, Dad? I just flew out for you honestly."

"Well... We could all go to dinner somewhere later?"

"Where to?"

"The Elmton? I haven't been there in a while," Dad suggested.

"Oh, sure. I'm sure Frankie will be happy to go there. That's where I took her for our first date."

"Really? I never knew that."

"You never asked, either." I chuckled. Dad never prodded too much into our personal lives growing up, as long as we weren't getting into serious trouble and kept our grades up. As a person, despite being an Aries, he's always been somewhat reserved. He minds his own business, spent his career working in oil fields and sometimes other blue-collar jobs, and has always been a loyal and stable provider and father.

"I suppose you have a point. I never did get too much into detail when you and Jeremy were growing up, eh?"

"As long as we weren't in jail or getting expelled, no, not really."

He heartily laughed after hearing that one.

"I left that to your mother. I just figured it was easier for me to stick to being the provider."

"Makes sense."

The rest of the day until we decided to leave for dinner was rather underwhelming. I watched a bit of TV, which included baseball.

Wait, today's MLB Opening Day! I hurriedly flipped the channel to the Cleveland Indians vs Kansas City Royals game. It's the top of the second inning, and it's KC 0 – CLE 1 now. Seems...promising, but I know how the Indians are. They'll find a way to blow it soon enough. It's a hallmark of Cleveland sports to find a way to ruin the season as soon as it starts. *Sigh.*

~ * ~

By the time dinner time came around, the four of us made our way to The Elmton. I'm *starving*. Holy shit.

Once we arrived, we quickly exited the car (which I drove), and walked inside. We were immediately greeted by a hostess with a smile.

"How many are in your group?"

"Four," I said.

"We've got a ten-minute wait. Is that okay?"

"Yes, that's fine."

"Can I get a name?"

"Jim."

"Alright, we'll call you when we have a table ready for your group."

"Sounds good, thanks."

I go back to Mom, Dad, and Frankie, who were a few feet away.

"They said it's going to be about a ten-minute wait, so I gave my name."

"Okay, that's fine. So, how's Vegas been treating you guys?" Mom asked. I was suddenly flooded with guilt that I definitely haven't visited the way I originally intended when I first moved out to Vegas.

Frankie's ears perked up, and I saw her raise an eyebrow at Mom's question. "It's been good, actually. I wasn't sure at first how much I'd like such a drastic change, but I've come to adapt to the heat, and I've made some good friends over the years," she said.

"Oh, well that's good! I'm glad it's been treating you well. What about you, Jim?"

"Yeah, I got promoted to casino management within a couple of years. It's been busy, but good. Jeremy apparently got into investment banking once him and Giulia got settled there. She tells me that he just works constantly."

Mom had a look on her face that I didn't recognize. She seemed kind of resigned? It wasn't full-on disappointment, but it wasn't a positive expression that I was reading.

"Yeah... I had a feeling that would happen. Even when he was going to YSU a mere twenty minutes away from here, he barely ever came around or called. He was always buried in studying, or had football practice, or whatever else."

"Huh, I would have never guessed my little shit of a brother would be like that."

"Oh, stop it," Dad said, playfully smacking my right bicep with the back of his hand.

"Jim, party of four," I heard the hostess call.

"Sounds like that's our table," I added. The four of us followed the blonde hostess to an empty four-top table in the restaurant that had just been cleaned and set up for us. Frankie sat to my left, and Mom sat across from me with Dad next to her.

"Hi, welcome to The Elmton. My name is Jennifer. Can I get you guys something to drink to start?"

"Water for me," Frankie said.

"I'll take iced tea," I requested.

"Water for me," Dad said.

"Water," Mom said.

"Three waters and an iced tea. Oh, sir, did you want unsweet or sweet iced tea?"

"Sweet. Whatever flavor it is doesn't matter to me."

"Alright, I'll be right back with those drinks, and will go grab your server as well. Her name is Barbara."

"Awesome, thank you so much."

Jennifer wasted no time in getting our drinks back to us, as she took less than five minutes to return with the tray of three waters and my sweet tea. She placed them according to everyone's requests. Jennifer also put four straws on the table, and we each took one.

"Barbara will be by in just a minute."

"No rush. Thank you," Mom assured her.

A few minutes later, a redheaded woman shows up at our table dressed the same way, equipped with a pad and a couple of pens clipped to her pocket.

"Hi, I'm Barbara. I'll be your server this evening. I see you've got the drinks. Did you guys know what you want?"

"Is everyone good with one pepperoni and one cheese?" I asked.

"Yeah," they all said a few seconds apart from each other.

"Okay, we'll get one pepperoni and one cheese pizza, please," I told Barbara. She quickly wrote it down on her pad.

"Anything else?"

"No, I think that's it for right now."

"Alright, easy enough! I will get that order in, and I'll have it right out as soon as it's ready. Oh! I forgot to ask. Are we celebrating anything today?"

"It's Dad's birthday," I said, quickly shifting my eyes from Barbara to Dad for half a second.

"Happy birthday, sir!"

"Thank you," Dad said. Was he...*blushing*?! Dad wasn't one to show emotion publicly, never mind be bashful enough to blush.

What felt like forever was only twenty minutes before we got our pizzas, and Barbara was smiling as she carried one in each hand as she approached our table. The four of us had sat in silence for the most part. Personally, I'm bordering on exhausted myself. I haven't had a lot of sleep since our arrival, and although it's Dad's birthday today, I'm not getting younger either.

"Alright, I have one cheese pizza, and one pepperoni," Barbara said. A second worker put down two pizza tray stands before she placed one pizza on each. Barbara then pulled out a pizza cutter out of her apron pocket, and sat it on the table between the pizzas.

"Thank you," I said.

"Do you guys need anything else? Parmesan? Extra napkins?"

"Yes, both," Mom added.

"Alright, I'll be right back with those."

Barbara jetted off for a minute, and quickly returned with the parmesan shaker and extra napkins. She also brought some extra plates just in case.

"I brought a couple extra plates as well. Just in case you need them."

"Thank you, we truly appreciate it," Dad said.

"You're welcome. Enjoy, y'all," Barbara said before walking away. Either I'm losing it, or I've never noticed this entire time that Barbara had a Southern accent to her voice. It's not just the fact that she said y'all—there's definitely something there that doesn't sound like it originates from the Midwest.

The four of us took turns with the pizza cutter, slicing the pizza and taking what we wanted to our plates before adding parmesan and finally eating.

"Oh, wow, that's good," Frankie said, who had mostly been silent the whole time we've been here. She doesn't seem to be in the most talkative of moods tonight, but that's alright.

"Yeah, that's pretty good. Who picked this place?" Mom asked.

"He did," I said, diverting my eyes in Dad's direction.

"Great choice, honey," Mom said, satisfied with the decision to come here for his birthday.

Barbara returned a few minutes later, and had something else in her hand—the billfold.

"Are y'all enjoying everything?"

Of course, wait staff love to come to your table when you've got your mouth full of food. Everyone seemed to look at Barbara and nod in agreement while still chewing their current bite of pizza.

"I'll leave this bill here, but no rush. Take your time, and flag me down when you're ready."

I finished chewing and swallowed the bite of food I had in my mouth at that moment.

"Oh, no, hold on one second."

I reached into my rear pants pocket to take out my wallet, flipped it open, and took out a Visa credit card, which I promptly handed to Barbara.

"Here you go."

"Oh, thank you! I'll be back in a bit once I've processed this. Y'all take your time eating, though."

"No problem."

When Barbara returned, she had the billfold in her hand again, which contained my credit card in one of the pockets.

"Here you go, Mr. Rossi. We look forward to seeing you again."

"Thank you, Barbara. You've been a doll."

I grabbed the pen included in the billfold, and left her a 20% tip. The service has never been anything short of great, and tonight was no exception.

Maybe fifteen minutes later, it seems that everyone was done eating. We put any silverware and napkins stacked on top of our plates, and tried to clean up the table as best we could. It's been customary in the Rossi family for generations to be better towards wait staff in that regard.

After cleaning up, we promptly left the restaurant, and headed home for the night.

27: THIRTY-SEVEN

One particularly chilly night in early February, I initially woke up from a dead sleep to go downstairs to get a glass of water. My mouth was dry, and the awkward sensation and feeling propelled me to wake up in the first place. When I was coming back to bed, I heard Frankie talking on the phone...and crying. Hard. My beautiful, loving woman was in hysterics.

"Oh my God, honey, what's wrong? Are you okay?"

"No... I'm not okay. Not at all." Her face was red and puffy. Tears were running down her cheeks. The box of tissues on the nightstand was half-depleted. I don't think I was gone five minutes from our bedroom.

"What happened? Talk to me, love."

"I... My..." She couldn't find the words.

"It's okay. Let it out."

"Jim, my mom... she's gone."

"WHAT?! Oh, honey... Come here." I sat next to her on the side of the bed, opening my arms for her. She lay her head against my chest and continued to sob hysterically. I caressed her head, giving her gentle head scratches as I combed my fingers through her hair.

"Do you want to talk about it?" I asked her. Frankie is hit or miss when it comes to talking about her emotions. Sometimes she is willing to, but other times she would prefer to avoid the subject entirely. I have a feeling that this is going to be the latter, but you never know.

"She... Cancer..."

I could tell it was hard for her to speak. I know her mom had fought a hard battle with breast cancer. She got diagnosed a few years ago, and it's been driving Frankie crazy since—crazy with worry and fear. Unfortunately, the cancer has been pretty aggressive. To some degree, at least she's not suffering anymore.

"Come here, love. Lay down. I got you."

It seems like her phone call was over some time ago, but she still made sure to check that the line was completely dead before proceeding. She shifted her positioning in bed to cuddle me and moved towards the center of the bed, burying her face in my chest while she cried some more.

I wish I could take her pain away. However, I don't think that would benefit either of us. She must endure her own pain and grief. It's her cross to bear. However, that doesn't mean I can't be there for her, and I am willing to do exactly that. She deserves that and so much more.

Fifteen minutes of silence pass by, and her breathing starts to slow and return to normal. She's not actively crying as hard, but I can tell that she's still torn up. Her heart is irrevocably shattered right now, and I can't imagine what it must feel like to experience this firsthand.

I look over at the clock. 12:37 AM. I kiss the top of Frankie's head, as she hasn't moved from her position with her head still in my chest. The only difference between now and when she first shifted into this was that my shirt is now drenched in tears. It's okay. There is nothing I wouldn't do for Frankie.

"How are you feeling, sweetheart?"

I wiped some of her remaining tears with a tissue that she already had close to her with us in bed.

"I… Jim… My mom lost…her battle with breast cancer. The hospital called while you went downstairs. I woke up initially because…well…I'm a light sleeper, but then the phone rang. I picked up on the first ring because…I didn't want to have you…hear the commotion."

I looked into her beautiful eyes, which were still a little bit red from all the crying.

"I love you, Frankie. You know I'll always be here for you. Your mom was a wonderful woman to be able to raise you the way she did."

She closed her eyes and tightened her grasp on me while we cuddled. I moved her hair aside so that it was out of her face.

"I love you, too," she mumbled, barely audible. "I always will."

I checked the clock again. 1:30 AM. Within a few minutes, I was asleep. Frankie calmed down enough to go to sleep, too.

~ * ~

When we woke up, the real work began. Frankie had to individually call each of her older brothers—Vincent, Ralph, and Joe—to try and figure out how to coordinate a funeral service. She called her dad last.

"I must go back to Ohio to see my brothers and other family…" She sounded reluctant, depressed, and every negative emotion imaginable in that short sentence.

"I understand. Do you want me to go with you? Or do you want to handle this alone? I'm good with either way. Just let me know."

"I would like for you to go with… So I don't lose my mind."

"Alright, let me call and get the days off."

Frankie looked at me surprised. Dumbfounded, even.

"Wait, like, right now?"

"Well, yeah... This is a legitimate family emergency, Frankie."

"Oh. Okay then."

I picked up the phone and dialed the HR department at work.

"Human Resources," I heard the woman answer.

"Hi, my name is James Rossi. I'm a table games supervisor, swing shift. I need to take a week off, effective immediately."

"W--what's the reason, Mr. Rossi?"

"My mother-in-law just passed away."

The line went quiet for a moment, and I thought she ended the call at first.

"Oh, my goodness. Right. Go ahead and be with your wife. I'll put this through and get it approved."

"Thank you very much."

"Is there anything I can help you with?"

"Nope, that will be it."

"Alright. Very sorry for your loss. We'll see you when you get back."

"Will do. Appreciate it. Buh-bye."

I promptly hung up the line.

"Well, I'm off work for the next week now. How soon are we going to Ohio?" I asked her.

"As soon as possible. Tomorrow? That way we have a chance to pack tonight, and leave in the morning. Can Jeremy or Giulia bring us to the airport?"

"Yeah, I'm sure we can work that out."

~ * ~

Jeremy drove us to the airport the next morning, at the ass crack of dawn—4:56 AM. The flight out to Ohio from Vegas was 5-6 hours, and we didn't have time to waste. Ralph agreed to pick us up from Cleveland Airport, and even let us stay with him in his guest room for the planning and duration of the funeral processions.

The Mancinis were, as you can imagine, a hot mess. Frankie took the brunt of it. Her dad was now a widower at the age of 66. She and her brothers were now without a mother. Her nieces and nephews were now without a grandmother.

The ceremony was held at Saint Nicholas Church, which both of our families have gone to for generations. All three of Frankie's older brothers had the opportunity to speak about their mother, if they chose to. Vincent and Ralph took the opportunity, but Joe decided to opt out due to his own stage fright and timid nature. Her father also opted out because...well...he couldn't stop crying.

Finally, it was Frankie's turn. I watch as she approaches the lectern, clears her throat, and tries to compose herself as best she could. She took in a deep breath, and began speaking into the microphone.

"In lieu of a eulogy, I have decided to write a poem to honor my mom..."

The crowd, comprised of family and friends alike, were dead quiet, waiting in anticipation for what she would say next. I looked at her encouragingly. She quickly began, and read the following poem from a folded-up piece of paper she had brought with her.

"My tears will fall
My heart still aches
I long again
To see your face.

Your love will stay
Your light shines bright
I will miss you
Day and night.

I'll never forget
The lessons taught
This goes to show
Love can't be bought.

I love you, Mom,
More than you know.
The best I can do
Is to let it show.

I know one day
We'll meet again.
But until then
This is the end."

There wasn't a single dry eye in the entire church after that. The rest of the ceremony went on, and no one else in the audience said a word. Everyone was too involved in their own heads and feelings after that.

28: THIRTY-SIX

Thanksgiving has come around once again. Frankie and I find ourselves torn on how to spend it.

Obviously, it's not because of the food. Our parents aren't getting any younger, but now that Jeremy and Giulia have little David in their lives, they are starting traditions of their own in Vegas instead of looking towards going to Ohio to visit.

The thing about Vegas is that, like New York City, it's a city that never sleeps. This town is running 24/7, and there's no stopping the movement or growth, whether those are realized or potential. It would take nothing short of a miracle for someone to agree to swap days off with me to be able to get to Ohio for Thanksgiving at this point, since the holiday is next week. People are scrambling in every direction, trying to do all the required grocery shopping, so that they can prepare their turkey the way they want to cook and thaw it.

With the imminent arrival of Thanksgiving, retailers are also preparing to brace themselves for the day after—Black Friday. People truly do not give a fuck about each other when it comes to Black Friday. They camp outside of stores. They push and shove each other around at every store they visit just to compete to get the best deals on the items they want. Some are so unhinged that they start fights and get kicked out of the stores themselves, and promptly told not to come back unless they want to catch a trespassing charge (or worse, depending on the offender).

I excogitated the situation at hand. Do I tell Frankie that I want to keep to ourselves and just go somewhere for dinner? I'm not really in the mood to spend hours out of the house, and this is one of the rare holidays that I have off from work this year. I typically don't, since Vegas never sleeps, and people still gamble and make poor life choices on Thanksgiving, just as they do any other day of the year, holiday or not. She's more into holidays than I am, at least in most cases.

"Honey?"

"Yeah?"

"What are we doing for Thanksgiving this year?"

"Aren't we going over to Jeremy's?"

"I mean… we could. But do you *want* to go over there? It's obviously way too late to go visit back home."

"I don't see why not. Do you have something better in mind?"

"Well…no," I said sheepishly.

"Do they want you to give them a heads up, or do you think they'll just expect us?"

"I'm going to let Jeremy know as a courtesy. I'll call him later."

"What do you want for dinner tonight, meanwhile?" Frankie asked. I'm usually pretty good about knowing what I do and don't want to eat in *general*, but it takes me a little bit to process when the immediate question is brought to light.

"Shit, I don't know. What sounds good?"

"Um… Manicotti?"

"Yeah! We haven't had that in a while. Do we need to go to the store for any ingredients?"

Frankie contemplates for a moment. "Yeah, the main ones. I have spices already. We certainly don't have the shells, and there isn't enough ricotta. I think the little that's there might be going bad soon, too. I can get stuff for a little bit of Caesar salad if you're interested in that, too."

"Yeah, that sounds great. Alright, let's go to the store then."

At about 4 pm, we went to the nearest grocery store for the necessary ingredients. Frankie is much more efficient at finding her way around the store for specifics, so I just followed her lead, holding her hand as she sometimes forcibly pulled on mine telling me to pick up the pace. Because of this, we were in and out of the store within 15 minutes—a new record, I think. Since the store was only about five minutes down the road, we were back home quickly as well.

"Do you need help with anything, dear?" I asked her. Usually, I'll offer to clean to help her out.

"No, I think I'm alright."

"Okay, just let me know if that changes. Otherwise, just let me know when it's ready."

Now was probably just as good a time as any to call Jeremy to tell him to expect us for Thanksgiving. I picked up the phone, which sat on a nightstand on my side of the bed, and dialed his number. It rings twice, then I hear Giulia pick up.

"Hello?" she asks.

"Hey, it's Jimmy."

"Oh, hey Jim! What's up?"

"Do you have room for us next week for Thanksgiving?"

"Yes, of course! You're always welcome."

"Okay, we'll be there."

"Come about 2 pm. Hopefully, I'll have everything ready by then."

Despite living in the same city, and only about a ten-minute commute apart, I don't see Jeremy and Giulia nearly as often as one would think. Jeremy's always working because of his career, and Giulia has had her hands full with David, the first of my nephews. They're crazy enough to say they want to have *more* kids, too.

~ * ~

The day of Thanksgiving comes around, and Frankie insists that she wants to make biscotti to bring over, accompanied with a bottle of wine. She doesn't like to show up to gatherings like this without bringing something herself. I guess it's her way of not only showing gratitude, but wanting to feel useful as well. She finishes up cleaning and baking at 1:57 pm, but I'm not worried.

"Alright, let me change into something more presentable, and we can go." She was dressed, in her own words, like she was looking homeless. Loose-fitting shirt, baggy shorts, no bra—the whole nine yards. I didn't care what she was wearing (or not), but whatever makes her feel better, I guess.

Once Frankie emerged from the bedroom, she was wearing jeans and a burgundy blouse, with black ballet flats on her feet. I get a whiff of whatever perfume she's wearing, and it's one that I don't recognize, but it smells good. Some tones are sweet, but it has mostly a floral scent profile.

"You look and smell great, my dear," I remarked affectionately. I pulled her into me and gave her a wet kiss on the lips.

"Hey, watch the lipstick," she said, laughing. "But thank you."

"Ready to go?"

"Yes, I am now."

On our way out, Frankie grabs the biscotti and red wine to bring over. We head out to the car, which is sitting in the driveway, and I make sure to lock the front door behind us. I open the passenger side door for her before getting into the driver's side myself. I make sure she's buckled in, do the same, and off we go to Jeremy's.

Twelve minutes later, we pull up and parallel park next to the sidewalk. There are still a ton of other people who had the same idea. I guess Jeremy's neighbors also host their families for holidays as well. We get out of the car, Frankie making sure she gets everything before closing the door. I ring the door bell, and hear a faint yell of "coming!" from a distance. It sounds like Giulia.

The door deadbolt jostles as she unlocks the door, then finally opens it. It is, in fact, Giulia. Jeremy doesn't seem anywhere to be found at the moment.

"Hey, you two! Happy Thanksgiving. Come on in, and make yourselves at home." Giulia hugged us both individually before backing away, and I closed and locked the door behind us while we both removed our shoes. I was always raised to take your shoes off whenever you get home, and especially when you go into someone else's home. Frankie pops her shoes off too, faster than I take mine off.

"I brought you something," Frankie mentioned while heading towards Giulia. "Almond biscotti and wine."

"Frankie, Jesus Christ, you didn't have to do this!" Giulia's surprise seemed genuine.

"Well, I wanted to."

"Thank you, Frankie. You've always been so sweet. I'll put the biscotti aside for now. Do you want to get started on this bottle of wine, though?"

"Well...yeah."

Giulia grabs two wine glasses and a waiter's corkscrew to open the wine bottle, then proceeds to pour some into each of the glasses.

"Are you having any wine, Jimmy?" she asks me.

"No, I'm good for right now. Thank you, though. Where's my nephew David?"

"He's taking a nap right now. Don't be looking for him to wake him up, please."

"Well, can I turn the game on at least? Where's my brother?"

"Oh, yeah, turn the game on. Jeremy... I think he's out in the yard?"

I went to the living room table and found the TV remote. I quickly flipped through channels until I found the game I was looking for—the Minnesota Vikings at Detroit Lions. Home field advantage was...not present, to say the least. The game had just gone to the halftime break, and I saw the score was Vikings 20, Lions 0. In Pontiac, Michigan. Not a good day for the Lions.

A few minutes later, so right when the game came back on, I finally saw Jeremy appear. He was coming in from the backyard.

"Jeremy!" I exclaimed. I was happy to see him, of course, and he began to walk my direction. I was sitting on the couch.

"Hey bro!" he said as he hugged me.

"How are you these days?"

"Oh, you know... The usual of working constantly."

"Is it busy?"

"Every day it's something different, man."

"Boys, dinner is ready!" Giulia yelled for both of us.

"Be right there," I yelled back.

Jeremy and I walked towards the kitchen, and took our places at the dining table. Frankie left the seat to her right open for me, and Jeremy took the seat next to Giulia accordingly.

"Wait, hun, can you go check on David? See if he's awake yet?" Giulia questioned.

"Oh, right, I'll go check on him." Jeremy promptly headed up the stairs to check on my nephew. About two minutes later, he emerges with David in his arms, and makes his way back down the stairs carefully.

"Was he already awake?"

"It looks like he just barely woke up, honestly."

"Oh, alright. I have the highchair ready," Giulia said, motioning towards the highchair at the head of the table next to her seat that is situated on the side.

The table was set with a plate and the appropriate utensils for everyone. The turkey, situated in the middle of the table, had the carving knife placed directly next to it.

"Oh, before I forget, what do you guys want to drink? Frankie bought wine, and I have beer in the fridge," Giulia added.

"Beer for me, and water," I said.

Jeremy thought for a second before saying, "I will take a beer."

"So, wine for the women, and beer for the men. Got it." Giulia laughed at how this divided across those lines. She went to the fridge to grab two beers, then handed one to Jeremy and the other to me.

Jeremy rose from his chair to grab the carving knife, and carefully but quickly carved up the turkey. The various sides were already on the table in different places—stuffing/dressing, green bean casserole, cranberry sauce, mashed potatoes with gravy, roasted Brussel sprouts. The works, really.

"Are we doing grace?" Frankie asked.

The room went silent for what felt like an eternity as we looked at each other with blank stares.

"Nah, just dig in," Giulia said. She seemed proud of herself, as she should be. She just made all this food for everyone, and after taking my first bites of everything, I discovered that she's also an amazing cook.

The conversation was kept minimal, although what little conversation there was, was peaceful. We're not an arguing type of family on holidays. We just love food.

After everyone finished up their entrees, it was time for dessert, and Jeremy seemed the most excited for that out of everything. As usual. My brother has always had a wicked sweet tooth.

"I have pumpkin pie and pecan pie if anyone wants some," Giulia stated as she pulled out both pies.

"I'll take pecan pie."

"Pumpkin for me," Jeremy said.

"Hm... Pecan for me," Frankie hesitated.

"Alright, I'll have pumpkin," Giulia said.

She dished out the pieces of pie according to everyone's request, and the four of us sat on the couch to finish watching the football games.

Turns out the Lions didn't stand a chance. Better luck next year.

29: THIRTY-FIVE

Frankie and I have been in Vegas for close to a decade at this point. Surprisingly, the one thing we haven't done yet is buy a house. I wonder if she even wants to by now.

I'm lying in bed, wide awake right now when I should be asleep. When I was younger, I used to be one of those people who could fall asleep almost right as their head hit the pillow. At least when I was a kid that was the case, and I remember this very vividly so. As an adult, though, that hasn't been my experience, especially since I moved to Vegas. Frankie is next to me, and she's reading a book to try and go to sleep as well.

"Hey, Frankie..."

She shifts to grab her bookmark from the nightstand, then places it in her current position in the book. She then puts it on the nightstand. I'm not sure how I never noticed she was a big Stephen King fan—the book is titled *Misery*. If I had to guess, she might be around 40% through the book.

"Yes?"

"I want to buy a house. What do you think?"

"I was ready years ago to buy a house. What took you so long to come to this conclusion?"

"W—what? Seriously? Why didn't you say something years ago, then?"

"Probably about five years into living in this town, I was ready."

I rolled my eyes, scoffed, and facepalmed.

"Whoa, what was that for?" she asked.

"It's just—why have we never talked about it before? We talk about everything. All the time. Neither one of us shuts up."

"I don't know, I guess it just never came up."

"Well, do you know any realtors and mortgage lenders?"

"Hm... I can ask Rosa who she used when she bought her house last year, if that would help."

"Oh, I didn't realize that Rosa moved out here."

Frankie laughed as she looked into my eyes. It was as if I said or did something completely ridiculous that she wasn't expecting.

"Dear, she moved out here about a year after we did. You just don't see her as often as I do."

"I guess that's true. You don't see Andrew and Chauncy as often as I do, either, unless you decide to come along to a group outing with me."

Her eyes looked side to side for a second—left, right, then straight back at me. "That is also true."

"Okay, back on topic. How soon do you want to start house hunting? I have enough pay stubs to show a lender and all that."

"Well, today's…Wednesday, right? How about I call Rosa in the morning, and we can set something up for the weekend if the realtor is open to it and available?"

"That would work. Sunday or Monday would work best. Those are my days off right now."

"Sounds good. Anything else bothering you at this ungodly hour, sweety? I'm enervated."

"I don't think so. I'm bone-tired as well. Anything else can wait for the morning, I guess." I shrugged my shoulders.

"Okay, good." She reaches to turn off the light, then scoots back closer to me in bed.

"Good night, beautiful," I said, before leaning in to kiss her. She let out a slight moan as she parted her lips while kissing me. Being with Frankie and spending my life with her has never failed to bring me an immeasurable amount of joy and love. After making out for a couple of minutes, she pulls away.

"Good night, handsome. I love you so much."

"I love you, too, with all my heart." I kissed Frankie on her left cheek, then she nestled her head into my chest. I wrapped my arms around her, and felt as she put her left arm around my waist in response. I put my right leg over her hip, and situated my left one between hers, completely engulfing her in my embrace. Exhaustion took over, and after a few more minutes, I fell asleep.

~ * ~

It seems that Frankie is up and about, and I'm just waking up—at 9:35 AM. Something smells good, too. I rub my eyes and stretch, then slowly get out of the warm, comfortable queen bed that we share. I make my way to the living room, where Frankie is sitting reading *Misery* again. There's a cup of black coffee on the table in front of her, which is odd because I've never known her to drink coffee very often, never mind take it black. I approach her quietly.

"Since when do you drink coffee?" I asked as she was taking a sip from her cup.

"Oh… Well… I felt like having coffee today for some reason. I know, it's not very often that I drink the hot bean water."

"Yeah, never mind drinking it without creamer, sugar, or really anything else in it. Just black."

"There's still a lot left in the pot if you want some, dear," she said, nodding towards the kitchen. "I just made this pot not long ago, so it should still be hot."

"Oh, cool. Thank you." I walked towards the kitchen and approached the upper cabinet containing all the drinkware. I opened it and took out a solid white coffee mug, then grabbed the canister and poured some coffee for myself. I cautiously put my top lip to the cup to touch the coffee so I could get a sense of how hot it was. Yeah, no, that is lava. I'll give it a minute, so I don't burn off my lips and tongue.

"Did you get a chance to call Rosa yet about what realtor and lender she used?" I asked.

"Yes, about an hour ago. I was quiet so I didn't wake you."

"Babe, you know as well as I do that I can practically sleep through a war." She chuckled. "Yeah, you're right about that."

"What did she tell you?"

"The realtor's name is Debbie. I forgot what brokerage she was with, but I guess that doesn't matter if we like Debbie. Lender… I think she said his name was Don?"

"Did she give contact information for both Debbie and Don? I would like to meet with them on Monday if possible."

"Yes, I wrote it down." There is a small notebook on the table, along with a pen. She opens the notebook and flips to find the page that she wrote the phone numbers for Debbie and Don on, and hands it to me.

"Do you think Debbie would pick up at 10 am on a Saturday?"

She shrugged her shoulders. "May as well try."

I dialed the number for Debbie in Frankie's notebook, and heard ringing within a second. To my surprise, she answers the phone.

"Hi, this is Debbie," I hear on the other end of the line.

"Hi, Debbie. My name is James Rossi. My wife and I got your phone number from a friend of hers. We're looking to buy our first home."

"Oh, how wonderful to hear! What's her friend's name who referred you to me? Just because I'm curious to know," she asked.

"Rosa. I'm not sure of her last name. She's my wife's best friend. She said Rosa bought at some point last year?"

"Oh, I do remember Rosa! That's amazing to hear. How soon do you want to meet up? Did your wife tell you that I work with a lender named Don?"

"Yes, she did. Can we do Sunday or Monday? Those are my days off. The four of us can meet up. I can bring pay stubs or whatever you need."

"I can do 11 am on Monday if that works for you."

"That works great for me!" I said excitedly. Wow, this was getting real.

"Bring three months' pay stubs, two years of tax returns, your Driver's license, and…I think that's it," Debbie said.

"Alright, sounds great! I'll make sure I'm prepared for Monday and get those documents to bring with us. Where do you want to meet?"

"We can get lunch at the Peppermill while we discuss?"

"Sure, we'll see you there!"

"Have a good day, James."

"Thanks, you as well. Bye." I hung up the phone. I noticed Frankie looking at me expectantly.

"So... It sounds like we're meeting soon?" she asked.

"Yes, Monday at 11 am at the Peppermill. I need to get my documents together—pay stubs, tax returns, things like that."

"Oh, cool. We're going together?"

"What kind of question is that? You're my *wife*. Of course you're going with me."

"Okay," she said and flashed a smile.

~ * ~

As promised, we met with Debbie and Don at the Peppermill on Monday at 11 am. The four of us got a table shortly after meeting in front of the restaurant, and I made sure that Frankie carried my documents in her purse so they wouldn't get lost or damaged.

As you can imagine, Debbie did more of the talking, although Don spoke up when he needed to. Both are nice people, and they seemed to know what they were doing. Eventually, the topic of physically house hunting came up, since Don seemed satisfied that my financial documents would qualify me for purchasing a home.

"Francesca, do you—" Don started.

"Frankie, please. I go by Frankie."

"Alright, Frankie, are you going to be added to the loan as well?"

"Er, um... I never established any credit yet, so no. I do work, but I don't have credit to look at."

"Oh, I see. Makes sense." Don's face showed that he wanted to say something more, but he was holding it back with his mouth.

"Do you have any questions for us?" Debbie interjected. She's been quieter since Don took over the conversation.

"Well, hm... I guess, when do we get to start looking at houses?" Frankie asked.

"What are you looking for in a home, Frankie? James? Are you looking to have any kids to warrant a bigger home?"

"No, we're not having any kids. Come on, we're both 35... It's just not going to happen now. What we're looking for... We don't need anything crazy. She likes to cook, but we rarely have anyone over."

"What about a yard? Do you want a yard or no?"

Frankie and I exchanged a look of what felt like mutual understanding.

"Yeah… Not really. I don't want to take care of a yard in all honesty," I said.

"I don't either," Frankie added.

"Do you want any particular part of town?" Debbie questioned.

"Close to the Strip since I work at the Tropicana."

"Anything else you're looking for?"

We sat quietly to think for a minute. That minute felt like an eternity to pass. Finally, Frankie speaks up.

"No, I think that's really it. Big kitchen and close to the Strip, and not too much house to have to clean otherwise."

"Okay, that's very doable. Let me do some research, and we can get together on Sunday to go look around at possible homes that are within your budget."

"That sounds great! You've already been a big help."

Debbie kept her promise to us. The following Sunday, we met with her to go house hunting. To my surprise, it didn't take long before we found one that suited our needs that we loved.

As soon as Frankie and I decided on the house we wanted, we put in an offer. The seller and listing agent were eager to accept it since they had motivation to sell. They were moving out of the state, and wanted the proceeds to apply to a new house in the area they were moving to.

Shockingly, once we opened escrow, the process was fairly quick. The 30-day escrow period went by fast, and we got all our inspections, repairs, etc. done in a timely fashion.

After the deal transaction was sent to the Clark County Recorder, we got the keys to our new home the next day from Debbie. At last, we were homeowners in Vegas. What a relief.

30: THIRTY-FOUR

It appears that Jeremy and Giulia have wasted no time trying to perpetuate the next generation of the Rossi family. I'm sure they...consummated their marriage relatively quickly, too.

On September 12, 1987 at 12:53 pm, the first of my nephews was born. Jeremy and Giulia decided to name him David Jason Rossi. Of course, they had to wait a couple of days before they could take him home. Once they brought David home, however, the two of them were very eager for Frankie and I to meet the newest addition to the family.

Jeremy invited us over to their new apartment, and when we walked inside their home, we were greeted by him and a very exhausted, disheveled-looking Giulia. Frankie shot me a look that said she was glad that wasn't her life, although she was also happy to have a nephew.

"Hi, Giulia," Frankie said, extending a one-arm hug since Giulia was holding David in her other arm. Giulia hugged her back as best she could.

"Hi, Frankie dear," Giulia responded warmly. "Hi, Jimmy."

"Good to see you."

I saw Jeremy walking towards us from the kitchen, a glass of water in his hand.

"Hey, Jer. How's being a dad treating you?"

"Shockingly, he's been pretty good. He's not too fussy, and we're able to get a couple of hours of sleep at a time. We've been taking turns regarding who's getting out of bed to tend to him."

"Oh, I guess that's good that he's not too fussy then."

"I'm still in a good amount of pain, though. It's only been a week. Doctor said it'll probably take me about six weeks to heal," Giulia abruptly added.

I could tell Frankie felt kind of awkward about this whole situation. She's never been hugely maternal towards human babies, but she's supportive of Jeremy and Giulia at least.

"Er, uh... How did you deliver? Like was it a natural birth or was it a C-

120

section?"

"Natural birth. I begged for that epidural, too. Lord have mercy, I needed it so much."

"Oh, I'm sure you did..." Frankie said with a drop of sarcasm.

"Jim, why didn't you ever have kids?" Jeremy asks, his gaze bouncing between Frankie and I.

"We never really had a desire," she said. "Our lives are fulfilled and happy without kids."

"What do you do with all your spare time?" he questioned.

"Whatever we want, honestly," I added.

It's kind of strange that we're being questioned by my own family. I've never once said growing up that I wanted kids, and Frankie has always been the same way.

"Are we done asking personal questions about our sex life?" Frankie asked. She was clearly not having it.

"Anyway... How have you guys been? We haven't seen y'all in a few weeks maybe." Giulia was obviously wanting to change the subject to avoid this conversation turning sour.

"We're alright. Work has been a little crazy with Labor Day just having passed, and you know how drunk people get when they start losing money left and right."

"Ah... Yes. That will do it," Jeremy said. He's been quiet since the conversation went sideways.

"Some of them have balls, though. They try and play dumb when I can clearly catch them counting cards and shit. It doesn't fly because I'm not stupid. I know how to throw them out as soon as I can catch it and prove that's what's happening."

"Counting cards in what? People do that?"

Giulia, bless her heart, doesn't seem to know how crafty people can get when they're gambling.

"People count cards all the time. Mostly while playing blackjack. If I'm overseeing a poker pit, it's not necessarily card counting that gets people in trouble. It's that they get too drunk to function and start falling while they walk, or are throwing alcohol everywhere, or just getting belligerent."

"Shit, how often are you having to throw people out, Jim?" Giulia stared at me with wide eyes and her mouth agape.

"Maybe once a month. I mean, I wasn't really keeping track of that, either. Just what it feels like."

"Really?" Even Frankie seemed surprised, even though I tell her nearly everything at home once I get the opportunity to do so.

"Yeah. Enough about me. What are you doing with your life, Jeremy? You have another mouth to feed now."

"Well, the answer is probably not something you would expect, bro."

"Come on, what is it?"

"Investment banking."

"Shut the fuck up. Seriously? Do you like it? It pays pretty well, I'd imagine."

"I do like it, and it pays very well. Giulia does work a bit to keep herself from going stir crazy and getting bored, but for the most part, I provide for everything and can do so comfortably."

"What are you doing, then, Giulia?"

"I got into baking, actually, and people will sometimes have me bake for their party or event. Or if they just want something specific."

"Oh, wow, I wouldn't expect that either," Frankie said. "It seems to come out of nowhere. How did you get into it?"

"My mother and I used to bake all the time when I was younger. I learned it from her and the other women in my family."

"Makes more sense that way. I can't imagine baking all the time unless you've got a passion for it, especially pastries and sweets in general," I chimed.

"Can I hold him?" I asked Giulia, motioning to David.

"Oh, yeah, of course! He's *your* nephew." She smiles as she hands baby David over to me, and I'm careful to support his head and body weight.

I looked down at the baby I now held in my arms. He looks slightly more like Giulia, but I can tell that the Rossi genes are there as well. It's the lip shape that gives it away for me. I have a seat on the couch next to Frankie, who just recently sat down, and gave her a kiss on the cheek. It will be quite the adventure to see what kind of boy and man David grows up to be.

"Thank God he doesn't seem to have your ugly mug so far, Jer," I said playfully.

"*My* ugly mug? You're my older brother, so what's that supposed to say about you?"

"That I'm better looking." I laughed heartily, but Jeremy doesn't seem to be amused. The ladies are laughing, too.

"Uh huh, sure you are."

"I mean, I did tell that to everyone at your wedding reception."

I watched as he rolled his eyes. Nothing has changed since we were kids growing up in Struthers. We're always sick of each other's antics and bullshit, but we still love each other. Mostly.

"You did. Love that for me."

"You know I love you, Jer."

"Love you, too, Jim. Sometimes."

"Put the football game on. You need to get David here into sports already. A week is too long."

Giulia rolled her eyes, tired of both of us. "Oh, good heavens, you two."

31: THIRTY-THREE

April 6, 1986 is the day that Jeremy and Giulia chose to get married. As the best man, it is one of my duties to roast the shit out of him…and say some good things, too, I suppose.

Unsurprisingly, Jeremy and Giulia chose the same venue for their wedding that Frankie and I had ours at a few years ago. Since it's early spring, and the weather in Vegas isn't yet horrific, any ladies in attendance could get away with sleeveless dresses if that's what they opted for. Jeremy decided that anyone on his side, including Frankie and I, was to wear something orange or have that as an accent color. It's long been his favorite color, which is weird because he was born towards the end of fall. Mine is blue, more towards a royal blue shade, so I had my groomsmen wear that when Frankie and I wed. Frankie had her bridesmaids and other friends wear royal purple, so the color schemes were surprisingly complementary. One didn't necessarily overwhelm or overshadow the other.

I opted for a solid black suit, black dress shoes, a white button-down shirt, gold cuff links, and a bright orange bow tie. My suit jacket has a welt pocket that stores a black handkerchief.

Frankie, on the other hand, chose a solid orange dress with white open-toed heels.

I thought I had a big wedding. No. My brother is putting me to *shame* on that front. I feel like this clown has invited the entire first-string, second-string, *and* third-string players of the Youngstown State football team, plus the coaching staff, plus Giulia's family, her bridesmaids, and her friends. Basically, everyone and their mom.

Our own parents also flew in yesterday. They spent a good portion of their time getting to know Giulia's family and parents, since we're about to be integrating two Italian families once again. Just what we need—more branches to the family tree. As if the Rossis and Mancinis weren't prolific enough, and now we're adding the Silvestris.

Last night, at the bachelor party, it was...quite something, to say the least. I'm not entirely sure that I can find a word strong enough to describe the debauchery that occurred. Wild is too weak of a word. Crazy is definitely way too tame. Insane might be getting there. Throughout our entire lives, I've never seen Jeremy this drunk. Ever. At 33, well... Let's say that the hangover this morning was the opposite of pleasant. I woke up with a pounding headache, and I was nauseous. Frankie had to run to the store to get me painkillers because we ran out. Jeremy and Giulia are still in their 20s (Jeremy being 27 and Giulia is 26), so I hope it's not as bad for them. Then again, I'm not sure what Giulia did last night at her bachelorette, but I can imagine that the night went similarly to ours. For everyone else's sake, I hope that they're not too badly hungover like I am, or else this is going to be a physically painful ceremony.

In my very hungover state, I found my parents talking to Jeremy as I emerged from the men's restroom. The three of them seemed focused on each other, so me approaching from outside their peripheral view might catch them off guard.

"Well, hello there," I said, making my presence known.

"JIMMY!" Mom exclaimed, throwing her arms around me and gripping me tightly in a hug. After she released me from her embrace, I also hugged Dad. From a short distance, I saw Frankie talking with a couple of Giulia's bridesmaids.

"Hey, Jim," Dad says with a smile. You would think that someone who's as fiery as Dad would be more outwardly emotive, but that doesn't seem to be the case.

"Hi, Dad." People were walking around and chatting all around us, and for a moment, it was like I had tuned them all out and could only hear my parents and Jeremy.

"Do you have your best man speech ready?"

"Yup," I said, pulling a few pieces of paper from my right-side interior suit jacket pocket.

"Have you, er, actually rehearsed it in front of a mirror or anything, though?" Dad looked concerned for once.

"Of course. I'm not going into this completely blind. That would be irresponsible and embarrassing, at the very least. I have it written down here, too."

"Do you have the rings as well?"

"Yes, Dad. They're in my pocket on the other side of my jacket. Shit, I didn't think I was going to be interrogated at Jeremy's wedding..."

"Sorry. I guess I just remember how nervous Andrew was at yours some years ago."

"Andrew? Nervous? Not at all. He was confident at my wedding and had everything under control."

"Strange. Maybe I'm remembering someone else, and I can't remember."

"I would bet money on that. I know Andrew better than he knows himself some days."

Eventually, Frankie concludes her conversation with some of Giulia's bridesmaids who are casually roaming about before the official ceremony commences.

"Doing alright over here, dear?" she asks me.

"Yeah, we're just talking."

"Hi Maria, hi Gio," Frankie says to my parents.

"Oh, hello, beautiful!" Mom says, giving Frankie a hug.

At 2:00 pm sharp, the wedding ceremony begins. A few straggling attendees find their way to their seats posthaste.

Music begins playing, and I look around.

"Please rise for the bride."

Everyone quickly stands, and I watch as rows of my friends and family turn their attention towards the middle of the aisle. Giulia and her dad have their arms interlocked as he brings her down the aisle to give her away.

I watch as Jeremy begins to choke and tear up as Giulia makes her way down the aisle, her dad parting ways just before she reaches Jeremy.

"We are gathered here on this beautiful day to witness the union of Jeremy Angelo Rossi and Giulia Isabella Silvestri in holy matrimony. This is a day of great celebration for everyone in attendance.

As Jeremy and Giulia embark on this journey, they will be able to nurture a love that makes them better versions of themselves. Marriage is a garden we sow with love, and harvest in personal growth.

Jeremy and Giulia, on your journey together, keep your spouse in the space of highest priority in your heart. It is paramount that you never take each other for granted, and are thankful for every opportunity to spend time with one another.

Always remember these words—love is patient and kind. Love is not jealous, boastful, proud, or rude. It does not demand its own way. It is not irritable, and it keeps no record or score of being wronged. It does not rejoice about injustice, but rejoices whenever the truth wins out. Love never gives up, never loses faith, is always hopeful, and endures through every circumstance."

He pauses for a moment before continuing.

"You have chosen to write your vows, and it is with these words you express your binding promises to love, honor, and cherish one another. If you are ready to make these promises to each other, I invite you to now face each other and declare your intentions. When you're ready, you may begin."

"I'll go first," Jeremy said.

"Please proceed," responded the officiant. Jeremy pulled out a somewhat crumbled piece of paper from his right rear pants pocket, which had some words scribbled on it in his terrible handwriting.

"Giulia, I knew you would be someone special from the first day I met you in college. You are funny, bold, gorgeous, and incredibly intelligent. But most of all, you put up with my shit."

Everyone in attendance chuckled at the last sentence.

"The fact of the matter is, we have been through a lot together since we first met. I never thought that I would be the kind of guy to settle down and get married, but you proved me wrong in the very best of ways. I love you so much, and I promise to be there for you, and with you, for as long as my heart is beating. I choose you, in this lifetime and every lifetime after that, Giulia Isabella Silvestri."

Tears formed in Giulia's eyes, and her makeup, which she had spent *hours* doing just before, began to run. She tries to wipe the running tears from her face with her hands without making a mess of them.

"Jeremy, my dear... As a little girl, I spent a lot of time thinking about when and if I would ever find love. When we met, I knew that I found that and so much more. From the first 'I love you' to today, we have grown closer together with every day and every situation. I want to grow old with you. I want to spend the rest of my life with you. You go by many names to me—my soulmate, my partner, my lover, and as of today, my husband. One day, our children will call you daddy.

Together, there is nothing we can't achieve or persevere through. I promise to remain loyal to you, to continue to love you, and to be as supportive of a wife as I possibly can. We are not perfect people, but we fit together like pieces of a puzzle. I choose you, in this lifetime and every lifetime after that, Jeremy Angelo Rossi."

The officiant looked between Jeremy, Giulia, and I. Jeremy glanced at me expectantly, raising an eyebrow, and I pulled the ring boxes out of my vest pocket, holding them next to each other in my right hand.

"Thank you for sharing your vows with all of us. The rings you are about to place on each other's fingers are symbols of the love you expressed. They will remind you of the vows you have just spoken for all to hear, and of the eternal love that you have for one another."

"Jeremy, place the ring on Giulia's finger, and repeat after me."

Jeremy opens up the ring box that contains Giulia's ring, and puts the box in his pocket after removing the ring.

"As this ring encircles your finger, from this moment forward, so will my love forever encircle you. You will never walk alone. My heart will be your shelter. My arms will be your home. We will walk through life as partners and best friends. I promise to do my best to love, cherish, and accept you—just the way you are. I give you my heart until the end of time. I have no greater gift to give."

Jeremy obliges and repeated the words of the officiant, phrase by phrase, as he looks directly into Giulia's eyes.

"Now, Giulia, place the ring on Jeremy's finger, and repeat after me."

Jeremy extends his left hand, and she places the ring on his finger. The officiant has her repeat the same words, but with his name in it, phrase by phrase. Jeremy starts to well up crying, which is a rare sight to see in and of itself.

"By the power invested in me by the Clark County Clerk, and the State of Nevada, I now pronounce you husband and wife. Jeremy, you may kiss your beautiful bride."

Jeremy plants a passionate kiss on Giulia's lips, quickly messing up her bright pink lipstick.

The officiant turns to everyone in the procession.

"Ladies and gentlemen, it is my honor to present for the first time, Mr. and Mrs. Rossi!"

~ * ~

A couple of hours later, it was time for the wedding reception. This is my time to shine. The time to embarrass Jeremy in front of our new in-laws, his friends, and everybody else who knows him and Giulia. I've waited my whole life for this, and that is not an exaggeration.

Some of our friends were already drunk when they arrived at the reception, if not at least buzzed. They must have started drinking immediately after the wedding.

As the best man, my speech comes last in the order of speakers, so I'd better make a great impression. Jeremy, Giulia, Dad, Giulia's dad, and the maid of honor have already taken their turns. Finally, the attention of everyone in the room turned to me. I take a cursory look at Frankie, take a deep breath, and rise from my seat. I walk towards the front of the room where everyone can see and hear me, and collect myself once again before I begin the speech.

"I appreciate that you all are here today to witness my little brother, Jeremy, wed the love of his life. For those of you who don't know me, my name is James, but most call me Jim or Jimmy. I'm the better-looking older brother of this guy."

I shot a look over at Jeremy, and everyone laughed.

"In all seriousness, I never thought that today would ever happen. I've known Jeremy our entire lives, and he has never been one to be tied down. Giulia, I hope you know what you're in for because he's a handful. I remember getting into playing football when we were kids, and Jeremy got mad because he thought our parents weren't letting him get into sports, too. Turns out that was a lie since he ended up being the starting quarterback for Youngstown State for three out of the four years he played in college.

My brother is a sweet, caring guy, and I truly wish nothing but the best for the two of you, and any children you have. Giulia, you will always have my support for whatever you and Jeremy need. Take care of him, and we will make damn sure to take care of you."

I grabbed my glass of champagne and signaled to everyone to join me.

"Everyone, please raise your glass. To my brother and his beautiful wife, Giulia, may your love story write itself for years to come with a fire that never dies out. May your lives be enhanced by having each other in it. At this point, I am elated to say: Giulia, welcome to the Rossi family. We're more than happy to have you, and welcome you with open arms and hearts."

Everyone raises their glass, jolts them together, and takes a drink.

32: THIRTY-TWO

Jeremy and I went out for a few drinks one night after I got off work at 11 pm. I could tell that he was restless and maybe a bit anxious about something, judging by his body language and behavior. He was swinging his right leg while sitting on the barstool, a surefire sign that something was going on that he wasn't telling me right now.

I decided to ask about it. Jeremy was not typically like this. He's usually full of energy, a pain in the ass, and when we were younger, a complete menace to society.

"Hey, Jer, you alright? You're acting a little...off?" I inquired, taking another swig of my beer.

"Yeah, um... I actually have something to ask you."

"Okay, what's up?" This could go so many different ways. I hope that it's not one of the bad ones.

"So, you know that Giulia and I have been dating for a while... Four years, even."

"Right." Where is this going exactly?

"Well... She doesn't know, and I'm not sure if she suspects anything, but I bought a ring several months ago. I'm so nervous to propose, but I do know that I want to spend the rest of my life with her and have a family of my own."

"You're serious?" I never thought that my kid brother, Jeremy Angelo Rossi, would be one to settle down. Never mind be telling me that he's ready to become a father. I guess he's 26 at this point, so it makes sense for most people, but that doesn't change the initial shock factor.

"Yeah, of course I'm serious. What did you do? How did you propose to Frankie? I need ideas."

"Well, I took her to Mill Creek Park in Youngstown. I had the ring several months before, like you, but we were together two years to the day when I proposed. I told her to pretty much be dressed and ready to go on that day by 2 pm or something, and I picked her up. I don't think she suspected anything, but her response was genuine. She cried, and of course said yes."

"Wow, how am I supposed to top that?" Poor guy seems discouraged.

"Um... I mean I don't know Giulia all *that* well. Where does she spend her free time since you guys moved out here?"

"Well, she likes to go to shows and concerts."

"Does she like Grateful Dead? They're playing at the Aladdin Theatre on Friday, November 30."

"Wait... Did you just say Grateful Dead?"

"Yeah..."

"That's her favorite band. Oh my God. Thank you. I'm going to get two tickets, and propose to her there."

"Y—you're welcome, Jer?"

How would he not know her favorite band right off the top? That's crazy to me.

"I'm glad that you seem to have put *so* much thought into this, my guy," I said, my tone oozing with sarcasm.

He laughed. He knew I was right. My brother was not one to do a lot of planning. That was always delegated to me growing up since his ass could barely show up on time to an event he *didn't* plan.

"I know, I know," he said, rolling his eyes. "I'm nervous, man. That's all there really is to it. Like what if I fuck this up and she says no?"

"I'm sure she will say yes. She's been with you this long, hasn't she? Has she tried nudging you towards marriage and starting a family before?"

"Oh, yeah, she talks all the time about *when* we have kids, and not *if* we have kids."

"Then don't worry about it, Jer. You got this. If she didn't see a future with you, she wouldn't say those types of things."

"I guess you're right about that."

"I *know* I'm right. I've been married to Frankie for almost seven years already. Wow... That's crazy..."

"Alright, alright. I get your point. I'll have to do it between songs, or if there's an intermission."

~ * ~

Maybe about six weeks later, I was at work, and I saw my brother come up to me in the casino. I was promoted to management within the week I last saw him, so I was still trying to settle into the new role. I could tell that he was excited about something. The man was practically bouncing on the balls of his feet and skipping around as he approached me. I bet something went *very* right for him.

"Hey, Jer, what's up?"

"She said yes! Giulia said yes to marrying me!"

"Oh my God, congratulations bro!"

We hugged each other. Here's the guy that I never thought would even settle down with a girlfriend, never mind getting married and have kids. Genuinely, I'm happy for him.

"Do you have a wedding date set yet? How did you do it?" I asked him.

"Date isn't set just yet, but we're trying to figure that out. Remember how I got Grateful Dead tickets? Well, there was an intermission during the show, and after a lot of people emptied out to buy merch, I gave a little speech and got down on one knee. She cried when she figured out what was happening and said yes."

"Frankie cried quite a bit, too. Do you have a best man in mind yet?"

I watched the gears turn in his eyes as he contemplated the question.

"Well... Uh... I was thinking you could be my best man if that's okay with you?"

"I'm honored, Jer. Yes, I'll be your best man."

"Thank you! Thank you! Thank you!" he said, hugging me again. It's rare that I see Jeremy this happy and excited about something.

"Come over to the house after I'm off work, yeah? Or let me know when you've chosen a wedding date, and we can start planning?"

"I'll let you know for sure!" He's smiling from ear to ear, beaming with pride and happiness.

"Sounds good. Catch you later, Jer."

I watched as Jeremy left my pit and drifted off into the distance.

33: THIRTY-ONE

Friday night in Vegas can go any number of ways, depending on your lifestyle and taste. For once, I had a Friday night off, so I decided to go out with the guys. Frankie is perfectly fine, elated even, to stay home and read books while I'm out. She's always been pretty low maintenance in that regard.

I end up going out with the guys to Bootlegger Bistro. It's a favorite venue of ours besides the Italian American Club. Andrew, my brother Jeremy, Chauncy, and a couple of others are here with me.

"Hey, Jimmy, come check this out," I heard Andrew call from somewhat of a distance.

"Coming," I said, quickly making my way towards the sound of his voice. I wonder what was happening. I got to about a foot away from Andrew, and what he wanted wasn't immediately obvious.

"Hey, what was it?"

"Look up at the game that's on," Andrew said, pointing to a TV that was mounted overhead. I followed his hand and came to find a game of men's college basketball. Specifically, this one happened to be a rivalry, and somehow, I didn't know beforehand that this game was on tonight of all evenings. It was Michigan at Ohio State, 3:47 left in the second half, and Ohio State was carrying a 15-point lead. I'm not complaining—that made my heart happy.

"Did you know they were playing tonight?" I asked him. I feel as if I've been left out of something because everyone knows I love my Buckeyes.

"Not really, I wasn't paying attention. I happened to see the game on, and I know you hate Michigan."

I laughed because he was right. I truly, fiercely hate that school up north. I can't even say "that team up north" because it extends across all sports, although the worst of the rivalry is certainly college football.

I watched for the remainder of the game, keeping a steady drinking pace on the beer that I had in my hand. The glass was about halfway full when I sat on a barstool to watch the game. Suddenly, I feel someone tap me on my right shoulder. The touch wasn't familiar, so I wasn't sure who it was right off the bat.

"What the—?" I turned around to face whoever tapped me.

"Hey, kiddo." I looked at the man before me up and down, and realized that I knew exactly who it was.

"COACH HENNEFORTH?!"

"You got it," he said, laughing at me in surprise.

"Oh my God! Where did you come from?!" I quickly embraced him in a hug, and was flooded with a swarm of emotions in the moment. I didn't think that I'd ever run into my former high school football coach like this of all people, especially in this manner.

"Ha, well… I moved to Vegas right after you guys graduated in 1970. I never had a chance to tell you that that's what I intended to do."

"Oh, wow, so you've been here a while… What brings you here tonight of all evenings, though?"

"The wife and I decided to come out. We don't go out a whole lot, but we wanted to tonight."

I stared at him for a second. I didn't know he was married. Then again, this man never really talked about his personal life when he was making us do drills and run plays at practice.

"She's here with you?"

"Honey, come here," he says, motioning in the direction of a woman about six feet away. She makes her way over to the two of us.

"Hi, I'm Jenna," she says, offering me her hand. I give her a firm shake but try not to be overbearing about it.

"Hi, Jenna, I'm Jimmy. I used to play football for him when I was in high school."

"Oh, really? Well, it's great to meet you, Jimmy! What position did you play?"

"Middle linebacker."

"That's cool," she said, smiling. "What did you end up doing after you graduated?"

"I got drafted, so I served for a couple of years before going out. Reduction in force and all that. Then a couple of years later, I got married and moved out here."

"You're married now? How long?" Coach asked me. He seemed surprised, but I'm in my thirties now—it shouldn't be *that* surprising.

"Yes, for...about to be six years."

"Who's the missus? Did she go to Struthers High?"

"Yeah, she did. Francesca Mancini. Or Frankie as most people would call her."

"My goodness, yes! I remember Frankie! That's wonderful, Jimmy. I never would have guessed."

"Yeah, I wouldn't have guessed either," I said, chuckling nervously. It seems to have been taken well, since the two of them laughed along with me. Sometimes I don't understand what I did to deserve Frankie—she's beautiful, smart, and puts up with my shit better than most people.

"What are you doing for work these days, then?" he asked.

"Oh, I'm working in the casinos. I started as a craps dealer, but now I'm dealing Texas Hold Em poker."

"What casino?"

"The Tropicana. What about you? Are you still teaching and coaching football?"

"Yeah, I still teach high school math. Statistics, these days."

Out of the corner of my eye, I see Jeremy heading towards me.

"Hey, Jer, what's up?" I asked, projecting my voice but not to the point of yelling.

"Bro, come here a minute."

"Alright, give me one second."

I looked back at Coach and Jenna.

"It was great catching up with you some, but I'm out with the guys right now, and they're calling for me."

"Oh, no problem at all! It was a pleasure meeting you, Jimmy," Jenna said.

"So glad to see you, Jim. Don't be a stranger," Coach added.

I hugged them individually, then got up from the barstool I was sitting at to make my way towards Jeremy and my group of guys.

"What's up?" I asked him.

"Drew wants to do a round of shots."

I looked over at Andrew. "Do I want to know what we're doing shots of?"

"Jaeger bombs."

I visibly gagged and wretched in front of them. "You know I hate Jaeger, dude."

"So... Does that mean you're going to whimp out and not do the shot with us, or...?" he taunted.

I let out a deep, exasperated sigh. "Give me the shot."

"That's the spirit!" He handed me a shot glass. They must have ordered the round while I was chatting with Coach and Jenna.

"What are we drinking to anyway?"

"To lifelong friendship and not ending up in jail yet," Andrew said with a huge shit-eating grin.

"Oh, good heavens..." I facepalmed. Hard.

"To us!" he said, and the group of us clicked our shot glasses together a moment before we each slammed back the contents.

I immediately regret my decision—I *hate* Jaeger. But it was nice to get the group together. We don't do this as often as I'd like, and it makes me happy.

34: (DIRTY) THIRTY

The date today is September 28, 1982. You know what that means? Today's my 30th birthday. That is wild. I have mixed feelings about turning 30.

I managed to take the day off work because I have a sneaking suspicion that my friends have something up their sleeve. At the moment, Frankie is on the balcony of our apartment. I go outside to join her.

"Frankie, do you know if anyone is doing anything today? No one is talking to me…"

"I don't have a clue," she said.

Here's the moment where I *do* have to question the validity of the words being said by the love of my life. Yes, I love her, but how do I know she's not hiding something? Maybe she's been in cahoots with my friends and swore them all to secrecy? That would be pretty crazy since I'm adept at finding out the truth and getting to the bottom of things.

"Are you suuuuuure?"

"Jimmy, why would I lie to you? I'm your wife."

"It just seems suspicious that not a single person has called me today or shown up at our door."

As if it's right on cue, the phone rings, and I walk over to pick up the receiver.

"Hello?"

"Hey, it's Andrew."

"Oh, hey, Andrew!"

"Happy 30th birthday, Jimmy!"

"Oh God, you remembered how old I am now?" I cringed slightly.

"Pretty hard to forget when we've literally grown up together and are exactly a month apart in age."

"I mean… You have a point."

"Do you have any plans later?"

"No, and I was just talking about that with Frankie."

"Meet me at the Italian American Club at 7 pm for dinner. My treat."

"On Sahara?"

"Well, yeah, that's the only one that I know of."

"Alright, we'll see you there."

"Later," Andrew said.

"Bye."

In the same second, I hang up the receiver. This feels off… Andrew isn't one to plan things. It's usually *me* that's doing the planning if we're having a guys' night or something.

"That seems…odd."

"I wouldn't worry much about it," Frankie remarked.

"Usually, Andrew doesn't shut up, though."

"Maybe he's got errands to do as well."

"Yeah, I suppose that's true."

That phone call lived rent-free in my head for the rest of the day. It's just not typical behavior of Andrew.

"Happy birthday, handsome," Frankie said before kissing me.

"Thank you, my love. So… What do you want to do before 7 pm? It's only noon, and I feel like that's a million years away right now."

"We can go get brunch somewhere?"

"Yeah, I could eat."

"What about the Peppermill?"

"Mm… That *does* sound good…" My mouth was watering at the idea of going to Peppermill.

"Okay, let me put on some shoes and grab my purse, and then we can go."

"Sure, no problem."

As far as wives or partners go, Frankie was extremely easy to live and be with. She's level-headed and rational, which I've always appreciated about her. Yet, at the same time, she's very loving and affectionate towards me. She's the best of both worlds, and I couldn't have asked for a better woman to have at my side.

A few minutes later, she emerges from the bedroom—with shoes and her purse, like she promised.

"Ready?"

"Yeah, I'm ready," she said.

I open the front door of our apartment, and the two of us go down the steps to the car. I opened her door and let her in before I went around to the driver's side to start the engine.

It takes us about ten minutes to arrive at the Peppermill, and we are greeted by a friendly hostess when we walk in the front door.

"Hi. How many?"

"Two, please."

"Table or booth?"

Frankie and I look at each other. She seems to prefer a booth most of the time.

"Booth, if you have it."

"Of course. Follow me." She grabs two menus, and shows us to a circular booth. I let Frankie get in before I sit down.

"What can I get started for you for drinks? Are we celebrating anything?"

"Water would be good," Frankie said.

"For you, sir?"

"Water, too, for right now. Today's my 30th birthday since you asked."

"Oh my goodness! Happy birthday!"

"Thank you," I said, smiling.

"Alright, I'll be back with those waters to give you a minute to look over the menu. My name is Kelly. Just holler if you need me."

Kelly walks away, which leaves Frankie and I to look at the menu.

"This menu is *huge*," Frankie noticed.

"Yeah, no kidding."

We sat in silence for a couple of minutes while we scanned every single item listed.

"Anything grabbing your attention, beautiful?"

"The Garden Omelet looks good. I would add cheese."

"I was thinking of the Maserati Omelet. How do you feel about orange juice right now? Or is it too late for that?"

"Since when is there a time limit on when you can drink orange juice?" She makes a good point.

"True. So, two glasses of orange juice?"

"Yeah, sounds good."

Kelly returns, bringing two glasses of water with her and sets them on the table in front of us. She takes two straws out of her left pocket, placing them on the table, then takes a pen and notepad out of her right pocket.

"Have you guys decided on what you'd like to eat?"

"We have."

"What can I get started for you, ma'am?"

"I'll have the Garden Omelet, please. Can you add cheese?"

"What kind of cheese?"

"American. Can we both get orange juice as well?"

"Sure." Kelly scribbles down Frankie's order along with the two glasses of OJ.

"For you, sir?"

"I'll have the Maserati Omelet, please."

"Will that be all for the two of you?"

"Yes, that's everything," I tell her.

"Great! I'll be back with the orange juice after I put this order through to the kitchen."

"Thank you so much."

About a minute later, Kelly comes back with the two glasses of orange juice.

Frankie grabs one glass, and I take the other.

"Cheers to making it to thirty," she said.

"Ugh, don't remind me," I added, jokingly. We clicked our glasses together, and each takes a sip of the fresh-squeezed orange juice.

"Oh, wow, that's good." I don't remember the last time I had fresh-squeezed orange juice.

"Yeah, wow, that's delicious."

Twenty minutes later, our food arrives.

"Maserati Omelet for you, sir," Kelly says as she places the hot plate in front of me, "and the Garden Omelet for the lady."

She then places it in front of Frankie. "Can I get you guys anything else?"

"No, that'll be it," Frankie said.

"We're good."

"Alright, enjoy."

Frankie and I cut into our respective omelets and take our first bites.

"This is excellent."

"Truly. Why don't we come here more often?"

"Great question."

Clearly, we were both hungry, as not much was said while we cleared off our plates and emptied the glasses of orange juice and water. When I was taking my last bite, Kelly approached us again.

"How is everything?"

"Terrible," I said sarcastically, winking at her.

She laughed. "Oh, I'm sure you couldn't stand to look at it, so you ate it all."

"That's right."

"I'll bring the check, then?"

"Yes, please."

She comes back with the check, and I quickly pay it before she walks away, leaving a 20% tip on top of the bill.

"Keep the change," I insisted.

"Oh, thank you so much! I hope you have a great birthday," Kelly said as she smiled.

"Thank you, I appreciate it."

Frankie and I walked out, holding hands, on the way to the car. We didn't have to fight much traffic on the way home, thankfully.

~ * ~

"Frankie, how close are you to being ready?" I looked at my watch—it's 6:40 pm. I hate being late.

"Almost done. Give me 5 minutes," I hear her call from the bathroom. She can take forever to get ready, but it's all worth it.

"Alright. Come out when you're done."

Turns out she overestimated this time. She was ready in three minutes, not five.

"Ready to go, dear?"

She smiled. "I am now."

"You look beautiful, as always." Sometimes, I wonder how I managed to pull this bombshell of a woman.

"Thank you, dear."

"Let's go." We head to the car and begin on our route to the Italian American Club. Sometimes finding parking can be a struggle there, but we got there by 6:53 pm. As we approach the door, I noticed Andrew waiting for us.

"Happy dirty thirty!" he said. The two of us embrace for a hug, and he hugs Frankie as well.

"Ha, thanks."

The three of us go inside, and what the fuck is this…?

"SURPRISE!"

Andrew managed to get *all* of my friends here, even ones that still live in Ohio. Is that Jeremy?!

"Andrew, what did you do?!"

"I thought it would be fun to have everyone visit for your birthday!"

"Man, you really didn't have to do all this for me! But thank you." I feel my face turn beet red as I blush.

"Frankie helped," Andrew admitted.

I facepalmed. Of *course* she and Andrew would be co-conspirators for a surprise birthday party. The two of them definitely know how to hide shit from me.

"Frankie…"

She grinned widely. Possibly the biggest shit-eating grin I've ever seen. "You're welcome."

"I love you so much, Frankie. You know that?" I hugged her again.

"JEREMY!"

I saw my brother look up at me as I bolted towards him.

"Happy birthday, big bro," he says as we hug.

"Hi, Giulia."

"Happy birthday, Jimmy!"

Everyone, at some point, wished me a happy birthday. We ate food, and drank an ungodly amount of alcohol. If their goal was to get me shitfaced tonight, they succeeded. I was stumbling by the time we were leaving the Italian American Club right around midnight. Slurring my words started happening about thirty minutes in. Frankie had to drive us home—at 1 am.

Even if I'm obliterated, it was a blast. I wouldn't want to ring in my 30s any other way.

35: TWENTY-NINE

Several months after Jeremy graduated from Youngstown State, I get a phone call from him.

I picked up the receiver on the second ring. "Hello?"

"It's Jer."

"Oh, hey, little bro. What's up?"

"Guess who's moving to Vegas?"

"You and Giulia?"

"You guessed it!"

"When? How soon are you going to start the drive out west?"

"Tomorrow."

"Seriously? I assume you've done more planning than Frankie and I did when we first moved? As it's been some months since you guys graduated from YSU?"

"Yes, we did have more time to plan it. She wouldn't go on a whim like Frankie."

I laughed. He was right, though—Frankie was surprisingly okay with deciding on a whim to move out west. Giulia is her own woman, so that doesn't surprise me she wanted to actually plan things out.

"Ha, well... Frankie surprised *me* with that, too."

"True. Hey, so, where are you staying again?"

"The Rexford. Did you want to look at moving into an apartment here?"

"Yeah, for sure. I think it would be good to be close to you since we don't really know anyone else out that way."

"I mean, that's fair."

"We'll be there in a few days," Jeremy said, and I could faintly hear him trying to compute the mental math.

"I look forward to it, bro."

"Oh, one last question... What's your apartment number?"

"Um... 209."

"Be careful out there. See you when you get here."

"Alright, see ya."

Jeremy hung up the line, and I heard dial tone.

Now...where's Frankie? I start scouring the apartment looking for her. I found her in the bathroom looking through the cabinet underneath the sink.

"FRANKIE! GUESS WHAT?!"

"Jimmy, what the fuck?! You came out of nowhere!"

"Sorry sweetheart."

"But what is it?!"

"Jeremy and Giulia are moving to Vegas! I just got off the phone with him, and he's leaving Ohio tomorrow to start their trek across the country."

"No way?! Now you don't have to worry about not seeing him since he'll be here in a few days."

"I know!" I started jumping up and down—similarly to how I would as a kid when I was *super* excited.

"Oh, goodness. You're like a little kid right now with how excited you are," she said, laughing at my expression and behavior. "It's adorable."

"Frankie, it's my kid brother. Of course I'm excited."

"I know, dear. I never said it was a bad thing," she said, smiling.

~ * ~

Four days later, I was taking a nap in the late morning when I heard a knock at the door.

Who the hell...?

I unlocked the deadbolt, and turned the handle to open the door. Jeremy and Giulia stand before me.

"JEREMY!"

I immediately grabbed my brother, hug him, and nearly squeezed every ounce of air out of his lungs.

"Hey, hey, I need to breathe."

"Like hell you do," I said jokingly.

"Happy to see me, eh?"

"Of course I am. Hi, Giulia," I said, also offering her a hug. "Come on in."

Frankie rounds a corner. She must have just came from the master bathroom.

"Oh my goodness! Hi Jeremy! Hi Giulia!" Like me, she runs up to Giulia and my brother, offering both of them a hug.

"Heyyyy Frankie!" Jeremy interjects.

"Can I get you guys anything? Water? Snacks or food?"

"I'm starving, and water would be great," Giulia said.

"Yeah, I'll take a water."

"Have a seat, guys. I'll have the waters in a second. Giulia, I made bucatini cacio e pepe last night. Do you want some of that?"

"Girl, what? I haven't had cacio e pepe in a while. Yes, I would *love* some. Thank you so much!" Giulia's face lit up with excitement, as it should— Frankie's a great cook.

"Ha, alright, I'll get you a plate. Jeremy, do you want some, too?"

"You know what... I should probably eat. Yeah, I'll have some."

Frankie goes back to the kitchen to retrieve two glasses and fills them with water, promptly bringing them over to Jeremy and Giulia. She then takes the bucatini cacio e pepe out of the fridge and dishes out a serving for Jeremy and Giulia each, making sure to heat it before giving it to them at the kitchen table along with silverware.

"The plates are hot. Might want to give it a second," Frankie warned.

"Parmesan?" Jeremy inquired.

"Oh, duh. How could I *forget* the parmesan?! Hold on a second."

Frankie goes back to the fridge and takes out a container of parmesan, then grabs a small spoon, bringing both to the dining table.

"Here you go. That's parmesan."

"Thank you, Frankie."

Jeremy scooped out some parmesan over the top of his pasta, then handed the serving spoon to Giulia for her to do the same if she desired. She did likewise, although she took less cheese than Jeremy. My brother is a cheese fiend.

Jeremy twirls his fork around in the pasta to get some, and takes his first bite.

"Oh my God, this comes close to Mom's, Jim."

"Yeah, I know. Frankie's a great cook."

"You really are, Frankie," Giulia chimed in.

"Thank you both," Frankie said as she basked in the positive affirmations. I think I even saw her blush slightly, and it's scarce that she does so.

"Jer, you said you might look for a place in this complex?"

"Yeah. I've got a few months' of living expenses saved just in case, but I'm thinking of applying to Caesars to work in their finance and accounting department. Seems like it would be a good gig."

"Yes, Caesars will take care of you if you can get in with them. I've met some people who work for them, and they seem happy with it."

"Is it okay if we crash here for the night?" Giulia said, interrupting Jeremy and I's casual conversation. "We'll look for our own place in the morning."

I looked at Frankie because I don't make decisions like this unilaterally. I *always* make sure to get her input and opinion first.

"I'm good with it if you are, dear," I assured her.

"Yeah, you guys can stay in the second bedroom this evening," she said. 'Make yourself comfortable."

"You're the best, Frankie!" Jeremy was excited to be here, and I was very glad to have my brother back.

I did have to go to work later, so I laid down for a nap shortly after that interaction. Everyone was respectful of the fact I was sleeping, too—Frankie seemed to have it under control pretty well.

I left for work about 3:30 pm, as I started my shift at 4:00 pm. It only takes me about 15 minutes each direction for my commute. I'm almost always early. Bring late or cutting it close gives me extreme anxiety, and I've been this way for as long as I can remember.

The Tropicana gaming floor was mostly tame—as much as a place that allows people to get drunk while throwing away money *can* be tame. I think I only had to have my pit boss throw out one belligerently drunk guy the whole evening, and that's including when my graveyard relief dealer showed up to take over my table.

By the time I got home a bit after midnight, everyone was sound asleep. The lights were turned off, I could hear Jeremy snoring from the guest bedroom (he's always been a loud snorer), and I tried to not make a sound when I went into our bedroom. Frankie was laying on her side, one arm outstretched over the edge of the bed, and the other resting under her face. I undressed down to my boxer-briefs, crawled in bed with her, and gave her a kiss on the cheek. It didn't take me long to drift off to sleep, but not before I told Frankie how much I love her.

36: TWENTY-EIGHT

I went outside to check the mail, and I grabbed the contents out of the receptacle. I thumb through the stack—ads, more ads, the electric bill from Nevada Energy, and…what's this? I observe and feel the envelope, and it has a thickness to it that would indicate there's a card inside. It's from a familiar address, too. It's from my younger brother, Jeremy. I reach into my right front pocket and retrieve the pocketknife, sliding it under the top of the envelope while being careful not to damage the contents inside. I opened it and pulled out the card.

On the front of the card is a picture of a cap and gown with a cute design on it. I opened it to the interior part of the card. It begins:

```
You are cordially invited to my graduation from
          Youngstown State University.
```

Holy shit, has it really been that long that my younger brother is about to graduate *college*? I feel like I just got married yesterday, but it's been three years since that happened. He had just graduated high school a few months before I proposed to Frankie. Have I not been back to Ohio in two years? It feels like a blur. Since moving to Vegas, my life with Frankie has been nothing short of a whirlwind. The growing, booming gambling industry in Vegas has kept me busy with Chauncy. When I haven't been at work as a dealer of some sort, I've been helping him run the sportsbooks. I've always had a head for math and statistics—it just comes naturally, and I excelled at it in school any time it's come up.

I work the swing shift most weeks, with the rare meeting being held in the morning, so I'm asleep most of the morning unless I have something to do like a doctor's appointment or other errands. Frankie, being the sweetheart and godsend that she is, likes to cook and makes sure I have food to bring with me to work when I leave in the afternoon. She also tends to take care of whatever the household may need, and I probably don't thank her enough for everything she does, but I do appreciate it greatly.

It's only 2:05pm—I have to work in a few hours, but Frankie should be around. I go back inside the apartment, and Frankie is going through one of the drawers in her dresser in our bedroom. I slowly walked up behind her, as she's elbow-deep looking for something it seems.

"Hey, babe."

She flinched and responded reflexively. "Oh, my sweet baby Jesus, dear. You scared the crap out of me."

"Sorry, sweetheart. Didn't mean to scare you."

She turns her body around completely to face me.

"What's up?"

"Well… Jeremy is graduating from YSU soon. I just got the invitation in the mail."

She looked at me wide-eyed in disbelief.

"Wait, *what*?! He's old enough to be graduating *college*?!"

"Frankie, he's 22 now… So yeah, he's old enough."

"We haven't been back to Ohio since we moved here, Jimmy."

"That's exactly what I said. Crazy how time flies, huh? Anyway, did you want to go? It's a few months out, so I can make arrangements with my work with plenty of notice."

"Yeah, let's go. It might be nice to see everyone for a few days or so. Catch up and all that."

"Alright, I'll call the airline tomorrow. Do you just want to go for the day, or do you want to spend some time back home to visit people?"

"I guess we could stay for a couple of days. I'm sure my parents and brothers would be happy to see us."

The next day, before I went to work, I called American Airlines to book the trip. Jeremy's graduation was on Friday, May 8, 1981, so I booked the dates as leaving Vegas on May 7 and returning on May 11. That would give us some time to travel, and also a couple of days to spend time with friends after the graduation ceremony itself. We would fly into Cleveland Hopkins Airport, and Frankie's brother Vince said he'd pick us up when we arrived and drop us off when we had to return to Vegas. I've always liked the guy, even if he did threaten my life when I first met him.

~ * ~

The months pass, and finally, we get to fly back to Ohio to see Jeremy graduate from Youngstown State with a Bachelor's in finance. Apparently, going on two years without seeing your family—when you initially told them you'd visit every year—doesn't do your memory (or your family relations) any favors. Sure, we've talked on the phone a good amount, but getting to see them is another story. I made sure to pack nice clothes for the trip, being the bougie and classy guy that I am. Frankie packed her clothes similarly.

Spring in Ohio is objectively the best—it's not so hot that you're breathing water, but it's also no longer snowing. It's a great, happy medium. Winter and summer are torturous for different reasons. I cannot stress enough how much I loathe snow with every fiber of my being and the fire of a thousand suns. Shoveling snow is awful. Driving on ice and snow before the roads are plowed and cleaned is awful. Having to wear a million layers of clothing just to not freeze to death outside during the winter is awful. No part of this is a pleasurable experience. On the other hand, feeling like you're breathing water when you go outside—even though you just took a shower ten minutes ago, and your hair still isn't dry—is ridiculous. I'm already spoiled by Vegas, even if the summer heat is the closest thing to a hate crime I'll ever experience.

We get in pretty late, so I had Andrew—my best friend since kindergarten—pick us up. We're still young enough that staying up late isn't an issue. I can only imagine that Jeremy is fast asleep so he's not a zombie in the morning. Once we saw Andrew's car pull up curbside, Frankie and I happily greeted him, even though we're both completely exhausted.

Andrew gets out of the car, the engine idling, and approaches me first.

"Hey man, it's been a while," he says, hugging me.

"I know, I'm sorry I haven't come back for a while."

"You're good. I understand." He outstretches his arms to hug Frankie as well.

"Hey Frankie, good to see you, too."

Frankie pulls away slightly. "It's been a while. Since the wedding, maybe?"

"Yeah, that sounds about right. Are you keeping this clown in line in Vegas?"

Frankie laughed. "All he does is work and sleep most of the time, Andrew."

"Sounds about right. He's always been a workaholic."

"He hasn't changed at all in that regard."

"Can I take both of your bags and load them in the trunk?"

"Yeah, of course," I added.

"Go ahead and get in while I do that, then," Andrew said while grabbing Frankie's bag first, unlocking the trunk, and putting it in before going back for mine.

I open the rear passenger side door, and have Frankie get in before I slide in next to her. Andrew circles back around to the driver's side after he closed the trunk.

"You guys good?"

"Yeah, we're good."

"I'm taking you to your parents' house, I assume, Jimmy?"

"Sure are. I never threw out my key. I know my parents well enough that the locks aren't changed."

From there, the conversation didn't last long. Frankie and I were exhausted. She passed out in the car first, laying her head on my chest, and I followed suit within a few minutes. Andrew must have taken note. For the rest of the hour and a half long drive, the car was quiet until we arrived at my childhood home.

"Alright, you two, we're here," Andrew said, gently jostling me awake.

"Oh... Okay. Help me with the bags?" I said, rubbing my eyes.

"Yeah, of course."

The three of us get out of the car, and Andrew circles around to the trunk to open it. I unclip my keys from the belt loop on the front of my pants, picking out my house key before handing them to Frankie.

"Here, go unlock and open the door while I carry the bags inside. Do you remember where I used to sleep upstairs?"

"I do remember," she said sleepily. Her eyes are still glossed over after being woken up.

"Alright, head upstairs and try to be quiet. It's pretty late."

I looked at my watch. 11:53 pm.

"Okay, love."

"Thank you for the ride, Andrew. I can always count on you."

"Any time, man. I'll see you in a few days to take you back to the airport?"

"Yes, if not sooner. I'm sure Jeremy won't mind if you join us for dinner after the graduation ceremony. I'll ask him in the morning."

"Sounds good."

Frankie and I each give Andrew a departing hug before he drives off. She then heads for the front door of the house, my key in her left hand, and I follow a few paces behind her. Once we're both inside, I lock the door behind us, and we head up the stairs as gingerly as possible, so that we don't wake anyone up. Especially Jeremy.

We go to my old room, and it's the same way I left it—except Mom made the beds (there are two twin beds on opposite sides of the small room) and cleaned it, obviously. I put our bags down in the middle of the room. We dress down some, and just before we get into bed, I see Frankie looking at me. I take a few steps towards her, and embrace her, my arms around her waist.

"Good night, beautiful," I said, kissing her passionately before pulling away.

"Good night," she said, smiling.

It didn't take long for us to fall back asleep.

We woke up at about 8:30 am, and promptly headed down to the kitchen. Unsurprisingly, Mom was in there making something for breakfast.

"It smells good in here," I said as I walked in, making my presence known.

Mom almost got whiplash for how fast she turned her head in our direction.

"OH MY GOD! JIMMY!" she yelled excitedly as she ran up to me.

"Hi, Mom." I gave her a warm hug.

"Hi, Frankie. Nice to see you, too."

I heard footsteps descending a few minutes later. Jeremy must have just woken up.

"Hey, big bro!" he said, running to give me a hug, then hugging Frankie.

I laughed. "Hey, kid."

"When did you get in? I didn't hear anything, and I'm a light sleeper," he inquired.

"We got here a little before midnight. Andrew picked us up from the airport and dropped us off here."

"Well, y'all were quiet as a mouse."

"That was the intention."

"What—what time is the ceremony, Jeremy?" Frankie asked.

"5 pm tonight."

"Are you all ready? Have you got your cap and gown and a suit to go underneath it?"

"Of course. Giulia helped me pick it out, obviously. You know I have zero fashion sense without her or Mom's help."

I saw Frankie chuckle at the veracity of that statement. Unlike me, Jeremy does—in fact—have no sense of fashion.

"What time do you have to be there? Usually, they want you at the venue much earlier than the ceremony itself."

Jeremy looked for the flyer he received from the school and located it on the counter. "It says here... Graduates need to be at the school two hours before, so 3 pm."

"That sounds about right. You'd have to leave here by 2:30 at the latest to get there with about 15 minutes to spare to find a place to park. Considering it takes about 15 minutes to *get* there."

"Seems reasonable. I'd probably leave here at 2 pm, in all honesty," Jeremy said as he worked out the logistics in his head.

"What do you want to do the rest of the day before you have to get ready and head out?"

"Hm... You guys want to go get Handel's later? Like in a couple hours? I haven't had it in a while."

"Hell yeah, let's go! They don't have them out in Vegas." Man... I was *very* excited at the idea of going to Handel's and getting my favorite chocolate chunk.

At about noon, we went to get Handel's—Mom, Jeremy, Frankie, and I. Dad was doing yard work, but said to get him the same as whatever I order, in a cup. The four of us approach the counter.

"Hi, welcome to Handel's. What can I get started for you?"

Frankie goes first. "I would like a single of the Buckeye, please. In a bowl."

"Okay, got it. What else?"

"I would like a single of Butter Pecan in a bowl," Mom requests.

"Okay, got it. For you, sir?" The employee looks at Jeremy.

"Can I get... a single of Cake Batter in a cone, please?"

"Of course. And for you?" Finally, it's my turn.

"I would like two singles of Chocolate Chunk in bowls, please. One's to take home for Dad."

"Will that be everything for you guys?"

"Yes," I said confidently.

She told me the total, and I paid for the four of us. I'm not going to make Jeremy pay, and I certainly won't let Mom or Frankie do it.

"Thank you, Jimmy," Mom said.

"Yeah, thank you," Frankie added.

Jeremy nodded a "thank you" as well while he dug into the glob of ice cream sitting atop his waffle cone.

After we got back to the house, we mostly kept to ourselves individually until it was time for Jeremy to get dressed and head to the YSU campus. To my surprise, he got ready fairly quickly and kept his cap, gown, tassel, and cords with him in the back seat until he arrived.

"See you guys there in a bit?"

"Yes, of course," I said, smiling.

"Alright, then I'm going to head to campus." He heads out the side door of the house and walks to his car. Once he unlocks it and gets in, he quickly puts it into reverse, getting down the long driveway and making his way to Youngstown State.

Unlike my brother, I tend to take forever to get ready, so I went back upstairs with Frankie right before he left to start changing my attire. Frankie did the same.

"Are you excited to see your brother graduate?" she asked me.

"Of course, I am. I'm proud of him."

I put my socks on first, then my pants and belt. When I got to putting on my dress shirt, I asked Frankie for a hand in making sure my collar wasn't all crazy.

"Frankie, can you fix my collar, please?"

"Sure. Kneel so I can reach."

I chuckled at the request while also remembering that she's short, and obliged her. She takes a moment to straighten out my collar, making sure it's even and in place on all sides.

"You should be good now," she says.

"Thank you, my love." I turn around and kiss her beautiful lips. She hasn't put on her classic red lipstick yet, which she wears most days, especially when we have to dress up to go somewhere.

She's wearing a floral dress with pink heels, her red lipstick, and modest makeup. I think she wants to keep the focus on Jeremy.

With the ceremony starting at 5 pm, we left at 4 pm because we knew everyone and their mom is going to be in attendance to see all the graduates. As if we're any better—four of us are going to support Jeremy! Thankfully, I have a good idea of where I'm going on this campus still, even though it's been a while since I personally attended. Doesn't seem like much has changed since then. Finally, I'm successful in finding a parking spot. I pull into it, check the sides to make sure I'm not parked like a jackass, and remove the key from the engine. Everyone opens their respective door, and gets out of the car.

"Alright, now let's see how to find our way to... What's the building we're supposed to go to?"

I pulled the invitation from my right back pocket to check the precise location. "Beeghley gymnasium, got it." After a quick scan of our surroundings as the four of us walk closer to the main campus, I noticed that there are physical signs with arrows telling us where to go for the ceremony.

"Looks like they thought this out in advance," Frankie commented.

"They sure did."

We followed the signs until we reached Beeghley. Upon approaching the main entrance, a security guard checks the purses of Mom and Frankie before they're individually allowed through. Dad and I just had to show the contents of our pockets, which were underwhelming. I just had the car keys and my wallet. Dad only brought his wallet and a handkerchief.

Although there were several people already in attendance, I think if we arrived any *later*, that we wouldn't have been able to find four seats next to each other as easily. We quickly make our way and arrange ourselves in order—Dad on the left, Mom next to him, I'm to Mom's right, and Frankie on the other side of me.

"Wow, I think I was still in Vietnam when this building opened," I blurted out.

"So, this is your first time seeing it?" Dad asked.

"Yeah, for sure."

"Oh, that's interesting," Mom added.

"Well… What do you think of it, then?" Frankie wondered.

"It's nice. They did a good job."

We didn't talk much after that, as we were all taking in everything around us—the graduates, the atmosphere, and all of the family members and loved ones in attendance with us.

A man in his mid-50s walks to the middle of the stage, speaking into a microphone that is fixed on a lectern. He is similar in height to me if I had to guess, and has thick eyebrows, dark features, and is wearing a black suit.

"Friends, family, and most importantly, the graduating class of 1980… Welcome to the commencement ceremony of Youngstown State University."

The crowd cheers in excitement and anticipation for what is about to happen.

"For those of you who don't know me, my name is John J Coffelt, and I am the university president. I have been serving in this role since 1973."

President Coffelt continues for a few minutes, orating a speech that he has clearly written out ahead of time, although the extra preparation doesn't detract from the experience. Rather, it *enhanced* the experience, so I was grateful that he is poised in his delivery. Following the conclusion of his own speech, he introduced a few other dignitaries, who also gave their own inspirational or motivational speech.

After what feels like forever, it's finally time for the rows of graduates to take the spotlight and center stage. The chairs are organized in several rows, but two main groups, where there is a separation down the middle to create an aisle. The first row stands up, and makes their way to the side of the stage steps. Each graduate is called by their name and major individually. As they make their way to the other side of the stage, they are presented their degree from President Coffelt, then shake a couple other hands from college officials. Upon departure from the stage, they quickly make their way back down to their seats. Everyone is donning a black cap and gown, a white/red tassel, and a variety of formal attire underneath their gowns.

From the looks and sounds of it, the graduates are in alphabetical order by last name, and I finally spot Jeremy closer to the back. That makes sense—R for Rossi is towards the end of the alphabet, after all. Jeremy was easy to spot because he decorated his cap in an obnoxious fashion. He has his jersey number, #8, smack in the middle of the cap. To the right of that is a poorly drawn football, and to the right of the #8 is a penguin (the mascot of Youngstown State) that is drawn, somehow, even worse than the football. Oh, Jeremy… Stick with finance. Don't become a starving artist any time soon. Hopefully Head Coach Narduzzi has better things to say about his performance on field than his artistry.

Twenty minutes pass, and they're going quickly and efficiently through all of the graduates. I finally see Jeremy, waiting at the bottom of the steps—it's about *damn* time—for his name to be called.

"Jeremy Angelo Rossi, Bachelor's of Finance," President Coffelt announces. Mom, Dad, Frankie, and I all go crazy to cheer him on, and we saw him look around for us as he walks across the stage to retrieve his degree and shake everyone's hands.

Jeremy exits the stage, fluidly following the person that directly preceded him back to his seat in the audience. I see him smiling on the way, as he should.

Moving on to the rest of the alphabet, we hear a name that sounds familiar. "Giulia Silvestri, Bachelor of English."

The four of us quickly exchange glances.

"I think that's Jeremy's girlfriend he mentioned," Frankie noticed.

"I think so, too," I said. "Can't wait to meet her."

Another hour goes by, and finally, this ridiculously long commencement ceremony is *over*. We quickly head outside and wait for Jeremy and Giulia at the front of the building. A few minutes later, we see them walking towards us. Giulia looks visibly uncomfortable from the heels she's wearing. I'm sure Frankie can empathize.

"Jimmy, Frankie, this is my girlfriend, Giulia," Jeremy says when they come up to us.

"Hi, I'm Jimmy. I'm his older brother," I said while shaking Giulia's hand.

"Nice to meet you, Jimmy."

"I'm Frankie, Jimmy's wife," Frankie interjects, also shaking Giulia's hand.

"Very nice to meet you both."

"I was more surprised that Jeremy found a woman who can put up with his antics."

Giulia laughed as soon as I finished the sentence. Loudly.

"Oh, come on. He's not *that* bad..."

"Nah, I'm just giving him shit. My brother's a good guy. At least now he is."
I playfully nudged Jeremy on his left shoulder. He smiled and laughed it off.

"So, what do you guys plan on doing with work now that you've graduated?"
Mom asked.

"Oh, um... We were thinking of moving out to Vegas actually to start our
careers. Jeremy really misses you, Jimmy."

"Really? That's a bit of a surprise..."

"Yeah, I'm bored and alone over here, bro."

"Well, I guess let us know how soon you want to move out, and we will
figure out a plan from there."

"Alright, we'll do that for sure. Are you guys hungry? I'm starving."

"Yeah, I haven't ate since Handel's earlier."

"Want to go to Belleria?" Dad asked.

"Belleria sounds *amazing* right now," Giulia added.

"Then it's decided. We'll meet you guys there, Jer."

"Can't wait. I haven't had it in a while," he said.

37: TWENTY-SEVEN

It took some time to get settled, but Vegas has treated us well since we decided to move from Ohio. After a year here, it is starting to feel like home.

I got a job as a craps dealer at the Tropicana Hotel. I started playing poker, craps, and roulette a few years ago back in Ohio, practically right when I got sent to the Ohio National Guard upon return from Vietnam. I needed something to do after hours, and my group of friends got me involved in that.

For the past year, we have been staying in condos called The Rexford, located at 1700 Rexford Drive, Las Vegas, NV 89104. If you're familiar with Vegas in the '70s, it's in the Beverly Green district—not too far from the Las Vegas Country Club.

It's been a good time up to this point, but it's certainly been an adjustment. The summer is no bullshit. Never have I been to a climate so dry that I get practically daily nosebleeds. It's terrible. Frankie has been in the same boat since our arrival. Also, I have never had my sinuses act up this much in my entire life. You would think that I'd do more research about a city before uprooting my and Frankie's lives there, but that is not the case. One day, I just decided that I was sick and tired of Ohio, and that I wanted a change. Thank heavens that she was cool about it and wasn't dead set on remaining in Ohio for the rest of our lives. I can't wrap my mind around the concept of being stuck in the same small town in the Midwest for your entire human life without ever having the inspiration to explore, move, and live. I love my family, but sometimes, you need a break from your old lifestyle and the opportunity to grow, carve your own path, and form an identity that you're happy with in the long run. Moving thousands of miles away from home is truly the best way to do it if you ask me.

With just Frankie and I in an apartment together, our lives are mostly peaceful outside of my sometimes-volatile work schedule in the casino. We agreed long ago that children aren't something either of us wanted—the two of us value freedom way too much for all that commotion. Of course, we'll buy a house here once we feel ready to do so in a couple of years or so. I need more working history in the state of Nevada before I think I'm ready to make that plunge.

Something that I have yet to give any serious introspective or reflective thought to is whether or not I'd like to try to go to school again. At 27, I haven't been to school since before I got shipped off to Vietnam when I was 19. It's been a few years since, and it begs the question of how much knowledge I would have to relearn. If I do go back to school, do I want to continue my pursuit in accountancy? How many of my credits from Youngstown State would transfer, if any? Would I be able to handle both school and my full-time casino job at the same time, along with whatever needs to be done at home?

At the moment, Frankie is out doing her own thing, so I have the house to myself, other than the cat we adopted a few months ago. He's orange and about three years old. And…not that bright. His name is Apollo. Apollo ran out in front of my car one night on my way home from work, and I was quick enough to come to a screeching halt so I could grab him and take him home. After we checked to make sure that he didn't belong to anyone, Frankie and I decided to keep him. Neither of us grew up with cats in Ohio, so he's our first cat, but he certainly wouldn't be our last. I think he finally feels like this is his home, and that his life on the streets was less than amazing.

Apollo approaches me and meows, looking up at me expectantly. I can tell that he wants pets, so I extend my hand and give him head scratches. He purrs loudly, and rubs his head in my hand, signaling he wants more pets and attention. Frankie loves on him too, and sometimes I feel myself getting weirdly jealous that he bonds with *her* more than *me*—and *I'm* the one that rescued the little ingrate from the road late at night!

"Treats?" I asked Apollo. He screams louder, and as I begin my short walk from the bedroom to the kitchen pantry, I notice that he follows me every step of the way. Yeah, he definitely wants treats, the little garbage can. This guy will do anything and everything for food and treats. I mean…same. I also love food.

Once I open the pantry, I locate the small bag of cat treats that we keep on hand for Apollo. He starts meowing louder and more often as I pull apart the sides of the bag to open it. I reached in and pull out a few treats—six of them. I counted.

I put one on the floor directly in front of Apollo, and he continues to look at *me* with the most confused, empty-headed look with those big green eyes. God, he's so stupid. He's lucky he's handsome.

"It's right here, bud," I said, pointing to the treat that is literally four inches in front of him. He looked down at my hand and was able to spot the treat quickly this time. He meows again, so I put a single treat in the palm of my hand for him to eat. He eats that one. I chucked the remaining four treats at various distances since he's getting fat, and could use the entertainment while he shovels down the treats like a vacuum.

Once he finished the last of the treats I gave him, I held up my empty hands. "No more, bud. You ate them all." He meows yet again, trying to summon a single brain cell capable of comprehending what just happened. Unfortunately, his attempt was not successful.

Within a few minutes, Apollo goes from being calm to tearing up the apartment. I guess people call this the zoomies? I call it Apollo being a menace to society and the state of my clean home. He's running *everywhere*—from the kitchen to the bedroom, to the living room, back to the kitchen, onto counters and surfaces. Anywhere you can think of in the average residence, he's got his orange paws all over it right now.

I realize that I haven't talked to Jeremy in a hot minute. Since I left Ohio as a matter of fact.

I pick up the phone that's on an end table near the couch in the living room, and started dialing.

3-3-0… What the hell was my brother's number again? I think for a moment, and it comes to me quickly. If I'm forgetting my own brother's phone number, that *definitely* means I'm not talking to the guy enough. After I dial the final number in his phone number, I hear the line ring.

"Hello?" I hear him answer.

"Jer, it's me."

"Jimmy? Is that you?"

"Yeah, bro. It's me."

"Oh my God. I haven't heard from you in forever. How's Vegas?"

"These summers are something else, but I like it. It's been a good change of pace and scenery. What all do you have going on these days?"

"Oh, you know… School. Playing football."

"Where are you playing and attending?"

"Youngstown State. I'm going to graduate in the spring with my Bachelor's in finance."

"Oh, wow! I'm proud of you, Jer. You've come a long way. Are you doing well in class too?"

"Enough to keep my place on the roster, I guess," he said shyly. "You were always the better student, Jimmy."

I laughed. He's right, and makes a good point.

"Did you get a full ride?"

"From high school? Yeah. I got a full-ride scholarship."

"Good for you! Have a girlfriend or anything yet?"

"I've been seeing this girl Giulia for a little bit. I really like her."

"Yeah? What is great about her?"

I hear Jeremy go silent for a moment as he contemplates the question. If I know Jeremy at all, he's about to go on a rant once he finds the words.

"Well, for one, she puts up with my shit. I think that's a feat in and of itself," he states confidently. The two of us laugh, but we both know it's true. He can be quite a handful.

"Alright, what else?"

"Besides the fact she's gorgeous? I love that she's smart, patient, and goofy.

I can be myself around her. I think I'm in love, Jim."

"Ohhhhhh my GOODNESS! My little bro, Jeremy, in LOVE?!"

"Yes. I know. It's very hard to believe."

"I can't WAIT to meet her, Jeremy! You should come visit us in Vegas with her. Make a little trip out of it."

"Well, if you come to my graduation in the spring, you can meet her. We're both graduating. What about you? How are you and Frankie?"

"I love her more every day. She's out doing her own thing right now. Oh! We adopted a cat a few months ago."

"What? Really? Bro, we've never had cats around growing up."

"Well, I found this orange cat when he ran in front of my car late at night coming home from work. Didn't belong to anyone, so we took him in."

"And how's that working out for you?"

"He's adjusting well, to my surprise. I think he likes Frankie more than me some days. Even if he's dumber than a brick most days."

"Are you sure you even like this cat?"

"Of course I do. He's orange, and I would throw myself into a burning building for him. His name is Apollo."

Jeremy let out a belly laugh, which I haven't heard in long enough that I've since forgotten what his laugh sounds like. I do miss him sometimes.

"Alright, Jimmy, I do have to head out to practice in a few minutes."

"Oh, okay. Please don't be a stranger. Here, I'll give you my new Vegas phone number."

I told him the ten-digit phone number, starting with the 702 area code.

"Okay, thanks. I got it written down. I'll call you at some point next week maybe?"

"Sounds good, Jer."

"Bye, Jimmy. It was good to hear from you."

"Bye, Jer."

I heard him hang up the receiver on the other end, and was now met with dial tone.

38: TWENTY-SIX

After we got married, Frankie and I began living together once we found an apartment in Youngstown. Our lease would be up in a little over a month. On a quiet Saturday afternoon, Frankie was folding and hanging clothes when I dropped the bombshell question.

"Frankie, how do you feel about moving out of Ohio?" I'm aware that asking this question can go a few ways.

Frankie stopped what she was doing dead in her tracks. She looks me in the eyes and pauses for a few seconds that feel like an eternity.

"I'm not opposed. Why do you ask?"

"What do you say we move to Vegas?"

Again, she paused and looked at me dead in the eyes.

"Why Vegas? Isn't it crazy hot?"

"I'm *tired* of the Midwest and Ohio. There has to be more to life and the United States than these sleepy small towns. There's not enough opportunity here either."

"What about your parents and Jeremy?"

"We can always visit. I just am tired of Ohio."

"Have you been thinking about this for a while? Because it sounds like you've put in some thought."

"Yeah, I have. I'm so bored of this place."

"How are you going to find a job out there?"

"My friend Chauncy runs sports books out that way, and he said he can get me set up with a job in a casino."

"Have I met Chauncy?"

"Of course you have. Jimmy Vaccaro."

"Oh! Yes. I do remember him. He's from around here, isn't he?"

"He is. He moved out there a few years ago."

"Wouldn't I need a job, too?"

"I mean, if you want, but I should be able to handle it fine on my own."

"How soon are you wanting to move?"

I had to take a moment to pause and think about it. Part of me wants to say that I want to move immediately, but I'm not sure how willing Frankie is to do that. On the other hand, I haven't even told Mom and Dad that I want to move out of Ohio, never mind Jeremy or any of my other friends who have remained here. I would have to tell *them* first, I think, for this to make sense.

"That's a great question. How soon are *you* willing to move? I haven't even told my parents this. You're the first person I've brought it up to."

"Well, personally, I don't have anything major tying me here. I am good with whenever you want to go."

"How quick can you help me pack up our belongings?"

"It would probably take me a few days to a week. We don't have *that* much stuff in here."

"A month would work."

"So, whose parents are we going to tell first? Yours or mine?"

She looked into my eyes pensively.

"I guess mine."

The next day, we drove about 20 minutes from our Youngstown apartment to Struthers. At this point, all of Frankie's older brothers have moved out, so her parents have been empty nesters for a bit.

I got out of the car when we arrived to open Frankie's passenger side door, then the two of us held hands as we approached the door. I rang the doorbell, and was met by Anna when the door was opened.

"Oh! Hi sweetheart. Hi Jimmy. Come in," she said, holding the door open for us.

"Hi, Mom," Frankie said. The two of them exchanged a warm hug. I closed the door behind us.

"To what do we owe the pleasure?"

"Ha, well… We've got some news."

"You're giving us grandchildren?"

"Oh, no, not that. Definitely not that," I remarked, somewhat nervously.

Anna frowned. I know she wanted us to give her grandkids, but that was simply not happening.

"Then what is it?"

"Well… Frankie and I are moving to Vegas."

"You're moving WHERE?!"

"Yes, you heard that right. Vegas. As in Las Vegas, Nevada."

"Why? What's wrong with Ohio?"

"I'm bored of it, and Frankie already agreed to it. My friend Jimmy Vaccaro has been running sportsbooks out there for a few years already, and he's willing to get me set up with a job once I get there."

"Frankie, is this true?"

"Yes, Mom. It is."

"How soon are you wanting to go?"

"In about a month."

"Goodness, me! That's so soon it feels like. This is really what you want to do, though?"

"Yes. Don't worry, we will come back to visit at least once a year."

"Jimmy, it's a big choice to up and move across the country. What if you don't make it out there? Are you moving somewhere else, or are you coming back here?"

"I'm not worried about not making it. I've always been smart and will find my way. I would move somewhere else if I had to, in the unlikely event that I don't 'make it' out in Vegas."

"As long as you two are supported and keep yourselves afloat, I guess I'm just going to have to trust you to do the right thing. You know we're always here for the two of you if you need us."

"We appreciate that very much."

We didn't stay long after that. We figured it was best to tell both sets of parents on the same day if possible. Since our parents didn't live far apart, in our childhood homes, we drove to my parents' house and had the same conversation. Mom didn't react well. Dad seemed initially concerned, but otherwise a bit indifferent.

"James Antonio Rossi, what the HELL do you MEAN you're moving to Vegas?!" Mom said scornfully.

"I didn't stutter, did I?"

"Boy, I will beat your ass if you talk to me like that again, and you know it."

Yeah, I do know it. Mom's a sweetheart, but she's got that famous Italian temper. Frankie does, too, but hers is not quite as pronounced as Mom's.

"Sorry, Mom. But yeah, our lease is up in a little over a month on our apartment, so it's perfect timing."

"I can't stop you from doing this, can I?" Mom asked.

"Nope. Frankie and I have already decided on it together."

Mom sighed, and Dad looked between Mom, Frankie, and I for a moment. Sometimes he's more unpredictable than Mom, in the sense that his emotions and reactions are difficult to read. Mom is, at least, easy to read and make sense of in that regard. She wears her heart on her sleeve.

"Alright... Will we get to see you before you go?"

"Of course. You guys and Frankie's parents both."

"I hope Vegas treats you well, Jim," Dad said. He's been quiet most of the time we've been having this interaction—at least up until now.

Once we got home from my parents, we wasted no time to notify our apartment complex that we intended to vacate and not renew our lease once it ends.

~ * ~

A month passed quickly. Frankie and I spent considerable time together determining item by item of what we were taking on our cross-country venture versus throwing out with the next trash collection.

The day before we are set to leave, we congregate at my parents' house. The Mancinis—all five of them (Frankie's parents and her three older brothers)— join us, and we make sure that Jeremy is home as well. All our stuff is packed in a U-Haul and my car. It's been packed to the brim for a few days.

"So what makes you want to go to Vegas, Jimmy?" Ralph asked. He's the oldest of the Mancini siblings.

"I just need a change, man. There's more to life and this country than Youngstown and Struthers. You know?"

"Yeah, I get it. I haven't traveled much myself."

"Can we come visit once you're settled?" Vincent asked. He's the older middle child, only younger than Ralph.

"Yeah, of course!" Frankie added.

Finally, Joseph—the youngest Mancini brother, and closest in age to Frankie—chimed in.

"I'm going to miss you, little sis," he said. He is usually the quiet one out of the brothers, and I saw him get a bit teary-eyed.

"I'll miss you too, Joe," she said, embracing him in a hug.

Seeing Frankie with all of her brothers in the same room is comical due to the height difference. She's the shortest, but definitely has the most attitude out of her siblings. God, I love this woman.

The rest of the evening went without a hitch, which is shocking for having ten full-blooded Italians in the same place. Everyone had their feelings about us moving, but that was expected. We're about to make the biggest move of our lives, and head 2,134 miles from home.

The next morning, we woke up sort of early—7:00 am. I wanted to get a head start on the road ahead of us, knowing full well that it would take a few days to reach Vegas. I planned out our route through most of the northern states. The route goes from the I-680 through some of the Youngstown metro, then I-80 for a lot of the westward route. Once you exit Nebraska, the I-80 ends, then you jump onto I-76 to get through Colorado and a good chunk of Utah. We had to do some weird maneuvers through Utah and northern Nevada, but finally, we made it to Vegas via the US 95.

Frankie and I didn't do a lot of stopping to sightsee on the way. We were *determined* to get to Vegas as quickly as possible. Of course, we did find small hotels and such to sleep in each day of the trip.

When we finally arrived in Vegas, we chose to stay the first night at the MGM Grand. All of our stuff was loaded into the car and U-Haul. We would worry about where we're going to stay in the morning.

At that point, we knew that this was going to be the mere beginning to the rest of our lives.

39: TWENTY-FIVE

It's the morning of Halloween in 1977. Frankie and I are about to head on an aircraft to Vegas to be married tomorrow, November 1. We've invited a few of our closest friends, including the strongest relationships within the bridal party or groomsmen. We're the last ones to fly out; I've heard from others that they left a couple days ago just to party. Leave it to a Libra and Aquarius to wait for the last minute to do something. Some of the guys have even moved out to Vegas by this point already.

Our flight out of Cleveland Hopkins airport was an early one—6:00 am Eastern Time. We figured that by the time we got to Vegas, we could check into our hotel, pass out, and worry about the rest later. There is no way on God's green Earth that either of us are going to be chipper that early in the morning. Neither of us are morning people.

My brother Jeremy took us to the airport since his sleep schedule is all out of whack anyway, and he didn't mind driving. He'll be coming to Vegas later in the day like a sensible person. We arrive at the airport right about two hours before departure—3:55 am. Jesus, why did we do this?!

I get out of the car first, then open Frankie's backseat door. Jeremy pops the trunk, and we get our suitcases out plus Frankie's purse. Before closing the front passenger door, we bid my brother farewell.

"We'll see you later, Jer?" I asked.

"Yes, my flight leaves at 1:30pm today."

"Alright. Get home safe and go to sleep if you can."

"I will certainly try," he said, snickering while letting out a laugh.

Frankie grabbed the handle of her suitcase to extend it, and I do likewise with mine, rolling them through the entrance. We were flying American Airlines, and approached the gate counter, where we met with an airline agent wearing branded attire. She smiles warmly at the two of us.

"Hello, we're flying to Vegas today, and need our boarding passes, please," I said to her.

"Alright, can I see an ID from both of you?"

I grabbed my wallet out of my back left pocket, and pull my driver's license out of it. Frankie fumbles through her bag, grabs her wallet, and does the same.

"Thank you, James, and... Francesca?"

"Just Frankie is fine," she corrected.

"Appreciate it, Frankie. What are you going to be doing in Vegas?"

"We're getting married. Tomorrow is the wedding."

The agent looks between both of us. "Congratulations! I hope that your wedding is wonderful, and you have many happy years together as a couple."

"Thank you so much," Frankie said smiling.

"Give me just a moment, and I'll get your boarding passes. Are you checking these bags?"

"Yes, please."

"Alright, I'll get bag tags for those, too."

"Thank you so much."

The process takes about fifteen minutes. She hands us our boarding passes and gives back our driver's licenses to each of us respectively.

"James and Frankie, you are good to go. I hope you have a great time in Vegas, and a long and loving marriage for years to come."

"Thank you," Frankie said.

"Thanks, we appreciate it."

The two of us make our way to the security checkpoint. Frankie only has her purse with her now since we left our bags with the American Airlines agent at check in. I just have my wallet in my back pocket, my keys, and the jacket that I'm wearing.

Upon arrival at the security checkpoint, there were three security agents that were available, and lines formed in front of them individually. We make our way to the one with the shortest line. Apparently only crazy people fly this early. Luckily, we didn't wait more than a few minutes.

The agent is a heavyset gentleman who looks to be in his 40s, with a patchy beard, etc.

"May I see your ID and boarding pass, sir?"

I hand the documents to him. I just carried my license in my hand with my boarding pass since I figured I'd need it immediately again anyway.

He looks at them, then me, and gestures me to proceed forward. Frankie goes through the same motions. After being patted down, and Frankie had her purse searched manually, we looked for our gate. I looked at my watch—4:45 am. We still had some time. Boarding typically starts 45 minutes prior to departure, and we have a 6:00 am departure. Perfect, we have just under 30 minutes to relax a little bit once we get to our gate.

~ * ~

Once we arrive in Vegas, we are exhausted. We retrieve the rental car that I booked with our trip and head to our hotel—we're staying at the Golden Nugget. I give the front desk employee my ID and credit card for the room reservation, and she gives us two room keys. God bless Las Vegas for being open 24 hours. I open the room door with my key, and hold it open for Frankie to come in. We threw our bags on the ground haphazardly, get comfortable, and pass out to sleep as soon as our heads hit the pillow.

After we woke up several hours later, around 7:30 am Pacific, Frankie hurriedly got what she needed, and began to make her way to another room—Rosa's room. Rosa, her best friend since childhood, has a room at the Golden Nugget as well. The girls in her bridal party are going to help her get ready.

"You're not going to eat something first?"

"I'll worry about it later," she said.

"Well, alright then. I'll see you later, beautiful."

I kissed her, then she quickly broke free of my hug to head out. Wow, do I have a mixed bag of emotions going on. I'm getting MARRIED today?!?! Of course, I love Frankie with everything I've got, but that still sounds crazy to me.

I went down to the lobby on the first floor of the hotel, and they had some breakfast items. Coffee, eggs, bacon, muffins—standard continental breakfast. Boy, do I need coffee. I take mine black. I grabbed a cup and waited for the guy in front of me in line to finish what he was doing, then proceeded to pour coffee into my cup with the carafe. I put some eggs, bacon, and sausage on a plate and took a set of utensils that were wrapped in napkins. I eat my breakfast quickly, but take my time sipping on the coffee. I may look a bit disheveled right now, but I don't care. I'm going to shower later anyway before I get ready. I'm sitting at a 2-top table by myself when a woman close in age approaches me from my left side. There's an open table of the same size directly next to me.

"Hi, is anyone sitting here?"

"No, all yours."

"What brings you to Vegas?"

"I'm getting married today. My soon-to-be-wife is already getting ready with her girls."

"Oh, uh, that's nice. Congrats."

This is awkward. Is she trying to hit on me? I don't know if it's that or if she's being friendly. I finish my coffee, take my plate and silverware over to the staff, and go back up to my room.

I unlock the door, go in, and close it behind me. Inhale, exhale. Inhale, exhale. My heart is pounding. Is it possible for the groom to mess up a wedding ceremony for something stupid and menial? The wedding starts at 2:00 pm, so I was told to be there by 1:30 pm at the latest. I'll probably show up around 1:00 just because my nerves are on edge.

I spot a notepad and pen on the desk in the room. I should probably write out my vows so I don't forget them in the moment. I grabbed both the pen and notepad and sat on the bed with my back leaning against the wall. What do I write about the most important, beautiful, and amazing woman I've ever met?

I sat in silence for a while, racking my brain for *something* that would be equal parts memorable and meaningful. Finally, I began writing.

Frankie,

From the first moment I met you, you had a light in you that I couldn't help but be drawn to. You are kind and sweet, beautiful inside and out, smart, and so effortlessly witty that you keep me on my toes. But most of all, you are the piece of my life that always felt like it was waiting to fall into place.

I spent years too nervous to tell you how I felt, but standing here today, there is no hesitation. I love you, and I will love you for the rest of my days. I promise to be your steady place, your partner in laughter and life, and to never take for granted the gift that is you. I choose you, forever and always, Francesca Regina Mancini.

I remove the piece of paper from the pad, fold it in half, and place it on the desk. I put the pen next to it, putting the cap back on so that it doesn't dry out. Time has gone by surprisingly fast this morning, and I noticed the clock on the nightstand next to the bed says 10:30 am. I should start getting ready. I start the shower, turning the handle to my desired temperature and letting it warm up for a minute before I stick my hand in to check. I am not a fan of ice-cold showers, even if I had to endure that in the Army. After the water isn't going to freeze my appendages off, I get in, and complete my shower quickly. I don't have a ton of time to waste today.

Once I dry off and put on my boxer briefs, I pull my attire out of my suitcase: a black tuxedo, black dress shoes, a royal blue necktie, Dior Eau Sauvage cologne, black socks, a white long-sleeve dress shirt, round gold cufflinks, and my Rolex Explorer II watch. Next, I grab my hair styling gel, comb, and antiperspirant. I start with the easy part: putting on the socks first, then pants and shoes. With my hair still wet, I return to the bathroom with my comb and styling gel, then the antiperspirant. I apply the gel to my right hand first, then work it into my hair while I fix it the way I want with the comb. After I'm satisfied with that, I wash my hands and dry them off before I apply Eau Sauvage and let it sit for a couple of minutes. The shirt and vest go on quickly, then I remembered that I haven't had to tie a tie for a while. I look in the mirror with one end of the tie in each hand, thinking of how to do this. I remembered after a minute of staring into the void, and tie it into a standard Windsor knot. Before I affix the cufflinks to my shirt, I straighten out the collar so that it doesn't look all crazy. With the cufflinks in place to my liking, I put on the jacket, and look at myself in the mirror again, checking for any stray hairs or something out of place. Lastly, I put the Rolex on my left wrist, positioning the face perfectly in the middle.

I checked the time. 12:55 pm. The venue we chose was Chapel of the Flowers, which is only 1.8 miles away. I double checked to make sure I have everything. I can't imagine that Vegas would be busy on a Tuesday afternoon. I make my way through the halls of the hotel, down through the casino, and finally arrived at the parking garage. When I get to the car, I unlock it, insert the key into the ignition, and turn over the engine. I give it a minute before putting the car into reverse out of my parking spot, and heading on my way.

Since Andrew is my best man, I let him hold on to the rings for a couple of days—meaning he brought them with him from Ohio for today's ceremony. Rosa, the maid of honor and Frankie's best friend, had one of her young nephews volunteer to be the ring-bearer and a niece to serve as flower girl. Since Frankie only has brothers and no sisters to bond with, Rosa and Frankie have become as close as sisters through their lifelong friendship.

I arrive at Chapel of the Flowers at 1:10 pm, put the car into park, and get out once I remove the key, locking it before walking towards the entrance. Immediately, I'm met with several rows of seats, high ceilings, and beautifully decorated scenery. They have truly put a ton of effort into making this remarkable. As I'm looking around the currently empty venue, I find the restrooms—and Andrew is coming out of the men's.

"Oh, hey man! You made it!"

"Jim, you know damn well I would never miss your wedding for the world."

"Do you have the rings?"

"Of course," Andrew said, gesturing towards his left chest pocket.

"Where's Jeremy? Have you seen him yet?"

"Yeah, we happened to book hotel rooms right next to each other. Didn't plan that. He should be here soon. He's probably getting ready."

"Ah, alright. What hotel?"

"Nugget something?"

"The Golden Nugget? That's where *we're* staying!"

"No shit? What floor?"

"Room 408, so 4ᵗʰ floor."

"Nice, we're on the 6ᵗʰ floor."

Before long, our entourage of people began showing up. Rosa, Andrew's girlfriend Stacey, Frankie's parents and brothers, and Jeremy are among the early birds. Andrew and my other groomsmen are wearing navy suits with light blue bowties. Frankie opted to have her bridesmaids wear purple dresses.

Mom comes up to me, and she's already crying. Oh, Mom…

"Hi, sweet pea!" she exclaimed, extending her arms to hug me.

"Hi, Mom," I said, embracing her warmly.

"Are you excited? I can't believe my baby is getting MARRIED today…"

"I'm very excited, but I'm nervous, too. I just want everything to go smoothly."

"I'm sure you'll be fine."

She goes to hug Andrew as well, then Dad approaches and greets me as well.

"Vegas, huh?"

"Yep. Go big or go home."

While the four of us are chatting, more people are making their way in, talking amongst each other and taking their seats. There's so much going on around me that it's proving difficult to keep up with the whereabouts of every individual person. Some of these people are brand new to me, especially those who are from West Virginia from when Frankie lived there prior to moving to Ohio.

The wedding starts at 2:00 pm on the nose. At 1:55 pm, the officiant announces, "Five minutes until we start the ceremony. Everyone, please take your seats and settle down."

As promised, the officiant—dutifully in place for the wedding—begins to take control of the ceremony. I'm at the front, off to the side, Andrew just a few paces behind me. He clears his throat.

Music begins playing, and I look around.

"Please rise for the bride."

Everyone quickly stands, and I watch as rows of my friends and family turn their attention towards the middle of the aisle. Frankie and her dad, Eugene, have their arms interlocked as he brings her down the aisle to give her away.

Holy shit, she is *stunning*. I start to tear up, but do my best to keep my composure. I felt Andrew give me a reassuring pat on my right shoulder.

"We are gathered here on this beautiful day to witness the union of James Antonio Rossi and Francesca Regina Mancini in holy matrimony. This is a day of great celebration, for a married life – a shared life – and is a great blessing.

As James and Francesca embark on this journey, they will be able to nurture a love that makes them better versions of themselves. Marriage is a garden we sow with love, and harvest in personal growth.

James and Francesca, on your journey together, keep your spouse in the space of highest priority in your heart. The love that you share must be guarded and cherished forever, for it is your most valuable treasure.

Always remember these words—love is patient and kind. Love is not jealous, boastful, proud, or rude. It does not demand its own way. It is not irritable, and it keeps no record or score of being wronged. It does not rejoice about injustice, but rejoices whenever the truth wins out. Love never gives up, never loses faith, is always hopeful, and endures through every circumstance."

He pauses for a moment before continuing.

"You have chosen to write your vows, and it is with these words you express your binding promises to love, honor, and cherish one another. If you are ready to make these promises to each other, I invite you to now face each other and declare your intentions. When you're ready, you may begin."

"I'll go first," I said.

"Please proceed," responded the officiant. I pull out the small paper from my right pocket, which was still neatly folded in half.

"Frankie, from the first moment I met you, you had a light in you that I couldn't help but be drawn to. You are kind and sweet, beautiful inside and out, smart, and so effortlessly witty that you keep me on my toes. But most of all, you are the piece of my life that always felt like it was waiting to fall into place.

I spent years too nervous to tell you how I felt, but standing here today, there is no hesitation. I love you, and I will love you for the rest of my days. I promise to be your steady place, your partner in laughter and life, and to never take for granted the gift that is you. I choose you, forever and always, Francesca Regina Mancini."

Tears formed in Frankie's eyes, although she tried hard to keep her composure so that she could read her own vows.

"James, Jimmy, my sweetheart… I have gone most of my life wondering if I would ever be accepted, loved, and supported. All of that happened, and more, when I met you. From the first 'I love you' to today, you have been my rock, my cheerleader, my everything. I promise to grow with you, to support you through whatever may come our way, to cherish you, and to always honor and respect you. You go by many names to me—my soulmate, my partner, my lover, and as of today, my husband. I promise to remember that soulmates always endure, even during times of struggle and discontent.

I promise to be by your side for every future step of life's journey together. I promise to continue my unwavering loyalty to you, and I vow that your arms are the ones I want wrapped around me at the beginning and end of each day. We are not perfect; we are human beings. But we are perfect for each other. I choose you, forever and always, James Antonio Rossi."

The officiant looks at Frankie, then Andrew, then me. I glance at Andrew as he pulls the ring box that has our rings in it out of his left pocket, holding it in his hand for the moment.

"Thank you for sharing your vows with all of us. The rings you are about to place on each other's fingers are symbols of the love you expressed. They will remind you of the vows you have just spoken for all to hear, and of the eternal love that you have for one another."

"James, place the ring on Francesca's finger, and repeat after me."

I carefully grasp the ring I bought for Frankie, and place it on her left hand, which is extended in front of me.

"As this ring encircles your finger, from this moment forward, so will my love forever encircle you. You will never walk alone. My heart will be your shelter. My arms will be your home. We will walk through life as partners and best friends. I promise to do my best to love, cherish, and accept you—just the way you are. I give you my heart until the end of time. I have no greater gift to give."

I oblige and repeat the words of the officiant, phrase by phrase, as I look directly into Frankie's eyes.

"Now, Francesca, place the ring on James's finger, and repeat after me."

I extend my left hand, and she places the ring on my finger. The officiant has her repeat the same words, but with my name in it, phrase by phrase. I find myself lost in her eyes in the moment.

"By the power invested in me by the Clark County Clerk, and the State of Nevada, I now pronounce you husband and wife. James, you may kiss your beautiful bride."

Without hesitation, I plant the most passionate, wet, and loving kiss onto Frankie's lips, easily smudging her red lipstick.

The officiant turns to everyone in the procession.

"Ladies and gentlemen, it is my honor to present for the first time, Mr. and Mrs. Rossi!"

40: TWENTY-FOUR

I am certain of something, and I'm not usually known for being decisive—since, you know, I'm a Libra. The one piece of information that I am convinced of, wholeheartedly and with my full chest, is that I want to spend the rest of my life with Frankie.

A few months ago, I went out to buy a ring. You know that excited feeling you get when you buy someone a gift—whether that's for their birthday, an anniversary, a milestone, or just because—and you can't wait to give it to them? You're trying not to spoil the surprise? That's part of what I'm feeling like right now, as well as nervous out of my skin because I'm planning on asking this incredible woman to marry me and spend the rest of our lives together. Trying to hide a ring box when she likes to look through nearly everything is also more difficult than I thought it would be.

I'm hoping that she doesn't suspect anything in particular. We've been together for a couple years, and I knew about six months in that I wanted to spend forever with her by my side. Instead of sticking to Struthers, I've planned to take her to Mill Creek Metro Park in Youngstown, which is only about fifteen minutes away driving. I don't recall Frankie ever saying that she's been there, but it's nice. It's a huge park, so I think Fellows Riverside Gardens is the secluded and romantic choice. You can imagine that I don't want anyone to fuck up my moment when I'm already terrified.

I told Frankie that I would be at her house approximately 1:30 pm, so that would give us time to be at Mill Creek Park by 2:00pm. We can go eat afterwards, as I'm sure she's going to want to, but I prefer the warmth of day in an attempt to calm my nerves.

I shower, style my hair, put on some cologne, and head out the door at 1:20 pm to go pick up Frankie. When I arrive a few minutes later, she's already standing outside, since she's expecting me.

"Hi sweetheart," I said as I approached her and kissed her before I opened the car door to let her in. She leans in to the kiss and gets in the car. I close it before I go back around to the driver's side.

"Hi babe. Where are we going?"

"We're heading to Youngstown for a bit—Mill Creek Park. I've passed it a number of times when I've been in Youngstown, but never got a chance to go."

"Oh, okay. That sounds good to me." She smiled, putting a bobby pin in her hair along the right side.

Traffic was surprisingly bad going into Youngstown, so we arrive at 1:57pm. I find a place to park, and I found a map of the park. I had been told about Fellows Riverside Gardens, but never had a chance to go myself, so I'm not all that familiar with the layout. Rolling fields of grass surround us, and the light brick paths are lined on either side with various flowers in all kinds of colors. It's remarkably beautiful, and we find a gazebo that's out of the way. No one is within it, and there aren't any people for at least a few hundred yards. The gazebo has a blue roof with off-white trimmings, settled within and surrounded by luscious green grass.

We talked about anything that came to mind. We've always been able to talk each other's ears off. It doesn't matter what the topic is, where we're at, or anything else. She brings me peace, comfort, and love. I feel better when I'm with her. I feel like I can handle anything and everything. I love this woman with every fiber of my being, every beat of my heart, and every breath my lungs take. I can't imagine anyone else to beat life's trials and tribulations with me. It just doesn't exist. Somewhere between the calm, I get increasingly nervous with every minute that passes. I have observed her carefully today, and I don't think she has the faintest idea that I'm about to propose.

"Hey, Frankie?"

"Yeah?"

"I don't really know how to say this elegantly, but..."

"But what?"

"For the past two years that we've been together, we've been through so much. We've laughed until milk shot out our noses, we've cried, and we've had everything in between. All of it has been truly magical, and I have never wanted anyone else."

She looks at me quizzically. I reach into my back pocket with my right hand to grab the ring box, then get down on my right knee.

"Frankie, will you marry me?" I asked as I opened the ring box.

I watch as tears quickly surface on her beautiful face. Tears of happiness and pure joy.

"Yes! Yes, Jimmy, I will marry you!"

I put the ring on her left ring finger, and stand back up normally before kissing her. After kissing, she puts her face into my chest as she's trying to compose herself from crying.

For the next several months, we would be immersed deep into wedding planning. The date we settled on for the wedding was April 6, 1978. Frankie was both excited and nervous to send out wedding invitations, but she did so dutifully with plenty of lead time.

I asked Andrew to be my best man, since I've known him since literally kindergarten. Frankie asked Rosa to be her maid of honor. They've known each other about as long. She invited some of her childhood friends to be bridesmaids, which is expected.

Instead of having a wedding in Ohio, I thought that the west coast might be a cool idea. At some point, we agreed to get married in Vegas. Because why not? It *is* the entertainment capital of the world, after all.

Combining two Italian families is a riot. Frankie is the youngest of four siblings—she has three older brothers, all of which have threatened my life if I ever break her heart. It's fine, though. I get along with them otherwise.

41: TWENTY-THREE

Frankie and I have been dating for a year, and if this is what true, lasting love feels like, count me in. She has made me the happiest I've ever been in my life. She accepts me for who I am, counters all my witty remarks, and doesn't desire children. I just never had the paternal drive, I guess. A lot of my friends are already getting their girlfriends and wives pregnant, and I don't see any appeal to the lifestyle. That's my opinion, though. I would never force anyone to believe or live in ways inauthentic to them.

I must figure out what we will do for our anniversary, though. I'm not trying to be a shit boyfriend and won't let her think that I've forgotten the date—October 12, 1975.

I sit in my room with a yo-yo, the string hanging from the middle finger of my right hand. Extend, retract. Extend, retract. The faint noise of the yo-yo becomes metronomic as I lay here, thinking of how to plan this day out with Frankie.

I went downstairs to ask my parents because I'm at a loss. My mind is drawing nothing but blanks. Not sure where Dad went off to, but Mom is watching her shows on TV.

"Hey, Mom," I said.

"Oh, Jimmy, you scared me." She was deeply immersed in whatever she was watching, and I must have caught her off guard.

"Sorry. I meant to ask you…What do you suggest Frankie and I do today? It's our 1-year anniversary. I really can't think of anything, and she's going to kill me if I don't do something special probably."

"Hmm…" I watched as the wheels turned in Mom's eyes. She's deep in thought, just as I am.

"Think of something?"

"Why don't you take her to Geneva-on-the-Lake? We haven't been there for a decade or so by now."

"That's not a bad idea…"

"It shouldn't be freezing outside yet. The beach should still be a pleasant temperature."

"That's true. Yeah, I think I'm going to do that. Thanks, Mom!"

She smiled as we resumed watching her shows. I looked at my watch. It's only 8:07 am. Plenty of time to make it over to Frankie's, tell her to pack a small bag, and make it to Geneva-on-the-Lake. I went back upstairs to throw some of my things into a backpack—just enough for the day—then grab my car keys and head over to Frankie's. Upon arrival, I approach the front door and knocked.

Frankie's mom, Anna, answered the door.

"Hi Anna," I said, smiling.

"Oh, hello Jimmy. Are you looking for Frankie?"

"Yes, I am. Is she awake?"

"She's been up for a little bit. Please, come in. You know where her room is. Do you want some iced tea or water?"

"Iced tea would be great, thank you."

I walked into the kitchen with Anna, closing the door behind me. She grabs a pitcher of iced tea from the refrigerator, then grabs a glass from the cupboard.

"Do you want some ice in it?"

"Sure. Light ice, please."

"Alright."

She puts a few cubes of ice into my glass, then pours the iced tea. After scooting the glass over to me, she goes to grab a small container of sugar and a spoon. She hands those to me as well.

"Oh, thank you for the sugar."

"You're welcome."

I spoon a little bit of sugar into my iced tea glass, and stir thoroughly before taking a sip of it. Ahh…just right. Not too sweet, but not painfully bland either. I take the glass with me upstairs, and Frankie's room is at the end of a hallway. I knocked on her door.

"Come in," I hear her say.

I let myself in, and her face lights up like a Christmas tree.

"Jimmy!" She squeezes me tight in a hug, then kisses me. She's so cute when she's happy and excited.

"Happy anniversary, beautiful," I said as I looked into her eyes.

"You remembered!"

"Of course, I remembered our anniversary. I would never forget that."

"You're so sweet, Jimmy. I love you so much."

"Frankie, pack a bag. Just enough to go to the beach, maybe a change of clothes, and some toiletries. We're going to Geneva-on-the-Lake."

"What?! Really?!"

"Yes, really. I haven't been there in many years myself."

The realization that we are leaving as soon as possible resonates with Frankie. She immediately ran into her closet to look for a bag of suitable size and threw a few changes of clothes, her toiletries, and some makeup into it.

"Do I need to bring a bikini?" she asks.

"Well, I've got my swim trunks packed."

"Okay, I'll throw it in."

"Do you have everything now? You're not forgetting anything?"

"I think I'm ready now. I guess if I forget anything, we can always get it there."

"Alright, sounds fair to me. I planned to stay the night, and we will drive back tomorrow morning."

"Sounds fun! I'm ready when you are."

Frankie hands me her backpack, which I put on my shoulders promptly. I finish the glass of iced tea I walked up with, then hold it in my left hand while I grabbed Frankie's hand with my right. The two of us descend the stairs, and I place the empty glass on the dining table.

Anna sees us as we're about to head out.

"Where are you guys headed?"

"Geneva-on-the-Lake. Today is our anniversary. I'll bring her back tomorrow morning."

"Okay, I appreciate it. Happy anniversary, you two! Have fun up there. The weather forecast this morning said it should still be nice out."

"Thank you. Well, I guess we should get on our way."

"Bye, Mom!" Frankie said.

"See you tomorrow. Be careful," Anna said.

Frankie and I walk out of her house holding hands, and I'm careful not to slam the door when closing it. I throw her backpack next to mine on the backseat, then open the passenger door for her, closing it once she's settled. Once I get in and start the engine, I take a minute to pause and reflect on the fact I just told her to pack in a hurry because we're going on a day trip out of thin air.

I grabbed Frankie's left hand with my right and kissed it while looking in her eyes. "I love you so much, Frankie."

"I love you, too," she says, smiling from ear to ear.

"Ready to get on the road?"

"Of course!"

The two of us begin our commute north to Geneva-on-the-Lake, and I'm surprised that Frankie never asked to go to the bathroom in the hour and a half that it took to get there.

Once we arrive in the area, I find a place to park the car in front of a row of a few hotels.

"Are you hungry?" I ask Frankie.

"Yeah, I'm starving. I don't think I had time to eat breakfast before you showed up at my house earlier. I was only awake for like 45 minutes."

"Oh... Heh, sorry about that," I said, blushing slightly.

She laughed. "No, it's alright. I *was* wondering what we were going to do today, and I didn't expect this to come out of thin air."

"Well, let's find a place to get breakfast. Then maybe we can lay out in the sand for a little bit."

"That does sound nice."

The two of us settled on Mary's Kitchen, which was established in 1946. We walk inside holding hands, and approach the hostess.

"Good morning! How many people?" she asks.

"Two, please."

"Do you want a table inside or outside?"

Frankie and I look at each other for a second. "I don't have a preference. It's nice out," she says.

"Outside will work great," I told the hostess.

The hostess showed us to a 2-top table outside, bringing two menus with her and placing them in front of us individually after we took our seats. Of course, being the gentleman that I am, I pulled out Frankie's chair for her before I sat down.

"Have you guys been here before?"

"No," we say in damn near unison.

"Well, welcome to Mary's Kitchen! My name is Heather. Are you celebrating anything?"

"Today's our one-year anniversary," Frankie responds.

"Congratulations! I hope you have many more anniversaries to go. Can I get you started with some glasses of water?"

"Yes, that would be great. Can you please bring some lemons as well?"

"Of course! I'll be right back with those waters, and I'll go grab your server. Lauren will be your server today."

"Okay, thank you. We appreciate it."

Within a few minutes, she returned with two glasses of ice water, two straws, and a saucer of sliced lemons.

"Thank you, Heather," Frankie said.

Heather glanced over her shoulder in anticipation. "Oh, I see Lauren heading in this direction. She'll be over in just a second."

A second woman approaches our table in under a minute. Impressively fast, if I say so myself.

"Good morning! My name is Lauren. I'll be your server today. Did you have a chance to look at the menu? Are you ready to order?"

I glance over at Frankie, checking if she's ready. I always let her order first. Ladies first.

"I think I'm ready," Frankie says, making eye contact with Lauren.

"Alright, what will you be having?"

"I'll have the veggie omelet."

"What kind of toast would you like with that?"

"Hm… sourdough."

"Will that be all for you, ma'am?"

175

"For food, yes. Can I also get a hot tea when you have a chance?"

"Of course. And for you, sir?"

"I'll have the Classic, please."

"How would you like your eggs?"

"Scrambled."

"Choice of meat? Sausage, bacon, or ham?"

"Bacon."

"What kind of bread for the toast?"

"Wheat."

"Anything else?"

"I'll take a cup of coffee."

"Alright. Just to make sure I've got everything straight, one veggie omelet with sourdough toast, and one Classic with bacon and wheat toast."

"You got it!" Frankie said.

"Alright, I will get that started for you. Just flag me down if you need anything."

"Thank you," I said, taking a sip of my water.

It takes about twenty minutes for our food to come out, and I'm not going to lie—it's *delicious*.

"How is it?"

"This omelet is amazing," Frankie says, satisfied with her order.

Normally, we talk a lot, but I guess we were both too hungry to talk. We sit in silence as we eat our breakfast, and once we've both satisfactorily inhaled everything, I flagged down Lauren.

"Can I get our check, please?"

"Oh, sure. I'll be right back with that. Everything taste alright?"

"Fantastic. We will come back to eat here if we make it to Geneva in the future."

"Glad to hear it!" Lauren said, smiling.

She returns a few minutes later, and I pay to cover the cost of everything plus a 20% tip.

"Ready to head out?" I asked Frankie.

"Sure. What are we doing now?"

"We can change and go lay out on the beach, then worry about the hotel for tonight afterwards."

"Alright, sounds good. Let's get our bathing suits and towels out of the car."

We got up from our chairs, making sure to push them in before leaving the table. I grabbed Frankie's hand, interlacing our fingers. She kisses me on the right side of my face, her lips meeting stubble where my beard usually grows. God damn it, I need to shave. I still appreciate her love and affection.

Once we get back to the car, I unlock the passenger door of the back seat. I reach in and grab her bag first, then mine, promptly closing the door behind me and locking it. I noticed that Frankie was looking around for the public restroom along the shoreline.

"Looks like there's a restroom just up ahead," she said.

"Oh, yeah, I see it. Do you have a towel too?"

"Uh... I think so? Let me check." She begins to rummage through her bag, and comes up empty handed.

"Shit, I think I forgot it..."

I laughed. "It's fine, I packed two just in case."

She signed in relief. "Oh, thank God."

"Alright, let's go change, and then we can worry about finding a place to relax."

We make our way to the public restroom, splitting up as I go towards the men's and her the women's. I walk into a stall and lock the door before stripping naked, then pull my swim trunks out of my bag to put them on. Did I bring my sunscreen? I look frantically through my bag again, even though I shouldn't be overly worried about it. I tan pretty easily. After a few minutes of going through my possessions, I come up empty-handed on the sunscreen. Hopefully Frankie has some—she's a bit more pale than I am, and she turns into a lobster for a few days if she doesn't use sunscreen. I pack my street clothing into my backpack, zip it up, and walk out in front of the restrooms. Frankie isn't out here yet, so she must still be changing.

After a few more minutes, Frankie emerges from the women's restroom in a purple bikini.

"Oh...wow... You look amazing, babe," I said. The man part of my brain wanted to say something far more vulgar, but we're in public, and I don't want to embarrass her (or myself for that matter). She might slap me if I did.

"Thank you, handsome," she said, then angled her head up towards mine to kiss me. I pull her closer to me to kiss her.

"So where do you want to set up?"

Frankie walks out in front of me, and looks in every direction, scanning the shoreline and sandy beach for an opening.

"Hm... What about over there?" she says, pointing east. I see a spot that's not occupied by anyone approximately 50 feet away.

"Let's go," I said as I reached to hold her hand.

I grabbed the two towels out of my bag and lay them next to each other on the sand. Frankie grabbed a book she was reading out of her bag, and situates herself on one of the towels. Both of us have always been avid readers. She lays on her back, leaning the spine of the book against her legs. She also puts on her sunglasses since the sun is shining directly at us.

"Are you comfortable like that? Do you want a drink or anything? I can go grab us some drinks."

She thinks for a moment, putting a finger to her lips.

"Can you get me a tequila sunrise?"

"Alright. I'll go do that. I love you, sweetheart," I said, kissing her lips before I get up. I find a bar with ease and approach the counter.

"Hi, can I get a tequila sunrise and an old fashioned, please?"

"Of course. Can I see your ID?"

I pull out my wallet and show her my driver's license, and watch as she does the mental math to calculate my age. She hands it back to me.

The bartender looks at me inquisitively. "Thank you. Will that be all for you, sir?"

"Yes, ma'am."

She gives me a total, and I paid it while leaving a tip. The bar wasn't super busy, so she gets my drinks to me quickly.

I go back to the spot where Frankie is reading, and she looks surprised. Like she wasn't expecting me back so quick.

"Oh, that was fast," she said.

"Yeah, it wasn't crowded. Here's your tequila sunrise." I handed the cocktail to her.

"Thank you," she said, immediately taking a sip of it. I took a sip of my old fashioned at the same time.

"Oh, man, this is *awesome*," she remarked, satisfied with how the bartender made it.

"Glad she mixed it just right then. Mine is good, too."

I sit on my towel, holding my drink in my right hand, and using my left to prop myself up. It's a beautiful day, and I'm with a beautiful woman that I love with every fiber of my being. Life doesn't get any better.

42: TWENTY-TWO

I've gone through...a lot since returning from Vietnam. Not all of it has been for the better, either. People are truly not grateful for the men that have served in Vietnam up until now, and they certainly aren't going to change their tune for anyone after me. I'm trying not to take it personal, but it's difficult when you've had to see some of the guys that you went overseas with die from various causes—drug overdose, being shot and killed on the front lines, and everything in between.

On a Sunday morning, I decided to attend church with Jeremy and my parents. The four of us make our entrance into Saint Nicholas, and I saw a familiar face. Someone I haven't seen since the two of us were in high school. It's Frankie. She makes eye contact with me as she is walking towards the row that she and her parents are sitting in.

"James!"

"Oh my, Frankie. It's been a few years." I opened my arms to embrace her in a hug, and she takes the opportunity to give me a tight hug. She's a short girl, about 5'3", so her head comes at chest level for me in the process. She pulls back just enough to be able to have a conversation.

"How have you been? I haven't seen you since high school."

"Ah, well... I got back from Vietnam last year."

A look that consists of equal parts surprise and sorrow came across her face.

"Oh... Um... How was that? How long were you there?"

"Just a year. Then I got flown back to the U.S. to serve out another year in the Ohio National Guard, so that'll be up within the next several months."

"Are you okay? Did anything happen?" She seemed deeply concerned for my well-being for someone I haven't seen in five or six years.

"Yeah, I'm good. I really just missed Mom's cooking."

She laughed as she thought about her next response. "I bet you did."

"Hey Frankie... What do you say we go to dinner one day? How would you feel about that?"

Frankie cocks an eyebrow. "James... Are you asking me on a date right now?"

"What if I am?"

"Yes! Just let me know where and what time." Frankie was beaming with excitement. I had no idea she even liked me this much.

"What about at Elmton on 5th Street on Tuesday at 6 pm? Does that work for you?"

"Sure does! Oh... Looks like Mass is going to start in a minute. Let's talk after?"

"Sure. That sounds great."

That's crazy. I've liked Frankie for a long time, but never had the thought that she wanted me back. I've been too scared to ask her out until just now. I don't know where I got the courage from, but I'm glad it happened.

Mass goes by in an hour sharp, and everyone immediately starts to head out the door.

"Mom, Dad, I'll meet you at home. I'm going to meet up with someone."

Mom raised a curious eyebrow at me. "Who are you meeting up with?"

"Do you remember that girl Frankie I met in high school?"

"Yeah..."

"I'm going to talk to her a bit. I will find my way home later."

"Oh... Well, alright. Have fun."

I wait a minute on the right side of the church doors, and then Frankie finally comes out.

"Frankie!"

She looks around and makes eye contact with me.

"Oh! Hi Jimmy," she said as her beautiful face was graced with another smile.

"So, uh, what do you want to do? My parents and Jeremy already took off and headed home. I said I was going to meet up with you."

I watch as the gears turn in her eyes, trying to come up with ideas of things to do. "Hm..."

"We could go to Yellow Creek Park and hang out a bit? I haven't been there in a long time."

"Yeah, that sounds fun!"

The two of us walk to Yellow Creek Park, and the conversation flows seamlessly. There is not a dull moment with her, and being with her feels peaceful and comfortable. I feel as if my heart skips a beat when she looks at me straight on, her blue eyes glistening and sparkling. Wow, I have never given serious thought to how beautiful she is. She's stunning. She's always been a pretty girl, but it didn't occur to me just how much I liked her. I wish I had spoken up when we were in high school, but then there's a good chance that everything would be a lot different if that had been the case.

We arrive at Yellow Creek Park, and find a bench to sit on. I don't have any bread or food for the ducks here at the moment, but I have Frankie, and that's even better. She takes her seat first and adjusts the dress she's wearing so she doesn't have a wardrobe malfunction, although I wouldn't care if she did.

There is about a minute of silence between us, but it feels like an eternity. She twirls small sections of her long dark brown hair around with her fingers and seems potentially nervous about something. She is staring off into the distance.

"Frankie, there's something I want to tell you..."

She turns to face me, making direct eye contact. My heart is pounding out of my chest, and I can feel sweat starting to come. I hope I don't get rejected.

"Yes?"

"Well... I..."

She doesn't break eye contact, but does expect me to finish my sentence. I manage to graze the top of her hand with the tips of my fingers. She didn't flinch or negatively react.

"I've liked you since we met in high school. I still remember the day that you yelled for me across the hallway when I was going to class. I think you're beautiful, and I'm upset with myself for waiting this long to tell you."

"Jimmy, I—"

"I know, I just let that all out..."

"No, no. It's not that. Jimmy, I've liked you since high school, *too*! I always wondered what happened to you after graduation, and then earlier you told me that you went to Vietnam for a year. I—I don't know. My emotions are all over the place, and I'm not usually like this..."

"Frankie?"

"Jimmy?"

"Can I kiss you?"

"Yes. Please."

I grab her face with my right hand, and bring her as close to me as possible, then plant an open-mouthed kiss on her. She follows my lead easily, and the next thing you know, we're making out in broad daylight on a Sunday in Yellow Creek Park. I feel the fingers of her left hand running through my hair, while her right arm is around my waist. I put my left hand on her face as well, although briefly, and then put it on the back of her head to support her. I didn't notice this earlier, but we somehow have also shifted to be facing each other on the bench, one of our legs on either side of it. She's careful to not let her dress expose her and keeps everything covered.

"Wow," she said.

"That was...um...amazing." I feel myself blushing a bit. I took a look at my watch, and realized that I have to be home on time today because we're having some of my mom's side of the family over for dinner.

"So what do you want to do now?" she inquires.

"Well, I have to go home because my family is coming over for dinner later. I'm sure Mom's already been cooking up a storm. Can I walk you home?"

"Yeah, that would be nice."

As it turns out, Frankie and I only live a block apart from each other. That's very convenient. We make the walk from Yellow Creek Park to her home, and get there about 15-20 minutes later.

"See you Tuesday? I'll come by here and we can go together?"

"That sounds good."

"Alright, I'll catch you later." I kiss her again before we part ways, and I watch as she goes inside her house.

~ * ~

I asked my sergeant to leave work early on Tuesday so that I would have time to get home, change, shower, shave, and get ready to go on my date with Frankie. Shockingly, he approves it. I'm nervous, even though I just saw her two days ago, and it went *very* well, all things considered. I smell and look homeless upon leaving work, so I certainly need to clean myself up before seeing anyone, especially a beautiful woman.

Once I get home, I quickly run to my room to get an acceptable change of clothes, boxers, a bath towel, toothbrush, toothpaste, and socks, then bolt straight for the shower. The house was built by my grandpa and my dad, and they decided to put the shower in the basement. No idea why, but that's all I've ever known. I turn the water on, and let it run for about a minute for it to warm up. I'm not planning on freezing my balls off while I clean myself. After the water has reached a suitable temperature, I strip naked and go in, closing the curtain behind me. I wet my hair, then my body, and grab the loofah that I have hanging from the hook to the right of the shower faucet handle. I squeeze some body wash onto it, and lather it everywhere. Following that, I apply shampoo and conditioner, making sure to rinse thoroughly between each product. I'm trying to be quick about this since I would hate to leave Frankie waiting. After brushing my teeth, I quickly step on the mat outside the shower and dry myself off. I get dressed as quickly as possible, and put some pomade in my hair to style it nicely.

I'll come back later to organize all the stuff in the basement. I'm in a hurry to get out the door. I ran upstairs, grabbed my car keys, and drove over to Frankie's as fast as possible while narrowly avoiding a speeding ticket. I made it there in about ten minutes, and Elmton's wasn't horribly far thankfully. Once I'm at the door, I knock three times. Frankie's mom answers the door.

"Oh, hello Jimmy! Is Frankie expecting you?"

"Yes, she is. Is she ready?"

"Give me one second. Do you want to come in for a minute?"

"Sure, I appreciate it."

The two of us walk inside the house, and she calls for Frankie by yelling.

"Frankie! Jimmy's here looking for you!"

"I'll be down in a minute!" I hear Frankie yell from upstairs, albeit somewhat faintly. It ends up not being *one* minute, but more like *ten* minutes by the time

Frankie descends the stairs. Oh well, it's fine.

"Hi Jimmy," she said smiling.

"Oh, wow, Frankie. You look great!" My eyes glimmer as I look at her. God damn it, she is *stunning*!

"Thank you, Jimmy."

"Ready to head out?"

"Ready if you are."

"I'll have her back before it gets too late, Mrs. Mancini."

"Alright. You two have fun!" Her mom has always been such a sweet woman.

I open the passenger front door of my car for Frankie, wait until she's settled to close it, then circle around the front end of the car to get into the driver's seat. I insert the key and turn over the engine, and drive the two of us to Elmton. Since Struthers is so small, it's only about a five-minute drive. The parking lot is small, so it can be a struggle to find somewhere to park, depending on the day you come. I did find a spot, and pulled the front end of the car into it carefully and precisely. I walk around to the passenger side to open Frankie's door for her, and she gets out.

"Shall we?" I ask, offering my hand to her, palm facing up. She smiles and grabs my hand, interlacing our fingers. Wow, she already seems comfortable with me.

We walk into Elmton, and order a 16" cheese pizza to share. As for drinks, I order an iced tea (my usual whenever I go out to eat anywhere), and Frankie orders a Sprite. We both ask for a glass of ice water, too. Our drinks come out quickly. Initially, I grabbed two packets of Sweet-n-Low, and dump them both into my iced tea, making sure to stir thoroughly with the straw. Frankie unwraps her straw and sticks it into her Sprite.

"What have you been up to since the other day?" I asked her.

"Hm... Not a lot. I went to get groceries yesterday for the house, since Mom asked me to. Honestly, I've been excited for this, too, and haven't been able to sleep much."

"Really?" Shit, I can feel myself blushing.

"Yes, of course." Jesus Hussein Christ, how is she so distractingly beautiful?

For the next 2.5 hours, the two of us become lost in conversation, bouncing across topics easily and readily. She's not only beautiful, but incredibly intelligent, too. As the evening is winding down, I asked for the check. Within a few minutes, the server comes over with it, and I paid the bill in cash while giving a 20% tip.

The two of us go back to my car, and of course I open and hold the passenger side door for her. Once I go back around to the driver's seat and close my door, starting the vehicle, I let the car run for a minute before I put it into reverse to take her home.

"Hey Frankie, I've had a really great night with you."

"I enjoy your company, too, Jimmy."

"Frankie, would you...um..."

"What is it? It's okay, you can come out and say it."

"Do you want to be my girlfriend? I *really* like you."

"Yes, I would like that very much." She smiled, her eyes wide and glowing.

I lean across the center console, grabbed her face, and kissed her. How did I ever get so lucky?

"Alright, let's go home before your parents kill me for bringing you back too late."

"Sounds good," she said as she laughed.

We drove back to her house, and I parallel parked just to the left of the driveway along the sidewalk.

"Thank you for such a wonderful night," I told her.

"I had fun, too!"

I went to let her out of the car, and after I closed the door, I gave her another kiss...which turned into making out for a few minutes. Not that I mind.

"Good night, Frankie. I'll see you soon," I said, as I embraced her in a warm hug.

"Good night, Jimmy."

I watched as she approached the front door, unlocked it with her key, and went inside.

43: TWENTY-ONE

One night, I got a couple of hours of sleep before I heard someone barge in and yell, "Rossi!"

I saw a couple of the other guys lift their heads in response, but they laid back down. I bolted awake immediately, my heart pounding in my chest. "Sir?"

"Get your things together. You're being sent back stateside." Wait, was this real? I wasn't expecting it so soon.

"Right now, sir?"

I watched as the sergeant approached my bunk.

"Yes, right now. The pilot won't be waiting very long."

I looked at my watch, which I didn't take off apparently before falling asleep. It's...1:24 AM?!

"Alright, give me a second."

I hastily throw on my pants and jacket, lace up my boots, and then pack all of my other belongings into my duffel bag. We didn't come with much on the way here, so it didn't take long to pack everything. The whole process took two minutes—tops.

"I'm ready, sir."

Sergeant Mills sized me up quickly. "Follow me."

The two of us trek through the swamps and mud of the Vietnamese landscape. Sarge is holding a flashlight to illuminate the path, and I'm keeping an eye out for any potential surprise attacks. It's hardwired into my brain at this point.

With every step, I feel exhaustion trying to take over. It's not a short route that takes a couple of minutes tops. We end up having to travel what feels like a couple of *miles* on foot. Finally, we reach the plane, and the steps to board are descended for me.

"Is anyone else going back with me, Sarge?"

"Yes, there are a few others. Not a lot, though."

"Okay. Well...I guess I better climb aboard then unless--"

"Wait. Hold on a second."

Sergeant Mills reaches into his jacket pocket, and takes out a folded piece of paper.

"What's this?"

"Your new orders, since you're going back stateside."

"Oh. Right. Thank you, Sarge."

"Take care of yourself, Private Rossi."

He extended his right hand, and I shook his hand respectfully.

"I will. Good luck to you for however long you're out here, Sarge."

"Appreciate it."

I walked further away from Sarge and towards the steps to board the aircraft. Upon entry, I notice about seven other soldiers, most of who are passed out cold. I wonder how long *they've* been sleeping on this aircraft before I got here, as I seem to be the last one. It's crazy to think we were just woken up in the middle of the night, or taken out of whatever we were doing, and being told to pack up and go home. Since there are so few of us, the guys are spread out, and keeping their bag on the seat next to them. Once I'm settled in, the cabin door closes.

I heard the pilot pick up the intercom from the cockpit.

"Welcome aboard, gentlemen. I assume most of you are asleep. We are heading back to the United States, and will be touching down in Los Angeles as our point of entry. Keep your orders handy, as they will help us get you to your necessary destinations individually. We will be taking off shortly."

I strap myself in, and lay the seat back as much as it will allow, applying my head to the headrest. I guess we'll see how long it takes me to fall back asleep.

Although there aren't many of us aboard the aircraft right now, you wouldn't think that if you only heard the audio. Out of the seven, three are snoring *loudly*, mouths agape, and the whole nine yards.

I'm not quite ready to fall asleep yet, and I know it'll take me a little bit to get there. I get out the book I brought with me, and opened it to the dog-eared page. Yes, I know, I shouldn't dog-ear pages... Sue me. It's my copy, no one else's, and it's not like anyone's going to beat down my door to read this novel anyway. I managed to read about twenty pages, then I started feeling tired again. I looked at my watch. The time reads 2:47 AM. Has it been that long?

I adjusted myself in the chair, careful to not remove or jostle the seatbelt too much. No one's in the seat directly in front of me, so I'm able to stretch my legs out. I'm sure I won't always have the luxury of legroom like this on other flights once we get back to the United States. Los Angeles is full of people, and just trying to walk or drive around that city makes you feel like you're crowded in like sardines. I can't imagine that it'll get any better as the years go by. Not sure I'd ever want to visit Los Angeles on my own accord, but Vegas doesn't seem so bad. This is coming from a guy who has yet to make it to Vegas, but has every intention of going.

As the aircraft makes its way through the skies, we hit a little bit of turbulence, but the captain has things under control swiftly. I take a deep breath and close my eyes, starting to count in reverse. 100... 99... 98... 97... 96... 95...

Finally, mercifully, I fell asleep.

~ * ~

Several hours later, I was woken up by the pilot talking on the intercom again. That may have been some of the best sleep I've had in years, to my surprise.

"Gentlemen, we are about an hour away from touching down in Los Angeles. Please prepare yourselves accordingly."

I yawned and rubbed my eyes, then took a swig of some of the water I had in my bag. I literally just slept about 18 hours, and I still feel somewhat tired. Maybe it's all the nights where I didn't get enough sleep, or had to wake up throughout the night for my duties.

The captain kept true to his word. Within an hour, our aircraft touched down on the runway in Los Angeles. I pulled my orders document out of my jacket pocket that Sergeant Mills gave me just before we left Vietnam. I unfurled the paper, trying to smooth out the folds and creases. To my surprise, it says that I'm being returned to Ohio to finish out another year in the Ohio National Guard.

Thank God. I can't wait to see my parents again, and to have homemade Italian food for the first time since I left for Basic Training.

44: TWENTY

Why am I here? Why am I in Vietnam? I can't get answers for any of my questions from my chain of command, or any other soldier that's in South Vietnam for that matter.

Upon arrival into the country, the guys in my unit immediately try to settle ourselves in our living quarters. By no means is it the best environment. The terrain is swampy, and it's difficult to find our way around. Once the sun goes down, unless you have a high-powered flashlight, you are screwed if you try to navigate your way around on foot.

All of us hope to make it out alive, but deep down in our hearts, we know that won't happen. Some men will die, even though the oldest person in my platoon is *maybe* 22 years old. We're being led by a lieutenant who is about the same age, and is also scared shitless, yet is in charge of 30 of our lives. Joel, the lone medic, is beside himself, knowing that he is going to be targeted specifically for the fact that he *is* a medic. He's more likely to lose his life while doing his job of helping a wounded brother than at any other time on the battlefront. We are thousands of miles away from our homes, from the comforts of the United States, and only have each other to rely on. Crazy that we came here as strangers on a boat, and now we will have to trust each other with our *lives*.

Nothing prepares you for war. No matter how much training, education, and practice you have, nothing compares to the experience of being thrust into a foreign country and having to accommodate a whole new culture, people, and customs. Nobody tells you that the guy sleeping in the bunk next to you one night could have his body blown to pieces before dawn, and that you just have to move on despite the trauma that you just witnessed. Nobody tells you that hearing gunfire and innocent civilians dying in the streets will haunt you for years to come.

Each night, I'm asked to safeguard one of our military posts, and make sure that my fellow soldiers aren't doing anything *too* wild. Some guys have fallen victim to substance abuse, as there are still long periods of downtime that we have to deal with. Yes, believe it or not, war can be boring. At least this one is.

Mental health and morale are at an all-time low in our platoon. I've been in Vietnam for about a year, and the days all seem to run together. There is no differentiation between Monday and Tuesday, or Tuesday and Wednesday, and so on. Going by age alone, we should have our entire lives ahead of us. Not everybody sees it that way, however. The doom and gloom outlook has overtaken many—not just in my platoon, but every soldier in the Army, every airman in the Air Force, and every sailor in the Navy.

Unfortunately, many guys have subjected themselves to substance abuse and addiction—the more common drugs of choice being cocaine and heroin. Being away from everything we know and love has taken its toll, and the output has been less than glorious. At least once a week, whether I'm out and about with the infantry or staying close to our posts, I witness a drug overdose of some variety. I'm the one that has to report it to the chain of command. Sometimes, I witness it happen in real-time.

The Vietnamese forces sure do love their guerilla warfare tactics, too. You could be minding your own business, even while keeping a close eye and ear out for someone to ambush you, and you *still* won't sense them coming from some random direction you didn't account for. They also have the advantage of knowledge and familiarity, since it's their own country they have spent their entire lives in. Some of them are loaded with weapons, and some prefer hand-to-hand combat. There is no way of telling which kind of fighter you are going to face on the other end, so you need to be prepared for anything and everything.

Meanwhile, we've been here for a year, and I truly miss Mom's cooking. The food rations are deplorable, and disgusting is not a strong enough word to describe the taste (or lack thereof, really). Flavorless and unseasoned doesn't even begin to describe the God-awful state of it. I miss my friends that I grew up with, too. I wonder what Andrew has been up to. Or Stephanie. Or Frankie... I always did like Frankie, ever since we've met really, but I never had the balls to ask her on a date yet. To me, she's always been beautiful. Why am I like this?!

Growing up in Struthers, it doesn't take a rocket scientist to figure out that it's a very small town. Just about everyone knows each other, and newcomers or visitors stand out readily. That's how it is in the Midwest when you're not from a major metropolitan area. Neighbors know each other and talk. You probably know your mail carrier, and there's a good chance that they have seen you grow up when they stop by your house along their route. Every time you change schools, it's a lot of the same people, with the rare transfer or new student from year to year. It's not the most exciting all the time, but there's one word that it is—predictable. You can go outside and play, and your mom doesn't even worry about what you're doing unless she needs you or tells you to be back in time for dinner. Since my family knows nearly everyone with a child my age, making friends has been easy. You didn't have to put any effort into it, either. Simply go outside, and if there was a kid close enough in age, they'd probably be willing to talk to you and become friends.

What's crazy is that, during this whole stay, I've barely thought about my younger brother Jeremy. I'm sure he's being a menace to Mom and Dad, considering he should be a freshman at Struthers High School now. I sure remember the first time I stepped foot onto that campus. I was a nervous wreck.

45: NINETEEN

I shipped to Basic Training on January 7, 1971, from my home in Struthers, Ohio to Fort Jackson, South Carolina. When I tell you that the people here are a lot different than my small-town upbringing in the Midwest, believe me— they are.

When I first arrived, I was told to pack a couple of days' worth of clothing into a bag. Upon arrival, we were processed in addition to what we had to do in MEPS (at the local board). Every man had to get the standard buzz cut (I cringed and lamented as I said goodbye to my hair that I usually kept styling gel in), was given a ton of immunization shots (I lost track of the number honestly), and had to take aptitude tests to determine what MOS we would be sent to technical school for following Basic. According to how I scored, I'm going to be trained as an MP after I'm done with Basic Training. Did I mention that you also had to pay the civilian barber?

I feel like I'm fighting for my life here. These drill sergeants are not fucking around. My body is tired, my brain is depleted, and the food is average *at best*. God, I miss Mom's cooking so much right now.

I'm three weeks in, and have another five weeks to go. I'm not a morning person either, yet they have us awake before the sun comes up (like 4 AM), where we must run about 5-6 miles before we even get to *eat breakfast* in the chow hall. Yes, on an empty stomach. I don't think a single one of us ever got a full night's sleep either, considering we had to rotate who was on watch every night. What happened was that a soldier would have to be on watch for 1-2 hours, and after the previous soldier goes to bed (assuming you're able to fall asleep practically immediately, which I've never been able to do), the next one wakes up to complete his shift. This went on every night, and you better hope you got some semblance of sleep if you were the last one to stand watch before the drill sergeants came bursting through to wake everyone else up for morning drill. The United States military truly has a way of breaking down everything about you, to the point where you want to give up, and then build you back up the way that they want you to be. In many ways, it's pure indoctrination at the highest level, yet no one wants to talk about it.

In addition to all of that, the PT was *ruthless*. Alongside running, we had to do PT before breakfast and lunch, and the favorite exercise for this seemed to be the horizontal bars. The drill sergeants would make us *all* do about 88 horizontal bars. It was very obvious that many of the guys were not used to doing the horizontal bars, as you could see the blood being left behind on them before they had a chance to develop callouses on their hands. If you collapsed during training, you were given a *brief* recovery period, and then you were expected to get back up to complete the exercise. There is no such thing as "giving up" when you are being trained and conditioned to be an enemy-slaying, killing machine. That is the only thing that matters to the government and chain of command in times of war.

Something else that I'm not used to, and I'd argue the same for anyone else in my unit, is hand-to-hand combat training. This training also included the use of bayonets. We did a variety of different tasks that were meant to build up our individual and collective confidence, among which included grappling and pugil stick exercises.

Possibly one of the most prominent social changes is the complete and utter hatred of the Vietnamese that is being shoved down everyone's throats, almost as soon as you step off the bus at Basic Training. Although the war has been going on for a while now, even if there was no official declaration of war by the White House, the level of xenophobia towards practically anyone Asian (but especially the Vietnamese) didn't make a lot of sense to someone like me that grew up in a small town. You would think that it would affect me more, but I've simply been too busy with my own life up to this point to really notice. My hometown of Struthers is largely homogenous, and anyone outside of the different flavors of white was simply uncommon. It's not that I harbored hate for any given race.

Fort Jackson feels like a fucking prison, and I can't say I'd recommend the experience. Most people who have ever been in the military will tell you about the rigidity, the rules, and how getting screamed at by drill sergeants or other authority figures is just a way of life. Here, you don't get to have an opinion. You don't get to stand out. You do as you're told, without question. God help you if you speak out against your leadership… That's the fast track to getting your entire unit to hate you because the drill sergeant made *everyone* do even more PT when our bodies and minds were already exhausted.

~ * ~

After I scraped by finishing Basic Training, which I felt like I only survived by the skin of my teeth some days, I was then shipped off to Fort Leonard Wood, Missouri for AIT (advanced individual training) as an MP, with the MOS 31B.

One of the first disciplines you're taught as an MP is military police law and order. As you can imagine, this does vary quite a bit from what you'd expect from law enforcement in the civilian realm. To boot (no pun intended), MPs are sworn to uphold the Uniform Code of Military Justice (UCMJ), first and foremost. That is not a document that most civilians would have any knowledge of beyond knowing it *exists* as a document.

I'd never been outside of Ohio before getting drafted, and I also really miss my own bed right now. I can't really say that Fort Leonard Wood is any better. Actually, I think it's worse. There is a reason that they call the state of Missouri as Misery. There is *nothing* to do here! The guys in my unit seem alright, I guess. We all miss home, and it feels like everyone is from a different state.

Little was I aware that my American way of life would be changing in a couple months' time. After I finish AIT in Fort Jackson, I'm going back to Ohio for eight weeks, then I'll be on the next troop ship to Vietnam. They really aren't wasting anyone's time, as this war has been going on since I was three years old. How do I feel about it? I'm honestly scared shitless. But it doesn't matter how I feel, does it? The United States government doesn't care how you feel. What they care about is having enough men being shipped overseas to support and defend the Constitution of the United States against all enemies, foreign and domestic; that I will bear true faith and allegiance to the same; and that I will obey the orders of the President of the United States and the orders of the officers appointed over me, according to regulations and the Uniform Code of Military Justice. So help me God.

46: EIGHTEEN

On a typical afternoon in October, I went to go check the mail. Our mailbox resides right in front of our house within the grass of our front yard. I open the front door of the mailbox to take out the contents, and casually flip through the envelopes in my hand as I walk back to the side door of the house.

"That's for Dad... another for Dad... Mom... What's this?"

A single envelope is addressed to *me,* which is unusual because I don't get a ton of mail. I walk back inside the house, and place the envelopes—other than the one addressed to me—to the right of the kitchen sink just before the entryway into the kitchen. That's where we've always kept our mail as far as I'm aware. I take the envelope addressed to me up to my room, since I want some privacy while I read through this. I just felt like I *should* have privacy when reading my own mail.

I unfurl my pocketknife that I carry with me (you never know when you're going to need one), and slip it under the top fold of the envelope, making a slit to tear it open. I stick my hand in the envelope, and take out the paper that's inside. Upon opening the paper, it reads:

```
Selective Service System
ORDER TO REPORT FOR INDUCTION
```

```
You are hereby ordered for induction into the
Armed Forces of the United States, and to report
at Local Board #80 on November 1, 1970 at 8:30 AM.
```

There are a few paragraphs of text underneath that as well, some of it stating that if I don't appear and give a *damn good* reason to have an exemption, I will face fines and/or imprisonment.

I... What? I'm being *drafted?* It makes sense, I guess... I just turned 18 in the last few weeks, and the Vietnam War is still going on overseas. Mom will certainly not be amused by this. I'm not sure how Dad will feel about it, considering he was drafted as well, but he went during WWII.

I hear Mom and Dad talking about God knows what downstairs from my room, albeit very faintly. They're home, so I guess now is a good time to tell them the latest news…

I make my way downstairs from my room, the paper in my right hand, and go into the kitchen. The two of them are having a conversation peacefully. Too bad I'm about to ruin their day.

"Hey."

Both turn to face me, doing it almost at the exact same time.

"Oh, hey. What's up?" Dad inquires.

"Well… I have some news."

"What's that?" Mom asks, eyeing the paper.

"Um… My number was called for the draft…"

"WHAT?!" I knew Mom would react this way. She's predictable by now. I watch carefully as her eyes start to water. Dad, however, looks more curious than freaked out.

"Well… When do you have to report at the local board?" he asks.

"It says here on November 1 at 8:30 AM."

"Oh, wow, that's pretty soon…"

"MY BABY IS GOING TO VIETNAM?!?!"

"Yes, Mom, that's what it seems like." I sighed. She's crying hysterically. I hate seeing her like this. She collapsed into Dad's arms, her face buried in his chest. Being the older brother between Jeremy and I, there's pressure to keep up appearances and be responsible. If you're the oldest sibling, you understand my pain.

~ * ~

I am more afraid of prison than I am going to war, so I show up to the local board at 8:15 AM (since I prefer to be early, not just "on time") on November 1. (Truth is, I'm too handsome and intelligent for prison. I would never make it.) I bring the paper, my driver's license, and any other government-issued documentation with me in a folder. Upon arrival, I take a number and find an available chair to sit in while I wait to be called. My draft lottery number is five, so I will be one of the earlier ones.

After about fifteen minutes pass by, I hear my number called. "Number 5, Rossi." I approach the local board volunteer.

"Full legal name please?" he asks me. The man appears to be in his 40s, his salt and pepper hair sparse in some places, glasses on his face, and has a fair complexion. He's probably about an average build.

"James Antonio Rossi."

"Date of birth?"

"September 28, 1952."

"Legal address?"

"150 Omar Street, Struthers, OH 44471."

"Mr. Rossi, do you have an active passport currently?"

"No, sir, I would need one."

"May I see your Social Security Card and photo ID, please?"

I opened the folder I was carrying with me, and provided him with my Social Security Card. I reached into my back pocket to take out my Driver's License. He compares my name on both documents, then takes another look at me.

The gentleman asks me to have a seat again, but the next time that my name is called, I will be seen by the on-site physician for a medical and physical evaluation. I brought a book with me because I figured this wouldn't be quick or efficient. I mean, this is the United States government we're talking about.

In the 45 minutes that they had me waiting to be called back by the physician, I managed to read 50 more pages of my book. I've always been a fast reader, which is why I think I've done well in school.

"Rossi, James." I scan the room again, and see a man that's about 6' tall, rectangular glasses, a white doctor's coat, and a stethoscope hanging around his neck.

"Coming," I call back to him. He waits a minute for me to walk over to him, to where I'm about a foot in front of him.

"Can I see that folder you're holding? What's in it?"

"My legal documents. Social Security Card, driver's license, birth certificate. Things like that."

"Ah, right. Come on back with me."

I follow the physician down a hallway. We walk past ten patient rooms, five on either side of the hallway, then he opens the door to the sixth one on the right-hand side. He walks in first, then I follow behind him. He sits down on the physician's stool, and I sat towards the foot of the patient bed, my feet hanging off the bottom of it.

"Let's start with the easy information. How tall are you?"

"Five feet, ten inches." I watch as he writes this information down.

"Step on the scale, please."

I oblige, and observe as he moves the levers on the scale.

"Looks like... 170 lbs."

"Yeah, that sounds about right."

"James, are you able to provide a urine sample right now? That way we can get that to the lab while we do everything else?"

"Sure, I can do that."

The doctor grabs a small cup with a lid on it, and hands it to me.

"The restrooms are three doors down on the left-hand side. Women's restroom is to the right in that area, men's is to the left. Just come back into this room with the sample when you're done."

"Okay, will do."

I follow his directions and was able to locate the men's restroom quickly. I walk up to an empty urinal, and I'm quickly able to pee into this cup until it's full. I finish emptying my bladder into the urinal, and make sure to flush since I'm not a disgusting man. My mother raised me to be a lot cleaner and more respectful than that, particularly in public. I make sure to wash my hands before leaving the men's room, and take the urine sample with me back to the patient room that the doctor is in.

"Here's my urine sample," I said while handing it to him.

"Great, thanks. Let me get this to a nurse so that we can get it sent to the lab."

He opens the door back up, and looks for a nurse. "Bethany!"

A blonde woman who looks to be in her early 30s whips her head around to the doctor. "Yes?"

"Can you take this urine sample to the lab please?"

"Oh, sure. Be right over in a second."

She puts down the file folder that was in her hands, presumably another patient's chart, and does a slight jog over to the doctor to pick up my urine sample.

"Thanks," he says. She walks off with the urine sample and heads the opposite direction.

"Alright, next is going to be the vision test."

The doctor has me look at a Snellen eye chart, as is normal for a vision test, and cover my left eye to read it at different distances, then repeat the process with my right eye. Suddenly, he takes pause from what he's doing, and takes a good look at my facial expression.

"You good? You look a little shaken."

"Yeah, I'm fine, doc. Let's proceed."

"Okay, vision comes to 20/20."

The next item on the list of screening tests is to conduct a hearing test. Of course, I pass that with flying colors too.

"Last one, and then we'll get you out of here. The final test is the blood test. I'm going to take a few vials of your blood to also send to the lab. Do you happen to know your blood type off-hand?"

"Um... A positive."

"Do you have a preference of which arm to take blood from?"

"The right one has usually worked alright."

He grabs from his supply cabinet a needle, an arm tie, four vials, some gauze, a pair of latex gloves, and bandages. He puts the pair of gloves on, and ties the band around my right bicep. My veins become easily visible, as I don't exactly have fat on me from all the years playing football. I'm lean muscle and my body has been known to be vascular. He taps the veins in the middle of my right arm, finding one that he likes, and inserts the needle into my arm. Blood starts flowing through the tubing and into the vial. It flows quickly, so it doesn't take long before the four vials fill up—maybe a couple of minutes? Satisfied with the progress, the doctor immediately places the gauze onto the spot where he stuck me, then removing the needle and turning off the tourniquet.

"Hold that there for a second."

I place the index and middle fingers of my left hand onto the gauze to hold it in place.

He then places the bandage over the gauze, holding it in place. "Keep that on there for a bit. Maybe in like an hour you can take it off."

"Alright, I can do that. Anything else I need to do while I'm here?"

"No. That's everything as far as my part of this goes. You'll receive your orders in the mail within a couple weeks. This will tell you your ship date for Basic Training as well. Keep that document with you, as you'll be asked for it at Basic Training, AIT, and throughout your journey. You'll also receive a packing list for supplies and clothing you are responsible for bringing to Basic Training with you. Any other questions?"

I thought for a moment. "No, I think I'm alright for now."

"Thank you. Have a good one."

"You, too."

47: SEVENTEEN

I rolled onto my side, and opened one eye to check the time. I am suspiciously well-rested for a Friday.

"Shit! I'm late for school!"

I rocket out of bed, throwing on whatever clothes that halfway matched and were clean in my closet, along with a pair of black no-show socks and sneakers. I grab my backpack, hastily making sure that I have all my school stuff in it, and run out the door as fast as possible. Why didn't Mom wake me up?!

I rush down the stairs as fast as my legs can carry me. I take a cursory glance into Jeremy's room, and notice he's already gone. He probably woke up at the *correct* time, unlike me, and didn't bother to think that I also needed to be up for school.

Once I get to the kitchen, Mom looks at me like she's shooting daggers with her eyes.

"You're late," she said. Yes, thank you for that life-changing information, Captain Obvious. It's as if I have no idea.

"I know," I responded. I ran out the door, threw a leg over my bike, and sped off to school. I usually walk to school, but I want to get there faster so I can try to make up lost time. I pedal as fast as I can for the mile-long trek to school, only stopping at marked stop signs or stoplights. My actions are bordering on reckless, but that's not important right now.

It's not until I'm halfway to school that I realize I didn't even put gel in my hair this morning. Or brush my teeth. My hair is a bit unkempt, but it's still manageable at the moment if I put about ten seconds of effort into my appearance. Spending time in the mirror to make myself look handsome and presentable was very much out of the question. I look borderline homeless, even though I'm one of the captains of the varsity football team this year (at least on the defensive line) as a senior. I'm pretty sure I have an exam today, too, although I don't remember which class it's in. Welp, that's a dangerous thought, considering that means I also didn't study or prepare for it.

Upon arrival at school, I chain up my bike as quickly as possible, then bolt for my first class of the day—U.S. government. Some people would know it as civics. Mr. Hendricks is not going to be having any of my bullshit over this. He *hates* when students are late for his class.

Just as I'm about to turn the handle to get into his classroom, I'm winded. Between running and pedaling my bike, I need a moment to catch my breath. I finally reach my hand to the door handle, and slowly turn it downwards to open it and push the door inward.

I get met with a glare from Mr. Hendricks as I enter the classroom. I expected this behavior from him.

"You're late, Jim."

"I know... I'm sorry, Mr. Hendricks."

"Have a seat and follow along, please."

My desk today is the only one that's open, which is towards the left side of the classroom in the second row from the front. I suppose the lesson plan today was the function and purpose of the executive branch. Mr. Hendricks, also a strict teacher, is a very passionate social studies teacher. He's by far one of the best teachers I've experienced so far.

"Who remembers what the purpose of the executive branch is off the top of your head?"

I looked around the classroom for a moment to see if anyone else is paying enough attention to raise their hand and provide an answer. Mr. Hendricks is one of those teachers that will call on you on purpose without your hand being up because he knows he can bust people *not* paying attention.

I raise my hand.

"Jim?"

"To conduct diplomacy with other nations and enforce the laws."

"That is correct. Who's the head of the executive branch, Jim?"

"The President."

"Also correct. I see you've been paying attention."

I flashed a smile at Mr. Hendricks. It's kind of my job to pay attention—I'm a scholar athlete and carry a 3.8 cumulative GPA. Coach Henneforth checks our grades every *month* to make sure that we're not bombing our classes. He values performance in the classroom as much as he does on the field and in the weight room.

"Next question. What is the purpose of the judicial branch?"

My classmate Sarah raises her hand.

"Sarah?"

"To interpret the laws."

"That's correct! It appears only Jim and Sarah are paying any attention today. The rest of you need to read and study more by the looks and sounds of today's class session."

The final bell for first period mercifully rang five minutes later. Truthfully, I have no idea how I was pulling correct answers out of my ass during this class period, which I showed up half late to. I barely actually read the book itself and didn't take copious amounts of notes in class. I suppose I just have a good memory.

My schedule this school year is rough. First period, I have civics, then second period is...physics. I'm not the greatest at the sciences, but I *am* great at math. That's possibly my only saving grace because I'm barely carrying an 85% in my physics class.

As I walk just down the hall to physics, it hits me—that's what my exam is in today, and believe me when I say I didn't study a wink for the last two weeks. I've *known* about it for those two weeks, but I've been going to bed as soon as I get home from football practice and eating dinner for that *entire* two weeks. Oh good grief, I hope I don't bomb this exam...

I sit at an open desk and begin rummaging through my backpack to look for a pencil. I know better than to try doing any kind of math, especially physics, in pen. To my dismay, I *only* have pens. Well, this is inconvenient. I'm usually better prepared, but with how I bolted out of bed and the house this morning, it's also not surprising. I do, however, have my calculator, so that's a good thing. I pull it out and put it on my desk. I turn to my left to ask my classmate, Aaron, for a pencil.

"Hey... Aaron..."

He looks over at me. "Oh, hey, what's up?"

"Do you have an extra pencil I can borrow?"

"Yeah, of course! I got you. Hold on one second."

"You're the best. Thank you so much. I'll give it back to you as soon as I'm done."

He reaches into his backpack and pulls out a zippered pouch, the one I'm assuming contains writing utensils and other small school supplies. He grabs a pencil and an eraser, and hands both to me.

"Here you go."

"I appreciate you, man."

Two minutes later, the bell rings. Class is about to start, which means we're getting our exams momentarily.

Mr. Jones, my physics teacher, walks to the front and center of the class, a small stack of papers in his hand.

"Alright, everyone. I hope you've studied and prepared for this. Today's exam is covering energy and momentum. Have your pencils and calculators ready as I hand them out. There are ten questions, and there is enough room for you to show your work under each problem. You may attach additional pieces of paper if needed. When you are done with your exam, please bring it up to me at the front, and you may leave after that. I should have these graded and back to you by the start of class on Tuesday."

The class goes back to being dead silent as Mr. Jones hands out the exam papers, each containing three stapled sheets. As I'm reading the room, the nervousness is palpable. He puts a stack of blank exams on the desk of the person at the front of each row and has that person pass back the stack to everyone behind them. I pull a blank copy off the stack and pass it to the person behind me. Right away, I write my name on the blank line next to "Name:" on the exam—James Rossi. I've been told that, for a guy, my handwriting is above average. I write in all capital letters, making the J and R of my name slightly larger than the other letters.

I take a moment to collect myself and steady my heart rate and breath. To say I'm nervous about this is an understatement, considering I have had exactly *zero* preparation for this very exam.

I flip through the pages of the exam, reading each question first before I try to tackle this beast. My tried-and-true test-taking strategy is to find the easier questions first, complete those, and save the toughest for last. That way, you know you'll have enough time and can get your confidence up with the easy ones. There are five multiple-choice questions on this exam, and five that you just need to show your calculations and provide your final answer on a line next to "Solution:". The multiple-choice questions are the last five of the exam, so I start with those first. I immediately know the answers to three of them practically right off the top of my head, so I circle the letter next to the correct answer on each one. Returning to the other two multiple-choice questions, I take about a minute each to think before I can muster what I think are the right answers. I'm a little less confident about one of them. Going well so far.

As I'm about to start the other half of the exam, a.k.a. the problems that require me to show my work, I take a glance at the clock that's high on the wall next to the door. Forty minutes left of class. I've got plenty of time. I go a bit out of order on these questions, but it doesn't matter. Completing and passing it matters, not the order in which I answer each question.

I take about five minutes in total for each question, where two minutes of that is contemplating the best approach, and the other three minutes is spent with my calculator and showing the appropriate computations. Before I get out of my chair to turn in my exam, I glance over all ten of my answers one last time to make sure everything is complete and accurate. Once I'm satisfied that that's the case, I put the pencil and eraser that Aaron lent me back on his desk, and he nods in acknowledgment. I turned the exam in to Mr. Jones and promptly left the classroom with time to spare before I went to my English class.

~ * ~

Tuesday rolled back around, and I made it to school *on time* today...unlike Friday. That's a train wreck I don't want to experience ever again if I can help it, in all honesty. Mr. Jones kept to his word and had the stack of graded exams in his left arm at the front of the class. I can't read his expression, though... He's difficult to make heads or tails of.

"Class, you surprised me, and did very well on this exam. The average score was 87%. However, we did have one student who scored 100%..."

Every student looks around the classroom, thinking they can figure out who got the perfect score, judging only by looks and facial expressions. I just looked straight ahead and didn't look at anyone in particular.

"The student who got 100% is..."

I noticed that Mr. Jones was making *direct* eye contact with me instead of spreading the eye contact around the room.

"James Rossi."

My heart skipped a beat. My eyes grew three sizes. My brain can hardly process what's going on. WHAT?! How the *fuck* am *I* the one that got the perfect score?!

Everyone turns to look at me.

"Seriously?!" That's all I could muster out of my complete surprise. I didn't even *study*, and some of my classmates probably agonized over this exam.

"Yes. Seriously. Congratulations, young man, you've earned it."

Well, this is going to help my grade in this class. I still can't believe it *happened*, though.

48: SIXTEEN

A big disadvantage of living in a small town is that sometimes you must visit the nearest major city to obtain certain things. One of those things is getting my Driver's License from the Bureau of Motor Vehicles.

I got my learner's permit about six months ago, so today, I'm going to take my license test behind the wheel. Dad and I had to drive to Youngstown to the BMV on Mahoning Avenue and Meridian Road. With traffic, it's about a 20-minute drive, and it's not all that far from Austintown either. Upon arrival at the BMV, I get out of the passenger seat, and Dad emerges from the driver's seat. We approach the front door of the building together, and I take the handle to open it for both of us. An employee is standing just to the right of the entrance indoors, and she looks at the two of us expectantly.

"What are you two gentlemen here for today?"

Dad and I look at each other for a brief second.

"I'm here to take my driver's license test," I say to her. She has a name badge, and her name is handwritten on it—Megan.

"How old are you, young man?"

"I just turned 16 last week."

"Alright, well, fill out this form, take this number, and have a seat. When an employee is ready for you, they will call your number." She hands me a two-page form, a black pen, and a smaller slip of paper that has a number on it. I take the papers and pen from her with my right hand.

"Thank you so much," I said with a smile.

Dad and I wandered through the building, looking for two chairs next to each other. After a couple of minutes, we find them and take a seat. I guess it's not terribly busy on a Saturday morning. It could always be worse, especially if we went to Cleveland, which is an hour away. At least Youngstown is only about fifteen minutes away from here, give or take.

"Are you nervous?" he asks me.

"No, I wouldn't say so."

"I guess we've been practicing for a while. What about parallel parking? That usually gets people."

"I think I'll be fine. I'm not worried," I said confidently.

"As long as you're confident in your abilities, I think that's what matters."

"I agree with that statement."

Twenty minutes passed, and then I heard my name called and yelled from the other side of the building.

"Rossi, James. Counter four."

The closest employee counter to me was twenty, and the smaller numbers were at the *far* other end of the building. I start walking, then realize that I don't have a lot of time before they start calling another person, so I pick up my pace to a jog. Upon arrival, I introduced myself.

"Hi, I'm James Rossi."

The woman looks at me, sizing me up as much as she can from sitting on the other side of the counter. If I had to guess, she's probably in her 40s, but historically, I'm bad at guessing age. Her strawberry blonde hair is short, the ends hitting just above her shoulder, and she has dark brown eyes. Her glasses are nearly too big for her face, and they appear to be on some kind of chain to keep them affixed to her person.

"My colleague, Darren, will follow you to your vehicle to start on your driver's exam. He's on his way over right now."

I look to my left and see a male figure in the distance making his way towards me. I would say that he's about the same age as the woman behind the counter.

"Alright, thank you." I wait for Darren to approach me, and he shows up within a couple of minutes.

"Hi, I'm Darren. I'll be your examiner for your driving test today." He holds out his right hand, and I reach out with my right hand to shake his.

"Hi, Darren, I'm James. Nice to meet you." I flash a smile while making eye contact.

I see Darren's eyes glance over my shoulder at Dad. "Is this your father?"

"Yes, that's my dad."

Dad makes eye contact and offers his hand while introducing himself. "Hi, I'm Gio."

"Gio, you can come with. You'll just sit in the back seat of the car while we do the exam."

"Oh, alright. That sounds good to me."

"Follow me, gentlemen," Darren says to both of us. We follow Darren down to a side door of the BMV and out to a parking lot. Darren has me lead the way to Dad's car.

"James, you'll be driving your own vehicle for the exam. Or, well, it may be your Dad's car right now. Is that something you're comfortable handling?"

"Yes, that's what I learned on when he was teaching me."

"Then this should be a breeze for you," Darren said as he smiled at me.

When we reach Dad's vehicle, I unlock it so that the three of us can get in and situate ourselves. I then put the key into the ignition, step on the brake pedal, and turn the key so that the engine turns over.

"Good. Adjust your mirrors before you put it into reverse."

I look over at the driver's door, push the buttons for the left mirror first to get it to my liking, and repeat the process on the right one after that's been completed.

"Excellent. Back out of here slowly."

With my right hand, I put my right foot back on the brake and shift the car into reverse. I wait a minute for several other cars to circle the vehicle's rear, then creep backwards out of the parking spot.

"Great. Now put it in drive and turn right onto Mahoning Ave. Make sure to signal and look for other drivers."

I push in the clutch with my left foot, shift to first gear, and start to scoot the car towards Mahoning Ave. I turn on my right turn signal with the lever and look for oncoming traffic before slowly entering the lane.

"Good job. Drive up to Osborn Ave and turn left at the stop light. Don't speed, but make sure you keep your speed reasonable and follow the speed limit. Make sure to signal, too."

I obliged and shifted the car into second gear after pressing down on the clutch when I hit 2,000 rpm. As I approached Osborn Ave, I turned on my left turn signal.

"Smooth shifting and turn signal timing. Great job. A lot of people don't do as well on shifting between gears with the manual transmission right away. How long have you been giving him lessons, Dad?"

"About a year. Pretty much as soon as we got his learner's permit."

Once the light turns green, I look both ways quickly before making my way through my turn in the intersection.

"Alright, next we're going to make a right on California Ave, and another right onto Dunlap Ave. Once we get back to Mahoning Ave, turn right and go back to the BMV."

Following Darren's directions and instructions, I maintain my composure and feel increasingly confident about the expected outcome. Finally, we return to the BMV.

"We're almost done. James, go to the back lot. There are four pillars where you will show me how to parallel park. After that's complete, I will give you your score."

Less than a minute later, we arrive at the explained parallel parking spot. I pull the car next to it, with only a few feet of distance. I look over at Darren, who's making notes on his paper and clipboard.

"How are you feeling?" he asks me.

I take a deep breath. "I'm feeling pretty good about everything."

"Well, whenever you're ready, go ahead and parallel park. I'll check your work after that's done and give you the result."

I shift the car back into reverse and start to point the rear of the car towards the right, where the pillars are. After I have a few inches of clearance, I turn the wheel the opposite way so that I can straighten out while in reverse. From there, I push in the clutch and return to first gear, scooting the car forward and correcting myself as much as possible. Finally, I put the car back into reverse, making sure I'm centered between the pillars. I have a good eye for distance and feel I'm right on the money.

"Done?" Darren asks.

"Yes, sir."

Darren opens his door to check how far away I am from the curb. I'm level on the concrete, not too close or far from the curb. I was right—I'm right on the money for that. He gets out of the car to check everything else as well and comes back in after about a minute. I watch nervously as Darren totals some numbers on a scrap piece of paper.

"Well, James... Do you want to know how you did? Dad, what about you?"

"Yes, please," I insisted.

"Yes," Dad responded.

"Congratulations, James! You needed a score of 80 to pass, and you scored a 95. You passed!"

I took a deep breath of relief. "Awesome! Love to hear it."

"Take this paper back inside, and have a seat. They'll call your name up at the photo counter to take your picture, and you will receive your new driver's license in the mail within a few days."

"Thank you so much, Darren!"

"You're welcome, James. It's been a pleasure. Be careful out there!"

49: FIFTEEN

The Struthers High School junior varsity football team, of which I'm the middle linebacker, has made it to the playoffs...and it's early January. This means we must play in the snow sometimes. This means I'm freezing *everything* off while trying to coordinate the plays to the rest of the D-line on the field, intercept the ball at any opportunity, and provide coverage in the middle of the field as I'm needed. While I'm happy that we have gone 12-2 during the regular season, that doesn't mean the work stops here. If you know football at all, or sports in general, you know that the ante is increased if you are lucky enough to make it into the postseason. You're playing against teams that have also earned their spot in the playoffs, and the fight to advance to the next level gets tougher with every game.

I would say that the season was great, but it wasn't. It was just *weird*. Despite a couple of clock management blunders, all the weird shit happened on the field rather than originating from the sideline.

For one thing, one week we played Poland Seminary, and there's 4:57 left in the fourth quarter. It's on 4th and 21 at Poland's 30-yard line since they kept tacking up the penalties and infractions, so you may as well just say 4th down and forever. They decided to try and make a play on it anyway. Who *does* that?! The logical solution would be for Poland Seminary to punt the ball away and hope for a touchback. Any sensible coach would have punted it on 4th and 2 or more, but I suppose logic wasn't present in the building on that day. My teammate Troy, who plays defensive end and wears jersey number 57, got called for roughing the passer. Unfortunately, that resulted in an automatic first down for Poland, but they were backed up another 15 yards to boot.

During a different game, maybe two weeks after we played Poland, we played Beaver Local as an away game. Rather than being towards the *end* of the game, this one happened with 12:31 on the clock in the first quarter. Keep in mind that we're not an NFL team here. We're high school students. With a score of zero for both teams, since Beaver had just gained possession of the ball for their opening drive of the game, they decided to go for a field goal...at 57 yards out. This kicker is all of 4'8", 90 pounds soaking wet, and doesn't have a cannon for a leg. Why did they attempt that with such a small kid? I'm still trying to figure it out.

Anyway, those are just the two weird experiences that I remember vividly. Our first opponent in the playoffs was Girard High School. They're good enough to be in the playoffs, but they're towards the bottom of the rankings early in the postseason. There is an 8-team playoff picture. The #1 team will play #8, #2 (us, Struthers) will play #7 (Girard), #3 will play #6, and #4 will play #5. From there, the teams pair up accordingly as it filters down into two, and those two play for the state championship. The other six teams are from around the state of Ohio, not just Mahoning County.

One day, I'm coming out of the locker room, and I see Andrew leaning against a couple of lockers in the hallway, waiting for me.

"Oh—hey, Andrew."

"How do you feel about the playoffs? Do you think Girard poses a threat?"

"Mm...I feel confident about *this* matchup, but I'm a bit nervous about going forward."

"What do you think will give you the edge?" he asked.

"Well, based on how I've seen them play throughout the season, and from what I've heard, they have a decent offense. If they drive up the score early in the game, they're more likely to win. However, I think we have a strong pass rush, and Troy is *amazing* at playing defensive end. I want to believe that he might get a couple more sacks in the playoffs if he brings his A-game. I think he's going to get up in the NFL one day."

"Well, you know what they say... Offense wins games, defense wins championships. You got this!"

I blushed a little bit.

"Thanks, man."

~ * ~

A week later, we finally played Girard and won. The score wasn't even close, either. We blew them out 45-14. That's a high-scoring game for high school football. By halftime, the score was 21-0. Although their attempts at a comeback were valiant and earnest, Girard simply could not overcome our defense. Troy managed to get a sack and miraculously avoided any roughing-the-passer calls. I managed to get a holding call against me, but it's fine. It was early in the game, and we still had two of our timeouts left by the end of the game. Coach Henneforth does a great job of clock management when it truly matters.

The following week, our opponent came from Cuyahoga County— Cleveland Heights High School. The Tigers came significantly more prepared than Girard, and they gave our defense a run for the money. We had to put our best offensive line out that could read their defense and find gaps to exploit. This game caused me to get a pass interference called against me. I did my best to keep a level head during this game, and even tried to prevent my teammates from becoming increasingly hot-headed, but that proved difficult. A couple of my teammates on the defensive line, as well as our kicker, were ready to pick fights during regulation. It was not worth getting more calls against our team by the referees, so logic eventually took over. Despite their best efforts to eliminate us, it ended up being a two-score game, with a final score of 35-21.

After defeating Cleveland Heights, our opponent for the semi-final was Geneva High School from Ashtabula County. I feel that we barely won this game by the skin of our teeth, and we defeated them 28-24. When we scored, they responded in kind. By the end of the game, neither team had any timeouts left. Their guys were just as physical as ours. Everything was tit-for-tat, and I felt like it was evenly matched. The biggest advantages we had were speed and the intuition to read their plays before they figured us out. We almost blew it with 2:43 left in the 4th quarter, but we held on and ate the clock as best we could, having the final possession of the game.

Finally, we made it to the state championship and faced West High School, which is based out of our state's capital, Columbus. The crowd was quite something at the championship, considering you're taking the students of a big city (and state capital) of Columbus, and putting them against a small town like Struthers. Either way, I'm elated that we got to the state championship. We fought hard, but we fought fair, although we earned two injuries during the game. Our left tackle, Michael, tore his Achilles and was carted off the field after Coach Henneforth and the referee looked at the severity of the injury.

The championship went into overtime. At the end of regulation, the score was 28-28. We won the coin toss and chose to receive the ball first in overtime. Overtime lasted fifteen minutes, and we managed to eat five minutes of that clock…and scored a touchdown on the opening drive of overtime when our quarterback rushed into the end zone for 15 yards.

Never in my wildest dreams did I think I would win a state championship during my freshman year of high school, yet here we are. We did it. I did it.

On the bus ride back to Struthers, we all took turns holding and kissing the state championship trophy. What a *rush* that was, and Coach Henneforth commended all our efforts and hard work during the regular season and post-season.

50: FOURTEEN

Being a guy isn't always the easiest, especially when you're fourteen, your voice hasn't completely deepened, and you haven't hit your adult height yet. In my opinion, puberty sucks the whole way around, no matter your biological sex or who you are. Hormones are raging, rational thought is at an all-time low, and your emotions are keeping pace with your hormonal fluctuations. You know what else is at an all-time high? My desire to get my first real girlfriend. Want to know how that's going? Like shit. Why is the female mind so convoluted and strange?

This is the year where I'm about to step onto a different campus than I've been going to for the past nine years.

But first, during the summer before it starts? Tryouts for the junior varsity football team. This is a two-week-long process, so I've—quite literally—got my work cut out for me. I'm trying out for middle linebacker, as I've always favored defensive positions ever since I started playing in the first place. I approach the football field as I walk along Garfield Street, sweating profusely since it's more humid than a normal summer. If I'm *already* this sweaty, I can't imagine how *sore* I'm going to be later. I've got cleats, a change of clothes, gloves, and shoulder pads in my bag. I finally approach the group on foot, sweat already dripping down my head and face.

The coach makes eye contact with me as he's standing on the 45-yard line on one end of the field. He has a clipboard and pen, and the papers being held contain the names of all the boys who signed up to try out for the team.

"Name?"

"James Rossi."

He looks through his roster and must flip through a few pages because it's in alphabetical order by last name, so the Rs are toward the end.

"You are trying out for…middle linebacker, it says here?"

"Yes, sir, that's correct."

"Alright. The defensive positions are towards the other 30-yard line. The

211

defensive coordinator will be with you today to get you situated. I'm the head coach. You can call me Coach or Coach Henneforth."

"Thanks, Coach."

I jogged over to where the other defensive players were and introduced myself to them. Among the guys I met, there was 1 defensive tackle, 1 safety, 1 left outside linebacker, 1 right outside linebacker, 1 cornerback, and 1 defensive end. Although we waited for more people to show up, it seemed like the defensive line was complete (that is, assuming all of us made the team). I didn't pay too much attention to what was happening on the offensive line or special teams from the jump, but I'm sure I'll get to know everybody eventually.

After everyone was checked in, Coach Henneforth called for everyone to gather for warmups and stretching. I had been playing football for a few years at this point, and I felt out of shape. How am I supposed to survive tryouts, never mind *practice,* if this is a constant? These coaches aren't messing around. After dynamic warmups and stretching concluded, we separated back into the three main groupings for more specific drills—offense, defense, and special teams.

Once all of us on the defensive line are gathered, the defensive coordinator walks away from Coach Henneforth and towards our end of the field. We moved towards the middle of the field (between both 45-yard lines) since the special teams guys need to use the field goal post for the kickers, and the end zone for the punters, so they're on one 35-yard line. The offensive line is on the other 35-yard line and using the other end zone.

"Alright, gentlemen. My name is Coach Jackson, and I'm the defensive coordinator. Besides Coach Henneforth, you'll be dealing mostly with me." You could have heard a pin drop on our side of the field. For the next 45 minutes, we're doing all kinds of drills—ranging from hand fighting to shedding blocks to sack drills. Of course, it depends somewhat on everyone's position, but Coach Jackson seemed to have the special ability to make the D-line work like an efficient, well-oiled machine.

After two weeks of grueling drills, learning the plays, and acquainting myself with the rest of the team beyond the defensive players, I ended up making the team, and they put me as a starter. It's rather unusual for a freshman to be a starter right away, but I suppose that my skills are good enough that the coaching staff believes I'm worthy of a starter spot. Typically, seniority will play a role in who gets the starter spot in most situations.

Throughout the season, I also noticed that I was getting taller. I started the school year at a mere 5'2", and I was 5'7" by the end of the regular season. I still have a few more inches to go to catch up to Dad, but I'm not that worried about it. I also started getting more muscle definition, my shoulders became broader, and my voice deepened. At any given point, I sound somewhat squeaky one minute, then the next minute, my voice is deep. It toggles between the two for the rest of the school year, but during the summer, it seems to fully mature into its normal, deep pitch.

Puberty is wild, man. It feels like one minute you're a short, squeaky, little kid, and the next thing you know, you've grown six inches (or more), sound like a grown man, and are building muscle mass fast as fuck. In the same breath, you can go from the opposite sex not even looking your direction, to all of a sudden, they chase you down. At least, that's the case if you're physically attractive to begin with.

What's also wild is how much your hormones affect absolutely *everything*. As a guy, you do pretty much everything to gain female attention from here on out. Why do you want to get your haircut a certain way? So girls notice you. Why do you want to work out and grow stronger? So, girls notice you and don't write you off as a weak punk. Why do you want to be tall? So, girls notice you *and* don't laugh at you for being short. Why do you try to get good grades in school? So your parents don't yell at you and threaten to kick you out of the house for being a degenerate...and because girls like that, too, I guess. None of that is even guaranteed to get a girl, either.

I can do without the random boners constantly, too. It seems like I can't do anything without the man downstairs thinking it's his place to be the star of the show. Too much information? Oh well. Bite me.

51: THIRTEEN

"Jim, pack a bag for the weekend. We're going to Geneva-on-the-Lake on Friday when you and Jeremy get home from school."

"Wait… really?" I have to make sure that I'm not going crazy and that I'm hearing this correctly. This was told to me on a Thursday night, so this is rather short notice. However, anyone who knows me understands that I'm always up for spontaneous adventures.

"Yes, really," Dad replied.

"Okay, well, I will go throw a bag together once I get to my room."

"Help your brother do the same, please."

I rolled my eyes because I know Jeremy will pack the craziest items of clothing he can find if those decisions are left to his own devices. I run up the stairs and head straight for my room. Hastily opening the closet door, I pull out my black duffel bag and throw clothes into it. Once I've packed everything but my toiletries (shower stuff, toothbrush, toothpaste, hair comb), I go to knock on Jeremy's door.

"Jer, are you in there?"

"Yeah," I hear from the other side of the door.

"Can I come in?"

"Okay." I open the door since it doesn't appear to be locked.

"Dad said to pack a bag for the weekend. We're going to Geneva-on-the-Lake tomorrow once we get home from school. Can I help you pack?"

"Okay."

The two of us pack a small bag for him with a weekend's worth of clothes. Since it's April, we aren't packing winter clothing. Instead, we're dressing for warmer weather since spring has officially arrived. Similarly, we pack everything but the toiletries, which we'll throw in quickly tomorrow. I walk back downstairs to find Mom and Dad in the kitchen, drinking tea.

"Okay, both of us have a bag packed for tomorrow."

"Glad to hear it. You boys should be getting to bed soon so you're not complaining you're tired in the morning to go to school."

I let out a sizable yawn, unintentionally, but it seemed to immediately validate Dad's claims that we should be getting to bed. I've been awake all day without any nap—I had to go to school, football practice, do homework, and shower once I got home, and I still had to fit dinner somewhere in that busy schedule.

"Yeah, that sounds like a good idea. Good night."

"Sleep well, sweet pea," Mom said.

"Good night, Jim."

I walked back up the stairs, crawled into bed under the covers, and passed out within a few minutes.

~ * ~

Mom and Dad kept their promise about going to Geneva-on-the-Lake the next day. As soon as Jeremy and I got home from school, they were loading up the car to head north.

Jeremy got on every last nerve on the 1.5-hour drive to Geneva-on-the-Lake. He kept asking if we were there yet every five minutes, and by the time we got there, I felt a sense of relief since he would finally shut up. We pull up to the Eagle Cliff Inn, where we will be staying for the weekend. After the four of us check in, we go back outside and head for the coast of Breakwater Beach.

Nobody told me that this was spring break for college students, and that there are some *gorgeous* college-aged girls in bikinis at all parts of the shoreline.

Mom is unfolding the beach towels and chairs, and Dad is putting up the umbrella. Jeremy is staring off into the distance, standing directly to my left. Everything seems to be normal. That is, until I see a breathtakingly gorgeous college girl run right across my field of vision.

I would guess she's about 5'7" and has nothing short of a model body that is *barely* covered by her hot pink bikini. She has a pronounced hourglass figure, complete with curvy hips, long legs, and an ample bosom. The only clothing I'm wearing is my swim trunks. I'm trying not to stare, but I can't help myself. It doesn't take long before I feel a tightening sensation as blood rushes to my penis.

Oh no… What's this feeling? I've never experienced anything like this before. I hope she doesn't notice! I would be completely mortified, especially because this girl is likely twice my age.

"Dad…"

He looks up from what he's doing and makes eye contact with me. "What's up?"

"Can I talk to you for a second?"

"Sure, about what?"

"In private, please…"

"Alright, let's take a walk."

The two of us start walking the opposite direction of Mom and Jeremy, looking for a private place to talk. We settle on behind the bathroom structure (an enclosed area with men's and women's restrooms and a roof over it) since there aren't many people there right now. Dad leans against the wall and propped himself on his left foot.

"What did you want to talk about?"

"Well… I don't know how to say this…" As you can imagine, I'm nervous to try and explain to Dad what just happened with my own body.

"Go on, just spit it out. No need to be nervous or shy."

"Um… While you and Mom were setting things up, I saw a pretty girl, and… my penis started to get hard, I think…"

Dad looks around, as if to make sure that no one could hear what he was about to say. "You…just got your first erection?"

"I think so. Is that what it's called?"

"It is. Have you experienced this before?"

"No, not that I remember."

"Oh, Jim… You're starting to become a young man, you know."

"I am? I don't feel like that, though."

"You are. Before you know it, you're going to get a bit taller and will probably end up around my height. Your voice will get deeper. You'll get facial hair and will have to shave every day like I do. Well, unless you *want* to grow a beard."

"When will all of this happen?"

"Well, it depends on the person. As for me, I got my first erection right around your age, and my voice started to get deeper within a few months. I think it finally got to sounding like it does today when I turned 16 or 17 years old. I didn't get my growth spurt all at once. It happened gradually over time, but I was fully grown just before I turned 18. Maybe you'll be the same, but there's always a chance it'll be a bit different."

"Oh, I see. That's good to know, I guess."

"There's nothing to be ashamed of, Jim. Getting an erection is normal. It will happen all the time, if I'm honest, especially if you're around pretty girls. Has it gone away by now?"

"Yeah, it faded out just before we walked over here."

"Sounds about right."

"So, Dad…what do I do about it when it happens again?"

"Well, if you can't…handle it right away, I usually find a way to hide it in my pants or short legs as best I can."

"Okay, I will figure it out then."

The two of us walk back towards Mom and Jeremy. Mom is sunbathing, and Jeremy seems to be running around like a wild child. No surprises there. I approach the shoreline and stand directly in the path of where the water ripples onto the sand. The cool water feels nice on my feet; it's warm outside.

Later in the day, we went back to the room. There are two king-size beds— one for my parents, and one for Jeremy and I. Why do I have to share a bed with this kid? I hate it. I wish Mom and Dad would have booked a room for themselves and another for us so that Jeremy and I could have our own beds. He's seven, he's old enough to sleep in his bed by now. Mom and Dad said that I could stay behind in the room if I wanted since they would take Jeremy to some kids' attraction near the beach. I can't remember what it was to save my life, but it doesn't matter. Finally, I can get some peace and alone time.

I lay in bed, the only noise being that of the air conditioner unit in the room, allowing my mind to wander. It turns out that that's a terrible idea. My mind decides it's time to revisit the beautiful college girl that I saw earlier. Within a matter of seconds, my penis is hard again. Since I didn't have a chance to really…react earlier, I begin to wonder what "handling it" (Dad's words, not mine) would *feel* like while thinking about a woman. I sigh as I unbutton and unzip my shorts to take it out from my boxer-briefs. I grab it at the base and start to stroke up and down, varying the speed and grip to see what gets me going. I waste no time to figure out what feels the best, and my breath starts to pick up the pace as I get increasingly aroused. My hand tries to keep up with my breath and desire, and with each stroke, I inch closer to climax.

"Oh, God… oh, God… oh… FUCK!"

It was at that moment that I came. It shot everywhere, and now I have a huge mess to clean up in a hurry before Mom, Dad, and Jeremy get back. *Shit!*

Thankfully, the towels are white, so there's nothing to color stain. While my penis goes back to its normal, flaccid state, I search for the smallest washcloth and find it quickly. I run the water in the shower from the faucet for a minute, then kneel in the tub to rinse myself off. After a meticulous check to ensure I got all of my mess cleaned up down there, I wash my hands in the sink and dry myself off in both places. Ten minutes after getting dressed and trying to make it look like nothing happened, I heard the hotel door jostle. Mom, Dad, and Jeremy have returned.

52: TWELVE

There stands a girl, I'd say about my age, four tables away from me in the cafeteria. It's lunchtime at school, and I can't take my eyes off her. She's standing at the head of a table with a few other girls sitting on the bench on either side. I'm not even feeling hungry, although I know I *should* eat for my own sake. I'm sitting with a few friends, and finally, someone interrupts me to snap me out of staring.

"Jim, what are you doing?" It's Andrew, whom I've known since I started at Saint Nicholas in kindergarten.

"Oh...hi. She's gorgeous." I looked at him, then quickly pointed my eyes towards the direction of the girl I've been helplessly staring at. He turns his head to match my line of sight.

"Who? Natalia?"

"Is that her name? The brunette with the hazel eyes standing at the end of the table over there?"

"Yeah, that's Natalia. She's out of your league, dude. She's into gymnastics—she competes and everything."

"But I like her."

"Have you ever *talked* to her?"

"No...but I want to..." I said shyly. I could feel my face blush a bit.

"Then go up to her. What's stopping you?" Andrew *did* have a point there. However, the idea of approaching a girl that pretty makes my heart pound so hard it feels like it's about to escape the confines of my chest.

"What if she hates me?"

"You don't know if you don't try." Andrew is trying his hardest to be encouraging, but I'm still a ball of nerves.

"Alright... Here goes nothing, I guess." I cautiously get up from my seat at the table and walk over to Natalia. I straightened up my posture, as I'm trying to project way more confidence that I do *not* currently have. After a few seconds, I'm mere inches away from Natalia's left side.

"Hi, Natalia..."

She whips her head around to look at me, her ponytail flipping with the movement. Her hazel eyes have specks of green, brown, and blue in them—kind of in a tie-dye pattern. She's even more stunning in person, and I'm so nervous that I feel like I'm about to throw up. I watch her facial expressions change as she sizes me up from head to toe. At the moment, I'm only about 5'1", and my voice is still mostly high-pitched and squeaky, although you can tell it's starting to change. Puberty hasn't quite made its way to me yet.

"Um? Who are you?" I could sense something of a mocking tone in her voice. This isn't going the way I wanted it to.

"My name is James, but you can call me Jimmy or Jim."

"Ew. I won't be talking to you. Get away from me, you freak."

I feel tears well up in my eyes as I look into hers. I'm embarrassed—no, humiliated. She won't even give me a chance.

"I... I'm sorry to bother you," I said as I turned my head and started walking away from her, going back to my table with Andrew. Once I get back to the table, I sit down and bury my red, puffy, crying face into my hands. Andrew was taking his drink out of his lunchbox at that moment, then looked up at me.

"Oh my God, are you okay?"

"She called me a freak," I said, my voice trembling as I was crying. It was a full-on ugly cry at this point. I need a tissue...or a few.

"I'm sorry..." I continued crying and tried not to be too loud. I didn't want to draw more attention to myself than I may have already. Andrew extends his arms out in a hug to offer me comfort. I walk around to the other side of the table, sit next to Andrew, and lean into the hug.

"Thank you for the hug," I said, burying my face into Andrew so no one could see how red and puffy it was from crying.

"We've been friends since kindergarten, Jim. You're like a brother to me by now." He hands me his unused napkin so I can wipe my tears with it.

"I know, I know...You've always been a good friend."

Finally, after a few more minutes, I can calm myself enough that my voice no longer shakes when I talk.

"Thank you. I appreciate you a lot, Andrew. I like you more than my brother..."

Andrew sat there and laughed at what I just said. "I mean, to be fair...he's like six. He's chaos incarnate at that age and will be for a while." He had a valid point...

Once lunch was over, the bell rang, and the cafeteria emptied as students swarmed the hallways to get to their next class. We only have a five-minute passing period, so it would be best for the average student to hurry up and get to class as quickly as possible. There's not a lot of room to talk or lollygag during that time.

After lunch this year, I have math. I had it first thing in the morning last year. Even though I excel at math, it's not the first thing I want to do when I wake up early in the morning. Andrew and I do have this class together this year—we didn't have any classes in common last year—so it was nice to have a friend when the material is getting progressively more challenging by the day, or at least that's how it feels. The two of us walk to math class together, talking about whatever comes to mind at the moment. From afar, I hear someone call my name.

"James!"

I looked around to see if anyone else near me could be mistaken and have the same name as I do. That isn't the case—no one else noticed or paid that much attention.

"Me?" I asked, while pointing at myself. Surely there's got to be another guy named James in this school, you'd think. As I look straight in front of me, a girl is running directly at me. I can't make out her features from a distance. I'm just barely outside the threshold of my math classroom door as this is happening. Finally, she stops in front of me, visibly exhausted and out of breath. She must have run a distance to be this winded.

"Yes, you. Hi. My name is Francesca, but you can call me Frankie. I know this is short notice, but would you like to hang out after school?"

"Um…sure. I should have some time. Do you want to go anywhere in particular?"

"I'm not sure," she says shyly. "How about we meet in the front after school, and we decide from there? We should probably go to class first."

"That works for me. See you later."

I wonder why she was trying to find *me* specifically. I'm not used to being pursued, I guess, by a girl. Aren't guys supposed to be the ones who pursue women? Or what if she just wants to be my friend?

I couldn't stop thinking about that brief introduction the rest of the day. My other classes didn't seem to matter because I wasn't paying attention to what was going on anyway. I'm unsure if any of my other classmates found out that I was mentally "checked out" or bothered to notice, but I hope it wasn't obvious.

After what feels like forever, the school day ends with the final bell ringing. I pick up my walking pace, making my way through the crowd of other students to get to the front of the school. Somehow, Frankie seems to have beat me here. I wonder if her last class was just by the door because that's the only logical reason I can muster for how she got there before I did. What a wild day this has been—I get shot down by one girl, and another one is chasing after me in less than an hour. The crazy thing is I don't remember meeting Frankie before now… Is it just that my memory is bad, or is it the first time I'm legitimately meeting her?

"Hey," I said shyly. I watch her face light up, her blue eyes widening with a sparkle in them. This is a *much* better experience than what happened to Natalia earlier.

"Hi, James!" She outstretched her arms, then wrapped them around me in a warm hug. I hugged her back, enjoying the moment.

"So, uh, why did you yell at me from across the hall? You can call me Jim or Jimmy, by the way."

Frankie looks up and around to think and find the words she wants to communicate to me. She puckers her lips and moves them to the right side of her face. For all this attention and possible affection, she seems shy.

"I..."

"Do you want to go to the park? Mauthe Park is less than a mile from here. We can talk as we head there."

She smiled. "Yeah, that would be nice."

The two of us made our way to Mauthe Park, and she became more talkative once we left the general vicinity of Saint Nicholas School.

"Have you always gone to Saint Nicholas?" I asked.

"Well, no. I just moved here last year."

"Where did you move from?"

"I'm originally from Elkins, West Virginia."

"Oh, cool. I have always lived in Struthers. My younger brother Jeremy goes to Saint Nicholas, too, but he's in first grade. I'm six years older."

"I have three older brothers, so I'm the youngest." Oh, boy. A girl with three older brothers. I'm sure they're used to beating people up for her because they tend to be protective... I would know; *I'm* an older brother myself.

"What do you think of Ohio?"

"It's similar to West Virginia enough that I don't notice many differences." She shrugged.

"I see. You never answered my question, though. Why did you yell for *me* across the hallway?"

She hung her head as if she was embarrassed. Otherwise, I'm not certain about how to read body language. I'm not well-versed in how girls and women behave either.

"I... Well... One of my friends said she met you years ago, but she was too shy to say something. Then, when I finally came up to you, I realized that I thought you were cute."

I blushed. Hard. "Oh, um...Thanks, I guess. Who's the friend?"

"Her name is Stephanie."

"Oh, wow. I haven't seen Stephanie since I started school here in *kindergarten*. She was always kind of quiet if I remember her correctly. I'm still friends with Andrew, whom I met at the same time in kindergarten. When did *you* meet her?"

"Last year. I met her at lunch on my first day at Saint Nicholas. There was an empty seat next to her, and I asked if I could sit there. I guess we're friends now."

Once we got to Mauthe Park, we headed immediately for the swing set and got on the two swings together. The two of us pump our legs to give us some air and height, and we take turns jumping off them mid-air, hoping we don't injure ourselves. After ten minutes of this, we take up a spot in the grass nearby and talk. Any and every topic under the sun seems to come up. Before we know it, it's 5:00 pm, and I need to go home. I'm sure she does, too.

"Well, Frankie, I think I should be getting home. It's getting dark out, and Mom is probably wondering when I'm going to walk in so I can eat dinner with my parents and brother."

"Oh, crap, yeah. I need to get home too," she says.

"Will I see you at school tomorrow?"

"Yes, of course!"

"Don't be a stranger. If you find me in the cafeteria, come sit with Andrew and I. Bring Stephanie too if she's up for it."

"I will do that. Have a good night."

We give each other a hug for a few seconds, then walk our separate ways.

53: ELEVEN

I haven't been this nervous since my first day of kindergarten. I'm about to start middle school, and to say that I have mixed feelings would be quite an understatement. You know that feeling you get when you realize that you have six teachers instead of one? That's what's going through my head right now, and let me tell you—it's not great. I haven't tried to look for any of my classrooms on campus before now, so it's going to be *fun* trying to figure out where everything is.

I show up at school with a new spiral-bound notebook, a few pens and pencils, and my lunchbox, all neatly contained within my backpack. You would think that, for a school I've attended *since* kindergarten, I'd know the layout by now. That's not the case since they do like to move teachers around as more are hired and others leave over the years. As I walk through the front doors, I am met instantly with a swarm of other students. Some are brand new, transferred from other places within Mahoning County, and others are like me, having been coming here for some time. Surely, everything in between exists, too. I ask what looks like a teacher for directions on how to get to my first class. After giving me some directions, I found it within five minutes. I see an open desk in the middle of the classroom, placing my backpack on the floor between my feet.

The teacher's name, "Mr. Gabbard," is written on the chalkboard. He's about 5'10", clean-shaven, and a generic-looking white guy with short dark brown hair and blue eyes. I wouldn't say he's ripped, but he looks like he works out more than just occasionally or when he feels like it. He's probably in his early thirties, so he's not geriatric either by any means.

The morning bell rings at 7:30 AM sharp, and we begin by standing and reciting the Pledge of Allegiance. After that concludes, Mr. Gabbard begins to introduce himself.

"Alright, class, good morning, and welcome to 6th-grade mathematics. I'll be your teacher this year, and you'll be seeing me first thing every morning for the next several months. My name is Mr. Gabbard, and you can call me that or Mr. G. I don't care which, and both work just fine. Do we have any new students with us today?" He pauses, then scans the classroom, seeing no raised hands.

"Since we all seem to be returning students here, I will skip past the parts you already know. I hope you've had a great summer, and I will do my best not to be boring and put you to sleep, as I know math isn't everyone's favorite." Several students start to chuckle or mumble in agreement with that last sentence.

After taking attendance, Mr. Gabbard changed to talking about the syllabus. Unfortunately, there is absolutely nothing interesting about the syllabus. It doesn't make sense to anyone but the faculty and administration. This discussion took the entire first class, and I could tell by looking around the classroom that almost everyone had either dissociated or started nodding off to sleep. Some were doing the old-fashioned head nod where you're sitting up, but as you doze off to sleep, your head starts bobbing up and down. Others just laid their head on their arms, crossed over the top of their desk. Then there were a small handful that didn't give a shit. Those few were leaning back in their chair, their head hanging the entire way back, mouths open, and were even snoring. How *I* managed to stay awake is anyone's guess.

After fifty minutes, we are finally put out of our misery, and the bell rings. Math class is over. I unzipped my backpack to take out the paper schedule I had written down and glanced at what I got next and where. Two doors down, on the opposite side of the hallway, I have English as my second class. Even though Mr. Gabbard put me to sleep, math has often been my strong suit. English, however, mmm…not so much. I've never been too much of a reader, and writing essays is not my forte.

Regardless of my personal feelings towards the subject, I walk into the classroom for English. This time, the teacher is a woman. She, too, has written her name on the board – Ms. Cox. Like Mr. Gabbard, she's fairly young, looking to be in her mid-30s. She is significantly more beautiful than he is. Her dark brown hair is wavy and lays about four inches past her shoulder length. Bright green eyes stare back at me from the front of the classroom as I take my seat. She's wearing a loosely fitting baby blue button-down short-sleeve blouse and a black skirt with 3-inch black heels. She's about 5'5", has a curvy yet slender build, and is…um…well-endowed. Hopefully, she doesn't see me blushing in my seat. I feel my face getting warmer.

The bell rings, indicating the start of the class. She wastes no time in getting the course started.

"Well, good morning, class! I'm Ms. Cox, and I'll be your English teacher for the year. Does anyone have questions before we get started?"

A girl in my class raised her hand almost immediately.

"Can I use the bathroom?"

"Sure. It's down the hall to the left. What was your name?"

"Cassidy," the little girl replied. Cassidy is wearing a knee-length bright pink dress with black close-toed shoes, and her light brown hair is in two pigtails—one on each side of her head. Her eyes are a dark brown.

"Yes, you can go ahead, Cassidy. Hurry back soon," Ms. Cox said with a smile. Wow, she's even prettier when she smiles.

Cassidy exits the classroom quietly once she gets up from her seat. Upon return, she opens the door and pokes her head in sheepishly before returning to her seat. She couldn't have been there for five minutes, which was likely an urgent matter.

From there, Ms. Cox decides that the first lesson of the day (and school year) will be a grammar lesson. Something about sentence structure and whatever else. I'm *way* too distracted by Ms. Cox to pay much attention right now.

After another 45 minutes, the bell rings, and I'm off to my next class, which happens to be...gym. Great, why do I have to have *gym* right before lunch? That's such a terrible idea since I have overactive sweat glands that never quit. After lunch, the remainder of my six classes go in the following order: science, theology/religious education, and Latin. Yes, I was forced to take Latin. No, I don't like it either. The other classes weren't interesting to describe or talk about, so there's no point in wasting my breath.

I get through the rest of the school day without a hitch, but I am *exhausted*. Did I sleep enough last night? No. Do I plan to get enough sleep tonight? Also, no. If growing up means that I'm going to be tired all the time, then why would anyone want to get older? Again, it sounds like a terrible idea.

After the final bell rings, I must go find where Jeremy is. He came to school with me today since he just started kindergarten. The two of us make our way home on foot. On the way, the two of us stopped by Dollar General just down the road from my house and got a bottle of Coca-Cola because I was thirsty, and it just sounded like it was going to hit the spot right now. I pop off the cap and take my first sip.

"Ah..." I say aloud, satisfied with my purchase. I look over at Jeremy, and he's making a weird facial expression. It's not quite a grimace, but it's not a smile, either. It's something in between that I don't know how to describe.

"Are you okay, little bro?" I inquire.

"Yeah, just thinking," he says.

"Well, alright then. Here, grab my hand." I extend my right hand towards his left. He grabs it firmly, and we begin the walk home.

54: TEN

Not sure about you, but I'm not the biggest fan of church. I'm full-blooded Italian, so unfortunately, my parents have forced me to go since birth, where I was baptized within my earliest days of life. That doesn't mean I have to like it, though.

On any given Sunday, the four of us are dragged to church, donning some of our best attire. We attend Saint Nicholas Church in Struthers, and that started with my grandparents when they immigrated from Italy, and my parents were children themselves. We live centrally in Struthers, so we scarcely go far to get wherever is necessary. The town of Struthers itself is not large, but it's also rare that we go into the proper Youngstown or Cleveland metro areas for anything.

If you know anything about the Catholic religion, you know that we take certain Sundays very seriously. Today is one of those Sundays, as it's Palm Sunday – the week before Easter. For as long as I can remember, and from what my parents tell me, Saint Nicholas folds up palm tree leaves into little handheld crosses that they hand out on Palm Sunday. You grab one on your way into the doors of the church from the ushers that are scattered about the main perimeter. Mom made me dress significantly nicer than I normally do, of course, to be suitable for the occasion. I am just eager to go back home and change into something more comfortable, but that won't be for a while from now, unfortunately. *Sigh.*

We are about to approach the front of the church, and surely, there are three ushers greeting people and handing out the crosses. Mom, Dad, and Jeremy take one individually, and the usher doesn't speak a word to them. For whatever reason, he decided to talk to *me* personally.

"Well, hello there, young man! You look very handsome today," he says as he hands me my cross.

"Thanks," I said, taking it from his hand.

"What is your name?"

"James, but most people call me Jim or Jimmy."

The usher is a bit older than I am, easily in his 60s, and old enough to be my grandpa. He still has quite the mane of hair, albeit his hair has lost any color it once had and gone white. I would say he's just barely shorter than Dad and stands at around 5'8" (Dad is 5'10" for reference). He has medium brown eyes and a pale complexion, and his brow-line glasses sit atop the bridge of his nose. He's wearing dark brown dress shoes, khaki pants, and a heather grey sweater vest. There is no doubt that he looks the part.

"Very nice to meet you, Jimmy. I'm Victor," he says, extending his free right hand as an offer to shake mine. I extend my right hand to meet his and give it a firm shake.

"Nice to meet you, too, Victor."

Mom and Dad realize that I'm not immediately behind them since Victor had stopped me for conversation. They're not far – just a few paces ahead of me, and they're now indoors.

"You coming?" I hear Dad say as he's calling for me.

"Yeah, be right there." I ran quickly to catch up with the rest of my family so that we could all find a place to sit together. Mom was holding Jeremy's hand so he wouldn't run off...as he often does. That kid, I swear. The four of us searched the several rows of pews for enough space to sit together, and we decided on one closer to the rightmost wall of the building and somewhat towards the back. We are on the inner end of the row, so people would have to walk past us to get in and out of their seats or use the restroom.

At the start of the procession with the palms, Father Mike opened the copy of the New American Bible that sat atop the lectern on the altar and started to read Mark 11:1-10. A couple of songs are led by the choir, and then the first and second readings start, each with intermissions. The first reading is from Isaiah 50:4-7, and the second reading comes from Philippians 2:6-11. There is also a verse before the gospel, which reads from Philippians 2:8-9. Finally, when Mass gets to the point of the gospel reading for today, it takes a while... Mark 14:1—15:47.

Throughout Mass, I can't sit still. Remember how I said I don't like church? It shows. I swing my feet, extending out in front of me first, then underneath the seat pews, slightly kicking them upon impact. I'm sure I drove everyone around me nuts—not just Mom and Dad. Jeremy isn't any better. My attention span can be compared to that of a goldfish. I'm surprised I didn't get any dirty looks from Mom or Dad, but I got them from the people on either side of us and the row directly in front of ours.

It's almost as if the angels heard me when, after an hour, Mass finally concluded. I've been waiting for this moment since we left the house this morning! I'm so eager to go back home, change into a T-shirt and shorts, and play with my toys. Or do *anything* else that doesn't involve being at church right now. I'm hungry, too, since talking about Jesus can do that to a person. I don't know, I just want food.

"I want to go home," I pleaded to Mom and Dad.

"Well, we need to go to Rulli Brothers first. We need groceries for the week."

I let out an exasperated sigh. I know that it's necessary to go to the store, but I want food *now!*

"Fine," I said while physically slumping. Jeremy seems to be running around like a maniac. I saw Mom roll her eyes and scoff like she's *very* sick of his shit.

"Jeremy, behave. Come here, we're leaving," Mom demanded. Jeremy runs up to her, stopping a few inches short of her feet.

The four of us take the short drive to Rulli Brothers. While we course through the aisles, Mom pushing the shopping cart, we stop for various items that are typical to an Italian household. These items include pasta noodles of various types, an assortment of fresh vegetables, fruit, milk, and any sauce that Mom wasn't feeling like making herself for the whole week. In addition, we picked up a pound of ground beef and a pound of ground pork. I have no idea what Mom is planning on making, but my mouth is already watering at the idea. Once we get back to the house, the three of us help Mom unload everything from the trunk and put everything in its place within the kitchen, loading the cabinets and the fridge to near capacity.

"Thank you for the help, boys," Mom declares. I've never thought anything of it to help Mom with whatever she needs. Call me a Mama's Boy, I guess.

"You're welcome," I said.

"What are you making tonight, dear?" Dad asks.

"I was thinking spaghetti and meatballs," she suggests.

"With the ground beef *and* the ground pork?"

"Yeah, that's how *my* mother has always made it, Gio."

"Sounds great. I'll try to keep the boys busy while you cook, then."

"That would be a real help," Mom said with a hint of relief in her voice.

"Boys, want to go throw the football?"

Jeremy and I look at each other, then back at Dad, our eyes sparkling with excitement and anticipation.

"Yeah!" we say in unison. Dad runs down into the basement to grab the football, and when he comes back up, the three of us head out the front door to the yard. Dad throws it to me, I throw it to Jeremy, and Jeremy...tries to throw it back to Dad. He's not that strong with a football yet, but he'll get there. We continue another round of this, then we start switching up the order to keep everyone on their toes. Jeremy caught the ball with his face a couple of times, and of course, I laughed. It's my job as the older brother to laugh at my younger brother when he gets hurt, isn't it? At one point, the ball hit him square on the tip of his nose.

"Ow!" he said.

"Oh, please, you'll be fine," I said.

"It hurts!"

"Don't be a baby, Jeremy."

I see Dad walking closer to us to inspect Jeremy's face and fixating on his nose. Dad gently puts his right hand on the left side of Jeremy's face and looks briefly at Jeremy in the eyes.

"Does this hurt?" Dad asks as he puts his thumb on the tip of Jeremy's nose.

"Yes," Jeremy says, whimpering.

"Do you want to put ice on it?"

"Yes, please."

"Alright, go inside and ask Mom for some. She should be able to get it for you from the freezer."

Dutifully, Jeremy rushes up the patio steps, back in the front door, and makes a beeline for the kitchen. I follow behind him.

"Mom, can I have ice?"

"What do you need ice for?"

"Jimmy threw a football at me, and it hit me on the nose. It hurts."

I'm trying my best not to laugh at my brother's misery and pain, but it's proving rather difficult. I did let out a chuckle. Mom gives me a death glare for my behavior, so that's my cue to zip it. She handed him a medium-sized bag of ice—not too big or small. Just enough for it to envelop his nose so that it doesn't hurt as much. After a couple of minutes of Jeremy holding the bag of ice on his nose, she chimes in.

"How are you feeling?"

"A little better," Jeremy says.

"Not as tender or hurting as much?"

"No."

"Alright, keep the ice for as long as you need it. Are you hungry or thirsty?"

"No. I'm sleepy."

"Okay. Go take a nap then, Jeremy."

Jeremy slowly started walking towards the stairs, then made his way up them, still holding the bag of ice to his face and covering his nose with it. Mom turns her attention towards me, now that he's out of the picture for a while.

"Did you really throw the ball directly at his face?" she wonders.

"No, I wasn't aiming for it. He wasn't paying attention."

She lets out a sigh and rolls her eyes again. "Yeah, that sounds about right for him."

55: NINE

Since I was practically born, I have watched and followed various sports, such as football, basketball, and baseball. Now, I want to wear a jersey of my own.

I hear the side door open, and it seemed that Dad had just gotten home from work. I'm peeking from the hallway that connects the kitchen to the living room. He approaches Mom first.

"Hi, honey. How has today been?" he says, kissing her lips and embracing her in a hug. She pulls away momentarily, just enough to be able to respond.

"I'm alright. How was work?"

"Ah, same old. Where are the boys?"

"Hi, Daddy!" I said. Jeremy comes bolting down the stairs at light speed.

"Hi Dad," he says.

"Heyyyy! How are my favorite boys?"

"Daddy, can I ask you something?"

"Sure, Jimbo, what's up?"

"Can I play football?"

He gasped before he took a moment to think about his response.

"You want to play football, eh?"

"Yes."

He shoots a look over to Mom, who is wide-eyed and agape.

"Honey, you look like you just saw a ghost. Are you okay? What do you think of Jimbo getting into football? We could send him to a skills camp or something to get him up to par."

She looks at Dad, then to me, and back to Dad. "Well... Hmm... As long as he keeps up his grades in school, I don't see a problem. I can investigate some programs and skills camps tomorrow."

"Thank you, Mom! Thank you, Daddy!" I jump up and down in pure, unbridled happiness and give them the tightest hug I can muster. I see Jeremy looking over at me, shooting daggers with his eyes.

"Why does he always get to do all the fun things?" Jeremy said.

Dad looked at him, very confused. I feel equally confused.

"Jeremy, you've never once asked to get into sports yet. What are you going on about?"

"What if I want to play baseball?"

"I think baseball starts at four years old. When you're old enough next year, we can talk about it, alright?" Dad was trying to appease my brother, but I'm not sure if he's having it. He's kind of hard to read, considering he's only three years old.

"I guess..."

Mom is looking between Dad, Jeremy, and I while this interaction is taking place, mostly silent.

"Jeremy, your brother has been into football for two years already. You weren't even old enough at the time to remember him getting a football for Christmas."

"Okay. Fine. I get it."

"Jeremy, quit being a brat."

"I'm not!" he says as he storms off with his arms folded. He's being a brat. At least, that's my opinion. I glance over at Mom, and her expression is less than pleased with my behavior. I know the look well, unfortunately.

"Jimmy, that wasn't necessary, and you know it."

"Sorry, Mom..."

"Don't apologize to *me*... It's your brother that you owe the apology to."

"Okay." I hung my head in shame as I went to go look for Jeremy. He's sitting on the floor in the living room, playing with a toy. He must have heard my footsteps because he was facing me by the time I arrived a few inches away from him.

"I'm sorry for being mean to you, Jeremy."

"It's okay. I forgive you." We hug each other, and that puts the topic to rest.

"Do you *really* want to play baseball?"

"Maybe. It looks cool." He shrugs his shoulders.

"We could always go with some of my friends to play. See if you like it."

"Yeah. I would like that," Jeremy says as he smiles. He may get on *every* single nerve in my body, but I do love my brother. I mean, he's the only one I've got.

"Okay. When we go to play baseball next, you can come with me."

Jeremy looked up and away like he was deep in thought about something.

"Do you have an extra mitt that would fit me?"

I thought for a second, realizing that I just might have one small enough to fit his hand.

"I think I do...Did you want to go outside and throw the ball?"

"Yeah!"

"Okay, go to the front yard, and I'll meet you in a couple minutes. I need to go grab the mitts and ball."

Jeremy abides, and I watch as he exits the front door, going onto the front porch, then taking the steps to the front yard. I run upstairs, bolt into my room, and look through the items in my closet. The two mitts are in a shoe box that wasn't previously being used, and the ball was in one of them. Thankfully, the mitts are the same size. Carrying everything in my arms, I rush back down the stairs and go out the front door to meet him. I walk down the porch steps at a normal pace since I've caught up to everything now.

"Alright, Jeremy, let's start with the basics. Are you right-handed or left-handed? You put the mitt on the hand opposite of your dominant hand."

"Um... right-handed." He had to think about that one for a moment.

"Alright, put the mitt on your left hand. I'm right-handed, too." Jeremy does as I ask.

"I'm going to back up a few paces, and I'm going to throw it to you. I will try to be easy so you have a chance of catching it. Put your gloved hand up to catch it, then throw it with the other one."

"Okay, let's try."

I back up about ten feet and gently throw the ball overhand to my brother. As the ball leaves my hand, I watch as he tracks it with his eyes. He then goes to try to catch it. He sticks his gloved left hand up just in time, and the ball lands centered in the mitt.

"Good job! Now throw it back to me."

Jeremy carefully sizes me up and backs up a few steps. Then, in a series of swift but smooth movements, he rotates on his right plant foot, brings his left knee up before he steps forward, brings back his right hand behind his head, and throws it squarely to me. I jumped up to catch it since it was just above head level. I wonder where he learned to do this.

"Wow, that was great! Where did you learn how to throw like that?"

"I pay attention sometimes when you are watching baseball," he says. That's surprising. I thought he just zoned out all the time and didn't bother to pay an ounce of attention. About two hours of this goes by, and finally, the sun looks like it's going down. We head back inside because, before we know it, Mom is calling us both in for dinner.

56: EIGHT

Have you ever tried to teach a younger sibling something, such as how to read? I'm letting you know it's a disaster, especially when they don't sit still (not that I sit still very much, either).

I'm sitting next to Jeremy with a picture book on the living room floor. He's got the "terrible twos," as the adults call it, and he's not fully potty trained yet, so Mom and Dad are having the time of their lives as well. Imagine that last sentence with an eye roll.

I open the picture book and flip past the title page and other information that nobody cares about. I start on the first page, pointing to each word as I slowly read it aloud to Jeremy, encouraging him to repeat the words back to me. He stares at the book for a few seconds while we do this, and I get the occasional utterance of a word from him. Of course, he doesn't know how to pronounce everything just yet, but he's trying...when he's not trying to put another toy in his mouth or screaming. Why did Mom and Dad give me a younger brother, exactly? This goes on peacefully for a couple of minutes before he decides to smack me across the face out of nowhere. Why do I even bother with this kid? He's such a pain in the ass.

I get up from the floor and walk towards the kitchen. My mouth has been doing more running than my legs today, and I'm thirsty. I grab the small step ladder from the coat closet to get myself a clean glass and turn on the sink to put water into it. (Don't worry, our water supply in Ohio is clean.) I take two gulps of the water in my glass before I hear Jeremy start to scream and cry again. What did he do *now*?!

I rush back to the living room and find Jeremy showing me his right index finger, which is bleeding. I sigh, exasperated, and can't figure out what he could have done on God's green earth to have this outcome from a distance. I walk closer to him and see that it's just a little paper cut. He's so dramatic.

"Boo boo," he says to me, tears still welling in his eyes. I roll my eyes as I head towards the bathroom, which is adjacent to the kitchen. We have first-aid supplies in the medicine cabinet in the downstairs bathroom. It was then that I remembered I'm still a little short to reach it, so I get the step ladder out of the kitchen to help. I grabbed the smallest band-aid I could find, a small rag with a dab of soapy water on it, plus a small tube of ointment, and brought the items over. I clean the cut with soapy water, and he cries louder, but I tighten my grip on Jeremy to get him to stay still. After drying it off, I apply the ointment and then the bandage.

"Better?"

Jeremy smiled and giggled before he gave me a quick hug. I guess he's cute sometimes. When he's not being chaotic or destructive.

About ten minutes later, I hear a familiar chime that gets louder as it moves closer to my house. The ice cream truck has arrived. I look around for Mom because I need a few dollars to go get some ice cream. Chocolate ice cream sounds *really* good right now. I find her in the bathroom, cleaning the sink and tub.

"Mom, can I have a dollar?"

"What for?"

"I want ice cream. The ice cream truck is coming."

"Okay, I guess that's fine. I'll keep an eye on your brother." She reaches into her purse and gives me a few dollar bills.

"Thanks, Mom!"

I ran out the side door of the house as fast as my legs could carry me. This ice cream truck moves pretty fast and doesn't stay still for very long. After running after this truck for about a minute, I finally get to his window.

"What can I get started for you today, son?" he says. He's an older gentleman, in his late 50s, but seems youthful at heart.

"Chocolate ice cream, please."

"Would you like it in a cone or a cup?"

"Cone, please."

"Single scoop?"

"Yes, please."

"Alright, that will be $0.25. Will that be all for you today?"

"Yes, that's it."

I hand him a $1 bill, and he gives me back $0.75 in change. After putting the change in my pocket, he hands me a cone with the fattest single scoop of chocolate ice cream I've ever seen in my short life.

"Thank you so much," I said just before I licked the glob that sat atop this waffle cone.

"You're very welcome, young man."

I start walking back home, this time more cautiously so I don't spill or splatter the gargantuan ice cream serving that I'm holding in my right hand. I go back in the way I left out through the side door of the house.

After about a minute, I returned to the house and looked for Mom to give her the change I hadn't used on ice cream. She's not in the kitchen, my parents' room, or the living room. I stand atop the stairs leading to the basement and call for her name.

"Mom?"

Faintly, I hear her respond from below. "Yes?"

"I'm back. Where do you want the change?"

There's a pause for a few seconds.

"Just put it on the counter to the right of the kitchen sink."

"Okay."

I carry the $0.75 in my pocket and place it in the spot that she requested in the kitchen. Immediately after, I head up to my room and get out my Scrabble board. Sometimes, I like to see how many words I can come up with on my own, moving up the dozen stairs quickly. Rarely do I find myself playing this with my friends since most of them don't seem interested enough in playing the game.

Thirty minutes later, I heard footsteps coming up the stairs leading to my room. Jeremy's room is just across a short hallway from mine. They don't sound like Mom's footsteps; hers are too light. These sound like heavier footsteps, so it's got to be Dad by process of elimination.

Although my door is open, he knocks on it. I turn my head to look at him and see what he wants.

"Hi, Dad."

"Hey, what do you have going on there?"

"I'm just playing Scrabble by myself right now."

"How would you feel about going to the park?" he inquired.

"Mauthe?"

"Nah, I was thinking of going up to Yellow Creek Park."

"Have we been there before?"

"Come to think of it, I don't think I've ever taken you. I used to go all the time as a kid myself, though. Uncle Greg and I loved going."

"Um...sure. Let me just put my shoes on."

"Alright. I'll wait for you downstairs. Come out the side door when you're ready." He leaves the general vicinity of my room and the upstairs, and I excitedly put on my sneakers and lace them up. I ran down the stairs as quickly as possible, trying not to lose my balance on the way there. As I was about to walk out the house's side door, Mom stopped me.

"Where do you think you're going, young man?"

"To Yellow Creek Park. With Dad."

"Oh… Well, alright. Just be back for dinner."

"Okay, Mom. I love you."

I ran out the door the rest of the way and went to the car in the shed. Dad had the engine running already.

"You ready?" he says, looking at me expectantly.

"I'm ready."

Dad puts the car into reverse and starts to make his way down the long driveway. We may have one of the longest driveways on this block of our neighborhood. Once the rear of the car crosses into Omar Street, Dad shifts into drive and begins navigating to Yellow Creek Park. To my surprise, it's only 1.2 miles away. That's walking distance in my book. I've been to Yellow Creek a few times before, so I'm not sure why this is a surprise to me. Maybe I just never paid enough attention.

Once we parked and got out of the car at Yellow Creek, I noticed that Dad was rummaging with something in his pocket while his eyes were looking forward.

"What are you messing with?" I asked, looking towards his pocket.

"Oh, I brought some food for the ducks."

"What is it, though?"

"Just some food."

We make our way across the wooden bridge that connects the opposite sides of the park to slightly lower ground, and I hold on to Dad's forearm in the process. Throughout the park, including the area we're currently in, are large grassy areas and even some wooded areas. Below the bridge is a small lake that ducks and various species of fish and other water creatures call home. Trees provide structure throughout the park, and I'm no stranger to sitting under one of them for shade and enjoying the moment.

Once we are close enough to the lake, Dad unfurls his left hand from his pocket and allows me to grab a few pieces of food for any ducks that come our way.

A female duck waddles her way closer to us. She seems young and looks up at me like she's *expecting* food. I guess a lot of people come here to feed the ducks and fish. I place two pieces of food on the ground, and she happily bends her neck down and grabs them with her beak to consume them. Coming up behind her is a duckling, which I assume is her baby. The duckling copies the behavior of her mother, approaching me and looking at me for food.

"Dad, can I have more?"

"Sure," he says, as he grabs more out of his pocket and hands it to me.

"Is that all of it?"

"Yeah, I think so."

I grasp the rest of the food and start dispersing it on the ground for the momma duck and her duckling to feast on. After they've eaten all of it, we walk around the park a little bit and stop under a tree for a few minutes before we head back to the car to go home.

57: SEVEN

Dad just put the Christmas tree up, and of course, he wants help from Mom and I to decorate it and put the lights on. Jeremy's first birthday is in three days, so he's still a bit too young to be successful in helping with the holiday decorations.

I love Christmas, and I love all the presents I get. The food is always good, too, since Mom is a great cook (and so are the rest of the women in my family).

We start by unboxing everything (we have a synthetic one since Dad didn't feel like going to a Christmas tree farm for a real one). We then proceed with the base, then the various lengths of branches, until we reach the top. Our tree topper is a female angel that glows and glistens.

"Honey, where are the lights?" he asks Mom.

"I think they're still in the garage. It doesn't make sense that they're not in the same box as the tree."

"We just put the whole tree up, and no lights are around."

"Oh, that's weird. I thought I put them there last year. I'll go look."

"Thanks, dear. Might want to see if the ornaments are in there too."

"Jim! Gio!" Mom was yelling from a distance. I rounded the corner of the kitchen and saw that she was carrying a large box full of stuff and needed help coming in the side door.

"Coming!" I scurried quickly to meet her, opening the door to let her in since her hands were full. Dad followed behind me to grab the box from her hands.

"Thank you, boys."

Dad and I walk back to the living room, and he takes items out of the box. The lights come out first, although they're tangled in with the ornaments, so it takes a few minutes to untangle and separate it from everything else. We start to hang all the lights, then plug everything in, and I hear my stomach growl. A lot.

"Dad, I'm hungry."

As if right on cue, Dad's stomach makes a similar sound in response. "You know what, I am too. I wonder what your mom is up to."

"Gio! Jim!"

"What?" Dad yells back.

"I made meatball subs and bruschetta on ciabatta bread." Dad and I walk into the kitchen, and Mom already has our lunch plated and at the table with settings, plus one for her.

"How did you know we were hungry?" Dad asked.

"Oh…I think I know my boys by now. Where's Jeremy?"

"He's upstairs taking a nap. Do you want me to wake him?"

"No, no. Let him sleep. We can have a nice lunch by ourselves here."

The three of us took a bite out of Mom's meatball subs, almost in synchronized unison.

"Mmmmm," Dad moans. He seems to love it.

"This is great, Mom," I said after I finished chewing and swallowing the massive bite I just took out of my sub.

"I'm glad you like it," she says, just before she takes her first bite and chases it by sipping her water.

"Yes, this is excellent, honey. Delicious as always," Dad adds, finally coming up for air.

"Hey Dad…"

"Yes?"

"Can I get a football for Christmas?"

Mom and Dad glance at each other and seem to nod in agreement.

"I don't see why not. What got you interested in football?"

"We watch football all the time, Dad…"

"I guess that's a valid point, kiddo. What about you, honey? What do you want for Christmas?"

"Oh…I don't know…"

Dad and I keep eating our sandwiches while Mom tries to come up with an answer. Being the youngest of four siblings, and not coming from a wealthy family, Mom has become hesitant to ask for gifts on any occasion. Dad doesn't take no for an answer, though, as he does enjoy spoiling us when he's able to do so.

"There's got to be something," Dad insists.

"I guess another tote bag would be nice. One that I can fit a bunch of stuff in."

"Alright, I'll see what I can find. Any particular color or style?"

"A neutral color—like brown, gray, black, or white."

About an hour later, I hear what sounds like Jeremy making noise from upstairs. He must have just woken up from his nap.

"Jimmy, go up and see what your brother wants. I'll be there in a couple minutes."

"Okay, Mom." I make my way toward the living room and then climb the stairs. Once I arrive, I head to Jeremy's room, where he is lying in his crib. A God-awful smell assaults my nostrils. It smells like literal *shit* in here.

"MOM!" I yell.

"Coming!" she responds.

"Bring a diaper!"

Within a couple of minutes, Mom arrives in Jeremy's room as well and is similarly assaulted by the stench of Jeremy's diaper.

"Jesus, child, you *smell!*" She pulls her shirt over her nose and mouth to try and thwart it off, but to no avail. I start gagging because of how awful it is. Dutifully, she undresses my brother from the waist down and finally opens the diaper by the sides. It's FULL. She gags a little and points towards the clean, unopened diaper and the baby wipes that she placed on the nightstand.

"Grab me those wipes, please." Her nose and mouth are still solidly under her shirt, so only her eyes are visible. I hand it to her, and she opens the container. She promptly begins to clean Jeremy's ass and nether regions.

"Now the clean diaper." Again, I hand it to her, and she opens it up, then positions Jeremy's body into it and seals it up. I take the soiled diaper and seal it back up, with the dirty baby wipes firmly inside it.

"All done?"

"All done," she says, lowering her shirt from her face to go back to normal. That was a less-than-great experience.

"Jimmy, bring that disgusting one downstairs and throw it in the dumpster outside. I don't need it stinking up the entire house and your father passing out from the stench. I'll be down with your brother in a moment."

I chuckled. "Okay, you got it." I run downstairs with the soiled diaper as quickly as I can, keeping about a one-inch grip on the thing between my right index finger and thumb. Dear God, this thing smells *awful!* How is it possible that such a small human can produce this strong of a stench? I bolt out the side door of the house and go around behind the garage, which is where we keep the garbage bin. I open the lid just barely enough to fit my hand and Jeremy's diaper, fling it in quickly, then drop the lid closed again. I walk back inside and feel like I'm able to breathe easier now that I don't have that stench following me everywhere.

58: SIX

I'm six years old, playing in my room with the train set that wraps around my room. Our house isn't huge, but it's enough for my parents and I. Right now, I'm an only child, but my mom has a huge pregnant belly. I know that my little brother is going to join us any day now. The date was December 8, 1958.

I hear my mom scream so loud it carries throughout our two-story house and basement.

"Gio! My water just broke!"

My dad, Giovanni, rushes downstairs from my parents' bedroom, which was adjacent to my own. Each hurried footstep seems louder than the previous, and I see the look of panic on his face as he makes his way down the twelve steps in our home.

"Shit! Merda! Just now? In the middle of the kitchen?!" Dad was clearly out of breath since he ran down the steps so fast in a panic.

"Si, amore mio. Just now."

My parents looked at each other, both surprised that this was happening. A few minutes passed, and I saw my mother buckle in half in the kitchen. I was at the top of the stairs when this happened.

"Gio…," my mom says. Her name is Maria.

"Yes, love?"

"I need to go to the hospital. These…these contractions. They hurt. They're bad. I need help."

"Jimbo! Get in the car! Your brother is on his way!" he exclaims.

I hurry down the steps as fast as my six-year-old legs will carry me and force my shoes on. I run to the car and get in the back. The three of us jump into the 1958 Ford Thunderbird, which my dad had just bought a few months prior. My dad gets into the driver's seat, shifts into reverse out of the driveway, and beelines it to the nearest hospital.

With traffic and all, it takes about twenty minutes. Mom is not amused in the slightest; her legs are hoisted on the dashboard, and her shoes are on the car floor beneath her. She's screaming in pain, and I feel bad for her, but I'm not sure what I can do at six years old.

We finally arrive at the hospital at 8:28 AM, and she runs out as fast as her legs will carry her very visibly pregnant body.

"GET THIS FUCKING BABY OUT OF ME!" she yells as she barges through the door, breathing heavy and restless. Medical staff swarm to her quickly and efficiently and carefully put her on the rolling bed. Dad and I are running right behind them, trying to keep up. Mom is breathing heavily, contractions less than a minute apart, and screaming about how much pain she's in. We rushed through the hallways of Labor and Delivery and finally got into our room within about three minutes, although it felt like an eternity with all the running. The four nurses who pushed my mom onto the bed in this room started to process an imminent delivery of my little brother. One of them began to talk to my mom, trying to calm her down.

"Ma'am, my name is Janine. I'm going to need to examine you for a second to see how dilated you are. Can I get your first and last name, please?"

"Yes, um…uh…my name is Maria Rossi."

"I assume these are your husband and son?"

"Yes. My husband is Gio, and my son is James."

"Okay, thank you for that information. I'm going to take a look now, so try to stay calm."

"I'll do my best."

I don't quite understand what's going on, but I think this nurse is about to tell my mom how soon my brother will be arriving.

"Oh…wow…you're right at 10 cm already. You're ready."

"He's coming?!" my mother questions.

"Maria, I'm going to need you to work with me here. I need you to start pushing as much as you can. I can see the top of your baby's head."

"Okay…"

My mom pushes as hard as she can, screaming and grunting while she goes. The nice nurse, Janine, tells her to keep going. She pushes several more times with all her might and is getting increasingly exhausted, but she powers through. After what probably seemed like forever to my mom, my brother finally arrived.

"Time of birth, December 8, 1958, at 9:01 AM Eastern Time. Eight pounds and six ounces." Janine pulls out her clipboard and writes down the information while taking some other notes about the situation. They cut the umbilical cord, cleaned up my brother, and handed him to my mom.

"He's beautiful," Mom says, with tears filling her eyes as she also cuddles my brother.

"Maria, what name should I put on the birth records for your new baby boy?" Janine asks.

"Jeremy. Jeremy Angelo Rossi."

Janine takes a glance at my newborn brother and says warmly, "Welcome to the world, baby Jeremy."

My mom looks over in my direction. "Hey, Jim, you want to come meet your baby brother?"

I ran excitedly towards my parents, and now my new brother. Yes, I was *very* excited to now have someone to play with!

"What is my new brother's name, Mom?"

"Jeremy."

"Hi, baby Jeremy," I said, looking into his dark brown eyes. Wow, he looks just like Dad and I. He looked back at me for just a moment, and I touched his little head. He whined a little, but he allowed my gentle touch and smiled very slightly. It seemed as if he was studying my face, taking in everything about the world he had just come into. I already knew I'm going to love him so much.

"Do we get to bring him home today, Mom?" I ask, with sparkles in my eyes. I wanted nothing more than to show my new brother the world and the home that I love so much.

"Not yet, love. In a couple days."

"Can I touch him? I want to hug him."

"Of course." She leans towards me, my brother Jeremy still cradled in her arms. I lean over to give him a gentle hug.

"Hi, little brother. I love you," I said, embracing his small body with genuine affection and kissing him on the forehead. From this point on, I knew I had a friend and playmate.

After a few more hours at the hospital, the three of us came home. The doctors told Mom and Dad that they'd need to keep an eye on my new brother for a couple of days, and then we could go pick him up and bring him home. Almost immediately upon entry, Mom goes into a frenzy trying to find *my* old baby stuff because now she's got a new addition to care for. Dad goes out to the garden, and I follow Mom to a storage closet that is just outside of my bedroom upstairs. She pulls out a folded-up crib and pulls it apart in a way that opens it structurally so that it can stand on its own.

A couple of days later, we bring Jeremy home. I walk into the kitchen, where both Mom and Dad are having a conversation.

"No more kids after this," Mom says.

"I'm happy with our two boys," Dad responds.

"I love you, honey," Mom said as she placed her head onto Dad's chest while hugging him.

"I love you with all my heart, *mia bella sposa*," he says as he looks deep into her eyes. He kisses the top of her head, and the two make their way upstairs to their room.

59: FIVE

It's my first day of kindergarten, and Mom wants to make sure that I get to school on time (and go to the right school, of course). She comes into my room, which is filled with my toys and my closet packed with clothes. Going through my wardrobe, she picks out an outfit for the day: a plain red polo, khaki cargo shorts, white ankle socks, and white sneakers. She makes my bed and then lays out the clothing items on top of the comforter. Then I averted my gaze to her.

"Go ahead and get ready, honey. I'll be in the kitchen ready for you when you're done. Don't forget to brush your teeth."

After she closes the door behind her leaving my room, I oblige to her instructions. I go into my bathroom to pick up my toothbrush, squeeze a small amount of toothpaste on it, and brush my teeth for about a minute, making sure to move it in circles around the surface of each tooth. After I feel satisfied with my progress, I spit out the toothpaste and bring three handfuls of water to my mouth so I can rinse and swish all of it out. Once I dry my face, focusing on my mouth, I go back into my bedroom to take off my pajamas and start to put on my outfit that Mom picked out. I undress my bottom half down to my boxers, then put on my socks, and then the shorts. Next, I take off my pajama top and put on the red polo in its place. I sit on the floor so that I can wiggle my feet into my sneakers and tie the laces, starting with the right foot, then following suit with the left one. Once I'm done, I go out to the kitchen to see Mom sitting in a chair, reading her book.

"I'm ready, Mom," I say as I make eye contact with her. She looks at me with some confusion in her expression.

"Honey, you didn't even brush your hair. It's a mess." She ran into my bathroom to grab my hairbrush and ran it through the curly ringlets of my dark brown hair. Once she feels satisfied that I look presentable, she kisses me on the cheek.

"Let's just grab your things, and I'll take you over to the school." She grabs a backpack from the kitchen counter on the flat surface to the right of the sink and hands it to me, which I then put on my shoulders. There are a few items here alongside it—a couple pens in a cup, a pad of pink Post-It sticky notes, and some Wrigley's Double Mint Chewing Gum. We exit the house through the side door.

After we make it to the end of the driveway, we start making our way to Saint Nicholas School. We head west to the end of Omar Street (the street where my house is situated), then north on Garfield Street, west on Helena Drive, and finally north on 5th Street. From our house, it's less than a mile, so it takes about 15 minutes to walk in each direction. We arrive at Saint Nicholas School at 7:20 AM, which is ten minutes early since the morning bell rings at 7:30. Outside the main double doors of the school is a fold-out table with two nice-looking ladies sitting behind it. Mom and I approach the table.

"Hi, today is my son's first day of school here. Where are we supposed to go?" Mom asks.

"What is your son's name, ma'am?" the lady with short blonde hair asks.

"Rossi. James Antonio Rossi."

"Alright, give me one moment…" The lady looks through a stack of papers that are in front of her, searching for my name.

"It looks like little James will be in room four with Miss Greco, Mrs. Rossi."

"Okay, great. Thanks!" Mom flashes the lady a quick smile and grabs my left hand with her right, and we make our way through the front doors. Once inside, we looked on both sides of the hallway for room number four. Odd numbers are on the left, and even numbers are on the right. Mom turns the handle to room four, and we walk in. Miss Greco is at the front, and several other kids are already there.

"Hi, Miss Greco?" Mom inquires.

"Hello! Who do we have here?"

"This is James Rossi. The ladies out front said that he is going to be in your class this year."

Miss Greco crouches down to become eye level with me, a smile coming across her face. The corners of her lips, which have bright red lipstick on them, turn up, and her pale blue eyes glisten with delight. She has long, wavy blonde hair, which she currently has parted on the right side, and a flower pin holding back the left. Her teeth are straight and pearly white.

"Well, hello, James. It will be great to have you in my class this year."

"You can call him Jimmy, too. Everyone calls him that," Mom adds.

"Okay, Jimmy. Why don't you go have a seat where you can find an open chair?"

I go to hug Mom before she goes home. "Bye, Mom, I love you."

"Have a good day, sweet pea. I love you, too. I'll see you after school at 2:30 pm". She crouched down to hug me and kissed the top of my head, then I watched as she walked out of the classroom door and left my view from the doorway.

Miss Greco turns her attention back to me and says, "Oh, Jimmy, you can put your lunch box in an open spot." She motions to the adjacent wall and points out the cupboard. I walk over to the cupboard and see that there are three empty spaces, so I choose the one towards the bottom right to put my lunchbox in. I then scanned the room visually to look for an empty chair and saw one in the corner opposite me, toward the back. I make my way over to have a seat.

I look to my right and see another boy. To my left is a girl. I look back at the boy first and introduce myself.

"Hi, I'm Jimmy."

"Hey, I'm Andrew," he says. I averted my attention to the left to look at the girl sitting there. She's twiddling her thumbs and is extremely shy.

"What's your name?" I asked her.

"Oh. Hi. I'm Stephanie." She breaks eye contact with me quickly and goes back to sitting quietly. She's pretty, even if she's shy, and has warm brown eyes and dark hair. Her complexion is pale, but she seems nice.

The three of us stick with each other throughout the rest of the day, and everything feels comfortable. Miss Greco kept us busy for the first few hours with activities like coloring pictures of various animals, story time, and some simple arithmetic. Of course, the classroom is chaos with all the time in between, too.

At about 11:30 AM, it was time for lunch. When I opened my lunch box, I saw Mom had packed me some minestrone she made the night before for dinner, a few red apple slices, some water, and crackers. I eventually got Stephanie to talk a little bit more, and she even gave me a hug at recess when we were playing on the jungle gym after eating lunch. Meanwhile, Andrew never stops talking, and I'm surprised I'm able to keep up with him.

While at recess, Stephanie decides to go jump rope with some of the other girls, while Andrew and I take to playing tetherball. The two of us pair up against some of the other boys in the class, and we win a few matches after offering best-of-three games. Turns out we're pretty good at it. This boy Zach kept claiming that we were cheating because he couldn't win when he played us. Stephanie eventually caught up to Andrew and I with a few minutes to spare before we had to go back indoors for the remainder of our first day of class.

Throughout the rest of the day, we play games like hide and seek and duck-duck-goose. Miss Greco also has us make our name cards that we keep in front of us on the tables, and I decorate mine with various sports balls surrounding my name – a football, a basketball, and a baseball, since those are my favorite sports.

The final bell rings at 2:30 pm sharp, and everyone makes a mad rush out the classroom door to leave the school. I look for Mom for a couple of minutes, trying to see past the swarm of other kids that are all different ages (Saint Nicholas School has kindergarten through eighth grade). Eventually, I spot her and run up to her happily.

"Hi, sweet boy!" she says, embracing me in a warm hug.

"Hi, Mom!"

"How was your first day at school? Did you make any friends?"

"Yes."

"Oh! I'm so happy for you! What are their names?" At this point, Mom is beaming.

"Andrew and Stephanie."

"I'm sure they're nice kids. I can't wait to meet them. Are you hungry? Or what do you want to do once we get home?"

"I want to nap."

"Okay, we can do that when we get home."

On our walk home, taking the same route (but in the opposite direction) as we did this morning, Mom asks me more about how the rest of the day went at school. I did lie down for a nap before playing outside some more before dinner time, making a mess of the piles of leaves that fell from the tree on the side of the house while I was playing.

Later that evening, I laid awake in my room, staring at the ceiling, thinking about how much fun I had had at kindergarten that day. Hopefully, I'll make more friends with the other kids in my class as the year goes on, too. Finally, after about an hour of thinking, I drift off into a deep sleep.

60: FOUR

Summer in Ohio is awesome. The fireflies (or, as I call them, lightning bugs) come out, the climate is humid, and you feel like you're breathing water some days. I guess it's better than living in the South this time of year. I would imagine that the rest of the Midwest is similar.

Besides my birthday, my favorite holiday is the 4th of July. Our next-door neighbor, Dan, likes to shoot off fireworks. Mom is never amused because he always leaves a huge mess of tiny pieces of paper (from the fireworks) in the street for at least a week. We like to do the normal things for my favorite holiday—Dad throws some hot dogs and burgers on the grill, we have some people around the neighborhood over, and we watch Dan light up our little stretch of Omar Street here in Struthers, Ohio.

Dan has a little boy named Tyler who's about a year older than me that I go over to play with quite often. At least a few days a week before Mom calls me inside for dinner. Tyler and I became instant friends since we're close in age and like to do what young boys do—tear up the neighborhood, run amok until dinner time, and have fun.

We just ate dinner about twenty minutes ago, and I go out the front door to the patio, which is surrounded by a black iron fence. The front of our house faces north along Omar Street, and there is a single chair that Dad sits in on the farthest east corner. To the west side of the patio, there is a recliner-type chair that Mom likes, and a bench with padded seats that I usually sit or lay on. Towards the northwest end of the patio are three cement steps, which were put there when Dad and Grandpa built the house just before I was born. The lightning bugs are out in force tonight, and once I fixate on one, I sometimes like to run around and catch them. It's amusing to see them light up in my hands. Then I release them after a few minutes, of course.

I sit on the bench, swinging my legs mindlessly as I look out into the distance. There's a gentle breeze that's occurring sporadically, but it's still humid out here. I hear the creak of the front door and look to my right. It's Dad. He sits in his designated chair and looks over his right shoulder at the shared side yard between our house and Dan's. Square in the middle is an oak tree that provides ample shade and cover. On one side of the branches is a tire swing, which Tyler and I have been known to swing on...and jump out of when we get high enough from the ground. The trick is not to break a leg or foot in the process.

"Where's Mom?"

Dad looks over at me in a way that's indicative that I just interrupted whatever he was thinking about.

"Oh... I'm sure she's just inside cleaning or something."

I go back inside for a moment to call for her.

"Mom?"

"In here, sweety." She seems to be calling me from my parents' bedroom, which shares a wall with the kitchen. I walk over and open the door to the bedroom.

"Are you okay, Mom?"

"I'm fine...I'm just exhausted," she says, burying her face into the pillow while lying on her stomach.

"I just wanted to be sure. I love you."

She turns her head to face me while still lying on the pillow and keeping the rest of her body in the same position. "I love you, too, sweet pea. What's your dad doing?"

"We're just on the porch."

"Oh, okay. Do you need anything?"

"No, I'm okay."

"Is it okay if I take a nap?"

"Okay, Mom. I will be quiet." I allowed myself to smile slightly, my expression genuine.

"Thank you, sweety. Please close the door on your way out."

I walk out of my parents' bedroom and oblige Mom's request by closing the door quickly behind me. I go to the living room and dig through my toy box. There's got to be something in here that I want to play with. My eyes sparkle and glisten as I locate a few of my favorite Army men figurines. I dig them out one by one, placing each one on the floor beside my feet. Once I'm satisfied that I've dug them all up, I begin to organize them as my imagination runs wild with ideas of a battlefield. I make a few sounds as I play, but I promised Mom that I would be quiet.

A couple of hours go by, and I hear footsteps approaching in my direction as I'm sitting on the couch looking out the window. It's Mom. She must have just woken up.

"Hi, sweet pea," she says, rubbing her eyes. "What have you been doing?"

"Just playing with my toys."

"You're such a good boy. Where's your dad?"

"I don't know."

"Oh...okay. I'll find him later. Can I get a hug?"

I walk up to Mom, and she crouches down to embrace me in a hug. She gives the best hugs.

"Are you hungry or thirsty?"

"I want juice."

She thinks for a moment to recall what we have on hand and in the house. "I think we have some apple juice. Would you like that?"

"Sure."

Mom heads into the kitchen and reaches above her head to open a cabinet containing the drinkware. She pulls out a plastic cup and sets it on the counter before opening the refrigerator to grab the apple juice. After twisting the cap off, she pours some into the 4-oz cup and hands it to me.

"Thank you, Mom."

"You're welcome, sweet pea. I love you so much."

61: THREE

Winter has arrived, and the forecast for today has stated that it will snow later today. Right now, it's 6:03 AM. It's currently December, a couple of weeks before Christmas, so that means we're about to be covered in it. Several inches of it, if not more.

Dad isn't happy about it. He's outside, complaining that he's cold when the white flakes haven't even begun to come yet. Mom seems to be indifferent to it. You would think that both parents would be used to it by now since we've been in the United States (never mind Ohio) for a few years.

I roll out of bed and go downstairs. As I am a few steps away from the bottom, I hear pans and glassware moving around in the kitchen. Mom must be causing the commotion, you would think.

"Mom?" I call out as I pass through the living room and come into the view of the kitchen. She's on her knees with some of the cabinet doors open, and it seems like she's organizing something.

"Oh, goodness! You're up early. Good morning, sweet pea." I must have caught her off guard, judging by that reaction.

"What are you doing?"

"I'm just doing some organizing. Nothing too crazy. Do you want anything to eat?"

"Um… French toast?"

"You know what… That does sound amazing right now," she says pensively. She gets the egg carton out of the fridge, still containing eight eggs out of the original dozen, and the loaf of wheat bread. She opened the cabinet door she had previously closed to get out a pan to cook everything in, along with a spatula, a medium-sized mixing bowl, and a whisk in the drawer just above it. Mom cracks four eggs into the mixing bowl, whisking them until scrambled, then puts the pan onto the stove and turns on the gas burner directly underneath it. Once she has coated the four slices of wheat bread that she took out with the eggs, she cooks them two at a time in the pan, making sure that both sides are evenly coated. As the last two are getting done cooking in the pan, she gets out two plates and transfers two to each plate. She opens the silverware drawer and gets out two forks and two butter knives. Then she pours two glasses of orange juice, one for each of us.

Mom looks at me for a moment and says, "Grab a plate and a glass of orange juice. Food is ready." I oblige, and I bring the plate, silverware, and orange juice over to the dining table. Mom grabs the others and sits in the chair directly to my left.

"Syrup?" I asked.

"Oh…duh!" She gets up, goes to the cabinet door to the right of the stove, and gets out the bottle of maple syrup, bringing it to the table in between us. I grabbed the bottle, flicked the cap upward to open it, and squeezed some syrup along both pieces of French toast. I spread it further with the butter knife. Mom does likewise and takes a sip of her orange juice before cutting up her first pieces of French toast and eating them. We spent the next twenty minutes or so eating our French toast, although I was only able to finish one of the pieces. The other went untouched, as I got full on the one piece plus orange juice.

"I'm full," I tell Mom.

"We can give it to your dad, assuming he wants it and is hungry," she suggested. She roams downstairs, going through the living room first, then the guest bedroom. Dad's not in any of those places, so she heads down to the basement. Once she reaches the bottom step of the basement, she finds Dad going through a tool chest.

"Honey? Are you hungry? What are you doing down here?"

Dad's back was to Mom for a moment, and he whipped his head around to bring his attention to her direction. He sizes her up quickly, noticing the plate of food in her right hand.

"French toast, it looks like?"

"Yes. Jimmy didn't finish it. I would've made you more if I didn't have to come looking for you."

"Yes, I'm hungry. Thank you, sweetheart. I'll be up in a second to eat it. Have you had your coffee yet?"

"I have," Mom said affirmatively.

"Would you mind pouring me a cup? Is it still hot?"

"Sure. I can do that. I'll see you in a minute." She then turns her attention to me. "Come on, Jimmy, let's go back upstairs."

Mom and I go back up the flight of ten stairs from the basement to the main floor and make a slight left to return to the kitchen. I started making my way towards my room when I heard glass break. I whip my head around to see what happened.

"*Merda!*" I hear Mom groan through clenched teeth.

"What happened?"

"Oh, I just broke my favorite coffee mug into pieces," she said, sadness covering her expression.

"I'm sorry…"

"It's not your fault, sweet pea. I got clumsy, and it fell from high up. It's fine. I'll clean it." She tiptoes around the kitchen, looking for a towel and a bucket to collect the broken glass shards into, and quickly tosses them into the trash can placed under the sink.

I carry on my way and kneel on the mat that sits by the front door of the house. Snow is now steadily falling, and it seems to have no intention of slowing down or stopping. I press my face against the glass in the middle of the door, my nose and lips making contact first. As I'm in this position, I hear a trail of footsteps and a deep voice come from behind me. It's Dad.

"What are you doing?" he says.

I turned my head slowly and made eye contact with Dad. He was scratching his face, and his beard was kept clean.

"Just watching snow."

"We're supposed to get a foot of the stuff today."

"Can I go outside and play?" I said, my eyes sparkling and full of wonder and hope. I softly smiled at Dad as well.

"I suppose. Just don't stay out too long, or you might even freeze to death."

About an hour later, I get dressed in snow-appropriate clothing. I put on about three layers, gloves, and a beanie to cover my head and ears. Once I'm done getting myself dressed for the brutality of the winter conditions, I walk next door and knock on the front door to see if Tyler can play with me in the snow. Dan answers the door and calls Tyler to let him know that I'm here. Upon seeing me, Tyler gets excited and runs back inside for a few minutes to get dressed the same way. The two of us run outside, and we have a blast. I wad up a snowball and threw it directly at Tyler's face. Naturally, he throws one back at me in the same place. We spend about an hour outside attacking each other with snowballs, build a snowman, and eventually go back inside to our respective homes. Mostly because our moms called us inside for lunch.

After eating lunch, I went back to the living room and turned on the TV. Surely there had to be something on. Football maybe? I flip through the channels using the up and down arrows on the remote while sitting on the carpet about three feet from the TV screen. Finally, I kept the channel stationary when I saw the Pittsburgh Steelers playing the Washington Redskins. It was towards the end of the game, though, with 2:58 remaining in the fourth quarter. I wasn't too concerned because I didn't get to watch the rest of the game until that point. However, I was happy to discover that the Steelers lost 28-17. It's always a good day when the Steelers lose in this house.

62: TWO

By November of 1954, I was scaling the stairs in both directions and being a menace. At least, that's what Mom has decided to call it.

Mom was *tired*. She hasn't spoken a word to me all day unless it's entirely necessary. It seems that she gets quiet when she's exhausted. The bags under her eyes are obvious.

"Mama," I whined. She glanced in my direction and made her way to me as quickly as she could, which wasn't very fast at all.

"Yes, my love?"

"I want food."

"Okay, let me see what I can make you." She kissed me on the cheek before going into the kitchen to scour the cabinets, refrigerator, and pantry. It was a Saturday afternoon, so we were due to go grocery shopping tomorrow.

"I've got some leftover pasta fagioli from last night. Is that okay?"

"Okay," I said. I didn't care; I just wanted *something*. I watched as she ladled some pasta fagioli from the container into a small pot and put it on the stove to warm it up for me. Then, she put a small amount into a bowl, placed it on the dining table, and inserted a spoon in front of me. She went back to grab a plastic cup and filled it with water.

"Here you go, sweety. Do you want some cheese on it?"

I nodded affirmatively, and she sprinkled some Parmesan on top of my soup.

"Thank you, Mama."

"You're welcome." She cradled my face with her right hand, looked into my eyes, then kissed my left cheek. I adjust myself in the chair and try to put a spoonful of the hot soup into my mouth. I burned my tongue in the process.

"Ow!"

"Did you burn your tongue?"

"Yes."

"You need to blow on it a little bit, sweet pea." She chuckled slightly as she went back to putting everything away to tidy the kitchen again. I grab another spoonful of pasta fagioli and heed Mom's instructions to blow on it for a few seconds before trying to eat it. That helped, and I did this until I didn't feel the need to blow on it anymore. I eat slowly to enjoy every bite while I look out the window. The blinds are up, so I can see outside our house. My current view is that of the shed, where Dad keeps the car parked, and the door usually remains shut. Birds are chirping, squirrels and chipmunks run amok, and it's a beautifully sunny autumn day. Once I've finished my meal, I take a few sips of my water before I bring the bowl and spoon back to Mom. She takes them from me and rinses them before placing them in the sink.

"I help."

"You certainly are, baby," Mom says, smiling. She brings me closer to her and hugs me.

I walk into the living room and kneel in front of my toy box. I sift through the toys that are in here—and I have many—and find my Jenga blocks. I dump the boxes of them on the floor and start organizing before I begin stacking them on top of each other. Dad comes down the stairs from my parents' bedroom.

"What do you have going on there, kiddo?" he says.

"I play."

"Looks like you're making a big mess, too."

I just looked at him and laughed, my eyes bright with amusement. I put three blocks next to each other on the floor, then three blocks on top of those, and so on. I built a tower as high as possible with the number of blocks I had. Then...I get behind the couch and charge at the newly built Jenga tower as fast as possible. Upon impact, the blocks come tumbling down, and a mess has been made. I smiled in delight at the destruction.

"Aaaaand there it is. The mess I just talked about," Dad said, sighing. He starts to pick up my Jenga blocks that I just made a disaster out of and puts them back in the container they were in. Then he puts that back into my toy box. Dad starts pacing around as if he's looking for Mom.

"Honey?"

"In here," Mom said, coming from the guest bedroom that was adjacent to the kitchen. Dad visually scans the immediate area he's in and finally makes visual contact with Mom. She's lying on the bed, sprawled out like a starfish, with her head looking straight at the ceiling in between the pillows.

"Oh, there you are. What are you doing in here, hon?"

"I'm just exhausted and didn't feel like going all the way upstairs."

"Can I get you anything?"

"Coffee. I want coffee." She grabs a pillow, puts it over her face, and lets out a deep, exasperated sigh. Mom didn't bother to move the rest of her body and just laid there.

"Okay, I'll make a pot."

"Thank you, dear," she says, the pillow still covering her face. I walked into the guest room to join Mom, but I stood next to the bed instead of lying on it with her.

"Hi, Mama."

"Hi."

"I love you."

"I love you, too," she responded, finally turning her head towards me and making eye contact.

I went back out to the living room and lay down on the couch. I'm feeling tired myself. A nap sounds like exactly what I need and want at this very moment.

I passed out on the couch for about an hour and a half. When I woke up, I panicked at first when I didn't immediately see Mom and Dad.

"Mama? Dad?" I yelled throughout the house, pacing as I spoke the words. I started checking everywhere. They're not in the kitchen or the guest room. Maybe Dad was in the shed or garden? I looked outside through the window in the kitchen that faces the back of the house and saw that Dad was watering the flowers that surrounded our garden area.

That's fine, but...where's Mom? I start on my way up the stairs, and at the top, towards the left, is my parents' bedroom. The door is closed, but I still want to know that she's okay. She must have laid down for a nap, too, considering how exhausted she was earlier.

I quietly walk back down the stairs and head straight for my toy box. I want to play with something, but I'm not sure what. Once I approach it, I open the lid and push it back to see what's inside. Immediately, the sight of several of my toy cars came into view, so I grabbed a couple in each of my hands. Before I could put the toy cars in my hands on the floor, a wheel came off one of them.

"Uh oh..."

I go to search for Dad to see if he's still outside and come to find that he is. He's in the shed. I go out through the front door, which is how most people get in and out when they come over. I put my shoes on, which are already lying near the doorway. I ran up to Dad with my broken toy car.

"Daddy!"

He looks around and notices that it's me approaching him. As soon as I'm about a foot away, he sees my outstretched hand containing my toy car.

"What's up?"

"It broke," I told him. I showed him the small tire that came off the car and the rest of the toy car, still mostly intact. He opens my hand slightly more to take a better look at the damage.

"Oh, yeah, I see the little tire came off. I'll fix it for you." He takes the toy car and small plastic tire from my hand and puts them on the workbench inside the shed. Various boxes and containers of tools are everywhere in the shed, as Dad tends to be handy. He grabs a pair of tweezers to pick up the plastic tire since it's so small while he holds my toy car in his other hand.

"Hm... Looks like it just attaches to this little metal piece that's supposed to be the axle." He attaches the tire to the metal piece of the toy car and does a couple of short runs of it on the surface of his workbench. Just want to make sure that the tire is secure and won't be coming back off anytime soon. His testing of the toy car renders a successful result.

"Here you go, champ," he says, giving the toy car back to me.

"Love you, Daddy," I said, happy that my toy car was fixed and I could play with it again. I hugged him, too. I ran back into the house with it and made my way to the living room.

Upon entry, my nose picks up a pleasant smell. It seems that Mom is making something in preparation for dinner. Mom is such a good cook. You can't help but be hungry any time she's in the kitchen.

"What are you making, Mom?"

"Lasagna. Your favorite!"

"It smells good."

"I put extra cheese on it because I know you like it better that way," Mom said with a smile. My face lit up like a Christmas tree because she was right—I *love* cheese, possibly to an unhealthy degree.

"When can we eat it?"

"Hm…In about 30 minutes. Go find your dad and let him know that dinner will be ready soon."

"Okay!"

I go back outside and look for Dad. It didn't take me long; it seemed that he was tending to the garden.

"Daddy, food is done soon."

"Oh, that—that sounds great. I'll be in soon. I'm just finishing up watering the plants."

About 35 minutes later, we are eating at the table together. Mom's cooking never disappoints. Dad's quick to get sauce on his shirt. I'm just happy to have all the extra cheese.

63: ONE

I just turned a year old a few days ago, and I heard Dad say that I'm about to meet someone new. I wonder who it might be.

"Your uncle Greg is coming over," he says.

I stare at him blankly.

"He's my older brother by two years."

"What time are we expecting your brother?" Mom asks.

"Think he told me that he'll be here about 4 pm?"

"Okay. It's only 8:41 am now. That gives me time to clean up the house. I'm making spaghetti and meatballs for dinner tonight. I know he likes to stay for dinner."

According to my parents, I was a quiet and timid baby. I would keep to myself mostly and wouldn't cause much of a scene when they would take me in public with them. (Mom told me I only fussed for food and attention. That tracks.) Soon after this exchange in the kitchen, Mom carried me into the living room and set me down on a blanket. She then grabbed a few of my toys, which I happily played with on my own. Mom dutifully cleaned the kitchen, as promised, and Dad went to run a few errands. I had a few toys I particularly liked. One was a toy car, the cast iron variety, that cost about $0.39 USD.

I started to smell the aroma of Mom's homemade cooking. The scent filled the entire downstairs, which included the living room and kitchen. Dad kept a garden outside our tiny home in Ohio, which consisted of a few essentials most Italian families would need: basil, tomato, parsley, garlic, and oregano. Mom would regularly go to the garden to see what she could harvest and use in her cooking. There is truly nothing better than fresh, homemade ingredients—especially her red sauce.

For the next few hours, Mom is frantically cleaning the house. Dusting, cleaning the windows, scrubbing down every surface that may get slightly dirty. Anything you can imagine cleaning a house, she was doing it. Dad was mowing the lawn and tending to the garden that was adjacent to the shed towards the back of the house.

As I play with my toys, the phone rings. We don't usually get many phone calls, but people show up and join us for dinner if they want to talk—you know, Italians living in a small town in Ohio.

Ring, ring! Ring, ring!

"Coming!" I hear Mom shout as she runs towards the phone. She hurriedly picks up the receiver.

"Hello?"

"Hey, it's Greg. Just wanted to know if it's okay with you that I bring Angela?"

Angela was Greg's wife, so she is my aunt.

"Oh, um, sure. I just figured she was coming with anyway?" Mom inquired.

"True. I'm not sure why I didn't think about it that way. Does 4 pm still work for you?"

"Yes, I'm just cleaning," she said, with a bit of annoyance in her voice. Mom always wants this house to be spotless, especially when we have anyone over for dinner—whether they have an invitation or not on any given night. People just tend to stop by and join us, although there's always a ton of food to go around.

"Alright, I'll let you get back to it. See you guys in a bit."

"Sounds good, Greg."

I heard the receiver get put back in its place as the call between Mom and Greg ended.

I start uttering what sounds like utter nonsense, and Mom suddenly takes notice.

"Ma…"

Mom runs as fast as her legs can carry her to the garden to call for Dad's attention.

"GIO! He's talking!"

"What? Really?"

"Come here! You've got to see this!"

The two of them rush inside with smiles from ear to ear. I turn my head to the right to see Mom and Dad with bright, excited eyes.

"Baby, say that again," she pleaded.

"Ma…ma…"

"Can you say *da-da*?"

"Ma…ma…"

I look at Mom, and her dark brown eyes are filled with happy tears. She's choking up as she's crying, and her mascara is running down her beautiful face. Mom was truly a stunning woman.

~ * ~

The clock strikes 4:00 pm, and I hear knocking at the door. The clock in the living room also begins its chime that happens with every change of the hour. Dad goes to unlock the door and opens it, with Greg and Angela on the other side.

"There's my big brother!" Dad says as he hugs Greg. "Hey, Angela."

"Nice to see you too, Gio," Angela says warmly, smiling as she goes to hug Dad as well.

Mom peeks out of the kitchen and into the living room, where Dad, Greg, and Angela are now sitting on the couch. She smiles at them while she puts the finishing touches on today's meal. I'm sitting on the floor with a few toys scattered about. Greg sees me and makes eye contact.

"And who have we got here?" he says, excited to see me.

"Greg, Angela…this is your nephew, James. He just turned a year old the other day."

"Oh my *goodness,* is he a handsome little boy!" Angela exclaims. "Jesus Christ, Gio, he looks just like you."

Confused, my dad looks at Greg. "You think so? He's got Maria's eyes, though."

"He's got your curly hair when you were that tiny, and he looks like trouble," Greg adds, laughing.

"Uh-huh, like you were *soooooo* much better behaved…" Dad says as he rolls his eyes.

"Ma…"

Greg looked at Dad in surprise. "When did he start talking?"

"Just earlier today. I was in the garden when Maria came barging about to come get my attention."

"No shit? How exciting!"

"Greg, can you quit cussing for five minutes? James is going to pick up all your foul language," I heard Mom yell. She's having none of Greg's antics right now.

"Whatever you say, *Maria…*" Uncle Greg retorted, then immediately scoffed while rolling his eyes.

"Guys, can we please get along?" Dad pleaded.

"Dinner's ready, gentlemen," Mom called from the kitchen. Food was always the common denominator that everyone could agree on in this house, if nothing else.

Greg and Angela got up from the couch and made their way to the kitchen. Mom had set up the table for five people already, and my highchair was behind one of the placemats. It seems that Mom sat me directly to her left. The spaghetti, meatballs, a bowl of extra sauce, a bowl of freshly grated Parmesan cheese, and garlic bread were in the center of the table, serving utensils already placed accordingly within the food.

"Honey, would you mind saying grace?"

"Sure," Dad says after a cursory glance at Mom. He pensively looks around the table, considering how to communicate grace in that moment. After quickly clearing his throat, he extends each of his hands outward, waiting for Mom to hold his right hand and Angela to grab the left. Greg and Angela grab each other's free hand as well.

"Dear Lord, please bless the food we are about to eat, and may it provide nourishment to our bodies and the hands that prepared it. Amen."

"Amen," everyone said in unison.

"Dig in, guys. What does everyone want to drink? Water? Wine?" Mom queried.

"Water is fine with me," Greg said.

"Same for me," Angela added.

Dad thought about it for a moment, then finally opened his mouth to speak. "What kind of wine do we have?"

Mom turns around the new, unopened bottle that's on the counter to read the label. She just purchased this wine the other day. "Hm, looks like this one is a Cabernet Sauvignon."

"Yeah, I'll take a glass of that."

"Two glasses of water and two glasses of wine. Jim has his cup of water, too. Easy enough."

Mom stands on her tiptoes and reaches into the higher cabinet just to the right of the stove to grab wine glasses, then uncorks the bottle of cabernet to pour out two glasses. She then reaches for two more glasses to pour the water into for Greg and Angela. Mom brings over the wine glasses for her and Dad first, then returns to the counter for Greg and Angela's water. At this point, Greg and Angela have already grabbed their first helping of spaghetti, meatballs, and bread. After placing all the drinks, she notices that Dad still hasn't served himself.

"You do plan on eating, right?" she inquires of him.

"I was just waiting for the wine, is all. Of course, I'm going to eat. Your food is always delicious," Dad said with a smile, then gave Mom a quick peck on the cheek. She smiled back at him, and the two of them exchanged a loving glance.

Immediately after, he reaches for the serving spoon in the pasta, dishing out a hearty amount onto his plate, then goes for the meatballs and bread. He then takes the spoon to sprinkle his helping of food with Parmesan. Once Mom is done serving herself the same way, she takes her fork and gives me a small amount of pasta and meatballs. I *love* cheese, so she makes sure to sprinkle some on my pasta as well. She cuts half of a meatball into smaller pieces for me as well, making it easier for me to eat. She hands me the child-sized fork, and I look at it for a moment. I stick it in the middle of the pasta on my small plate and use both of my hands to twirl it to get some pasta. Clumsily, I bring the fork to my mouth with pasta twirled around the metal part of it. I drop it on my plate and whine slightly. The sauce is already all over my face. Instead, I picked up a small chunk of meatball with my left hand, and that made it into my mouth. I chew slowly, tasting the flavors and seasonings, smiling and giggling while I look at Mom.

"Oh, honey... You're already making such a mess," she says, her face covered with concern. Mom grabs a napkin to wipe the pasta sauce off my face.

"Ma..." I say as I giggle at her some more. She picks up my fork, twirls it, and grabs some spaghetti.

"Open up," she tells me as she moves the fork closer to my mouth. I open my mouth in response and close it around the fork. I began to chew on what pasta made the journey. It wasn't enough—I started to cough because I choked on a piece of pasta. She pats my back repeatedly, trying to help me dislodge the pasta that got stuck in the wrong pipe. After a couple of minutes, my body righted itself, and I put out a hand towards my water cup. Mom hands it to me, and I grab it with both of my hands before putting it to my lips and drinking the water slowly.

"What have you been up to, Greg? Haven't talked to you in a bit," Dad said.

"Oh, you know...the usual, I guess. Nothing too crazy."

"You plan on having any kids any time soon?" Dad glances over at me, then returns his gaze to Greg.

Greg and Angela take a long look at each other as if communicating nonverbally, and then Greg returns his gaze to Dad.

"Yes, we will have them. Not just yet, though."

"Greg, we aren't getting any younger, you know..."

"I know, I know. Ma has been nagging me about it, too. Give it a rest."

"What about you, Angela? Are you keeping this clown in line at home?"

Angela laughed at the ridiculousness of what Dad had just said to her. What did she have to do to keep Greg in line, exactly?

"Oh, stop... He's not even that bad, and you know it," she remarked.

"You weren't the one he bullied all day for all of our lives, Angela."

"Cut the crap, Gio. We're adults now." Angela was through with Dad's bullshit.

The rest of our dinner continued mostly peacefully. The conversation bounced between topics without much fuss. By 5:15 pm, everyone went out to the front porch of the house, and Mom sat me on her lap on a bench that was situated against the right rail. Everyone talked some more for a while, and Uncle Greg and Aunt Angela went home at about 6:00 pm. We retired back indoors for the night.

64: BIRTH

The time is 1:30 PM on September 28, 1952. My mom, Maria, has been in labor for about three horrifically painful hours. If the neighbors couldn't hear her screaming bloody murder, they were probably deaf. As much as she's trying to be calm, the pain she's experiencing depicts a much different situation.

My dad, Giovanni (who usually goes by Gio), was in a panic. How was he supposed to soothe my mother, who was in pain and screaming for all to hear? He knew in the deepest parts of his soul that telling a pregnant Italian woman, who's currently going through labor and is about to be a first-time mom, to calm down is NOT the way to go. His better judgment and past experiences have told him that the opposite usually happens when it comes to women.

About twenty minutes pass by when she suddenly can't take it anymore. She's had enough, and she chose not to have a doula or midwife in the home early in the pregnancy.

"Gio!" she yells from the bedroom.

He pauses momentarily to make sure it was his name being called.

"Yes, hon?" he yelled back from the living room.

"We need to go to the hospital! NOW!"

He ran as fast as he could up the stairs and helped my mom down them. When they finally reached the bottom, he busted out the front door with the car keys to start the ignition. He came back for her and escorted her to the car sitting in the driveway.

The ride to St. Elizabeth Youngstown Hospital took another twenty minutes. During the car ride, Mom did everything possible to stay calm—taking deep breaths, sitting as comfortably as she could, and trying to converse with my dad. Staying calm was tougher than she thought.

The two of them finally arrived at St. Elizabeth. He takes her left hand, and they make their way to the emergency entrance quickly. Dad slams the door open and yells, "She's about to give birth!" It didn't take long before the staff of the emergency room took notice, and Mom was quickly put on a rolling bed and rushed back to Labor & Delivery.

The labor and delivery nurse, Brittney, was experienced and kept her wits about her. After getting some basic information from my parents, such as names and identities, she began to instruct my mom on what to do to bring me into the world. When my mom was asked if she wanted an epidural, she gave a resounding "yes."

Once everything was handled, it was time for my mom to start pushing.

"Maria, I'm going to need you to start pushing. Your cervix is fully dilated to 10 cm."

Dutifully, my mom starts pushing with all her might, screaming to the high heavens with each one. Several pushes go by, and Brittney says, "Keep going, I can feel your baby's head." As my mom continued to push and scream, more of my body came out.

Finally, I made my entrance into the world.

"Time of birth, 2:18 PM. Congratulations, Maria and Gio! Your baby boy has finally arrived," Brittney said as she cut the umbilical cord. Immediately after Brittney dried me off, I weighed 8 pounds, 4 ounces, and measured 21 inches. Brittney handed me to my mom, whose eyes were filled with joyous tears.

"He's beautiful," she says to my dad. He touches my small head as I cry, the sound filling the L&D room. After a few minutes had passed, Brittney came back over to my parents.

"Alright, Mr. and Mrs. Rossi, what are we naming him today?" she inquires. The two of them briefly glance at each other as if there's an unspoken agreement. They had picked out my name many months ago.

"James Antonio Rossi."

Smiling, Brittney took her pen and clipboard, which contained some papers. She began to write my name: "Welcome to the world, baby James. I'll give you guys some privacy."

I feel the warmth of my mom's touch, and she tenderly kisses my head and looks into my deep brown eyes.

"He's got a ton of dark hair already," my dad says.

"I'm sure you did, too. You still have a ton of hair."

Dad did a cursory look for Brittney but couldn't seem to find her right away. He locates a different nurse nearby and approaches her.

"Hello, pardon me. Do you happen to know where Brittney went?"

She looks at him, pondering what her response will be, then scans the Labor and Delivery wing herself.

"Hmmm… I'm not sure. I can try to go find her. What was it you needed? Is it something I could help you with?"

"Well, maybe," he said. "We're just wondering when we'll be able to take our son home."

"Oh, yes. You should be able to take him home in a couple days."

"Wonderful. Thank you."

"Was that all you needed?" the nurse asked. "My name is Alexa. If you need anything else, let me know."

"Yes, that was all."

"Okay, I will be around if you need anything. Brittney, too, once I find out where she is. Just holler."

It's only because of my mom's excellent photographic memory that I'm able to recount all of this in such detail. After four days, on October 2, I was finally ready to come home. The two-story Midwestern home in Struthers, Ohio—the one that I would come to love and cherish throughout my childhood—was built by my dad and my grandpa. While my dad drove, Mom cradled me in her arms in the car. According to her, I cried a little bit on the twenty-minute drive home, but I mostly stayed quiet.

I took in the big, bright world around me through the window, squinting when the sun got into my eyes. Finally, we arrived at our family home, and my dad came around to the passenger side door to help my mom out of the car since she was still carrying me. She gracefully and carefully exits, and my dad opens the front door of the house for her.

Once inside, she took me upstairs and tenderly placed me into a crib. "This will be your room, James," I heard her say. I squirmed a bit once she set me down, but quickly went peacefully to sleep. I wiggle around in the crib, trying to get comfortable. I can hear Mom and Dad in the next room, chatting casually and seeming relieved that I was finally here—at home, too.

About two hours later, I woke up from my nap and started fussing. I was hungry, and I began to cry for Mom. She took notice rather quickly. I heard the *thump, thump, thump* of her footsteps becoming closer as she picked up her pace to come to me.

"Hi, sweet baby. Are you hungry?" She picks me up from the crib and then sits in the chair about five feet away. She nestles me into her arms, then exposes a nipple for me to latch on to. After a few attempts and her trying to wiggle around a bit, I'm finally able to start drinking her milk. I suckle and drink quietly for a few minutes, and she gently touches my head and face with her free hand. She looks at me, and I see her warm brown eyes start to water. She's overwhelmed with the joy and love she has for me. Her smile widens as she holds me close, a tear slowly descending on her face.

I hear another set of footsteps a few minutes later. It's Dad. I wiggle in Mom's arms.

"Buon pomeriggio, neonato," he says warmly, gently touching my head. He looks at Mom and asks, "May I?"

She nods affirmatively and carefully places me in his arms. Thick, wavy locks of dark brown hair are characteristic of Dad. His eyes are dark blue, and a matching full beard defines his oval face. The scent of his cologne was still present, albeit faded, since it was getting later in the day. I felt secure in his grasp, his muscular hands and arms keeping me stable. In response, his mouth and lips smiled at me. He then looked at Mom, who caught his gaze immediately.

"He's a good-looking boy already," he said.

"He sure is. He looks more like you," she responded.

My parents spent the next several minutes picking apart my appearance, detailing which features I got from them individually and where I ended up unique. Dad beamed with pride as I—his first-born son—was finally in his arms. "You're going to be an amazing young man one day," he said to me.

"He's got a great man to look up to," Mom said, with love and appreciation for him. They share a passionate kiss while I'm still in Dad's arms, and at that very moment, all feels right.

ABOUT THE AUTHOR

Liz DelSignore was born and raised in the entertainment capital of the world—Las Vegas, Nevada, USA. During the day, Liz is a full-time IT professional. *From Death to Birth* is her first novel, which is loosely based on Liz's actual ancestors and relatives. Liz has a deep love for cats and will always have at least one in her home.